Dr. Nathan Pritikin
Jim Fixx
Dr. Ashley Montagu
Isaac Asimov
Arthur C. Clarke
Sir Bernard Lovell

Shere Hite
Milton Friedman
Anwar Sadat
Dr. Benjamin Spock
John Gardner
Andrei Sakharov

These are only a few of the many experts whose provocative insights into the future fill these pages, preparing and inspiring you for the world of tomorrow.

Also in **THE BOOK OF PREDICTIONS . . .**
a look at the Greatest Predictions of all time—and the Worst . . .

PLUS:

world-renowned psychics predict what life has in store for Jacqueline Onassis • Richard Nixon • Muhammad Ali • Johnny Carson—and many, many more.

PREDICTION: THIS LIVELY, THOUGHT-PROVOKING AND IMMENSELY ENTERTAINING BOOK WILL PROVIDE HOURS OF FUN AND FASCINATION FOR YOU AND YOUR FAMILY.

THE
PEOPLE'S ALMANAC®
PRESENTS

THE BOOK
OF
PREDICTIONS

BY
DAVID WALLECHINSKY
AMY WALLACE
IRVING WALLACE

BANTAM BOOKS
TORONTO · NEW YORK · LONDON · SYDNEY

THE PEOPLE'S ALMANAC® PRESENTS THE BOOK OF PREDICTIONS
*A Bantam Book / published in association with
William Morrow and Company*

PRINTING HISTORY
Morrow edition published January 1981
2 printings through November 1980
A Selection of Literary Guild
*Serialized in OMNI Magazine (Chapter 17), February 1981;
Book Digest; New York Times Special Features; Literary
Calvacade and Campus Life, May 1981.*
Bantam edition / December 1981

ISBN 0-553-20198-0

Published simultaneously in the United States and Canada

PRINTED IN THE UNITED STATES OF AMERICA

0 9 8 7 6 5 4 3 2 1

"All of us are fascinated by the future,
because that is where we
will live the rest of our lives."

—Criswell

Executive Editor:	Carol Orsag
Predictions Managing Editor:	Kristine H. Johnson
Senior Editors:	Fern Bryant
	Elizebethe Kempthorne
Associate Editors:	Anita Taylor
	Linda Schallan
	Diane Brown Shepard
Assistant Editor:	Judy Knipe
Staff Researchers:	Torene Svitil
	Helen Ginsburg
	Vicki Scott
	Loreen Leo
Editorial Aides:	Joanne Maloney
	Linda Laucella
	Lee Clayton
	Danny Biederman
	Patricia Begalla
Photograph Editor:	Claudia Peirce
Art Editor:	Sandra Forrest
Copy Editor:	Wayne Lawson
Psychic Consultant:	Richard De A'Morelli

THEY WROTE THE ORIGINAL MATERIAL

A.E.	Ann Elwood	J.H.	Jannika Hurwitt
A.K.	Aaron Kass	K.H.J.	Kristine H. Johnson
A.T.	Anita Taylor	L.L.L.	Loreen L. Leo
A.W.	Amy Wallace	L.O.	Laurel Overman
C.O.	Carol Orsag	L.S.	Linda Schallan
D.B.S.	Diane Brown Shepard	M.J.T.	Michael J. Toohey
D.E.B.	David E. Bresler	M.S.S.	Michael S. Smith
D.W.	David Wallechinsky	P.G.	Paul Gerber
F.B.	Fern Bryant	R.E.	Robert Embry
H.H.	Hal Hellman	R.J.F.	Rodger J. Fadness
I.W.	Irving Wallace	R.R.	Robert Reginald
J.A.D.	Julie A. Dad	S.D.	Sally Darnowsky
J.B.	Jeremy Beadle	W.A.D.	William A. DeGregorio
J.B.S.	J. B. Schallan	W.K.	Walter Kempthorne

Contents

Explosion . . . Notes for the Future . . . Future Pop . . .
Dial-a-Drug, Marijuanahol, and Chemical Religions
. . . The Pharmacy of the Future—7 Wonder Drugs
That Are on the Way . . . Cocaine Legalized, Sold in
Liquor Stores . . . The Three-Minute Mile, Robot
Football Teams, and Cricket in Yankee Stadium . . .
Legalized Gambling, Rugby in America, and New
Rules for Baseball . . . Baseball Records Shattered . . .
The 21st-Century Gladiators . . . 3-D TV and Pleasure
Islands . . . The Growing World of Leisure . . . Future
Recreation Environments . . . The Growth of Tourism
. . . Future Trends in Tourism . . . Publishers Phased
Out—Authors Free at Last . . . L'Envoi

WELCOME TO THE FUTURE

Ever since human beings first walked the earth, they have attempted—whether by extension of logic or through the use of magic—to divine what the unknown future holds in store for them. For a variety of reasons—to comfort themselves, to prepare themselves—human beings have been eager to know what tomorrow, the day after tomorrow, the next month, the next year, the years to come, will do to them and in what ways the future will affect their lives and their fate.

This same curiosity about the future encouraged us, as authors, to attempt to penetrate the invisible veil that hides tomorrow from us when we wrote two books, *The People's Almanac* and *The People's Almanac 2*, during the decade of the 1970s. In the first of these books, our opening chapter was entitled "The Other Side of the Looking Glass." Here, we invited scientists and psychics to offer prognostications about the years ahead. In our all-new follow-up *Almanac*, we again used our opening chapter, entitled "Around the Corner," to forecast happenings ahead that might affect our lives.

The response to these two chapters, reflected in the thousands of letters we received and continue to receive from our readers, was overwhelmingly enthusiastic and sounded one note. Everyone, it seemed, wanted us (by whatever means possible) to shed more light on the dim landscape ahead.

And so, because of the curiosity of our readers, and, indeed, because of our own curiosity, we set out to probe what might be foreseen of the next 20 years, the next 50 years.

We undertook this book, *The Book of Predictions*, which proved to be a fascinating involvement in the possibilities of what might occur during the rest of our lives. Now it is done. We make no claim that this is the first volume ever to deal with prophecy. Countless predictors of every shape and form have put to paper their ideas of what the future will bring to humans. From soothsayers and psychics of the distant past, like Nostradamus and Mother Shipton, to psychics of the present day, like Jeane Dixon and Alan Vaughan, we have been given visions of what to expect in the future. From authors like Edward Bellamy and H. G. Wells to scientists and scholars like Herman Kahn and Alvin Toffler, we have derived or been given more studied forecasts of what might take place in the years to come. Almost all of these writings, to the best of our knowledge, were limited to one individual's effort at portending the future.

With our work, *The Book of Predictions*, we reached further, tried to attempt more. Our design was to undertake at a given point in modern history, perhaps for the first time, a universal sum-up of what the leading minds alive on earth (in their own words) now forecast will happen to us and to all humanity during the remaining years of our time.

The Book of Predictions is divided into three parts. The first part is devoted to the forecasts of the most respected experts in a wide range of fields that involve your life. The second part is given over to the instinctive foresights of psychics and seers well known in their profession. The third part discusses colorful personalities and predictions of the past, but also contains forecasts of the future from sources as diverse as biblical prophets, noted contemporary journalists, Nobel Prize winners.

From the outset of this project, the main thrust of the authors and editors was to obtain predictions from experts in every area of human endeavor. By expert predictors we mean, according to the dictionary definition, people able to "foretell on the basis of observation, experience, or scientific reason." The experts are specialists whose specialties range through a whole spectrum of disciplines and interests—microbiology, pharmacology, economics, sports, music, urbanology, law, religion, fashion, literature, education, psychology, public health, sex, sociology, meteorology, military planning, archaeology, solar energy, climatology, physics, engineering, astronomy, anthropology. Many of them are renowned academics, others well-known science editors or writers, still others professional futurists. Occasionally, these experts have used words familiar to them but unfamiliar to most laypersons, and these words we have defined in a glossary.

When you open the pages of this book, you open a door to a preview of what some of the best minds in the world believe the future might be. To give you a sampling of the experts' guesses:

1985 Your home television set will have 300 channels carrying different programs.

Before 1990 The Soviet Union's present government will be overthrown by a social democratic faction within the Communist party.

1990 All automobiles will have electronic collision-avoidance hardware.

1992–2030 One million human beings will be living permanently in space colonies.

2010 A black Christian pope will move the Vatican to Jerusalem.

2010–2030 There will be no more night on Earth. Solar satellites, storing the sun's rays, will illuminate the nighttime hours, giving Earth a 24-hour day.

To round out our coverage of the future, we turned to leading psychics. We felt that these psychics, who, according to our dictionary, are "persons apparently sensitive to nonphysical forces or supernatural forces and influences," were proper persons to supplement the projections of logic employed by our experts. It is true that most psychics have a dismal track record of accuracy in public predictions. However, once in a while some psychics have made startlingly correct predictions. Some of these have been included in the third part of this book under "The 18 Greatest Predictors of All Time" and "The 6 Greatest Predictions of All Time."

This book, then, is an innovative gathering of those on Earth who are among the world's best futurists, a gathering of special persons who have undertaken to penetrate the invisible veil that bars Earth's people from knowledge of their tomorrows.

Besides illuminating the years ahead, this book may have value in other areas. As the well-known architect Marvin Adelson wrote us, "The collection will have served a useful purpose in stimulating dialogue about issues deserving attention, and as a unique historical record of contemporary expectation on a significant scale."

One lesson we learned from this project is that the future is up for grabs. While most of the population waits with resignation to find out what will happen next, there is an active minority which has plans for the rest of us. And these activists are sharply divided. Indeed, it sometimes seemed to us, while we were preparing *The Book of Predictions*, that some of our predictors are headed on a collision course with one another. In no field was this tendency more apparent than that of energy.

Several predictors are counting on nuclear power to meet our energy needs. And many of these are counting on the eventual development of controlled thermonuclear fusion power from hydrogen isotopes. This is scheduled for 1990 (Robert Truax), 2000 (Arthur C. Clarke), or 2010 (Willard Libby). Others—many others—predict that it will be solar power that will win out. Most of them expect some form of orbiting solar-power stations to be developed which will beam solar energy to Earth, to be distributed through existing electricity distribution grids. Roger Williams Wescott sees these stations in orbit by 1994, Harry Stine by 2001, Isaac Asimov by 2020.

Predictors Karl Hess and Ernest Callenbach envision a more decentralized solar future in which neighborhoods and individual homes will be self-sufficient in terms of energy. And Marvin Adelson suggests that home owners with solar collectors will become energy producers as well as consumers, replacing bills with income during sunny months. Other predictors see future energy being derived from wind, glaciers, refuse, and alcohol.

Given all these possibilities, it would seem that a society based on safe, renewable energy sources, such as the sun and wind, is achievable within 40 years (less if the solar industry were given the tax benefits and government research grants which the oil industry has received for over 60 years). Sadly, a solar-powered world is unlikely to happen so quickly, because oil and coal—the nonrenewable energy sources which form the basis of our current supply—are also the source of great profit.

There is probably enough oil around to keep us going for quite a while. But even if we retain access to the world's major oil reserves,

A family of four in the U.S. uses this much oil in a year.

they will still run out eventually. We owe it to our children's children to begin preparing now for a world without oil, coal, and nuclear power. And we must hope that safe energy self-sufficiency will be reached before we are forced to endure a nuclear meltdown or a war to protect oil fields in the Persian Gulf.

Because we think many of our readers may have a latent or hidden sense of prophecy, we are inviting you to try out your own secret gifts. At the end of this book we are sponsoring two contests to find the best predictors among you. It costs nothing to enter, and the best predictors will be rewarded with prizes and publication of their predictions.

As for the rest of our readers, we welcome your comments on *The Book of Predictions,* telling us what was most liked and what was least liked about it. Also, we welcome any new ideas you may have, stories you may have heard, and clippings you may possess, concerning predictions and prophecy. Anything we can use in another edition of this book, or in our forthcoming all-new editions of *The People's Almanac* and *The Book of Lists,* will be credited to you and will be paid for at our regular rates. Write to: *The Book of Predictions,* P.O. Box 49328, Los Angeles, Calif. 90049. Submissions we cannot use will be returned if you enclose a stamped self-addressed envelope.

In 1601 William Shakespeare wrote, "We know what we are, but know not what we may be."

To learn what we may be, we say to you, please turn these pages.

David Wallechinsky
Amy Wallace
Irving Wallace

THE BOOK
OF
PREDICTIONS

Part I

THE EXPERTS

1

PREDICTIONS ON ALMOST EVERYTHING

1999

The U.S. government will be moved from Washington, D.C., to Minneapolis, Minn.

2000

Computer printout terminals in every neighborhood will publish and bind any book you request right before your eyes.

1993–2030

International terrorists, using nuclear weapons, will destroy a major capital city in the world. This will lead to police states, which in turn will lead to a worldwide disarmament conference and the scrapping of nuclear-weapons systems.

THE ODDS ON TOMORROW

Predictor JIMMY "THE GREEK" SNYDER is the world's foremost oddsmaker. As scientifically as possible, he sets the odds on the outcome of everything from football to elections. A sports analyst for CBS-TV, Mr. Snyder is also a syndicated columnist and the head of Jimmy the Greek Snyder Public Relations in Las Vegas, Nev. We asked him to give us his odds on 11 possible future national and international happenings to take place by 1992. Here is his reply.

His Odds

• People will die in the next 10 years as the result of military use of nuclear weapons.
2–1: They will.

• People will die in the next 10 years as a result of a nuclear power plant accident.
2–1: They will not.

• A major California earthquake will occur in the next 10 years killing 500 or more people.
8–5: It will. (Hope I'm wrong.)

• Edward Kennedy will be elected president in the next 10 years.
1–1: Call it a toss-up.

• The U.S. government will announce, in the next 10 years, the existence of UFOs.
20–1: It will not.

• There will be federal legalization of marijuana within the next 10 years.
2–1: There will. (I don't smoke.)

• The Equal Rights Amendment will become law by 1992.
3–1: It will.

• Richard M. Nixon will run for state or federal office again in the next 10 years.
10–1: He will not.

Ten to one against.

• Someone will be convicted in the next 10 years of taking part in the J. F. Kennedy assassination.	10–1: No one will.
• U.S. ground troops will become involved in military actions somewhere in the world in the next 10 years.	10–1: They will.
• There will still be international Olympics in 1992.	10–1: There will be.

NUCLEAR DISARMAMENT FOLLOWS TERRORIST DESTRUCTION OF CITY

Predictor KARL HESS, a leading advocate of neighborhood self-reliance, is the author of *Community Technology*. Using small-scale social organization and alternate technology, he is helping to convert the Charles Town, W.Va., area into a community independent of big government, utility companies, supermarkets, giant transportation, etc. A welder by trade, Mr. Hess lives in a beautiful solar house, which he himself built at a total cost of $11,000.

• PREDICTIONS •

1982–1992

• The amorphous semiconductor, and similar devices which convert solar radiation directly to electricity, will make it possible for most energy to be generated locally, even on single houses. A crisis will develop in which major corporations and the U.S. government will press to continue central control of energy, with many communities wanting to break away into self-reliance. The communities, eventually, will carry the day.

• There will be a deterioration in large-scale public institutions. One which will collapse completely will be the public school system. In its place, one-room schools associated with particular neighborhoods and communities and local and small schools catering to every sort of interest will spring up. There will be a flowering of literacy, art, and science. Biology will replace physics as the most engrossing field of investigation and philosophical speculation during the period.

• Agriculture will begin to decline and gardening, or intensive growing of vegetables including growing without soil in hydroponic gardens, will begin to replace it. Yields per acre of highly fertilized, big-farm crops will decline, and the costs of fertilizers and pesticides

will increase to levels where they will be economically counter-productive. Famine will be narrowly averted worldwide as nations previously embarked on forced draft industrialization draw back to concentrate on food production.

1993–2030

• Waves of wildcat strikes will pit ordinary working people directly against big business and the bureaucracies of big labor. More demands for workplace democracy, in which working people fully share in decisions about their work, will replace wage demands as a central labor-management issue.

• There will be a collapse of most major currencies, marked by constant inflation. New currency will be issued in the U.S., for instance, to soften the appearance of inflation if not the impact. However, realistic people everywhere will begin turning to barter as a replacement for the trivialization of official currency.

• Urban areas will split up into separate neighborhoods with the sort of separate municipal power that most enjoyed before the growth of the city as a dominant administrative unit. Federations of these neighborhoods will constitute the new cities in the shells of the old.

• An international terrorist gang, using nuclear weapons, will devastate a major capital city. In the aftermath there will be a police-state clampdown in most countries, followed by a quick, widespread reaction in which popular pressure undermines the police states and sets the stage for a truly democratic and worldwide disarmament conference, leading to the scrapping of major weapon systems everywhere.

• The nation-state will be obsolete. Regional social organizations will be the major substitute, but autonomous local communities will be the basic social unit. Extended families will be the rule in those communities, but many will be based upon other associational forms, depending upon free choice.

SURVIVAL OF THE
HEALTHIEST—AND
MOST AFFLUENT

Predictor DAN LUNDBERG, considered America's foremost independent authority on retail gasoline, has made numerous accurate predictions concerning energy, including California's gas shortage in March, 1979. His *Lundberg Letter,* a weekly newsletter, is the leading publication on gasoline retailing in the petroleum industry and is subscribed to by oil companies, banks, the media, and state and federal agencies.

· PREDICTIONS ·

By 1982

· All unnecessary private passenger car pleasure driving will have been curtailed, and vehicular commercial traffic and bus transportation will be strictly controlled. Coupon rationing universal.

1985

· The federal government will have turned the corner in piling more and more regulations onto the energy distribution system, until nationalization will have occurred as a sheer necessity, from pipeline and other transportation systems to refining, and right down to the retail gasoline service station.
· The overwhelming weight of the federal bureaucracy will have overtaken all but the most affluent, the single *class* of citizens able to maintain themselves as did ordinary citizens during the 1970s. Citizens not extremely affluent, or in other advantaged private circumstances, will be like a vast disenfranchised horde of luckless persons doing the real productive work to carry all the rest, preoccupied with the one remaining issue, survival. Lawmakers and the constabulary will be a raddled political caretaking elite, filling the courts and jails with scofflaws, the violent, and other hapless victims. Punk rock will be sweet nostalgia.

1987

· Nature's remedy for the destruction of the planetary environment will have been applied in terms of a whole bewildering array of degenerating sicknesses and epidemics. We will find among the survivors only the most naturally healthy peoples of the world. Greatly reduced in numbers, they are discovering at long last that the only way to survive is to respect ecology in toto.

1990

• An archaeologist will come upon a copy of this book and wonder how it escaped the searing devastation of confrontation between Iceland and Malta. Finally able to produce the bomb, the countries weren't signatories to a final worldwide disarmament agreement. I am studying archaeology and know just where I'm going to preserve my personal copy of this book.

1993

• There will be a revival of marriage, an effort to restore the capability of childbearing. These people, like early Christians, will have disavowed civilization as well as all religious trappings and psychoanalysis.

2000

• The Planned Planet movement will have triumphed over all other systems of thought.

GLOBAL CONGRESS

Predictor ISAAC ASIMOV is a professor of biochemistry at Boston University School of Medicine and a popular science writer with over 200 books to his credit. Approximately one quarter of these books are science fiction or mysteries; the rest are nonfiction, taking the entire span of human knowledge as their province, from physics and mathematics to Shakespeare and the Bible.

• PREDICTIONS •

1985

• World oil production will fall below world needs.

1990

• North America will no longer be a reliable source for food export.

1995

• The nations of the world will meet (unwillingly) in a Global Congress to tackle seriously the problems of population, food, and energy.

2000

· Under global sponsorship, the construction of solar power stations in orbit about the earth will have begun.

2005

· A mining station will be in operation on the moon.

2010

· World population will have peaked at something like 7 billion.

2015

· The dismantling of the military machines of the world will have made international war impractical.

2020

· The flow of energy from solar-power space stations will have begun. Nuclear fusion stations will be under construction.

2025

· The Global Congress will be recognized as a permanent institution. The improvement in communications will have developed a world "lingua franca," which will be taught in schools.

2030

· The use of microcomputers and electronic computers will have revolutionized education, produced a global village, and prepared humanity for the thorough exploration of the solar system and the plans for eventual moves toward the stars.

· ALTERNATE PREDICTION ·

1995

· Call for Global Congress goes unheeded. In wretched scramble for energy and food, civilization dissolves in war, and the planet's capacity to support life of any kind is sharply reduced.

250 MILLION MIGRATE
TO ORBITING MINI-EARTHS

Predictor TIMOTHY LEARY has been called the messiah of LSD. A self-acclaimed visionary prophet, he popularized the idea of "turning on, tuning in, and dropping out." Leary was a well-respected professor of psychology when he had his first psychedelic experience in 1960. Subsequent drug experimentation led to his dismissal from Harvard in 1963. Although he spent several years in exile after escaping imprisonment on charges of marijuana possession, Leary resides in Hollywood, Calif. His writings include *The Politics of Ecstasy* and *Confessions of a Hope Fiend*.

• PREDICTIONS •

1982–1992

• All predictions for 1982–1992 must be qualified by geography. Where you are in 1992 will define nothing less than the species you belong to. The agonizing differences in political and scientific sophistication between North America and the other continents will accelerate so rapidly that, by the year 1992, it will be generally understood that there are many humanoid species defined by habitat and neuro-technology. And that North America is where the free individual is found.

• In North America, science will have produced a utopian civilization of aesthetic tolerance, intelligence, and sophistication. All handicaps and diseases, including aging and death, will be eliminated by recombinant DNA research. Psychological handicaps such as ugliness, stupidity, aggression, and fear of change can be cured by those who choose, voluntarily, to exercise the available medical and psychopharmacological options.

• South America, Africa, the Muslim world, Southeast Asia, and India—because of commitments to traditional, fanatic religions—will have collapsed into violence, famine, disease. By 1992 the entire world except for North America and Australia will be Communist-controlled. Western European nations will have become liberal, moderately prosperous satellites of the Soviet Union. Anti-Americanism, based on envy, will be global. Enormous migrations of intelligent, freedom-loving people to U.S.

• In North America: Look for an enthusiastic emergence of self-confident, self-sufficient, proud, tolerant, good-natured patriotism. The intelligent individualism of the "me generation" will become a continental life-style. North America first! State and regional pride! A glorification of our uniqueness! A tolerant, noncompetitive, mutually respectful racism.

• Can-America will be governed, not by corrupt politicians, but by electronic democratic consensus. The Republican and Democratic parties will be obsolete. The Carter-inspired Cold War II will have evolved into sophisticated isolationism. Cessation of foreign trade, particularly with exploitive powers like Japan. Look for a proud return to the pioneer, frontier, future-oriented Americanism of Washington's Farewell Address. "Billions for defense, but not one penny in tribute to the pirate multinationals."

• The economic-spiritual recession of the 1970s will be cured by space migration, space industrialization, solar satellite power. North America turns away from the primitive Euro-Asian world and moves into the high frontier. The spectacular successes of the 1981 Space Shuttles will rekindle the *Mayflower*–covered wagon spirit of adventure and exploration.

1993–2030

• The most important fork in human evolution in the next 50 years will involve space migration. The North American move into space will begin in 1995. By 2030 it will have duplicated the New World migrations of 1620–1970. (It took 350 years for the immigrant population of North America to rise from zero to 250 million.)

• Over 250 million people will be living on High Orbital Mini Earths (H.O.M.E.s). One hundred million will have been born on the new worlds. (These estimates compare nicely with the growth in number of passengers carried by civil airlines from 1948 to 1978.)

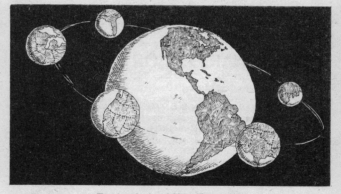

Two hundred and fifty million people
live on orbiting mini-earths.

• The Can-Am space colonists will live in village-type H.O.M.E.s averaging 1,000 souls per colony. The cost of a custom-landscaped, climate-controlled, four-acre lot with a private three-bedroom, two-bath home in space will be one-tenth that of the same back on the swarming Old World. And earth-side, this luxury will be available only to top government officials.

• Since the Can-Am space civilization is based on individualism, each H.O.M.E. colony will have its own flamboyantly unique lifestyle. An inconceivable efflorescence of new aesthetic-cultural lifestyles will inevitably emerge.

11

• The crowded Old Planet will have become totally communized, i.e., bureaucratized. Each nation in the Soviet Empire, and in the competing Chinese Empire, will be an insectoid society divided into rigid castes. Managerial, technical, and military elites. Docile worker-consumers. Enormous swarms of proles in the African-Asian lands kept tranquilly illiterate, less by the omnipresent police than by government-controlled television. The only crime, individualism, will have been stamped out or reduced to scattered undergrounds. The western European nations will maintain their 1970s material living standard by providing high-tech products for the Soviet Empire. Japan will do the same for the Chinese Empire.

• North America will remain an uneasy launching base and buffer zone between the Post-Terrestrial Confederation and the two terrestrial Communist monoliths. The latter will be held in check by fear of the retaliatory force of the Can-Am–H.O.M.E. alliance and by widespread bribery. The post-terrestrials will shower down new technologies, limitless cheap solar energy, advanced rejuvenation and neurological benefits which will be reserved for the ruling castes.

• Like flower pollen, the 250,000 H.O.M.E. gene-pool colonies will be scattering, some in orbits near the Old World, most moving out through the solar system, sailing farther and farther away from the titanic empires of the Brezhnevs and the Toyotas.

SCENARIOS FOR THE 80s

Predictor DAVID PEARCE SNYDER, life-styles editor of *The Futurist* magazine, is also a consulting futurist who teaches sociopolitical forecasting techniques to private and public-sector organizations. He has served as a lecturer for the U.S. Defense Intelligence School, for the Congressional Clearinghouse on the Future, and for White House staff programs.

• PREDICTIONS •

EVENTS THAT ARE 90% PROBABLE

1982–1983

• More than a dozen major U.S. corporations and large American cities are faced with bankruptcy; some are bailed out, but some firms go under. Several large European firms also collapse, but are nationalized. Brazil and the Philippines each default on $20–$30 billion in international indebtedness.

• Economic downturn reduces urban revenues; city services are cut back across the board. Police and fire department budgets in some cities must be cut 15%–20%; garbage is collected once a week, and many local ordinances are not enforced—e.g., public health, anti-pollution and building codes. Deteriorating quality of city life substantially slows the urban "renaissance" of the late 1970s.

• Proenvironment groups actively oppose nuclear and synfuel projects throughout the nation; protest demonstrations, legal action, and civil disobedience are increasingly accompanied by sabotage and other acts of violence.

1982–1984

• Cost of petroleum rises to cartel optimum price of $35–$45 per barrel.

• Older U.S. cities, particularly in the northeastern portion of the nation, are faced with a major new crisis: 100-year-old components of the urban infrastructure—e.g., water and sewage systems, subways, utility distribution networks, streets—have deteriorated beyond economical maintenance and repair. A costly National Urban Restoration Program is proposed, prompting a public debate over the future of large cities.

• Information crimes rise sharply. Computer fraud, commercial espionage, and theft of software, data, and copyrighted material become the most common form of grand larceny, and there is a burgeoning black market in stolen or bootlegged information products amounting to billions of dollars annually.

1983–1985

• Electronic Funds Transfer System (EFTS) is installed nationwide; use of cash begins to diminish—particularly in suburbs, business districts, and satellite cities—where electronic point-of-sale terminals are installed by most retailers.

• Flow of illegal aliens into the U.S. now exceeds 3.5 million per year, only half of whom are apprehended. Legal immigration now reaches 1 million per year, up from 750,000 per year in 1979.

• Mandatory minimum sentences are generally adopted for crimes involving firearms and multiple offenders; crimes against property—including white-collar crime—are increasingly punished by terms of mandatory public service.

1984–1986

• Trend toward a "sensate" society continues; marijuana is legalized under regulation, and some hallucinogens are licensed for recreational purposes. "Cerebral Entertainment Centers" spring up, first in offshore resort areas and then in the U.S. In these centers, patrons may undergo psychotropic experiences under professional guidance and in specially designed physical environments. Sweepstakes contestants are offered "17-Day All-Expense Paid Tour through Your Own Head."

1985–1987

• At least one half of all U.S. households are connected to an interactive video–data communications network, which permits shopping and working from the home and two-way discussions with the instructors of televised classes, political candidates, and public officials.
• A Universal Individual Identification Numbering System is adopted by the U.S. as a defense against a growing "underground" economy and the increasing influx of illegal aliens.

1986–1988

• At least one half of all U.S. households are equipped with an in-house computer of sufficient capacity to handle all bookkeeping, financial and tax management, energy monitoring and control, and all other domestic recordkeeping.

1987–1989

• Auto sales maintain a steady downward trend; only 70% of all U.S. households now own a car, down from 80% in 1980. Each household does, however, have an average of four light-duty conveyances, such as motorcycles, mopeds, bicycles, and small electric or pneumatic runabouts.

1988–1990

• Number of Hispanics in the U.S. exceeds the number of blacks for the first time; overall, minorities now make up more than 25% of the total U.S. population.

EVENTS THAT ARE 75% PROBABLE

1982–1984

• Casino gambling is legalized in 10 states. As a revenue-raising measure, gambling casinos are licensed to operate in such states as California, New York, Texas, Florida, and New Jersey, and the District of Columbia.
• Nuclear blackmail. Terrorists use a nuclear device to extract demands from the authorities of at least one major industrial power.
• Failure to solve stagflation and energy problems leads to a general increase in public cynicism. Rise in scofflawism, off-the-books business, and public distrust of all large institutions; radical splinter parties are formed, some of which attract a significant constituency.
• Technological disasters become widespread. Major air and shipping accidents, chemical spills, structural failures, and technological sabotage become increasingly common; previously rare or unknown diseases and pests assault humans, animals, and crops.

1983–1985

• Cities begin to lose population at an increasing rate as major growth industries move to exurban areas and workers follow. There is additional migration out of lower-middle-income neighborhoods, from which many unemployed or underemployed workers and their families relocate to rural areas, in hopes of living self-sufficient life-styles that are better than those afforded by deteriorating urban conditions.

1984–1986

• Large-scale production of coal in the western U.S. begins to ease the long-term energy shortage, although energy prices remain high.
• Popular opposition to nuclear power becomes politically overwhelming; government agrees to cease further plant construction and to phase out all nuclear power plants by the year 2000.

1985–1987

• Courts are generally open to television coverage. Both criminal and civil courtroom proceedings are increasingly carried on cable television, where they become so popular that they eventually lead to the elimination of soap operas and game shows from broadcast television.
• As "flextime" is increasingly adopted, there is less and less distinction between weekdays and weekends—and between day and night—in terms of work, commerce, and other daily activities; many retail outlets and public services are open 24 hours a day, 7 days a week.

1986–1988

• Congress establishes "social cost" excise taxes on harmful commodities or activities, so that those who consume such commodities (e.g., alcohol and tobacco) and those who engage in such activities

(e.g., operate an unsafe or polluting auto or manufacturing facility) will pay the costs that the society as a whole incurs thereby. A bottle of hard liquor costs $125, a double martini at a bar costs $20, and a pack of cigarettes costs $5; noncompliant motor vehicles are subject to a $100–$250 annual tax.

1987–1989

• Widespread adoption of preventative medicine—through health maintenance organizations (HMOs) and more rationalized lifestyles—aided by growing use of home diagnostic devices, begin to have positive measurable effects on American public health. As quality of health care has improved, costs have dropped steadily since the middle of the decade.
• Long-term disparities between economic classes in the U.S. grow perceptibly wider. Wealthier individuals and families hire many personal services—laundry, housecleaning, yard and home maintenance, etc.—from persons who possess insufficient job skills to find employment in the growth sectors of the economy.

1988–1990

• Long-term trends toward reduced marriage and childbearing continue throughout the decade. One third of all Americans now live alone (up from one fifth in 1980), and these "singles" are heavily dependent upon institutions for many personal support services. One half of all meals are now eaten outside the home, up from one third in 1980.
• Public and private corporations and government bureaucracies run nearly everything via EFTS and other electronic communications networks; small business has practically vanished, and nearly all goods and services are marketed through franchises or local outlets of nationwide organizations. Individual entrepreneurs, however, flourish in most technical, professional, and scientific fields.
• Travel and tourism becomes one of the world's five largest industries; 5–6 million foreigners visit the U.S. each year, versus less than 2 million in 1978; 20 million Americans go abroad each year, as compared with 10 million in 1978. Over 1 million foreign students come to the U.S. each year, up from 300,000 per year in 1978.

EVENTS THAT ARE 50% PROBABLE

1982–1983

• Congress establishes a National Service Corps (NSC) as a backup to the all-volunteer army. In peacetime, the service corps serves as a paraprofessional support arm to local police, fire, medical, and social service organizations, including traffic control, parking enforcement, disaster relief, paramedical, and paralegal services; the NSC also serves as a ready reserve during national emergencies.

1982–1984

• Nuclear power plant melts down in populous area somewhere in the world; tens of thousands of casualties result both from radiation and mass panic.

1984–1986

• Extremist political parties—both right- and left-wing—gain substantial popular support in the U.S. as traditional political parties are unable to resolve long-term economic and energy problems. Confrontation and violence increasingly mark political meetings; demagogues blame immigrants, native minorities, and working women for unemployment, and demand expulsion of foreigners and legislation limiting each household to one job. Others seek massive welfare reductions and high tariffs to protect domestic jobs.

1985–1987

• International terrorism spills over into the U.S. Extremist elements among black, Hispanic, American Indian, and Asian populations turn violent; bombings, kidnappings, and assassinations rise.

1986–1988

• Powerful laser hand-weapons are perfected but limited to special-duty military units, SWAT teams, and critical security functions. However, bootleg production and black market sales to underworld and terrorist groups begin within two years.

1987–1989

• Education is increasingly provided via electronic media and small computers in the home, starting with adult education, but gradually incorporating secondary and primary curricula. Neighborhood schools, in turn, increasingly serve as local resource and community extension service centers providing career counseling, educational testing and guidance, individual and family self-help programs, laboratory and other hands-on problem-solving classes for adults and children, etc. Many are staffed 24 hours a day.

1988–1990

• Increased air pollution from greatly expanded use of coal begins to have measurable negative impacts on public health.

ECOTOPIA

Predictor ERNEST CALLENBACH is the author of *Ecotopia*, a work of "politics fiction" which predicts the secession of the states of Washington, Oregon, and northern California in order to achieve an ecologically sane society. This meticulously detailed work has excited much interest and has been translated into seven languages. Callenbach is also the author of *The Ecotopian Encyclopedia for the 80s* and coauthor, with Christine Leefeldt, of *The Art of Friendship*. The founder and editor of the journal *Film Quarterly*, Mr. Callenbach is the science book editor at the University of California Press, Berkeley.

•   PREDICTIONS   •

1980s

• The traditional family will become even more of a statistical rarity; people will replace the biological family with friendship networks and new types of living groups, building emotional bonds as defenses against the competitive pressures of contemporary life and causing talk of a "We Decade."

By 1990

• The dominance of the automobile over American social, psychological, and economic life will be broken. With gas costs perhaps 10 times those of 1980, people will own fewer cars, drive them less, and increasingly utilize streetcars, buses, taxis, car pools, bicycles, and their own two feet. This decline of the private auto will significantly reduce air pollution—something no amount of ridicule or regulation of Detroit was able to accomplish. It will also enable us to begin rebuilding our cities as pleasant environments for people on foot.

1982–1992

• Smoking will *not* be stamped out. In fact, vast numbers of young people, especially women, will continue to become smokers. Lung cancer rates will climb even higher, like rates for other cancers. Some cancer mechanisms will be isolated, but no "cure" will be found—except to clean up chemical contamination of the biosphere. Feeble attempts will be made at this, but no real progress.
• Under the impact of rising prices, electric consumption will decline, making nuclear power stations even less necessary. Wind power will begin to be utilized for generating electricity, and power co-generated by industries will be "wheeled" to places where it's needed by utilities which have been forced to become common carriers for energy.

• "Passive" solar energy will provide most of the heat for new dwellings, which will be very well insulated, and for retrofitted old ones. "Active" solar systems will heat domestic water, cool air in summer, and provide industrial heat and steam. Rooftop photovoltaic electric generation will be beginning to replace utility grid electricity for moderate residential loads, and battery storage of electric energy will have become cost-competitive for such purposes.

1993–2030

• Instead of being printed, warehoused, and sent through the mails to bookstores, books and other printed matter will be "published" by computer storage. Printout terminals in every neighborhood will quickly and inexpensively produce a copy when a customer requests one; such terminals will also exist in rural areas, giving access to both specialized and general books to everyone in the society.
• Under the impact of gas shortages, areas of sprawl (urban or suburban) will coalesce into more compact neighborhoods, each possessing residential structures, shopping facilities, and sources of employment. City neighborhoods will become more cohesive. The equivalent of small towns will develop around suburban shopping centers or transit-line stations. Intervening areas will tend to wither.
• Recycling will become an omnipresent feature of life, personal and social. Sewage will be turned into fertilizer to produce more food, etc. Biosource plastics will be biodegraded back to fertilizer or remanufactured into new plastics; even portable houses will be recycled. Metals, much more precious because of rarity and their high energy content, will circulate in a greatly expanded scrap industry.
• Competition will be extended downward in the educational system, from college level to elementary. Families will choose from a range of schools with different educational emphases, paying tuition with publicly provided funds. Teachers will run these schools, taking the consequences if they fail to attract students. State and national testing services will help parents evaluate the schools' work.

By 2000

• Ultra-high-speed, magnetic-levitation, linear-motor trains (probably imported from Japan or Germany because of lagging U.S. technology) will become standard means of intercity transportation, displacing airplanes for distances up to around 1,000 kilometers. (We will finally have switched to the metric system!)
• People will increasingly live in extended families of up to a dozen people, in order to afford high mortgages and rents. They will work shorter hours. Their pay will buy about two thirds as many objects as in 1980, and they will watch much less TV and engage in much more gardening, participant sports, adult education, political activity, and friendly partying. They will be thinner, more active, less frantic, more secure, and physically and emotionally healthier than we are.
    Callenbach adds: The most significant prediction anybody could make is whether or not there will be a nuclear war. I have adopted a variation of "Pascal's Wager" on this question. The philosopher Pascal, faced with the equally awesome problem of whether God existed, decided it was prudent to act as if He did—preferring to bet on redemption rather than purgatory. Similarly, I prefer to bet there

will not be a nuclear war, since if there is, nobody will be around to check any of my predictions.

WASTE NOT, WANT NOT—
THE NO-FLUSH CRAZE

Predictor JEROME GOLDSTEIN, a strong advocate of recycling wastes, is the publisher and editor of both *In Business* and *Compost Science/Land Utilization*. A trustee of the Institute on Science and Man, Mr. Goldstein is also the author of *Recycling, Sensible Sludge, The New Food Chain*, and *Garbage As You Like It*.

• PREDICTIONS •

1982–1992

• The environmental pressures to turn wastes into resources will be joined by a new set of forces from the following areas: energy, economics, and legislation. In the search for alternative energy sources, wastes will be viewed as raw material for fuel and fertilizer. In this period, industry and cities will begin to discover that recycling wastes is cheaper than old-style dumping or burning. What's more, dumping and burning have been made illegal, and newspapers carry front-page accounts of astronomical fines. (The city of Philadelphia owes the federal government $15.2 million because of ocean-dumping violations.) Thirty-five states have enacted "bottle bills," requiring deposits on beverage containers. Twenty-three cities require residents to sort their garbage into containers of paper, glass, and metal—or cans will not be emptied. One hundred and thirty cities in the U.S. are composting municipal sewage sludge and/or garbage. Worldwide, the total has reached 640.
• The search for alternatives to centralized sewage-treatment plants intensifies, as small towns, rural communities, and condominium developers seek ways to develop cheaper waste-water management systems. In 1985, magazines like *Better Homes and Gardens* carry 50 advertisements for alternative toilets—flushless toilets that compost wastes; enclosed systems that turn out water "pure enough to drink." One toilet, in fact, uses a sound track that makes a flushing noise when the toilet lever is turned, even though no water is used in the system. Trade schools teach "country plumbers" how to improve septic tanks, as the moratoriums on sewage hookups and an abrupt drop-off in federal financing for sewage-treatment plans force home owners to clean up the old systems.
• The country rediscovers the mom-and-pop business. In every

commercial field, small business begins to flourish; the corner grocery store comes back to many corners, often replacing a vacated drive-in bank, gasoline station, or 7-Eleven. Kids discover how much fun it is to drink freshly made sodas at a locally owned luncheonette that has a first name, no golden arches, and loads of bike racks. City planners stop chasing "smokestacks" to fill up regional industrial parks and instead pass ordinances that encourage small businesses to come back to Main Street. The Harvard Business School announces that its executive-in-residence program that most recently installed an ex-GM president will replace him with the small-entrepreneur-of-the-year, but Harvard can't find a mom or pop who can afford the time off.

1993–2030

• Children read in school texts about the days when wastes were not treated as resources. It's difficult for them to understand, since 50 of the Fortune 500 companies employ wastes as a "raw material" in their manufacturing operations. Fifteen of those companies are in the energy field—six producing refuse-derived fuel for public utilities; 10 are in the land reclamation and fertilizer industry using composted wastes to restore strip-mined lands and to return nutrients to cropland. The other companies are in the methane and alcohol fuels-production area.

• The Chrysler Corporation diversifies into the alternative waste-water treatment field, announcing plans to manufacture and market 250,000 compost toilets of Swiss design. The new unit will be called Iococcer III. Environmentalists are split over the no-flush craze, which (1) saves water and reduces pollution, but (2) means that homes can now be built anywhere and everywhere.

• Congress passes legislation to dismantle the Small Business Administration, since the U.S. Department of Commerce is such an effective advocate for small business that no other support agency is needed.

A NEW AGE MOVEMENT

Predictors AMORY and HUNTER LOVINS are two of the foremost critics of the nuclear industry. Dr. Amory Lovins is the British representative of Friends of the Earth, Inc., a U.S.-based conservation group. An experimental physicist, he has concentrated on energy and resource strategy since about 1970. His clients have included several U.N. agencies, the U.S. Solar Energy Research Institute, and the U.S. Department of Energy. In 1979 he married Dr. Hunter Sheldon, a member of the City of Los Angeles Energy Management Board, who also served as the assistant director of the California Conservation Project from 1974 to 1979. They work as a team on energy policy.

• PREDICTIONS •

Mid-1980s

• Total energy use in the U.S. stops growing; nuclear-reactor manufacturing industry starts to collapse; cheap solar cells come on the market before we know what to do with them.

• Increasing public perception that cancer and some birth defects are largely caused by chemical pollution leads to stringent restrictions on the chemical industry, opposed by that industry and its allies in a decade-long fight as intense as that over nuclear power today. Manufacture of some major classes of organic compounds banned in 1990s. Chemical use of chlorine and other inorganic elements not handled by natural cycles comes under increasing fire by 1990.

• Water crises (due to both chemical contamination and scarcity) begin to become regional. Same mistakes initially made as with energy—being supply- rather than demand-oriented and lumping together all water needs without regard to water quality required—but wise water use becomes a major political issue in late 1980s and, as people learned from the lessons of the 1970s energy crisis, becomes rapidly accepted. Meanwhile, it's much more disruptive than energy was in the 1970s, and even more productive of centrifugal conflicts between regions, putting a severe strain on federalism.

Late 1980s

• Transition to an efficient, renewable-based energy future becomes unstoppable, highly visible, and generally accepted as the only alternative that makes economic and political sense. It happens from the bottom up; national governments are the last to know. Diverse, pluralistic societies with scope for grass-roots initiatives have a head start; more inflexible societies, by 1990, are being forced in the same direction by intractable political, economic, and environmental problems, but by then they cannot avoid a disruptive transition away from oil and gas. Nuclear power programs persist only in dictatorships and are in trouble even there.

• Networks start to take over visibly from hierarchies as the most effective and influential pattern of social organization. Diverse social movements—soft energy, environmentalism, women's and minority rights, peace, holistic health, whole food, and many others—increasingly coalesce into a recognizable and politically potent New Age movement that is more and more in conflict with a simultaneous trend toward greater militarism and greater efforts by centralized institutions to maintain and expand their social control. Result: visible start of profound cultural transformation such as we haven't had for centuries. Which way it comes out depends on you.

• The perception of limits gives rise to profound disillusionment and resentment among some who had been promised "your turn is next": urban minorities, blue-collar workers, and third-world populations. The collapse of the old American dream hastens calls for both revolution and charismatic leadership. Multinational corporations lose their legitimacy as institutions. These developments leave a vacuum of guiding values which emerging New Age values struggle to fill.

Late 1980s–Early 1990s

• Desertification of previously rich Midwestern farm areas becomes an obvious threat. Agribusiness starts to drop despite intensive chemical application and further narrowing of crop genetic base. Uncontrollable pest outbreaks and vulnerability to climatic instability increase the shift to smaller-scale and more organic farming and forestry methods, but by then one-half to two-thirds of original topsoil has been lost in many areas. The 1980 rate of U.S. soil loss—nine tons per acre per year, or one dump truck load per second—isn't reduced until 1990, too late to make the big savings. Urban farming and forestry seek to compensate for even less reliable supplies of food to the cities.

1995

• Problem of employment now seen as insoluble without redefinition. Failure of employment leads to a crisis in sense of self-worth.
• Failure of central solutions now generally accepted; indeed, the *cause* of problems is solutions. General consensus that the 1970s energy crisis and 1980s water and (later) soil-fertility crises were easy compared to worldwide problems of climate, ecological stability, chemical pollution, collapse of marine ecosystems, and deforestations that by now seem so collectively intractable. Some regions that started reforms early are doing fine, but many others are near biological collapse, and their side effects are spread widely. Paradoxically, as these problems become increasingly transnational, their solution, if any, comes increasingly from local projects sparked by small, unofficial groups, mainly with a strong biological emphasis. The groups emphasize decentralized local decision-making and participation, and technology appropriate to local environments and cultures, in contrast to top-down planning and implementation, and the massed technical resources of the international agencies and corporations.

1995–2005

• Effective collapse of the Soviet empire from internal political stress. Complete reshaping of Japanese economy well under way after a period of declining Japanese economic influence but increasing Japanese military influence. Unmanageable political stresses among Persian Gulf countries as some start to run out of oil before others. World crude oil prices over $75 per barrel (1980 dollars). Most new cars run on alcohols and other liquids from farm and forestry wastes, and get over 100 mpg.

2000

• Success of ecodevelopment strategy now proved by relative prosperity of developing countries that started it by early 1980s, but many others suffer continual famines and some epidemics, aggravated by widespread soil and water contamination and collapse of international credit. Gross national product (GNP) growth by now generally ridiculous as measure of welfare. Third-world problems mirrored in the most advanced countries. The paradoxes of countervailing forces include the simultaneous collapse of many urban services and growth of strong self-reliant urban neighborhoods. Attempts to pro-

23

vide services centrally cannot cope with demand and increased alienation. Vulnerability of all central systems widely perceived. The only solutions that work incorporate local control, self-reliance, diversity, and voluntarism. These help somewhat to cope with the serious social stresses engendered by extensive migrations triggered by the collapse of "modern" agriculture, as in the 1930s Dust Bowl.
• The energy problem is so well on its way to solution (via far more efficient energy use and benign renewable sources) in the more pluralistic market economies that it is hard to remember what all the fuss was about in 1980. Centrally planned, less adaptable economies took too long because their central elites thought they were part of the solution when they were really part of the problem. They are now overtaken by events. Explosive increase in intentional "solar villages" everywhere, especially in free societies. Much indoor agriculture in home- and village-scale bioshelters.

1980 on

• High and (at least for the first decade or two) increasing risk of nuclear war, nuclear terrorism, and—even without war—collapse of the international financial monetary system. With their usual unconscious wisdom, the people who started to increase their resilience and self-reliance in the 1970s saw this coming, and many get out in one piece.

Note from AMORY *and* HUNTER LOVINS: The most certain event from now is *plentiful surprises*. In 1974 we listed the 20 most likely surprises in energy. Near the top of the list were "Major reactor accident" and "Revolution in Iran." Item 20 was "Surprises we haven't thought of yet." There will be a great many of these—some, like more Middle Eastern political upheavals, easy to foresee in outline, but others from completely unexpected directions. We need to be ready for these psychological opportunities. Meanwhile, keep on your toes.

OPTIONAL MENSTRUATION IN 2020–2024

Predictor ROGER WILLIAMS WESCOTT graduated summa cum laude from Princeton University in 1945 and later was awarded a doctorate by the same institution. A former Rhodes scholar and past president of the Linguistic Association of Canada and the U.S., he co-edits the journals *Kronos* and *Futurics*. Among his books are *The Divine Animal* and *Language Origins*. Dr. Wescott is a professor of anthropology at Drew University in Madison, N.J.

• PREDICTIONS •

By 1984

• Increased earthquake activity—especially in land masses bordering the Pacific Ocean such as Japan and California—because of the close alignment of the Jovian, or outer, planets, which will have electromagnetic as well as gravitational effects on the inner planets, including our own.

1985–1989

• "Belt tightening" in most countries—due, in part, to the recent earthquake activity—reflects a critical shortage of nonrenewable fuels.

1990–1994

• Launching of orbiting and/or geosynchronous earth satellites, designed to facilitate weightless manufacture of industrial goods, transmission of solar energy (via microwaves) to the earth's surface, and the manned exploration of the solar system.

1995–1999

• The extinction of a considerable number of the earth's nonhuman species, especially among whales, whose warmth and intelligence our planet can ill afford to lose.

1999—last whale dies.

2000–2004

• The supplementation of our traditional academic and professional disciplines by a growing number of "interdisciplines," such as futuristics (the anticipation of the future), anomalistics (the comparative study of anomalies), noetics (the general investigation of consciousness), and polymathics (the integration of scientific with humanistic and "spiritual" disciplines).

2005–2009

• The end of international warfare, resulting either from the conquest of all nations by the victor in a third world war or from the voluntary surrender of sovereignty by all previously independent nations to a much strengthened United Nations organization.

2010–2014

• Globalization, or the gradual replacement of civilization in its technical sense (peasant farming for the support of urban centers in nation-states) with a new stage of culture, characterized by dispersed population, outer-space industry, and videophonic intercommunications among all individuals and groups.

2015–2019

• Penetration of the earth's mantle by a supranational "Project Manhole," exhaustive exploration of the ocean depths (involving discovery of a new group of invertebrates), and the settlement of other planets, moons, and asteroids.

2020–2024

• Optionalizing of menstruation and development of ectogenesis, or gestation in artificial wombs, enabling women, if they choose, to have reproductive involvement comparable to men.

2025–2030

• Supplementation of remedial medicine (disease prevention) not only by preventive medicine (public health programs) but increasingly by promotive medicine, the active and positive cultivation of health and happiness.

BY THE NUMBERS

Predictor JOSEPH MARTINO is an operations analyst at the Research Institute of the University of Dayton in Dayton, O. His work involves consulting, teaching, and researching in technological forecasting and long-range planning. Mr. Martino also serves as the technological forecasting editor for *The Futurist* magazine.

• Percent of U.S. households with TV games:

1982	10%
1987	50%
1992	90%

• Percent of retail sales made using some form of Point of Sale Electronic Funds Transfer from buyer's bank to store's account:

1983	10%
1989	50%
1995	90%

• Number of long-distance calls (millions per day) in the U.S.:

1985	83
1990	113
1995	156
2000	216

• Percent of schools (elementary and secondary) using Electronic Library Services:

1985	10%
1993	50%
2001	90%

• Percent of professional persons (doctors, engineers, etc.) using Electronic Library Services:

1985	10%
1995	50%
2004	90%

• Percent of first-class mail transmitted electronically rather than as letters (Electronic Mail):

1985	10%
1995	50%
2005	90%

• Percent of households having cable TV in the U.S.:

1987	50%
1998	90%
2000	99%

• Percent of U.S. households using prerecorded video disc (or equivalent) materials:

1990	10%
1998	50%
2006	90%

LAW OF GRAVITY REPEALED

Predictor ERSKINE CALDWELL, author of over 50 books and dozens of short stories, may be best known for his 1932 novel *Tobacco Road*, which tells the story of an impoverished and degenerate family of Southern sharecroppers. The books that followed, including *God's Little Acre, Journeyman,* and *Trouble in July,* were enormously popular, in part due to Caldwell's controversial and frank style, which led to several attempts to ban books by him. Mr. Caldwell has also published collections of his short stories and written several movie scripts. His recent books include *Annette* and *The Earnshaw Neighborhood*.

• PREDICTIONS •

1985

• Homes and offices will be equipped with a teletype or printout machine for reports of news, weather, and sports.
• One-passenger, three-wheel, solar-powered vehicles will replace present-day commuter single-passenger automobiles.

1990

• A different type of money will be in circulation. Not gold and not paper. It will be a computer type of exchange of credits and debits.
• Casino gambling will be legalized in most, if not all, of the states bordering the Atlantic, Gulf, and Pacific coasts.

1995

• There will be a law enacted that will require s.o.b.'s to wear at all times a badge proclaiming themselves as such.
• A major war will engulf the U.S. on our own soil, and there will be peace for a thousand years thereafter.

1999

• The U.S. government, including the Capitol, White House, taxis, spies, and call girls, will be moved and established in Minneapolis, Minn.

2000

• California from San Francisco to Los Angeles will at last become the victim of an earthquake and disappear into a black hole while being televised by ABC, NBC, CBS, and PBS.
• The misery of poverty will not have made close neighbors any more friendly than they were in 1980.

2030

• The law of gravity will be repealed and face-lifts will no longer be necessary.

THROUGH THE LOOKING GLASS

Predictor FELIX KAUFMANN is an economist and president of Science for Business, Inc., an international business consulting firm located in Ann Arbor, Mich. He has served as a consultant to U.S., European, and third-world government departments; several U.N. agencies; multinational corporations; and various financial, industrial, commercial, and research organizations. Mr. Kaufmann is also director of the futures program for the Hudson Institute.

• PREDICTIONS •

MEDICINE

1982–1992

• Enormously fast increase in the use of computers for medical record-keeping, billing, history-taking, test-ordering, diagnosis, advice on treatment and prescriptions, developing medical norms, monitoring health, discovering first signs of metabolic imbalance or incipient disease.
• The deaf can live quasi-normal lives through early training in the use of a vest-pocket converter of audio into characteristic optical signals.
• Highly successful implants of better-than-natural artificial hearts (now delayed mainly by worries about fate of radioactive power source after accidental death of owner).
• Four or five types of cancer routinely cured; promising approaches to most others.
• Routine use of microcomputer brain implants to control epilepsy, pathological loss of self-control, some psychoses.
• Spectacular successes with drugs in reliably improving mood, memory, learning, and lessening pathological guilt, fear, wrath, and shock, as well as many psychotic conditions.

1994

• Mass-manufactured implantable miniaturized artificial kidneys.

1995

• The blind can "see" with converter of optical to tactile (or hot and cold) signals.

By 1999

• All human infectious diseases successfully eradicated (destruction of causative organisms with antibiotics, chemotherapy, phages; control or eradication of vectors; mobilizing controlled response of human-immune systems).

By 2002

• Every kind of cancer totally curable in early stages; successfully treatable throughout.

2015

• Complete eradication of infectious and heritable diseases in humans and cultured plants and animals. Defective strains of animals and plants will be eliminated from the gene pool. In humans, currently employed methods will be perfected and widely applied: diagnosis of potential carriers of defective genes, genetic counseling, early diagnosis of embryo, in special cases operations.

POPULATION AND NUTRITION

1982–1992

• World nutrition problems solved in principle by drastic improvements in:
   1. Agriculture: desalination, genetics, pest control, growth stimulants, culturing new species.
   2. Aquaculture: aqueous animal husbandry, even more successful than terrestrial because of vastly higher fertility (especially when enhanced by scientific breeding techniques and control of predators and infection) and less limited growth potential (especially when stimulated with growth hormones and elevated temperatures).
   3. Microbial culture: cheap proteins, vitamins, and other nutrients.

Remaining question: Who pays for the food of the poor?

• Widespread availability of a new, cheap, convenient, aesthetic, safe contraceptive—reversible only by deliberate inactivation—which will be increasingly used by women in all cultures (surreptitiously if need be).

1995

• Parents can choose the gender of their child before conception. A significant change in gender proportions in societies where male offspring is regarded much more favorably than female, e.g., India.

2005

• Factory production of basic foodstuffs improves world nutrition outlook still further. Even the poor can be fed cheaply now.

2010

• World population levels off at about 7 billion (7×10^9) and remains at that level, more or less, until 2030.

2015

• Marked changes in societal institutions in regions and societies where young males preponderate over nubile females. Male homosexuality and polyandry (sanctioned in India, for instance, by mythological precedent of the Pandavas) will become normal life-styles. Increased female fertility rates, but sharply decreased birth-rates.

2025

• The 7,000-year-old trend of voluntary human clustering in cities is in reversal. Human habitations become loosely scattered over all pleasant (at least to some) areas of the earth. Wealth, almost space-capsule-like self-sufficiency of domicile, and—above all—vast improvements in communications technology will gradually make crowded living and commuting obsolete.

2030

• Except as a result of possible recent use of dirty nuclear weapons, it is not unreasonable to expect that beyond this date people of 21 years and under will no longer be deformed, sick, stupid, neurotic, undernourished, or even ugly. The two most important principles of successful child-rearing, which have long been known, will be almost universally applied:
  1. Full brain development needs good nutrition from conception and adequate stimulation from birth.
  2. The best way of preventing humans from succumbing to the stress of frustration or to the burdens of responsibility is to expose them from early childhood on to both occasional frustrations and regular responsibilities.

WORLD ECONOMICS

1982–1999

• The cost of capital will rise and the remainder of the 20th century will see an increasing shortage of investment capital, mainly as a result of:
  1. Much greater capital needs for extracting, processing, handling, transporting, and distributing essentials (food, fiber, fuel, energy).

2. Massive transfers of funds to third-world countries producing formerly cheap raw materials.
3. Competition for capital from these and other actively developing countries.
4. Severe competition from the public sector for capital which is in part derived from taxes (reducing profitability) and in part from government borrowing, which drives up both interest and taxes (to service the debt).
5. Massive need for modernization or replacement of existing manufacturing facilities, which are obsolescent or fall below constantly rising standards of health, safety, environmental protection, and acceptability to the new generation entering the labor force.
6. Decreasing returns on capital investments because of rising costs, coupled with public policies indifferent or hostile to profits in the private sector.

ECONOMICS IN DEVELOPED COUNTRIES

By 1982

• Construction of new factories for low-value products (steel, autos, textile, bulk chemicals, cement, shoes, etc.) is no longer economical because of rising costs and shrinking returns.
• New factories built only for high value-added items (drugs, biologicals, instruments, computers, machine tools, robots, high technology) or for items that can be made in totally automated, workerless factories.

1982–1992

• Labor shortages now existing mainly in repair and service jobs (mechanics, gardeners, plumbers, electricians, electronics repairmen) will spread as the new generation of entrants into the labor force will be much less willing than the retiring generation to do serious work in such uncongenial surroundings as old factories and mines.

1982–1999

• Continued inflation (double digit); governments realistically fear being ousted if they administer the bitter medicine needed to cure it.
• Sharply lower productivity in aging factories, due partly to continued lack of new industrial investment in them, partly to further deterioration of the attitude of the workers.

ECONOMICS IN COMMUNIST COUNTRIES

1982–1992

• Second-world countries will compete successfully for some of the

new factories that can no longer be profitably built in the first world. Their main competitive advantage is a relatively undemanding labor force which works long hours (though not very productively, either) and is not accustomed to striking. China, especially, is likely to be the recipient of numerous factories to supply the West with products that it can no longer manufacture, at least not economically.
• Although developed countries will be supplying technological and management know-how, there will be no significant foreign ownership of factories in the second world—not even in such countries as Yugoslavia and Romania, where the laws do not totally preclude it.

ECONOMICS IN DEVELOPING COUNTRIES

• With somewhat lower wages, much lower fringe benefits, and less restrictive regulations protecting employees, consumers, and the environment, developing countries will successfully compete for the new factories that are no longer profitable to build in the developed world. But foreign ownership of such factories, which will mostly be built with developed countries' technical assistance and know-how, will be outlawed in each country as soon as it is no longer dependent on the inflow of foreign capital (or as foreign capital ceases to be available for that purpose). Rough timetable:

Already

Libya, Iran.

1982

Nigeria (now permits only highly restricted foreign ownership, anyway).

1983

Mexico (in most cases allows only 40% foreign participation now).

1984

Venezuela, Ecuador, South Korea.

1985

Brazil, Indonesia.

MATERIALS

1982–1992

• Mixed carbon-silicon polymers combining some advantages of plastics with some of glasses (hardness, cheapness, inertness, strength).

• Thin, long fibers imparting tensile and structural-strength orders of magnitude higher than now available at competitive prices.

• Industrial use of space conditions—near-zero (absolute) temperature, pressure, and gravity—to manufacture very superior crystals (including large precious gems) and alloys for revolutionary new applications.

WEAPONS

By 1982

• Research on controlled chemical and biological warfare becomes respectable and, for the first time since World War I, first-rate scientists will be willing to work on (a) alternatives to vastly more destructive and lethal high explosives, bullets, and nuclear weapons; and (b) methods of controlling terrorism, violent crime, and civil riots without fatalities.

By 1984

• Widespread realization that manned aircraft are obsolete for use over enemy-held territory will result in cancellation of all new contracts for military aircraft of that type.

By 1990

• Nuclear device actually used or threatened against civilian targets by terrorists or blackmailers.

1993–2003

• Nuclear attack threatened or executed in international relations.

TECHNOLOGIES AND ENERGY

Before 1993

• Biofeedback and hypnosis fully respectable.

By 1993

• Mind control for malignant hypertension and other "incurable" diseases.

By 1995

• Scientific dowsing for water, minerals, lost or buried objects.

Scientific dowsing by 1995.

1995

• Several pilot plants in operation for producing electricity by controlled fusion of hydrogen isotopes.

By 2005

• Telepathy for some types of communication, criminology, etc.

2005

• Abundant and cheap electrical energy beginning to come on stream from controlled fusion and other sources (ocean temperature differentials, tides, wind, geothermal, solar).

2010

• Huge fusion power plants functioning all over the world. Efferent "cables" are thin superconducting wires cooled by liquid hydrogen, which then link up to huge aluminum-alloy peripheral cables. Energy ceases to be a limiting factor for development.

• Human habitations have individual power plants supplying most energy need, including recycling of wastes. Most of them will be in sunny climates and many will use solar energy.

CRIME, POVERTY, COMMUNISM, AND CHURCHGOING—ON THE RISE

Predictor ASHLEY MONTAGU, the British-born anthropologist and social biologist, has created controversy since the beginning of his career, when he wrote *Man's Most Dangerous Myth: The Fallacy of Race* (1942). He has since written more than 40 books, including *The Natural Superiority of Women* (1953). Dr. Montagu's *The Elephant Man: A Study in Human Dignity* (1971) is the basis of the 1979 Tony Award-winning play of the same name.

• PREDICTIONS •

1982–1992

• Huge increases in virtually all crime rates in most Western societies, with resulting increase in the corruption of such societies.
• The spread of communism to many nations of the third world, the Caribbean, and the Far East, largely as a consequence of American foreign policies.
• An increasing breakdown in moral values.
• An increase in churchgoing, but a decline in religion and in the quality of spiritual values—replaced by a crass materialism.
• Devastating increases in poverty and overpopulation. It is not overpopulation that causes poverty, but poverty that causes overpopulation—the power of the powerless.

1993–2030

• The high probability of a nuclear war, which will not, however, wipe out the whole of humanity.
• As a consequence of such a war, a U.N. that will for the first time really attempt to do something about disarmament and peace.
• The first genuine international attempt to raise the standards of living of the impoverished peoples.
• The first gropings toward a federation of the whole of humanity.
• The recognition that education is not instruction but the art and

science of being a humane, warm, loving being; that technology is not science; that we must always remain in control of what we do as scientists and technologists—otherwise we will become the victims of our creations; and that we must live as if to live and love were one.

NUCLEAR WAR KILLS
200 MILLION

Predictor EDMUND C. BERKELEY, a pioneer in the computer field, took part in building and operating the first automatic computers at Harvard University in 1944–1945. Six years later he started what is today the oldest magazine in the computer field, *Computers and People,* which he continues to edit. Mr. Berkeley has written 14 books on computers and other subjects, including *Giant Brains, or Machines That Think, The Computer Revolution,* and *Ride the East Wind: Parables of Yesterday and Today.*

• PREDICTIONS •

According to Mr. Berkeley: "These predictions are not specific as to time. They represent states or conditions which in my opinion will be reached about that time."

1985

• Automatic computer programming using plain ordinary language will replace from one quarter to one half of all human programming of computers.

1987

• A champion chess-playing computer program will be better than almost all grandmaster human chess players.

1990

• The computer will become a motorized book able to be carried around in a person's pocket, with many kinds of questions going in and many answers coming out (not all computers, but at least some like microcalculators now).

1992

• Every defined intellectual operation will be performed by a computer program faster and better and more accurately than by a human being. ("Defined" means able to be defined to a computer, or specified exactly. Example: winning a game of chess. Counterexample: driving a school bus.)
• Computers will become more common in the U.S. than cars.
• Operating a computer will be as prevalent and widespread as driving a car.
• A great many important social, economic, and industrial policy alternatives will be assessed and evaluated by large, well-designed computer programs dealing with society, economics, and industry.
• Participation in computer programs aimed at producing death, misery, destruction, and harm to human beings will be considered as evil, wicked, and antisocial as killing, torture, and crime.

2000

• The shortage of oil will compel a large-scale migration of people from colder parts of the world to warmer parts of the world.
• The forgetfulness and the superstitions of great masses of people will put many major advances in public health over the last 100 years into great jeopardy.
• The amount of public understanding of important questions of public policy in the U.S. will decrease as the media, especially TV, radio, and advertising, conceal more and more important information and appeal to lower and lower levels of people's minds. (See George Orwell's book *1984*.)
• As the minimum wage rises and governmental regulations increase, it will become increasingly difficult for small businesses to employ additional persons, to introduce innovations, and to perform profitably in competition.
• Monopolies and oligopolies will steadily increase in the U.S.
• More than 80% of the people in the U.S. will be supported by the work of less than 20%.
• More than 80% of the people over 16 in the U.S. and more than 90% of the people over 16 in the world will recognize that, starting in 1963 with the planned assassination of President John F. Kennedy, a power-control group—including Allen Dulles (CIA), Lyndon Johnson (vice-president), J. Edgar Hoover (FBI), Richard Nixon (presidential candidate), some members of the Joint Chiefs of Staff (Pentagon), and other persons—took over the U.S. presidency by a coup d'etat. Subsequently, the power control group arranged the assassinations of Robert Kennedy (senator) and the Rev. Martin Luther King, Jr. (Nobel Prize winner); the attempted assassination of George C. Wallace (governor of Alabama); the probable assassinations of Adlai Stevenson (U.N. ambassador) and Walter Reuther (United Auto Workers president); and certainly the assassinations of over 16 Black Panthers, including Fred Hampton, and over 20 witnesses. But the CIA and the FBI, as well as *The New York Times* and many other prominent elements of the media, will never admit this.

2030

• There will be a large-scale nuclear war in the northern hemisphere, springing from an insane dictator like Hitler; or a conspiracy of military, industrial, and dictatorship interests; or a combination of the two. The war will kill more than 200 million people and reduce much territory to radioactive ashes. (See *On the Beach* by Nevil Shute, *Triumph* by Philip Wylie, etc.)

WAR ELIMINATED

Predictor ROBERT TRUAX, a former research chief at Aerojet General Corporation, is a pioneer in rocketry. He has worked with the U.S. Navy, Air Force, and Department of Defense and has been involved with the Mercury space project and the Polaris missile. Mr. Truax is working in the backyard of his Saratoga, Calif., home on a rocket that will be capable of sending a man or woman to the edge of space. Assembled from old government equipment, it should be ready to launch the world's first civilian astronaut into space by 1981.

· PREDICTIONS ·

1990

· Controlled thermonuclear power will become a reality.

2000

· Fifty thousand people will be living and working in space.

2010

· The cause of aging will be found and a "cure" developed.

2030

· A United States of the World will be established, a world government of a free democratic type. War will be forever eliminated.

2060

· Means will be discovered to achieve earthly immortality—even circumventing accidental death.

• More people will be living in space than on the earth.

FARMING THE OCEANS,
THE MOON, ANTARCTICA

Predictor ANDREI D. SAKHAROV is one of the foremost physicists in the world. A major developer of the Soviet hydrogen bomb, Dr. Sakharov is also well known and highly respected for his strong stand on human rights in the Soviet Union. In 1970 he joined with other Soviet physicists to form the Committee for Human Rights, which openly condemns Soviet repression. For this and his other work, he was awarded the 1975 Nobel Prize for Peace. While Soviet authorities were displeased with Sakharov's stance for many years, they allowed him to continue his work until early 1980, when he was abruptly arrested, stripped of his awards, and exiled from Moscow.

• PREDICTIONS •

1. WORK TERRITORY vs. PRESERVE TERRITORY

There will be a gradual growth (completed long after 2024) of two types of territory out of the industrial world: Work Territory (WT), where people will spend most of their time, and Preserve Territory (PT), which will be set aside for maintaining the earth's ecological balance.

2. WORK TERRITORY

The WT will have intensive agriculture, and all industry will be concentrated in giant automated and semiautomated factories. Almost all the people will live in "supercities" in multistoried apartment buildings with artificially controlled climate and lighting.

3. PRESERVE TERRITORY

People in the PT will live in tents or in houses they have built themselves. Their basic work will be to preserve nature and themselves. People will be able to spend some 20% of their time in the PT.

4. FLYING CITIES

Artificial earth satellites will house vacuum metallurgy plants, hothouses, etc. They will serve as cosmic-research laboratories and way stations for long-distance flights.

5. SUBTERRANEAN CITIES

There will be a widely developed system of subterranean cities for sleep and entertainment, with service stations for underground transportation and mining.

6. AGRICULTURE

In the next few decades, a huge industry will be created to produce animal-protein substitutes. New forms of agriculture will arise, including marine, bacterial, microalgal, and fungal. The surface of the oceans, of Antarctica, and, ultimately, of the moon and the planets as well, will be gradually adapted for agricultural use.

7. COMMUNICATIONS

There will be a single global telephone and videophone system followed, more than 50 years from now, by a universal information system, which will give everyone access at any given moment to the contents of any book that has ever been published or any magazine or any fact.

8. ENERGY

During the next 50 years the importance of energy created from coal at huge power plants with pollution controls will become ever greater. Simultaneously, the production of atomic energy will become widespread, and by the end of that period so will energy created through fusion.

9. TRANSPORTATION

For family and individual transportation, the automobile will be replaced by a battery-powered vehicle on mechanical "legs" that will not disturb the grass cover or require asphalt roads.

10. COMPUTERS

Computers with larger memories and faster action will solve multifaceted problems, including weather forecasting, analysis of organic molecules, cosmological calculations, multifaceted production processes, and complex economic and sociological calculations.

11. PHYSICS AND CHEMISTRY

Synthetics superior to the natural materials in every significant way will be created. Automatons of the future will have efficient and easily directed "muscles," and there will be highly sensitive analyzers operating on the principle of an artificial "nose." Artificial diamonds will be created from graphite through special underground atomic blasts.

12. SPACE EXPLORATION

There will be greater attempts to establish communication with civilizations from other planets. Powerful telescopes set up at space laboratories or on the moon will permit us to see the planets orbiting the nearest stars. In 50 years, the economic exploitation of the surface of the moon and the asteroids will probably be under way.

I believe that mankind will find a rational solution to the complex problem of realizing the grand, necessary, and inevitable goals of progress without losing the humaneness of humanity and the naturalness of nature.

SOURCE: Andrei D. Sakharov, "Tomorrow: The View from Red Square," *Saturday Review*, August 24, 1974.

COMMUNISM OVERTHROWN IN U.S.S.R.

Predictor ANDREW M. GREELEY is a Catholic priest and professor of sociology at the University of Arizona in Tucson, Ariz. He also serves as the senior study director for the National Opinion Research Center at the University of Chicago. Father Greeley is the author of poetry, fiction, and nonfiction books including *The Jesus Myth* and *Religion in the Year 2000*.

• PREDICTIONS •

Before 1990

• The present Communist government in the Soviet Union will be overthrown either by a violent internal revolution or more likely by a "social democratic" faction within the party.
• Some of the constituent republics (the Ukraine, for example) will obtain authentic separate status. The Soviet colonies in Eastern Europe will then go the same route.
• The OPEC price cartel will be destroyed, perhaps by force of arms.
• More and more psychiatrists will warn of the serious dangers of sexual promiscuity. Permissiveness will go out of fashion.
• Pope John Paul II will convene an ecumenical council with full participation open to some non-Catholic groups.
• The Republican party will be replaced as one of the U.S.'s two major political parties.

Before 2030

• A safe and certain means of natural family planning will be discovered.
• Fusion energy will become a reality, solving the world's energy crisis and making possible universal affluence.
• The world's population will come into balance between births and deaths.

- Marxism will be little more than an interesting if obscure historical relic.
- Organic unity among many Christian denominations.

TEXAS AND ALASKA
THREATEN TO JOIN OPEC

Predictor MAGOROH MARUYAMA is an anthropologist who teaches at Southern Illinois University in Carbondale, Ill. His areas of special interest and accomplishment are cultural alternatives, urban and regional planning, and extraterrestrial community design. Dr. Maruyama is the editor of *Cultures of the Future* and *Cultures beyond Earth.* He is also the author of some 90 articles, which have been used in 30 disciplines throughout the world.

· PREDICTIONS ·

1982–1987

- Spanish (along with English) will become an official language in the U.S.

1982–1988

- Glacier ice movements can be used to generate electricity by sticking poles into an ice mass and letting the ice pull cables to turn generators.

1983–1990

- An efficient and inexpensive storage system for electricity will be invented. In addition, the transcontinental and intercontinental transmission of electricity by microwaves, lasers, and lightweight batteries will be developed.

By 1985

- Chinese and Spanish (along with English) will become the official languages of San Francisco and Vancouver.
- A movement away from homogeneity and towards a "harmonious combination of dissimilar elements" will begin in many areas of society—in consumer products, housing design, service industries, etc.

1985–1995

• Underwater cities in tropical and arctic regions, and subterranean cities in desert regions will be built.

1986–1998

• Desert countries and desert states, such as those in North, West, and East Africa, the Middle East, Central Asia, Mexico, and Australia, will begin to become rich as solar-energy sources.

By 1987

• If federal pressure against the oil industry increases, Texas and Alaska might separate from the U.S. and join the Organization of Petroleum Exporting Countries (OPEC). Or Texas might join Mexico and Alaska might join Canada in an oil policy deal.
• Because of labor immigrants from India, Asia, and Africa, the OPEC countries will become multicultural and multilingual. These laborers will send money to their families, thereby benefiting the economy of the home countries.

1989–1999

• Small-scale chemical and physical process industries, mostly automated, will be built in outer space.

By 1990

• Many scientists, engineers, and physicians will relocate from the U.S., Canada, Europe, and Japan to OPEC and solar-energy countries.

1998–2008

• Large-scale and heterogeneous communities and cultures will be established in outer space.

By 2000

• Technology will be used to revive and enhance traditional cultures in Africa and Asia. For example, the use of tape recorders in ritual performances, sending taped messages instead of letters, and the use of transceivers instead of the telephone. Native languages and oral literature will be revitalized by these means.

FOCUSING ON GLACIERS

Predictor GWEN SCHULTZ, a geography professor at the University of Wisconsin in Madison, works with the Wisconsin Geological and Natural History Survey. She is the author of numerous popular and scientific articles as well as several books, including *Glaciers and the Ice Age, Ice Age Lost*, and *Icebergs and Their Voyages*.

• PREDICTIONS •

By 1992

• Environmentalists will be alerting us to preserve glaciers in their natural, unspoiled condition, just as they warned us earlier to save forests, prairies, lakes, and so on. Today, when antipollution laws protect even the boundless atmosphere and ocean, glaciers are the only major natural feature still overlooked in the preserve-the-environment campaign. They are viewed as inhospitable, useless wastelands, but in another decade they will be considered valuable physical and aesthetic resources. Their worth as storers of fresh water, as regulators of climate, and as realms of natural beauty will be seen more clearly. By then the "health" and naturalness of small glaciers near populated areas will be noticeably impaired by effects of human activities. Even larger, more remote glaciers like those of Antarctica, Greenland, high mountains, and polar islands—the last genuinely virgin, wild territories on earth—will be adversely affected by civilization's encroachment and airborne fallout. The need to monitor glaciers will be increasingly apparent.

Before 2030

• Artificial melting of mountain glaciers will have significantly increased, openly or clandestinely. As populations grow and living standards rise, glaciers in some areas will be made to melt faster than normal to release more runoff into streams for irrigated agriculture in neighboring lowlands, or production of waterpower, or other industrial and domestic water needs. Or a glacier may be intentionally shrunk or removed to mine under it, free a harbor or mountain pass, or achieve a warmer local climate. Small-scale glacier melting has been done for centuries, mainly in Asian mountains, by dusting the ice surface by hand with dark, solar-heat-absorbing particles like soil, ashes, or coal dust. This practice will spread and employ more efficient techniques. Glacier dusting will be done more easily and widely by airplane; the ice will be blasted to break it up; and—if water needs are critical—nuclear power or heat-focusing space mirrors may be used. Glacier meltwater will be wanted more and more because it contains no troublesome or offensive impurities such as are found in most surface, ground, and reprocessed water. Glaciers most likely to be made to melt faster are those in mountains near arid

45

Glacier meltdown ahead.

lands, like those in inner Asia, which are headwaters of streams and rivers in China, the U.S.S.R., and South Asian countries. Experimental melting will be carried on in the western U.S. and Canada and in Europe, followed by dubious attempts to induce greater snowfall to replenish the glaciers. Melting will be accelerated mainly in times of climatic or other crises. Ultimately disputes will arise among communities and countries having conflicting interests in the glaciers and their meltwater, as boundaries commonly run through glaciered mountainous regions. Though environmental damage may be unnoticed, continued diminution of glaciers would upset nature's balance, locally at least, and cause some glaciers to disappear.
• Serious attempts will be made to bring icebergs to some coastal areas suffering from a shortage of fresh water. The favored source will be Antarctic waters, where there is a wide selection of large, stable, flat-topped bergs. Some bergs may be brought from Greenland, and small ones from Alaska and Chile. Where possible they will be transported along cool ocean currents. Formidable problems will be faced in transporting a berg or a train of bergs, and in mooring it (because almost 90% is underwater), and then in collecting and distributing the meltwater, once the berg is parked. Meltwater could be piped ashore, or quarried ice conveyed. Some chunks could be helicoptered inland to small reservoirs, or to pools as novelties. The problems will continue to be worked out, for icebergs are abundant and free, and they contain the purest water on earth—no hardness, no contaminants—being glacier ice, formed from snow, most of which fell long ago before harmful pollution and fallout existed. As water crises worsen, the icebergs' valuable meltwater, now wasted, will be earnestly sought. Where moored, imported bergs could change the local environment of marine life, create fog and cool breezes, and counteract overheating of waters by nuclear power plants.

• "Tourist erosion" will grow to destructive proportions due to increasing numbers of visitors to historic sites and natural-beauty areas. The term "tourist" here includes regular vacationers as well as researchers, technicians, educators, students, and others on field trips and expeditions who behave as tourists. "Erosion" here consists of tourists removing things or causing things to be removed, capriciously or deliberately, by various means. It is picking pieces off old monuments and buildings, touching works of art, plundering archaeological sites, trampling or overriding fragile vegetation, digging up "souvenir" plants, collecting biological specimens, chipping or carving into rock formations, tearing up land to build lodgings and access routes in wilderness regions, and much more. Each act may seem small, but the combined effect, though not measurable, will be great indeed.

• International commerce on a large scale will be taking place through the Arctic Ocean.

• The revelation will have come that, in general, the intelligence of scientists is less than that with which they have been credited, and the intelligence of "dumb" animals (large and little) is far greater than has been suspected. The same can be predicted regarding their respective abilities to communicate.

ILLITERACY INCREASES—NOVELS WRITTEN IN SIGN LANGUAGE

Predictor WILLARD ESPY is the author of numerous books concerned with the English language, including *The Game of Words*, *An Almanac of Words at Play*, and his latest, *Say It My Way*. A former reporter, editor, and radio interviewer, Mr. Espy has been a frequent contributor to *Harper's Magazine*, *Atlantic Monthly*, and *The Nation*.

• PREDICTIONS •

1987

• Nouns and verbs will agree to disagree.

1988

• The National Academy of Arts and Sciences will propose that Americans begin dropping 10 words a day from their vocabulary to make the language more democratic. Twelve percent of the nation will be silenced in the first week.

1989

• Language sports will replace baseball. National League teams will be Sister-Speak, Split-Talk, Black English, Gay Lingo, Standard English, Body English, and Banggangsprache.
• The first popular novel in sign language will appear.

By 1992

• The proportion of functionally illiterate Americans will rise to 27%.
• Highway and directional signs will have diversified into rudimentary hieroglyphics.

1992—traffic safety signs may be in rebus.

2023

• Congress will determine that all legislative proceedings shall be conducted in 17th-century French.

2027

• The Supreme Court will decide that nouns and verbs which continue to agree are in restraint of trade.

By 2030

• The proportion of functionally illiterate Americans will peak at 47%.
• Chinese scholars will begin instructing American educators in the art of combining direction signs so as to convey complex ideas.

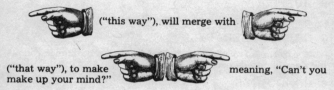

("this way"), will merge with

("that way"), to make make up your mind?" meaning, "Can't you

2030

• Standard English will wind up in the cellar for the 40th consecutive year.

NEW AND FUTURE WORDS

Language is constantly changing. New words appear in dictionaries—and old words disappear—as a result of a word-watching system used by lexicographers (dictionary authors and editors). A sampling of almost all English printed material—magazines, books, newspapers—is read by editors who analyze the current use of words. Words are marked for frequency of use and the context in which they are used. These citations will eventually determine which words will be incorporated into the dictionaries we use. The following words are likely candidates for future dictionaries.

1. ADVERTORIAL

A broadcast advertisement with editorial content and commentary rather than direct product promotion.

2. BAG LADY

A female vagrant, one who appears to carry all her belongings with her in shopping bags.

3. BALLOON EMBOLOTHERAPY

The treatment of a hemorrhaging blood vessel by insertion of a catheter with a tiny balloon end into the damaged vessel; the balloon is inflated, blocking the bleeding.

4. BOX

An oversized portable radio.

5. BULIMAREXIA

The physically and psychologically damaging cycle of starvation, binge eating, and purges arising from a desire to become or stay thin.

6. BUSTIER

A strapless, tight-fitting women's blouse.

7. CHRONOTHERAPY

The treatment to adjust the "internal clock" of insomniacs, allowing sleep at normal hours.

8. CONDOMIZE

To convert multiple-rental property to condominiums.

9. CORE MELTDOWN

The melting of a nuclear reactor's stainless steel fuel rods or the enriched uranium pellets they contain; this emergency state is caused by inadequate distribution or circulation of cooling liquid.

10. DISCO

The recorded dance music characterized by rapid and emphatic tempo, repetitive melody, and high volume. *adj:* of the life-style associated with this music; e.g., disco fashions.

11. EEJAY

Electronic journalism.

12. EUSTRESS

The positive, constructive response of the human organism to demands made on it.

13. FLOTATION MATTRESS

A water bed.

14. FLOUTMANSHIP

The political art of defying or scorning the obvious facts.

15. FOOD PROCESSOR

A kitchen machine that performs a variety of food preparation tasks, as slicing, chopping, mixing, etc.

16. GARBOLOGY

The study of a culture by examining its garbage.

17. GAS GUZZLER

An automobile that yields few miles per gallon of gasoline.

18. GASOHOL

The fuel for internal-combustion engines composed of gasoline and alcohol.

19. GENERIC

Of food marketing, packaged according to content only rather than brand name; a cost-cutting measure of some large grocery chain stores.

20. GLUON

A theoretical subatomic particle whose function it is to hold quarks together.

21. HYPOXIC TRAINING

The athletic training in which the body is forced to produce extra red blood cells by means of controlled stress accompanied by mild oxygen deprivation so as to be capable of extra oxygen uptake on demand.

22. IMAGING TEAM

A group of technicians who receive signals from space probes and convert them to pictures that are studied for scientific content.

23. JUMPER

An unskilled, short-term employee of the nuclear power industry who exposes himself to quick doses of relatively high radiation.

24. LIMERANCE

The ultimate, near obsessional, form of romantic love.

25. MAGNETOENCEPHALOGRAPHY

The noninvasive measurement of the electrical activity of the brain by analysis of the magnetic field produced by brain currents.

26. MINAUDIERE

A tiny, boxlike handbag for formal wear, often richly ornamented or carved and frequently worn on a cord or chain.

27. NECROMANIAC

A fanatic devotee of a dead entertainer.

28. NERD

A gauche, socially inept person.

29. NEVER NESTER

A person who will never marry or own a home.

30. NEW WAVE

Neo-Dadaist musical movement characterized by minimal, often harsh or erratic, instrumentation and insipid or violent lyrics; effect is heightened by intentionally bizarre behaviour and costumes of musicians; alternately called *no wave*.

31. PAYLOAD SPECIALIST

A nonastronaut space traveler who performs in-flight scientific experiments.

32. POLLERO

A person who helps Mexican nationals enter the U.S. illegally.

33. POLLO

An illegal Mexican immigrant to the U.S.

34. RISHON

In subatomic physics, hypothetical fundamental particle of which quarks may be composed.

35. ROLLER DISCO

Disco dancing done on roller skates.

36. SCRAM

In nuclear jargon, to activate a shutdown of a nuclear reactor by dropping control rods into the fuel core to stop the chain reaction.

37. SIABON

A hybrid ape produced from the mating of a male gibbon and a female siamang.

38. SLIDE

An open-toed, backless women's shoe, usually with a high heel.

39. SOCIOBIOLOGY

Discipline that views such characteristics of human society as male dominance and aggression, incest taboo, pair bonding, and division of labour as genetically (biologically) determined.

40. STOCKHOLM SYNDROME

The psychological state affecting persons held hostage, who under the extreme and prolonged stress of the situation begin to side with and often identify with their captors (term is derived from such an experience by hostages in a bank robbery in Stockholm, Sweden).

41. SYNFUEL

The synthetic substitute for the products of crude oil; derived from coal, shale oil, or vegetable products.

42. TAGGANTS

The microscopic plastic particles embedded in explosives to aid in identifying the explosives after they have been detonated as an anticrime aid.

43. THERMAHOL

The heating fuel composed of a combination of petroleum-based fuel oil and grain alcohol.

44. TINING

The shallow grooves cut into the road surface to prevent skidding and hydroplaning when the surface is wet.

45. TUBE TOP

Usually strapless, sleeveless women's blouse in the form of a tight-fitting, stretchy knit tube.

46. WIND SURFING

The sport in which participant stands aboard a surfboardlike platform equipped with a triangular sail and negotiates waves with the help of the wind.

47. WORKFARE

The welfare payments that are given on the condition that the beneficiary does necessary government work when such is needed.

48. XENOCURRENCY

The money circulating outside the country of its origin.

SOURCE: Reprinted with permission from the 1980 *Compton Year-book,* copyright © 1980 by Encyclopaedia Britannica, Inc., Chicago, Ill.

TELEPHONE SERVICES OF TOMORROW

Bell Laboratories reports that, given the present state of technology, it would be possible to market the following communications services. They won't be available to the general public, however, until a national telecommunications policy is instituted.

1. Your phone messages will be recorded so that you can hear them at a preselected time. The new service will also record messages from other callers when your phone is in use.
2. If the line is busy, additional calls will automatically come through as soon as the line is free.

3. You will be able to answer your calls selectively. People you do not want to talk to will receive a busy signal, be automatically routed to another phone, or receive a prerecorded message.
4. Calls from a pay phone will be billed to any authorized number. No operator, no credit card, no small change—just fast service.
5. You will have your own personal *nationwide* telephone number so that calls will reach you no matter where you are.
6. Emergency aid—police, firemen, or medical personnel—will be summoned by pressing a single button using the Touch-a-matic telephone.
7. A promising new cordless telephone will provide increased mobility in the home or office.
8. Customers will physically rearrange their own telephone equipment and even change services without waiting for a telephone installer.
9. With a direct link to customers' homes, public utilities will save energy by reducing electricity during a hot day. They will also be able to read meters without going to a customer's house.
10. Customers will call home and remotely control appliances or thermostats.
11. Home information systems will permit customers to communicate with computers over telephone lines, and any information requested will appear on your TV screen.

UNEARTHING THE PAST—
IN THE FUTURE

Predictor RICHARD MACNEISH, director of the Robert S. Peabody Foundation for Archaeology in Andover, Mass., estimates that he has spent 5,683 days participating in archaeological digs. He has published over 170 articles and numerous books, among which are five volumes on the prehistory of Tehuacan, Mexico. His current project is a multivolume series on the prehistory of Ayacucho, Peru.

• PREDICTIONS •

1982–2030

• A number of great breakthroughs will occur in Red China. One of these will be that plants (millet, soybeans, and perhaps rice, etc.) were first cultivated or first domesticated as much as 15,000 years ago, and here, too, there was a Neolithic Evolution, not a Neolithic Revolution. (The earliest evidence of the Neolithic in China we have at present is only about 5,000 to 6,000 years old, and many people think this is near the beginning of when it happened. My prediction of a find of 15,000 years is almost three times as old, and means that there was a long, slow development in evolution, not a 1,000-or-so-year revolution.)

• It will be found that the first villages with pottery began about 10,000 years ago in interior central China. (As of the present, the oldest pottery we have in China is only about 6,000 years old, so a guess that it started about 10,000 years ago is a radical departure from what has been found so far and from what most scholars would predict to be the beginning of the use of pottery.)

• Villages without agriculture will be found in coastal China dating to at least 15,000 years ago. (There are currently no known villages in China older than about 6,000 years, and the ones they have found so far have used some sort of agriculture. No one has dreamed that there are villages without agriculture in China, let alone that they are this old and located on the coast.)

• Agricultural beginnings in the Near East, somewhere in the "Hilly Flanks" (Zagros Mountains), will be pushed back to before 18,000 years ago. (As of now in the Near East, the oldest evidence that most scholars are willing to accept for the beginning of agriculture is about 11,000 years ago. On the basis of recent finds in Egypt, as well as the lack of very acute analysis of materials from the Near East, I think everybody is far too conservative, as well as wrong.)

• The first six-to-eight-million-year-old hominids with upright posture and Ramapithecus-like skulls will be discovered in South Asia, perhaps in or near the Swailik Hills of India. (The earliest recognized remains of man come from Africa and are between one million and three million years old. Anthropologists, because of Louis Leakey's work, have pretty much come to the conclusion that Africa is the cradle of mankind and that manlike beings with upright posture evolved in that one-to-three-million-year period. I think they are not only wrong as to the time but even the place.)

• An indisputable find of an occupation with bifacial tools will be excavated in Alaska or Northwest Canada dating to about 70,000 years ago. (Many archaeologists believe there is no reputable evidence for man in the New World before 12,000 years ago, and the majority of the others do not think the American Indian arrived in the New World much before 25,000 years ago. I think they are all far too conservative and haven't really looked at the evidence we have, let alone searched for the 70,000-year-old evidence we don't have.)

• Riverine villages without ceramics or (much) agriculture dating to 7,000 years ago will be found in the Maya lowlands of Central America. (At present, the earliest Maya material is about 3,000 years old, and it has agriculture which everybody believes is the basis for village life in the Maya lowlands. Again, I think the majority are wrong and new finds which my colleagues or I may make will prove this to be wrong.)

• An early skull with pre-Homo sapiens or Neanderthaloid characteristics, dating before 50,000 years ago, will be exhumed in the New World. (So far every skeleton ever found in the New World is that of modern Homo sapiens, and none are over 10,000 to 20,000 years old.)

• Paleolithic (Mousterian-like or Ordos-like) cultural remains will be found in Northeast Siberia, dating to 75,000 to 100,000 years ago. (Nothing has been found that is more than about 14,000 to 15,000 years old in northeastern Siberia, and even it is Mesolithic or Neolithic.)

• Pottery (possibly fiber-tempered) will be found in sites on the South American circum-Caribbean mainland area dating to before 4000 B.C. (Pottery found to date in the New World starts at about 2500 B.C. and seems to come from the Pacific coast of South America.)

---

50 BIGGEST U.S. METROPOLITAN AREAS IN 1990

	1980 Population	1990 Population	Percentage Change
1. New York	9,173,000	8,437,000	8.0%
2. Chicago	7,032,000	7,087,000	.8%
3. Los Angeles–Long Beach	7,027,000	7,012,000	.2%
4. Philadelphia	4,782,000	4,741,000	.9%
5. Detroit	4,346,000	4,258,000	2.0%
6. Boston	3,917,000	3,986,000	1.8%
7. Houston	2,740,000	3,754,000	37.0%
8. San Francisco–Oakland	3,210,000	3,314,000	3.2%
9. Dallas–Fort Worth	2,795,000	3,285,000	17.5%
10. Washington, D.C.	3,074,000	3,247,000	5.6%
11. Nassau–Suffolk, N.Y.	2,740,000	2,937,000	7.2%
12. Anaheim–Santa Ana–Garden Grove, Calif.	1,970,000	2,731,000	38.6%
13. San Diego	1,826,000	2,455,000	34.4%
14. Atlanta	1,930,000	2,334,000	20.9%
15. St. Louis	2,368,000	2,326,000	1.8%
16. Baltimore	2,176,000	2,287,000	5.1%
17. Minneapolis–St. Paul	2,065,000	2,170,000	5.1%
18. Pittsburgh	2,255,000	2,118,000	6.1%
19. Tampa–St. Petersburg	1,511,000	2,097,000	38.8%
20. Phoenix	1,381,000	1,964,000	42.2%
21. Denver–Boulder	1,560,000	1,963,000	25.8%
22. Newark	1,937,000	1,823,000	5.9%
23. Miami	1,513,000	1,806,000	19.4%
24. Cleveland	1,908,000	1,764,000	7.5%
25. Riverside–San Bernardino–Ontario, Calif.	1,375,000	1,659,000	20.7%
26. Ft. Lauderdale–Hollywood, Fla.	980,000	1,550,000	58.2%

		1980 Population		Percentage Change
27.	San Jose	1,280,000	1,539,000	20.2%
28.	Milwaukee	1,435,000	1,467,000	2.2%
29.	Seattle	1,428,000	1,432,000	.3%
30.	Cincinnati	1,371,000	1,355,000	1.2%
30.	Portland, Ore.	1,168,000	1,355,000	16.0%
32.	Kansas City	1,301,000	1,328,000	2.1%
33.	San Antonio	1,082,000	1,318,000	21.8%
34.	New Orleans	1,168,000	1,303,000	11.6%
35.	Buffalo	1,300,000	1,252,000	3.7%
36.	Columbus, O.	1,114,000	1,220,000	9.5%
37.	Indianapolis	1,156,000	1,203,000	4.1%
38.	Sacramento	982,000	1,200,000	22.2%
39.	Hartford–New Britain–Bristol, Conn.	1,058,000	1,082,000	2.3%
40.	Salt Lake City–Ogden	871,000	1,076,000	23.5%
41.	Memphis	907,000	987,000	8.8%
42.	Rochester	974,000	986,000	1.2%
43.	Orlando	657,000	951,000	44.7%
44.	Norfolk–Virginia Beach	831,000	942,000	13.4%
45.	Nashville	803,000	922,000	14.8%
46.	Honolulu	762,000	921,000	20.9%
47.	Louisville	889,000	911,000	2.5%
48.	Oklahoma City	797,000	908,000	13.9%
49.	Birmingham	820,000	877,000	7.0%
50.	Greensboro–Winston-Salem–High Point, N.C.	794,000	870,000	9.6%

SOURCE: Reprinted from *U.S. News & World Report,* copyright © 1979, U.S. News & World Report, Inc.

ANTHOLOGY OF EXPERTS

Seeking specialists in many fields to give their forecasts on what the years and decades ahead might offer us, we were surprised by the enthusiasm and cooperation of these experts. In fact, we received so many detailed predictions that we were unable to contain them within the pages of one book. From some of the best of these experts we have culled the most interesting and thoughtful of their exclusive forecasts.

From predictor ROY AMARA, president of the Institute for the Future, located in Menlo Park, Calif., who in 1955 planned and designed the first full-scale banking computer:

1982–1992

• The key economic question for most nations in the 1980s will revolve around the proper role of government in the economy. Each country will continue the search in its own way for new forms of partnership and arrangements between public and private sectors.

Beyond 1992

• In the private sector, employees and consumers will acquire a proportionately greater voice and influence in decision-making at the expense of professional managers, government, and shareholders. In the public sector, the first steps will be taken toward a real breakdown of national political barriers through the formation of strong (regional) economic associations spurred by new multinational corporate forms.

From predictor DR. ROBERT O. BECKER, research professor of surgery at the State University of New York's Upstate Medical Center in Syracuse, renowned for his pioneer work in bioelectronics:

1982–1992

• In the area of growth control, the use of small electrical currents to stimulate bone growth in humans will become an established medical treatment. Similar electrical techniques will be used to stimulate regeneration of joint cartilage in early cases of arthritis. Electrical stimulation combined with grafting or injection of appropriate cells will be used to stimulate regeneration of the spinal cord in patients with paraplegia.

1993–2030

• The concept of replacing defective or worn-out parts by transplants or implants of artificial devices will be replaced by the electrical stimulation of regenerative growth in the human. This will be applied, for example, to cardiac patients, where new heart muscle will be grown; in cases of kidney failure, new kidneys will be grown; and almost all body parts will be restored by regenerative techniques, including amputated extremities.

From predictor NEVILLE BROWN, senior lecturer in international politics at the University of Birmingham, in England, and author of *The Future Global Challenge:*

1983

• Serious issues of privacy, political toleration, etc., are raised by the need to protect military electronics against espionage.

1985

• The alienation of young professional people becomes a serious threat to the survival of Western democracy.

1993

• The U.S.S.R. draws level with the West in terms of military electronics.
• Israel, having formally annexed the West Bank and the Gaza in 1985, completes its extension of Israeli citizenship to the Arab inhabitants there.

From predictor LANE DEMOLL, former editor of *Rain: Journal of Appropriate Technology* and author of the book *Stepping Stones: Appropriate Technology and Beyond:*

1982–1992

• Americans will reduce their total energy use 75% by 1992, while substantially improving the overall quality of our lives. Self-reliance on a community and regional level will be the key. Locally available resources will provide most of the decreasing amounts of energy necessary. We will almost totally eliminate our need to mine new resources—recycling or reusing materials and returning bodily leftovers to the soil. We will relearn the value of cooperation, smallness, simplicity and tender loving care in all things—our farms, businesses, neighborhoods, and towns.

From predictor LOUIS ANTOINE DERNOI, consulting urbanologist and lecturer, is working with the German futures group in Berlin:

1987–2030

• Major human functions and activities will engage in a blending process due to physical, psychological, and moral pressures. (Blending aims to express a situation different from the present fragmented activities of Western populations. Few of us are lucky to have work or occupation that is, at least partly, also a pleasurable leisure engagement; work is mostly a bread-winning proposition only. Once blended, it will show traits of the artist's, craftsman's, scientist's work today: it will be carried out with enthusiasm, not as a toil but as a quasi-leisure engagement.) This is the percentage of people having achieved blending: 1987—10%; 1992—25%; 2010—50%; 2030—75%.

• The following shows the percent of the total population that will not work anymore in the system of 7 hours per day, 5 days per week, or have 2–3-week yearly vacations, or spend 60% of their life in one time-block of work: 1987—20%; 1992—40%; 2010—65%; 2030—85%.

From predictor DR. LEONARD J. DUHL, professor of public health and urban social policy at the University of California, Berkeley, and author of *The City and the University:*

1982–1992

• The search for alternatives (as opposed to Western notions of scientific rational realities) will lead to science dividing into two spheres—organized classical science and one more related to mystical, religious, and "right brain" notions. Such differences are already noticeable in the study of physics, for example, as opposed to psychology. This will lead to many new research techniques, values, etc.

1985

• Health will be more broadly defined and not left to the doctors; it is the union of the community at large. Medicine, like science, will incorporate alternatives (right-brain type and non-Western practices) and have two sides to it: treatment and healing. Much will be deprofessionalized. The emphasis in part will move from illness to health (or how to be healthy).

From predictor DR. RODERIC GORNEY, associate professor of psychiatry at the University of California, Los Angeles, and author of the book *The Human Agenda:*

By 1990

• General worldwide recognition that for the future the central criterion by which all human endeavors must be assessed is the impact they have on human fulfillment. Those two words will comprise a new definition of "the bottom line," which gradually will supplant the present one that deals with monetary profit and loss. Over time, this redefinition will affect all sorts of environmental, educational, social, economic, and developmental decisions.

From predictor DR. JOSEPH KUC, professor of plant pathology at the University of Kentucky in Lexington, Ky., and author or coauthor of 145 research publications:

1982–1992

• Pest control will depend less upon absolute control and more on tolerance of low levels of pests. Instead of pesticides, the new trend will be toward "biological control." Plants will be injected with hormones and other agents which elicit natural disease-resistance mechanisms in the plants.

1993–2030

• Agricultural wastes and crops will supply 10%–20% of the world's energy need. Energy production and distribution will become less centralized.
• If weather conditions are not favorable in Africa, Central Asia, and the Indian subcontinent, large segments of the population will suffer from starvation and malnutrition. The destruction of tropical rain forests, e.g., in Brazil, will change weather patterns and accelerate the development of deserts and marginally agricultural areas.

From predictor DR. OZAY MEHMET, professor of economics at the University of Ottawa in Ontario, Canada:

1982–1992

• The third world will be characterized by a conflict between egalitarianism and authoritarianism. As the have-nots intensify their demand for a larger share of the benefits of economic growth, several countries in Asia, Africa, and Latin America will experience violent revolutions and military coups. But the drive toward greater social justice will not be achieved until the end of the 20th century, except for a relatively few countries.

1982–2030

• The energy crisis will bring about far-reaching changes in the intensive capital and energy life-styles of industrialized countries. More and more consumer goods will be produced in, and imported from, third-world countries, implying greater dependency of the rich countries on the third-world countries. But the industrialized countries, principally the U.S., will maintain their comparative technological advantage, although by 2030 new competitors (e.g., China) might emerge.
• Changing economic realities in the international economy, which will worsen in the early 1980s, will, in the 1990s, increase the drive toward the "global village" based on economic interdependence. Such economic problems as inflation and unemployment will assume global proportions and become common problems requiring global solutions.

From predictor DR. JAMES F. MURPHY, professor in the department of recreation and leisure studies at Northeastern University in Boston, Mass., and the author of five textbooks:

1982–1992

• Development of "leisure ghettos" in which enclaves of individuals of similar life-styles begin to emerge as the dominant basis for segregation in society (e.g., when leisure opportunities and activities determine a person's behavior, choices, and social group more than one's age, gender, occupation, ethnic background, etc.).

• A reorganization at the federal Cabinet level will result in the creation of a Department of Leisure to promote and encourage satisfaction and fulfillment for all people. Work will no longer serve as the primary social organizing function in society.

1993–2030

• Establishment of nonwhite and "minority" standards of leisure conduct as the norm following the "pluralizing" by former nonaligned groups (e.g., blacks, Hispanics, women, disabled, gays, etc.) resulting in the resurfacing of extensive forms of competition, street scene celebrations, incorporation of all art forms into the fabric of city life, etc.

• The potential for leisure riots will increase. The lack of sufficient, diverse, accessible, consumption-oriented leisure opportunities and the growing availability of large blocks of free time will result in the clamoring for the dismantling and destruction of facilities which do not respond to increased demands for personal fulfillment.

• The emergence of outer-space leisure picnics—adventures into space by selected prominent and wealthy individuals—will become the new form of nouveau riche "pop leisure." For some individuals it will perhaps be the only means of escape from a world growing restless for redistribution of leisure-dependent resources.

From predictor STEPHEN PAPSON, a sociologist who teaches at St. Lawrence University in Canton, N.Y.:

1985

• The travel industry becomes increasingly efficient in providing information for destination selection. Computer and video technology will provide instantaneous information on the destination. For example, videotapes will be used as supplements or as replacements for the tourist brochure.

1995

• The travel industry becomes the world's largest industry. Due to increasing numbers of tourists, governments at all levels begin to set quotas on the number of tourists allowed to enter their jurisdictions. At first, limitations will be placed on peak travel periods and on specific areas. This will be extended to national borders and seasons.

Continuous present–2030

• Due to increasing standardization of tourist destinations in order to handle the number of tourists, the possibility of spontaneous, authentic encounters with members of different cultural groups declines. MacCannell's notion of "staged authenticity," in which encounters are contrived but appear as spontaneous, is the dominant experience of most tourists.

From predictor DR. ANTHONY PIETROPINTO, a practicing psychiatrist in New York City who is the medical director of the mental health program at Lutheran Medical Center in Brooklyn, N.Y., and coauthor of *Beyond the Male Myth: A Nationwide Survey:*

1982–1990

• There will be a marked change in sexual mores, with a restriction of premarital sexual activity to those men who have made a definite commitment to the women involved, a standard generally enforced by the women. This will be seen as necessary by women to maintain sexual versus nonsexual role division in the working world.
• The key issue for the women's liberation movement will be enabling women to combine successful careers with child-raising. Feminists will turn for leadership, not to single women, but almost exclusively to wives and mothers. Society will realize the folly of keeping our most gifted women from reproducing.

2010–2030

• A generation from now, the combination of women's greater longevity and equal education and job experience will produce a corps of female "elders" who will assume the majority of leadership positions in politics, business, and science. Feminist leadership will no longer be controlled by women under 45.
• Males and females will share equity but not equality. Women will be regarded as having unique and indispensable potentials in nearly all fields and will be deemed more suitable as work partners for men than peers of the same sex. Women will take leadership roles as often as men, with no stigma placed on the dominant woman or subordinate man. Stringent self-limitation with regard to sexual behavior and equal job ability will curb confusion between sex role and work role on the job.

2

PREDICTIONS ON OUTER SPACE

1993–2030

The first manned landings will be made on the planet Mars.

1993–2030

The majority of people leaving Earth for permanent jobs in outer space will be female.

2030

Spacekind will issue a Declaration of Independence from Earthkind.

LOOKING THROUGH
THE SPACE TELESCOPE

Predictor SIR BERNARD LOVELL is the founder and director of the prestigious Nuffield Radio Astronomy Laboratories at the University of Manchester in Cheshire, England. The recipient of numerous awards for his pioneering work in astronomy, Dr. Lovell has written popular and technical books, including *Science and Civilization*, *Discovering the Universe*, and *Out of the Zenith*.

• PREDICTIONS •

1982–1992

• The most important astronomical event of this period will be the launching of the large space telescope by the U.S. Space Shuttle. At present scheduled for 1983, the telescope will be free of the atmospheric disturbances which limit the performance of terrestrial telescopes. It seems likely to be the major influence on our developing knowledge of the structure, origin, and eventual fate of the universe.

• The development of the Soyuz-Salyut spaceship combination by the Soviet Union will lead to the establishment of permanent manned spaceships in orbit around the earth. Permanently orbiting

The Space Telescope.

manned spacecraft in immediate contact with the ground have important military and peaceful applications.
• The investigation of the planets will proceed by unmanned spacecraft. Further landings of instruments on Mars and Venus and close inspection of several other planets will be important features in the development of our understanding about the evolution of the solar system and particularly why the planet Earth is uniquely favored in possessing a habitable atmosphere.

1993–2030

• This period seems likely to witness a striking renewal of space flights by man to the moon and the first manned landings on the planet Mars. It is not possible to foresee at this moment whether the planetary exploits will be stimulated by competition between the U.S. and U.S.S.R. or whether the adventures will be a true international effort involving all nations that have developed competent space technologies.
• The urge to establish working colonies on the moon and in space will have arisen because of the increasing difficulties of pursuing certain astronomical studies from terrestrial bases. For example, the spread of military and commercial communication interests over the radio frequency band will probably wipe out the possibility of continuing radio astronomical studies from Earth.
• Many futuristic space concepts will have been demonstrated. With world population four or five times as great as at present, the demand for power will have stimulated the transmission of solar power from space. The large numbers of huge spacecraft required will alter the night sky to such an extent that most Earth-based astronomical observations will have ceased. Observations will be made from orbiting spacecraft or from observatories on the moon—and they will probably be manned.
• The major astronomical problems which confront us today will have been solved. But, as has happened in this century, their solution will have revealed features of the universe that we cannot envisage at present. Man will still feel that the next step forward will enable him to understand the totality of the universe. But by this time it will have been widely realized that a comprehension of the natural world and of man's place in the universe can be achieved only by a synthesis of all forms of knowledge.

ROBOTS MINE THE ASTEROIDS

Predictor NIGEL CALDER, editor of *New Scientist* magazine from 1956 to 1966, has since worked on a long succession of joint TV and book projects for the British Broadcasting Corporation (BBC). These include *The Violent Universe, Spaceships of the Mind,* and *Nuclear*

Nightmares. Winner of the 1972 UNESCO Kalinga Prize for Popularization of Science, Mr. Calder lives in West Sussex, England.

• PREDICTIONS •

1982–1987

• The risk of nuclear war is at a maximum owing to acute nervousness and mistrust among the nuclear-armed nations and special dangers in central Europe (a German bomb?) and the Middle East (Israeli and Islamic bombs). If it supervenes, a nuclear world war will negate most other predictions in this book.

1987–1992

• "Work riots" occur in many industrialized countries, as unemployment soars due to automation. Women's Lib is greatly set back, and there is renewed interest in domestic life. The badge-and-medal industry booms, as "unwanted" people assert their identities. Gambling is the chief leisure-time activity.

By 1992

• Industrialized nations by now have divided into two groups: those (e.g., Japan?) where grief and agitation about loss of jobs have led to repressive police states; and those (e.g., Britain?) which never took work so seriously, where a benign new social order emerges and people have a lot of fun.

1992–1999

• A big drive to self-sufficiency and to intensive and artificial methods of food production begins the gradual abolition of farming. Human settlements condense into compact, relatively small units, and large tracts of fertile land are returned to nature. Success with solar-chemical and nuclear-fusion techniques removes the anxieties about energy supplies.

By 2000

• Two negative predictions. The search for extraterrestrial intelligences is abandoned because there seems to be nobody there. And the much-advertised heating of the earth by the man-made carbon dioxide "greenhouse" fails to occur; instead there is renewed concern about cooling and an impending ice age.

By 2010

• An artificial brain as complex and as richly programmed as the human brain turns out to have conscious thoughts and emotions. Floating cities in mid-ocean help to spread people more evenly and rehearse some of the problems and opportunities of living in space.

By 2020

• Robots and self-reproducing machines go out into space to mine the moon and the asteroids and to prepare space for human habitation. A complete community is sealed up, on Earth, to discover the problems of biological isolation in eventual space settlements.

Robots mine the asteroids.

By 2030

• The first large human colony is established in free space. Its probable mission: to build a robot spaceship that will travel to another star. Transport around the solar system has become very easy, by solar sailing and nuclear-fusion rocketry. The colonization of space begins at last, on a much firmer basis than the old space shuttle.

The residential area of a space colony.

SLOW JOURNEY TO THE STARS

Predictor EDGAR MITCHELL was an astronaut on NASA's third mission to the moon, where he experienced "a blissful alteration of consciousness." As a result of this experience, he decided to devote himself to the exploration of extrasensory phenomena and founded the Institute of Noetic Sciences in San Francisco, Calif. Mr. Mitchell is the director of two computer software companies in West Palm Beach, Fla.

• PREDICTIONS •

1982–1992

• The decade of 1982–1992 will most likely see space activity, with a few major exceptions, continue to receive minimal attention and effort because of pressing world economic and sociopolitical problems. Unmanned interplanetary investigations will continue at a low level of activity but near-Earth applications, many using the space shuttle, which can be justified as contributing to the solution of energy and other socioeconomic problems, will be stepped up. This decade will be one of planning new programs for the future rather than funding new immediate programs and new hardware.

1992

• By 1992 and beyond, many economic problems of the previous decade will be moving toward solution, and space exploration will be revitalized by plans for large space stations for laboratories and workshops, orbiting solar-power stations, permanent scientific communities on the moon, manned exploration of other planets of the solar systems, and, most likely, by some breakthroughs in physics and biophysics which will eventually lead to manned exploration of the near stars in this galaxy.

TOWARD THE 21st CENTURY

Predictor ARTHUR C. CLARKE, author of almost 50 books, some 20 million copies of which have been printed in over 30 languages, is one of the most commercially successful science fiction writers in the world. He is also a highly respected scientist and has been awarded a Franklin Institute Gold Medal for his innovative work with communication satellites. His nonfiction includes such classics as *Interplanetary Flight, The Exploration of Space*, and *Profiles of the Future*. His prize-winning novels include *Rendezvous with Rama, Childhood's End*, and *2001: A Space Odyssey*. Mr. Clarke lives in Sri Lanka.

• PREDICTIONS •

Many years ago, in the opening words of *Profiles of the Future*, I stated: "It is impossible to predict the future, and all attempts to do so in any detail appear ludicrous within a very few years."

Strictly speaking, the very concept of prediction is logical nonsense, because it's a statement about the future—and how can one make any meaningful assertions about something that doesn't exist? (What color are a unicorn's eyes?) The best that can be done—and sometimes even this is a very poor best—is to outline the entire spectrum of possible futures and to assign probabilities to each item. This is not *prediction* but projection, or *extrapolation;* there is a profound difference between the two, which many people find hard to understand. Let me give an example.

If I said that the population of the U.S. on January 1, 2001, would be 236,453,328, that would be a *prediction*—and it would be wrong (barring fantastic luck!). However, a statistician might say that the population of the U.S. at that date has a *90% chance* of being between 220,000,000 and 240,000,000. That would be an *extrapolation,* and if he were good at his job, he'd have a fair chance of being right. He would have taken the existing birth, death, immigration, and emigration rates; made reasonable guesses about their future values; and done some arithmetic. But this procedure assumes that history won't produce any surprises, which it invariably does. The population of the U.S. in 2001 might be only a couple of million, if there had been a nuclear war. And if you think there's *no* possibility of a similar error in the other direction, consider this science fiction scenario: When the King (!) orders the multiple cloning of everyone named Kennedy, the population jumps in one year from 230,000,000 to 1,000,000,000+.

So, having proved the impossibility of prediction, here are my extrapolations, in the areas where I feel I can speak with any authority. I have given dates only to the nearest five years; anything else would be to convey a misleading impression of accuracy.

Most of the headings are self-explanatory, and I have omitted the two most important of all—the detection of extraterrestrial life and the detection of extraterrestrial intelligence. Either could happen tomorrow—or a thousand years from now. We have no hard facts on which to base even a guess, still less a *reasonable* extrapolation.

1985

• Permanent space station similar to Skylab, but in a higher orbit; carries 5–10 men.
• Electronic tutors. These will be the erudite descendants of today's computer toys—completely portable, cheap, capable of giving pro-

grammed instruction in almost any subject at any level of difficulty. They could trigger an educational explosion (particularly in developing countries) which could boost mankind out of the Stone Age.

1990

• Return to the moon.
• Wrist telephones. These will become possible with the construction of very large communications satellites and will start a social-economic revolution as great as that produced by the telephone itself a century earlier.

1995

• Lunar base established. The beginning of planetary colonization—the main theme of the 21st century.

2000

• Commercial fusion power. Era of cheap energy dawns.

2005

• Manned flight to Mars.

2010

• Space cities.

2020

• Mars base.

2030

• Manned exploration of the solar system. First robot interstellar probes.

ONCE WE WERE NOT ALONE

Predictor DR. GARRY HUNT is head of the Laboratory for Planetary Atmospheres at the University College in London. A regular broadcaster on BBC television and radio, in 1980 he produced a program on the solar system entitled *Worlds Apart*. Dr. Hunt also worked as an experimenter for NASA on the Voyager Mission to Jupiter and Saturn and on the Viking Mission to Mars.

• PREDICTIONS •

1986
• The giant white oval clouds which formed in the atmosphere of Jupiter in 1939 are suddenly seen to disappear, causing a dramatic change in the face of the planet.

1987
• Suddenly, after more than 50 years of speculation and study, a new planet is found in our solar system beyond the orbit of Pluto. Observations made using the Space Telescope find this 10th planet residing in the cold outer reaches of our solar system. The search continues for evidence of any neighboring satellites.

1989
• The Voyager spacecraft reaches Neptune, the farthest planet in its tour of the outer solar system. The pictures show that the planet is surrounded by a system of rings, composed of tiny particles which extend down to the cloud tops, just like those around Jupiter and Uranus.

1990
• For several years, men and women have been working successfully in Spacelab, a laboratory located above the earth's atmosphere, without the limitations of gravity. Suddenly, disaster strikes and the space station is damaged. A dramatic rescue is carried out, using a spacecraft launched from a space shuttle, to return the scientists safely to Earth. During this decade, similar missions have been made to deflect exhausted spacecraft, such as Tiros X, a weather satellite, and keep them from hitting large cities in North America.

1993–2030
• Toward the end of this period, there will be a dramatic mission to Mars involving a spacecraft that can move over the surface of the planet and then bring samples of material back for reexamination by Earth scientists. The spacecraft will be controlled from Earth, and the analysis of the surface material will be carried out in Spacelab above the atmosphere to avoid contamination of our planet. Core samples of Mars, obtained at the polar region and near the equator, show direct evidence that the planet has undergone climatic cycles in the past, at times quite different from those of Earth. This indicates that the planet itself has greater control of the environmental changes than have external effects, such as the sun. The soil samples extracted from several meters below the surface of the planet yield the most exciting and rewarding object of all time: a fossil of a tiny creature. At one time in the past, Mars possessed life. Early in the history of the solar system, we were not alone.
• Since the 1940s, the amount of carbon dioxide in the earth's atmosphere has been slowly but surely increasing to the extent that

enormous climate impacts are being forecast by the turn of the century. After several decades of very changeable weather, disasters that can be attributed to the increased CO_2 in the atmosphere start to affect our daily lives. The amount of polar ice is now greatly reduced compared with 1970, and the ocean has increased in volume, flooding low-lying areas such as the coastal parts of Holland and Florida. London is protected by the presence of the Thames barrier.

• International legislation reduces the use of coal burning by urging all the leading nations to make greater use of nuclear generating stations for the production of electricity. Legislation is also being attempted to prevent certain countries from continuing to cut down their large equatorial forests, which act as a "sink" for the atmospheric carbon dioxide. Man's activities are seen to be adversely affecting our weather and climate.

• After a gap of nearly 30 years, space people from Earth land on the moon. Large colonies are set up in selected areas. From the moon, the earth's atmosphere is constantly monitored. Minerals from the moon are brought back to Earth and examined for use in our rapidly advancing technology.

• The rapid developments in telecommunications through the use of satellite links have greatly reduced the need for business travel. No longer is it necessary to travel from London to Los Angeles for a two-day meeting. Now the conference delegates see each other on huge screens and transmit data and pictures on near real-time data links at costs far below the round-trip air fares.

ROBOTS CLASH IN SPACE

Predictor BEN BOVA is the executive editor of *OMNI*, one of the most popular magazines about the future, and past editor of *Analog*, one of the foremost science fiction magazines. He is a science fiction writer as well, with several books to his credit, including *The Weather Makers*, *Out of the Sun*, and *The Duelling Machine*.

• PREDICTIONS •

1984

• Permanent orbiting spacelab is launched into orbit by U.S. space shuttle.

1985

• Space shuttle makes first nonscientist passenger flights. Among earliest celebrities carried into orbit are people from show business, the media, and politics.

1987

• The Soviets land cosmonauts on the moon and set up a permanent lunar base for exploration, mining, and scientific research.

1988

• First test in orbit of high-power laser-beam weapons, by both the U.S. and the U.S.S.R.

1989

• Japan establishes a permanent orbital space station.

1993

• First prototype solar-power satellite successfully beams energy from space to earth.

1997

• The U.S. and U.S.S.R. engage in an unpublicized robotic war in space as both sides try to establish networks of laser-armed satellites to serve as ABM weapons.

2005

• Solar-power satellites, built by a consortium of multinational corporations, beam more energy to the earth than is produced from oil, coal, or uranium.

2015

• First true space colony is established in orbit between the earth and the moon.

2030

• The five space colonies in orbit between the earth and the moon declare their independence from all terrestrial nations and form their own government.

SOVIETS ESTABLISH
FIRST COLONY ON MOON

Predictor TRUDY E. BELL is a free-lance science writer and editor who specializes in astronomy and space. Her background includes six and a half years on the editorial board of *Scientific American* and one year as senior editor for *OMNI* magazine. She is also the author of more than 70 articles and book reviews on astronomy, space activities, and the history of astronomy.

• PREDICTIONS •

By 1985

• Japan will send interplanetary probes toward Venus and Halley's Comet, as will France—becoming the next nations behind the U.S. and the U.S.S.R. to send spacecraft beyond earth orbit.

By 1986

• The People's Republic of China will put an astronaut into orbit around the earth—becoming the third nation to put a man in space.

By 1987

• Commercial enterprises in space—particularly communications and earth-resources observations—will have become a substantial *international* market. Nations with their own satellites in orbit will include India, several Arab countries, and Brazil. West Germany will be a leader in space manufacturing processes, with the U.S. playing a belated game of catch-up.

By 1990

• The U.S.S.R. will establish a colony on the moon for both scientific research and military observation purposes—making the U.S. uneasy.

By 1995

• The U.S. will have established a modest astronomical observatory and research station on the far side of the moon and will begin experimenting with manufacturing processes using lunar materials.

By 2000

• *No* signs of extraterrestrial intelligence will have been detected elsewhere in the galaxy, and popular opinion about its existence will take another pendulum swing back toward the notion that we are the only intelligent life forms in the universe.

By 2010

• Vacations in space and space tourism, as a branch of high-priced adventure travel (analogous to today's commercial trips to the North Pole), will have become established—and will be an immediate success.

By 2030

• The U.S. will have established, as a separate military service branch, the U.S. Space Force, a spin-off from the U.S. Air Force, just as the air force was an earlier spin-off from the army and navy.

FIRST CHILD BORN IN SPACE

Predictor DR. GERALD FEINBERG is a theoretical physicist and professor at Columbia University in New York City. He is the author of two books about the future, *The Prometheus Project* and *Consequences of Growth,* and the coauthor of *Life beyond Earth,* a study of the possibilities of extraterrestrial life.

• PREDICTIONS •

1982–1992

• Conditions on Jupiter are found to be hospitable for various forms of unearthly life.
• New probes of Martian surface resolve questions about life on Mars that were left open by Viking probe.
• Tests of mass driver and ion rockets open way for large-scale exploration of solar system.

c. 2000

• First O'Neill-type space colony is built and inhabited. This colony would be an artificial planetoid made of lunar materials and powered by solar energy so as to be self-sufficient. (For further information, see Gerard O'Neill's *The High Frontier*.) First children born off Earth.

1992–2030

- Life discovered on Titan, a moon of Saturn.
- Manned (and womaned) expeditions to Mars, Titan, and Ganymede (the fourth satellite of Jupiter).
- Detection of extrasolar planets by space observatories.
- One million human beings live permanently in space colonies.

WOMEN LEAD SPACE COLONIZATION

Predictor GEORGE S. ROBINSON is the world's first attorney to receive a Ph.D. in space law. For the past nine years he has served as assistant general counsel of the Smithsonian Institution. He has also served as legal counsel for the Federal Aviation Administration and as an international relations specialist for NASA. Dr. Robinson is the author of numerous articles and books on space law, including *Living in Outer Space* and *Space Trek: The Endless Migration*.

· PREDICTIONS ·

1982–1992

- "Space law" will shift from civil to military in character as the U.S. Department of Defense acquires independent manned capability in space. The militarization of space will force the civilian efforts of NASA back under the jurisdiction of military authorities. Private enterprise will participate in space industrialization only with heavy military protection.
- There will be a voluntary realignment of national boundaries shared by Canada, the U.S., and Mexico. This realignment will serve as the basis for Western leadership in space industrialization. The U.S.S.R. will establish the first *permanent* space community with the first *permanent* inhabitants.
- Equatorial countries will emerge as the dominant nations or political alliances involved in the routine industrialization of space.

1982 on

- Although the genus *Homo* will remain the same, humans that function predominantly in space will be recognized as being in a different species from *sapiens*. The dependence of space inhabitants upon technology for their survival, together with a synthetic and alien

life-support environment, will foster values and behavior that are quite different from those of humans living on the earth.
• As our understanding of individual and group behavior becomes more advanced, the principles of social order will be based more on science than on ever changing morals and ethics. To give civilizations directions for survival, broader philosophical and theological constructs will be adopted.

1993–2030

• The majority of people leaving Earth for permanent or long-term habitation in space (manufacturing facilities or deep-space probes) will be female. Social order in space communities will be distinctly matriarchal.
• Violent, competitive theocracies will emerge in permanent earth-orbiting space communities and deep-space probes. Sexual relations in space communities will, in part, be influenced by relative isolation and lengthy separations of husbands and wives and of lovers. Audiovisual technology will play an important role in bringing individuals together, and electronic and pharmaceutical aids will be commonplace. Lessons of history will be repeated . . . and repeated . . . and repeated.
• In satellite space communities and manned deep-space probes, limited space and weight capacities will prevent the accumulation of personal property. Consequently, psychological substitutes for material wealth and power will take the form of the age-old marketable commodity that requires no physical space—secrets.

2030

• The first Declaration of Independence by Spacekind from Earthkind will be announced.

2030 on

• Direct genetic intervention will allow for the predetermination of human characteristics depending upon the circumstances in which the individual will function in space.

FORECAST 2001

Predictor G. HARRY STINE has worked in several fields including industrial research and development, astronautics, and forecasting since 1952. He has written more than 20 books on science and technology, including *The Space Enterprise* and *Century-21: The Hopeful Future*. Mr. Stine also participated in Operation Moon Base (1957), a U.S. Air Force study, and has been a consultant to the

Smithsonian Institution, the Institute for the Future, and the Hudson Institute.

• FORECASTS •

2001

I do not make predictions; if you want a prediction of the future, go see a fortune-teller. A prediction implies that an event will occur in the future with better than 99.9999% probability.

I make forecasts, and there is a difference. A forecast implies that there is a high probability but not a sure bet that something will occur.

A short-range forecast for 10 years or less is *always* overoptimistic; a long-range forecast for more than 10 years into the future is *always* conservative.

My forecasts of the future are based upon extrapolation of historic trends. There are two axioms that one must always keep in mind when doing this: (a) a reasonable and rational forecast will *always* err on the conservative side; and (b) the more outlandish and fantastic a forecast appears to be when it is made, the more likely it is to occur.

With the above caveats, I can make a generalized forecast for the year 2001:

We will be able to do anything we want to do, provided we are willing to pay for it and to live with all the consequences.

I have extracted the following forecasts from my book *Century-21: The Hopeful Future*. They are forecasts of things that I expect to see in the next 21 years. However, due to political and/or economic factors, they carry with them a −5/+25 year variation as to when they might occur. In physical technology, developments may include:

• Establishment of a central data facility with wide public access from library, business, and home terminals, utilizing very large communications satellites in geosynchronous earth orbit.

• Large-scale use of new structural materials of high strength and low weight, many of them made in space.

• Three-dimensional holographic television for business conference purposes and, in Century-21, for home entertainment purposes.

• Revision of gravitational theories leading in Century-21 to the possibilities of new modes of transportation including interstellar travel.

• Development and widespread use of microelectronic modules and memory units for such prosaic purposes as true "picture windows" (i.e., windows on which are projected electronic images, as in television).

• Development and use of the photoelectrolysis process—by which water molecules are broken down into hydrogen and oxygen—as an energy source for widespread use on earth, leading to a "hydrogen economy."

• Development and use of photochemical energy sources in which light energy causes chemical reactions of great energy release to occur, leading to the replacement of the Otto and Diesel cycle engines in most ground transportation vehicles by Century-21.

• Routine access to near-earth orbit with fully reusable space vehicles capable of orbiting payloads for less than $10 per pound.

• Space factories in orbit producing new materials and pharmaceuticals in weightlessness.
• At least 20 solar-power satellites (SPS) operating in geosynchronous earth orbit by 2021, each producing 10 gigawatts (equal to 1 billion watts) of electricity, which is beamed to earth for use on existing electric-power grids. By 2025, because of the large-scale relocation of energy-consumptive industrial processes into space, nearly all the baseload energy requirements of earth will be assumed by the SPS system, allowing a shutdown of all nukes and placing of coal-fired plants on standby for peaking.

Century-21 is going to see the sort of progress in biotechnology that we have seen in physical technology in the 20th century. Although this will just be getting under way by 2001, we can expect the following developments in biotechnology:
• Development of immunizing agents that can protect against most bacterial and viral diseases, including the cure for the common cold.
• Artificial generation of protein for food through *in vitro* cellular processes.
• Chromosome typing for detecting abnormalities in humans within weeks after conception and, in Century-21, gene mapping *before* conception to permit the conception of the best possible child.
• Cloning of human organs, leading to a cloning of replacement organs in Century-21.
• Development of insect-control chemicals for specific insect targets, with no effects on the physiology of human beings or other animals.
• Chemicals that will accelerate perception and learning, especially among retardates.
• Significant contribution of microbial systems to the world's food supplies.
• Psycho-chemicals for specific behavior modification in humans and animals.
• Cures for all observed and known forms of cancer.
• Stimulation of the nervous system by externally applied electronic signals, leading to the direct communication between a human and a computer.
• Computer analysis and mapping of the human nervous system, permitting direct programming and inputting of a computer by a human being.
• Plant genetic technology permitting economically improved caloric productivity per hectare by a factor of 10 or more.
• Chemical control of human aging permitting an extension of life span to 150 years for 50% of the population of 2001 and up to 250 years for 75% of the population of 2050.
• Neuro repair surgery permitting the repair and eventual regeneration of individual neurons.
• Electronic alteration of brain functions leading to electro-psychiatry (the application of electromagnetic fields to the brain) and an end to the electro-shock therapy of 1980.
• Beginnings of genetic engineering, including genetic manipulation to eliminate congenital defects.
• A wide variety of different and effective contraceptive drugs and methods for both sexes, including "morning after" drugs.
• Identification of biological and psychological effects of exposure of human beings to strong electromagnetic and electrostatic fields.

• Identification of a totally new form of "radiation" or "aura" possessed by living organisms whose propagation through space does not obey the inverse-square law and is not limited by the speed of light.

The development of the social sciences and of social institutions will, as it always has, lag behind the development of physical and biological technology. However, because of the absolute requirement to bring rigor to the social sciences and to unify the human race on Planet Earth, we will see the maturation of "metalaw," which is a system of law applying to the relationships between intelligent entities of all kinds, including human beings, and which is based upon Haley's Principle: "Do unto others as they would have you do unto them."

It's going to be an exciting future, and I intend to stick around to take part in it as long as possible!

PRIVATELY OWNED ROCKETS

Predictor EWALD HEER is the director of research programs in space mechanics at the Jet Propulsion Laboratory of the California Institute of Technology in Pasadena, Calif. His past experience includes research and design at McDonnell Douglas, Hewitt Robbins, and other aerospace companies. He also served as the program manager of NASA's lunar exploration office. Mr. Heer is the editor of *Remotely Manned Systems* and *Robots and Manipulator Systems I & II*.

• PREDICTIONS •

1990

• Communications in space will use light waves produced by high-power lasers requiring comparatively small but rigid optical lens systems. This will replace communication by microwaves, which requires comparatively large antennae.
• Direct broadcasting from space satellite to home receivers will be introduced.
• One-of-a-kind (i.e., custom-made) items will be inexpensively designed and manufactured, and will become generally affordable through computerized analysis and robot technology.
• Automatic and "intelligent" management and management-

control systems—including universal credit, auditing, and banking—will come into general use.

• Household computers will come into general use to run the household and communicate with the outside world. They may be used on a metered basis for translating, teaching, information retrieval, medical diagnosis, computation, design, and analysis and as an intellectual collaborator.

1995

• Based on an extensive weather-satellite system and associated developments in information management, it will be possible to make long-range weather forecasts.

2000

• The oceans will be used extensively for extraction of mineral resources and sources of energy. Ocean-floor and subfloor mining will be accomplished by automated systems and remotely controlled robots.

• Cargo launching into space will become so economically attractive that solar-energy-collecting systems and industrial complexes will be built in space on a large scale by private enterprises.

2010

• The use of rockets for private and commercial transportation to terrestrial and extraterrestrial locations will be possible, both technically and economically.

2020–2030

• Permanent lunar bases will be built for commercial and scientific exploitation of lunar resources. The installation will also be used to launch remotely guided robot systems programmed for exploration and mining in the asteroid belt.

MYSTERIES OF THE UNIVERSE TO BE SOLVED

Predictor RICHARD BERRY is the editor of *Astronomy* magazine. A Vietnam veteran, Mr. Berry has built rocket payloads to fly through the aurora, measured air pollution with laser beams, taught physics, and engineered space hardware used during the Apollo-Soyuz mission of 1975.

• PREDICTIONS •

1980s

• There will be a rise in the popularity of astronomy as a hobby. You'll see a sharp increase in the number of telescopes, private observatories, and even the appearance of special astronomy retreats (like ski chalets, but where guests spend a week or more with access to a big telescope). There will be an even more dramatic rise in TV shows, video disc programs, and movies about space and astronomy.

1985

• Enough people will have flown on the Space Shuttle so that shuttle consciousness will begin to alter the way large numbers of people view the earth and its place in the universe. A subtle effect at first, you'll begin to experience it when you know somebody who knows somebody who's been in space. It won't hit you full force until *you* know somebody who's been in space—or you get there yourself!

1987

• The Space Telescope will revolutionize astronomy. Its ability to penetrate deep into space will turn up several major discoveries—probably entirely new classes of objects—that were essentially unimagined before this powerful orbiting observatory began its work.

By 1990

• Video media will begin to step into the role now filled by magazines and books. Coupled with increasing computational power in the hands of people, there will be an explosion of computer-generated cartoon movies, composition of music via computer, the introduction and spread of video/screen newsletters of very small, highly specialized circulation, and a decentralization of information dissemination despite government and monopoly attempts to regulate it.

1995

• The U.S. will lose its early lead in manned space exploration—perhaps decisively—to other nations.
• Astronomers will have come close to answering the major scientific questions about the universe, including: the history and origin of the solar system, how our galaxy and other galaxies formed after the Big Bang, how galaxies spiral and why, and the nature of quasars and other high-energy beasties. While this prediction could be made every decade, this time there will be sufficient detail and supporting evidence for the scenario. Even more predictably, astronomers will have difficulty communicating their discoveries to the public.

2000–2005

• Rather later than most scenarists predict, a permanent manned station will be established on the moon. The reason: costs in energy, money, and logistic support will turn out to be greater than the enthusiasts expected. Once established, the base will be permanent. It will not be American.

2005

• Weather will become understandable at long last, partly because of large, fast computers, and partly because the study of the other planets with atmospheres (Venus, Mars, Jupiter, and Saturn)—both close-up via probes and synoptically via the Space Telescope—will finally provide the missing links to meteorologists.

2010

• Major resource shortages—similar to the oil crises of the 1970s—will occur for other vital industrial materials such as mercury, copper, tin, silver, cadmium. Unless extraterrestrial sources of these materials are exploited, shortages will be accompanied by political blackmail.

HUMANS COLONIZE 8 PLANETS

Predictors L. STEPHEN WOLFE and R. L. WYSACK are the authors of *Handbook for Space Pioneers,* a nonfiction reference book on space colonization. Mr. Wolfe is a project manager on industrial energy conservation projects for Carter Engineers in La Jolla, Calif. Mr. Wysack is a draftsman and industrial engineer currently working for International Harvester's Solar Turbines Group.

• PREDICTIONS •

1985

• The first satellite launch system developed by a private company places its first satellites in orbit. Among them is a spy satellite for the People's Republic of China. The company offers launching prices lower than those offered by NASA's Space Shuttle and the Eurospace agency's Ariane launch systems.

1986

• The first privately financed antenna farm, an array of independently operable communications and data-gathering devices, is placed in orbit by the Space Shuttle. It reduces the cost of intercity telephone and data transmission by a factor of 10. By the stroke of one technological revolution, all of AT&T Long Line's existing equipment is made obsolete.

1988

• In violation of the spirit, though not the strict letter, of the first nuclear disarmament treaty, the U.S.S.R. places a "permanent" space station in orbit for military purposes. Continuously operated by military cosmonauts, the station is used to observe foreign military installations and movements and to search for strategic mineral deposits worldwide. It contains nonnuclear rockets capable of destroying U.S. intelligence satellites in orbit without warning.
• In this year the first Japanese astronaut makes a flight in a launch vehicle built by Japan.

1991

• The U.S. launches its first "permanent" space station in response to the Russian move. In addition to its military purposes, the station becomes an important center for nonmilitary space research, including earth resources, space manufacturing, and zero-gravity medical techniques.

1996

• The first privately developed launch system capable of putting a human being in orbit becomes available to all people. It is so profitable that a dozen imitators flock to the market. The principal purpose of the service is repair of orbiting communications equipment, but small nations, research institutions, and large manufacturing concerns take advantage of the service to advance their research programs.

1998

• Private launch service companies inaugurate the first tourist service to space. Though it is very expensive, all flights are booked a year in advance.

2000

• Japan stuns the world by placing the first prototype solar-power generating station in orbit. The enormous array of solar cells converts sunlight to electricity, which is beamed by high-intensity laser to a distribution center in the mountains of northern Honshu. Though small by the standards that are soon to come, this 50-megawatt power plant sounds the death knell for fossil fuels.

2005

• The race for space energy production is on in earnest. Japan has launched 2,000 megawatts of space-generating capacity. A consortium of multinational companies financed by American and European interests has already launched a 1,500-megawatt powersat and has an additional 3,000 megawatts of capacity on the drawing boards.

2006

• Astronomical observatories in space employing revolutionary light-gathering and spectrographic techniques discover direct evidence that earth-sized planets orbit the two larger stars of the Alpha Centauri system, the nearest star system to our own sun.

2008

• A private space consortium establishes a permanent moon base for the mining and refining of low-cost materials for building power-generating satellites.

2010

• The first human being lands on Mars. No evidence of life is found.
• In this same year NASA launches *Ambassador I*, the first interstellar data-gathering probe, on a 20-year mission to the Alpha Centauri system.

2012

• A competing manufacturer of power-generating satellites captures the first asteroid and brings it to earth orbit. The asteroid contains a variety of important metals, oxygen, and water, all of which are needed to construct orbiting power stations and living quarters for their maintenance personnel. This one asteroid will provide materials for more than 60,000 megawatts of satellite generating capacity.
• In this same year the U.S.S.R. deploys its first powersat, but also asks for participation in future ventures with capitalist enterprises.

2020

• American, Japanese, and European interests have become the largest suppliers of energy to the world. Solar-power satellites delivering power through conventional electric distribution systems now account for 45% of world energy consumption.

2022

• A "permanent" scientific station, similar to those in Antarctica in the 1960s and 1970s, is built on Mars. Much is learned about comparative planetology. A few complex organic molecules, possible precursors to life as we know it, are found, but nothing resembling even the simplest of Earth's life forms is discovered.

2025

• War and the threat of war disappear for the first time in history. By this date 90% of Earth's households are linked by satellite communication, which provides education, entertainment, personal communications, purchasing, and financial services. A common world language is understood by 90% of Earth's people. It is an evolved form of what is now English. Illiteracy and ignorance are virtually wiped from this planet.

2028

• Solar-power satellites now supply 90% of the world's energy. Controlled nuclear fusion emerges as a practical source of power. For safety reasons, the first large-scale fusion plants are built in space, employing masers to beam power to earth-based distribution systems.

2030

• Evidence of life as we know it emerges from the data transmissions of *Ambassador I* in the Alpha Centauri system. The probe reports four planets orbiting Alpha Centauri A. Spectrographic analysis indicates that the third planet from the star is rich in oxygen, nitrogen, and water and has a temperature range similar to Earth's. The possibility of reopening the frontier rekindles humanity's desire for interstellar exploration, and several nations begin plans for launching manned vehicles to the Alpha Centauri system.

2040

• International Council for Space Exploration (ICSE) is formed to consolidate worldwide efforts to explore space. Individual nations and private corporations still maintain separate organizations for commercial uses of space.

2050

• *Freedom IV*, the first interstellar spaceship carrying humans, departs for the Alpha Centauri star system, 4.3 light-years from Earth.

2074

• *Freedom IV* returns to Earth to report the discovery of the first habitable planet for humans orbiting Alpha Centauri A, the largest star in the Alpha Centauri system. The planet is larger than Earth, with a dense oxygen-nitrogen atmosphere and a gravitational field at the surface 27% higher than Earth's.

2087

• A young physicist named Raymond Krauchunas succeeds in the development of a unified field theory first proposed by Einstein 150

87

years before. The UFT provides a theoretical basis for faster-than-light travel and opens the possibility of large-scale expansion of the galaxy.

2112

• The *Albert Einstein,* the first starship capable of faster-than-light travel, departs on an exploratory mission to 10 star systems.

2122

• The first colony of 2,000 people settles on the habitable planet in the Alpha Centauri system. They name the planet Wyzdom in honor of its discoverer, Captain Jan De Wyze of the *Freedom IV.* The first colony fares badly in the hostile environment, and in two years they have placed a dictatorial leader in charge. Employing an unprecedented political strategy, the dictator introduces a system of radical free enterprise. Within seven years the colony is well established and prospering, and the dictator steps down in favor of an elected government.

2153

• A second habitable planet is discovered in the star system of 82 Eridani. This planet is also larger than Earth, though smaller than Wyzdom. It is covered entirely by ocean, with no continental land masses, although thousands of islands dot its surface. The discoverers name the planet Poseidous.

2177

• The first human colony settles on Poseidous and benefits from the well-documented experiences of Wyzdom's first settlers. On two of the planet's largest islands, competing economic systems are established, one socialist, the other free enterprise based on the Wyzdom model.

2217

• Space explorers from Earth encounter the first spaceship of an alien species. The situation is potentially hostile, but the alien races learn to communicate with each other and begin a long and mutually profitable period of cooperation in the exploration of space and the advancement of science. Because this other species, which humans call the Ardotian race, lives on a much warmer planet than Earth, no conflicts arise between them over the desire to colonize the same planets.

2291

• The Ardot civilization encounters yet another species with interstellar capability. Humans name them the Chlorzi, and the three races form the Galactic Association of Intelligent Life for the purpose of promoting exploration of the galaxy and the advancement of their common knowledge.

TRIANGULUS DEXTERALIS
(COMMON NAME : TRUP)

HEIGHT: 130 - 150 CM
WEIGHT: 40 - 80 KG
(RANGES OF 95 % OF POPULATION)

POPULATION ESTIMATE: 20-40 MILLION

In the year 2310, humans land on the planet Yom
and there encounter the local inhabitants, known as Trups.

2365

• The Chlorzi discover another planet suitable for human life and offer it to us for colonization. To this date, humans have discovered and colonized seven planets within a radius of 60 light-years. None of these planets is occupied by an advanceable life form capable of creating its own civilization.

2380

• The first colonists land on Athena, the eighth planet to be colonized by humankind, yet the outward migration has just begun. Athena lies a scant 78 light-years from Earth, but the Milky Way galaxy measures 90,000 light-years across and 10,000 light-years thick at its center!

• ALTERNATE PREDICTION •
(If The Above Don't Come True)

2000

• If the development of space power has not begun, within 10 years conflicts over dwindling fossil fuel reserves will precipitate war between the U.S. and the U.S.S.R. Escalation to full-scale nuclear war will occur rapidly. Two billion deaths and the destruction of modern civilization will precede humankind's entry into the new "dark age" lasting 600 years!

3

PREDICTIONS ON TOMORROW'S WARS AND OTHER DISASTERS

1982

Khomeini's successors in Iran will be defeated by a coalition of Kurds and liberal minorities supported by the U.S. and U.S.S.R.

1983

Saudi Arabia and Libya will lose their wealth, and democratic forms of government will take over in both nations.

1988

The Soviet Union's secret preparations for a nuclear "first strike" against the U.S. will be exposed, and the U.S. will strike first, killing and injuring 100 million Soviet citizens.

MAJOR POWERS INVADE IRAN, AFGHANS EVICT SOVIETS, GERMANY REUNITED

Predictor COLONEL T. N. DUPUY, now retired from active army duty, is a military historian and research executive with over 50 books to his name. Among his better-known works are *Military History of World War I* (12 vols.), *Military History of World War II* (19 vols.), and *Elusive Victory: The Arab-Israeli Wars, 1947–1974*. His most recent book, *Numbers, Predictions, and War,* presents a theoretical formula with which to predict the outcome of battles and wars both in the past and in the future.

• PREDICTIONS •

1980–1993

• Chaos in Iran. A combination of internal power struggles and separatist movements in Baluchistan, Kurdistan, Khuzistan, and Azerbaijan, complicated by Soviet occupation of part of Azerbaijan, Iraqi seizure of Khuzistan, and combined U.S., Saudi, and Egyptian occupation of the northern shore of the Strait of Hormuz. Settled by nuclear confrontation of U.S. and U.S.S.R.; all foreign forces withdraw as part of a worldwide peace settlement; a U.S.-supported Bakhtiar regime restores stability in Iran.

1983–1995

• U.S., Saudi Arabia, and Egypt initiate a "Marshall Plan for the 80s"; Oman joins in 1985, followed by Sudan, Somalia, Eritrea, and Ethiopia (following Soviet and Cuban withdrawal from these areas after the resolution of a nuclear crisis).

1984–2000

• Worldwide nuclear proliferation. Leads to intense U.S. negotiations to establish a strengthened U.N. Nuclear Commission and an effective Security Council Emergency Force (SCEF).

1986–1990

• Undeclared war across the Iron Curtain. East and West Germans, defying Soviets and U.S. (locked in their confrontation over Iran), make selective raids across the Iron Curtain at each other's forces, but avoid involving other NATO or Warsaw Pact nations.

1988–1999

• Unrest and rebellion in Soviet Turkestan ruthlessly suppressed by Soviets. However, this leads to Soviet expulsion from Azerbaijan and Afghanistan.

1990

• Union of China, Taiwan, and Mongolia during unrest in U.S.S.R. and the U.S.-Soviet nuclear crisis. New China threatens U.S.S.R.

1990–1993

• Three-year nuclear crisis of U.S. and U.S.S.R. Both sides fire nuclear weapons in sea near major cities: U.S. in Gulf of Finland, near Leningrad; U.S.S.R. off Sandy Hook, N.J. Resolved by agreement on Iran and on mutual withdrawal of forces from Central Europe; U.S. withdraws to U.K., Ireland, Spain, and Iceland; U.S.S.R. to within its own national boundaries.

1990–2000

• Introduction of computer-controlled robot tankettes results in sweeping changes in military organizations around the world; weapon adopted by SCEF.

1991

• Following death of Kim Il Sung, revolution in North Korea; negotiations between north and south; reunion; U.S. withdraws; new Korea is unaligned.

1999

• Reunification of Germany; United Germany abandons sovereignty to U.N. Security Council in return for permanent seat on Security Council; disbandment of both German armies; Germany garrisoned by SCEF.

THE DAY THE BOMB WENT OFF— YOU ARE THERE

It was a sunny summer morning in the Chicago Loop. The usual bumper-to-bumper jam of cars and trucks. On the sidewalks, the usual crowd of shoppers, tourists, messengers, office workers heading out to an early lunch. It was Friday.

At 11:27, a 20-megaton nuclear bomb exploded a few feet above street level at the corner of La Salle and Adams. First the incredible flash of light and heat. In less than one-millionth of a second, the temperature rose to 150 million degrees Fahrenheit—more than four times the temperature at the center of the sun.

The roar followed immediately but there, in the center of the city and for miles around, no one was left to hear it. There was only the heat. And the dust.

Imagine that it happened. We will not speculate here on why it happened—on whose fault it was, on the series of diplomatic bluffs and blunders and miscalculations here and there that made it happen. It happened.

Even in the macromagnitudes of nuclear weaponry, a 20-megaton bomb is large—the equivalent of 20 million tons of TNT, though such comparisons have little meaning. The yield of a 20-megaton bomb is some 1,500 times as great as the yield of the bomb that was dropped on Hiroshima in 1945.

The U.S. does not admit to deploying any 20-megaton bombs in its nuclear arsenal. With its superiority in missile numbers and missile accuracy, the U.S. prefers weapons of lower yield. But the Soviet Union's 200 SS-9 intercontinental ballistic missiles are believed to carry warheads in the 20-megaton range, and they—along with lesser bombs—are presumably targeted on the 50 largest cities in the U.S.

In the event of a nuclear war, a total of some 100 to 200 megatons would be directed at a metropolitan area like Chicago's.

The bomb that exploded in the Loop left a crater 600 ft. deep and nearly a mile and a half in diameter. The crater's lip, extending almost to the shore of Lake Michigan on the east, was 200 ft. high and would be, after the cloud of radioactive debris and dust had settled or dissipated, the tallest "object" visible in the area of the blast.

For the moment, though, there was just the incandescent fireball, rising and expanding outward at enormous speed, reaching a height and breadth of three or four miles, illuminating the sky, so that 100 mi. away, over Milwaukee, the flash blinded the crew of a Chicago-bound airliner.

Around Ground Zero, everything—steel-and-concrete skyscrapers, roads and bridges, thousands of tons of earth, hundreds of thousands of people—instantly evaporated.

At the edge of the fireball, a thin shell of superheated, supercompressed gas acquired a momentum of its own and was propelled outward as a blast of immense extent and power, picking up objects from disintegrating buildings, snatching huge boulders and reducing them to vapor that would solidify, eventually, into radioactive dust.

Three seconds had elapsed since the bomb went off.

A high-altitude blast at one to three miles above ground level would have inflicted considerably greater blast damage, but the surface blast has its own "advantage": by maximizing the amount of debris sucked up in the nuclear explosion, it multiplies the long-range radiological effects, threatening the survival of living things hundreds of miles from the target area. And even the blast radius of a surface detonation is powerful enough to ignite fires more than 20 mi. from Ground Zero—more than 30 mi. if clouds help to reflect the flash.

Within a minute, the familiar shape of the mushroom cloud began to form over Chicago, symmetrical and strikingly beautiful in various shades of red and reddish brown. The color was provided by some 80 tons of nitric and nitrous oxides synthesized in the high temperatures and nuclear radiations. In time these compounds would be borne aloft to reduce the ozone in the upper atmosphere.

The mushroom cloud expanded for 10 or 15 minutes, reaching a mature height of 20 to 25 mi. and extending 70 to 80 mi. across the sky.

Hiroshima—five weeks after the bomb was dropped.

To a distance of five miles from Ground Zero—to affluent Evanston on the north, well past working-class Cicero on the west, beyond the University of Chicago campus on the south, there was—nothing. A few seconds after the bomb went off, the fireball appeared, brighter than 5,000 suns. Those who saw the sudden flash of blinding light experienced instant and painless death from the extreme heat long before the noise and shock wave reached them.

Glass melted. Concrete surfaces disintegrated under thermal stress. Anything combustible exploded into raging flames. Even reinforced, blast-resistant structures collapsed, along with highway spans and bridges.

The blast wave arrived about 15 seconds later, buffeting the few man-made remnants that had not been pulverized. With the shock came torrid wind, traveling at some 300 mph, carrying dust and embers and fragments, blowing down vents and tunnels to suffocate the few surviving human beings who had been sheltered below ground level.

After about 10 seconds, the wind reversed direction, drawn back toward Ground Zero.

The enormously high temperatures from the fireball of a nuclear weapon generate enough light and heat to ignite simultaneous fires over huge areas. In these areas the heated air forms a rising column, resembling on a vast scale the airflow in a fireplace. Cool air drifts into the fire zone to replace the rising hot air. As the fires gain strength, burning hotter and more violently, the chimney effect intensifies, sucking in more air and causing the fire to burn hotter still.

About 20 minutes after the atomic bomb attack on Hiroshima, a mild wind began to blow from all directions toward the center of the city. Within two or three hours, the wind developed a speed of 30 to 40 mph and air temperatures rose steadily toward 2,000°F as fires burned out of control for a distance of 1.2 mi. from Ground Zero. The wind was accompanied by light, radioactive rain over the center of the city and heavier rain around the periphery. It was a firestorm, and it destroyed about 2,800 acres.

A 20-megaton bomb could, under similar conditions, generate a firestorm that would devastate an area some 500 times as large.

On the freeways radiating from the Loop, automobiles, trucks, and buses were simultaneously evaporated and blown away, their particles sucked up into the fireball to become components of the radioactive cloud.

Along the Stevenson Expressway, some seven or eight miles from Ground Zero, scores of oil storage tanks exploded—ruptured by the shock wave and then ignited from the grass and shrubbery burning around them.

At this range, too, aluminum siding on homes evaporated and some concrete surfaces exploded under thermal stress. The few buildings still standing were in danger of imminent collapse—and all were engulfed by flames. Highway spans caved in. Asphalt blistered and melted.

Clothing caught fire, and people were charred by intense light and heat. Their charcoal limbs would, in some instances, render their shapes recognizably human.

With greater distance from Ground Zero, the effects diminished. About 10 mi. from the Loop, in the area around the Brookfield Zoo, the fireball was merely brighter than a thousand suns. Glass did not melt, but shattered window fragments flew through the air at about 135 mph. All trees were burning even before the shock wave uprooted most of them.

Railroad bridges collapsed, and railroad cars were blown from their tracks. Automobiles were smashed and twisted into grotesque shapes. One- and two-story wood frame homes, already burning, were demolished by the shock wave, which also knocked down cinder-block walls and brick apartment buildings.

Those who had taken shelter underground—or, more probably, just happened to be there—survived for 15 minutes or a half hour longer than those who were exposed. They suffocated as oxygen was drawn away by the firestorm that soon raged overhead.

At O'Hare Airport, the world's busiest, aircraft engaged in landing or takeoff crashed and burned. Planes on the ground were buffeted into each other and adjacent hangars, their fuselages bent and partially crushed by the shock wave. Some 30 seconds before the shock wave struck, aluminum surfaces facing the fireball had melted and the aircraft interiors had been set aflame.

The enormous temperatures associated with all nuclear weapons, regardless of yield, result from fission, the process in which certain atomic nuclei become unstable and disintegrate. (Even a fusion bomb like the one here described gains about half its energy from fission.) As the nuclei break up and form new atoms, they yield neutrons and immense amounts of energy. The atoms created by fission are so radioactive that if one could collect two ounces of them one minute after their creation, they would match the activity of 30,000 tons of radium and its decay products.

When a 20-megaton nuclear bomb goes off, it produces more than half a ton of this material. One minute after detonation, it is as radioactive as 30 million tons of radium. Though this radioactivity declines within one day by a factor of 3,000, the material still has the radioactivity of 10,000 tons of radium.

If one could instantly remove the entire fission inventory from the largest commercial nuclear power plant (3,000 megawatts thermal) and simultaneously detonate a 20-megaton nuclear bomb, 30 minutes after the "experiment," the activity from the bomb would be about 100,000 times as great as the activity contained in the reactor's fission inventory.

The astronomically hot fireball indiscriminately incorporates all those materials into a superheated gas and mixes them with millions of tons of earth and target debris. The mixture condenses into droplets of liquid and then solidifies into particles ranging in diameter from one-thousandth to one-fiftieth of an inch. The particles incorporate all of the extremely dangerous radiological residues, and are borne aloft to deliver death hundreds of miles from the target.

In addition, many neutrons escape the exploding weapon to be absorbed by the earth and air in the immediate blast area. This leads to the production of a wide variety of neutron-activated radioactive isotopes of such elements as sodium, chlorine, manganese, zinc, copper, and silicon, as well as radioactive carbon transmuted from nitrogen in the air.

All of these substances, dangerous to varying extents, remain active in the blast area to jeopardize survivors and would-be rescuers.

In the pleasant western suburb of Hinsdale, some 16 mi. from the Loop, the manicured lawns surrounded by wooden picket fences on tree-shaded Chicago Avenue caught fire first. Leaves in the trees ignited next, and then the picket fences themselves. Paint evaporated off house exteriors. Children on bicycles screamed as they were blinded by the flash of the fireball. An instant later, their skin was charred. Autos collided as their tires and upholstery burst into flame.

The white wooden cupola on the brick village hall blazed, and even the all-stone Unitarian Church on Maple Street was burning— ignited by the curtains on the windows facing east.

The shock wave arrived some 50 seconds later, tearing the roofs off houses, blowing in side panels, spreading burning debris.

At about the same distance north of the city, Ravinia Park's summer festival was to have featured an all-Mozart program that

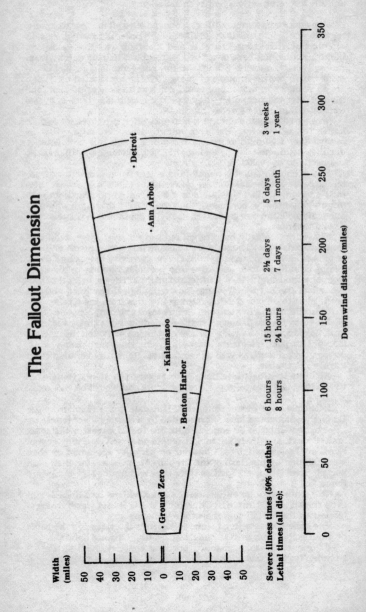

The Fallout Dimension

Width (miles)

50
40
30
20
10
0
10
20
30
40
50

• Ground Zero   • Benton Harbor   • Kalamazoo   • Ann Arbor   • Detroit

Severe illness times (50% deaths):   6 hours   15 hours   2½ days   5 days   3 weeks
Lethal times (all die):   8 hours   24 hours   7 days   1 month   1 year

0   50   100   150   200   250   300   350

Downwind distance (miles)

The diagram above shows the distances and times at which a 20-mph wind would deliver lethal fallout (650 rads) and severe but less than lethal fallout (450 rads) from the cloud of debris generated by a 20-megaton nuclear bomb (with a 50% fission yield) detonated near ground surface.

At a distance of 200 mi. downwind, for example, unprotected persons would receive a severely sublethal dose of radiation within two and a half days, and a lethal dose within seven days.

Even with excellent medical care, the 450-rad exposure would eventually kill about 50% of a young adult population. And in the conditions of a nuclear attack, it is unlikely that such care would be available to more than a tiny fraction of the exposed population.

The symptoms of radiation injury resulting from a nuclear detonation can vary considerably, depending on an individual's age, state of health, and constitution, and on whether the exposure is from a distance or through direct contact or ingestion.

Direct contact with radioactive dust may cause a sensation of burning and itching of the skin, and eye irritation. Within six hours of exposure to 450 rads, individuals experience headaches, nausea, dizziness, and a general feeling of illness that persists for a day or two, followed by a period of extreme fatigue.

After several days, or even weeks, the initial symptoms return. Their severity requires constant hospital care—blood transfusions, antibiotics, and perhaps bone-marrow transplants. Loss of body hair becomes noticeable, but more serious symptoms are bloody diarrhea and urine caused by spontaneous bleeding of the kidneys and intestines. Bleeding may also occur from the gums and lips.

Skin areas become puffy and discolored as diffuse skin hemorrhaging sets in. Lesions develop where there has been direct contact with radioactive dust. Because the body's count of white blood cells has been reduced, multiple infections develop. Emaciation and delirium are common.

Strong individuals who receive competent medical support for a period of three or four months gradually recover from the ordeal of radiation poisoning—unless they succumb to tuberculosis or other diseases caused by their lowered resistance to infection. Body hair eventually grows back. With six months or a year of convalescence in an antiseptic environment, about half the victims survive.

Some of them, however, will ultimately return for treatment of leukemia, carcinoma, cataracts, or other long-range disabilities induced by their exposure to high levels of ionizing radiation.

SOURCE: By Theodore Postol. Reprinted by permission from *The Progressive*, 408 West Gorham Street, Madison, Wis. 53703. Copyright © 1978, The Progressive, Inc.

Friday evening. There would be no Mozart and no Ravinia Park. By 11:30 A.M., that agreeably green place was a burning wasteland.

About 21 mi. southwest of the Loop, the Argonne National Laboratory sprawls on some 1,700 acres of parkland. Its 5,000 employees had engaged in a broad variety of research efforts, many of them centered on the development of nuclear power. Argonne and its predecessor, the Metallurgical Laboratory of the University of Chicago, were instrumental in developing the atomic bomb.

Argonne researchers who happened to be looking out a window on that Friday morning—gazing, perhaps, toward the Sears Tower barely visible on the skyline to the northeast—suddenly saw a flash that filled the sky with the brightness (from their vantage point) of 50 to 80 suns. They were blinded, their clothing ignited on their bodies, and exposed skin areas suffered extremely severe third-degree burns.

Here, too, leaves and grass and many readily combustible materials caught fire at once. The shock wave, which arrived a minute and a half later, caused only minimal damage, except as it spread burning debris. But the fires soon raged out of control, for here, as for many miles around, there was neither power nor water pressure nor emergency equipment nor any human will but the impulse to surrender to the hysteria of total disaster.

And soon after all this happened, the radioactive cloud, carried by the prevailing winds, began drifting toward the east at about 20 mph.

By the time the mushroom cloud has completed its 15-minute process of stabilization, it is directly overhead for distances up to 40 mi. from Ground Zero. Fires are still burning as radioactive particles begin settling on the landscape. The radiation level rises rapidly to exceed 4,000 to 5,000 roentgens per hour, delivering a lethal dose within seven to eight minutes. Individuals driven out-of-doors by fire are directly exposed.

Within an hour or so, elements of the cloud begin to arrive about 40 mi. downwind. The density and activity of the particles is such that a belt four to five miles wide quickly develops radiation levels of more than 3,000 roentgens per hour. By this point, activity is diminishing, so that it requires an exposure of 10 to 20 minutes to absorb a deadly dose. Within a larger belt, up to 10 mi. wide, fewer particles are falling, allowing up to a half hour's exposure before a fatal dosage is absorbed.

As the cloud moves downwind, expanding and dropping particles, the fallout level becomes unpredictable, though it remains, in many places, extremely high.

No one knows how many Americans might die from blast and fire and radiation sickness in a nuclear attack. Casualty projections are a matter of heated controversy within the government and outside it. A reasonable conjecture is that an all-out nuclear attack might claim 160 million lives—about three quarters of the population. In a particularly strategic concentrated metropolitan area subject to a direct strike—Chicago, for example—virtually the entire population could be expected to perish.

But American casualties would, of course, not be the only ones. No matter how it happened or whose fault it was, there would be a counterstrike, and the indiscriminate murder of one nation's citizens—ours or theirs—would be avenged by the indiscriminate murder of the other's.

Moving slowly to the east, Chicago's radioactive cloud brushed Indiana and was blown into Michigan, dropping silent death along the way, drifting inexorably toward Detroit. But it didn't matter, for at a few seconds before 11:27 that Friday morning, a 20-megaton bomb had exploded in Detroit, too.

SOURCE: By Erwin Knoll and Theodore Postol. Reprinted by permission from *The Progressive*, 408 West Gorham Street, Madison, Wis. 53703. Copyright © 1978, The Progressive, Inc.

NUCLEAR WEAPONS UNLEASHED IN INDIA-PAKISTAN WAR

Predictor LENNY SIEGEL has been the director of the Pacific Studies Center in Mountain View, Calif., since 1970. His many articles on U.S.-Asian relations have appeared in the *San Francisco Chronicle* and the *Grapevine*, as well as in such international periodicals as *Afrique-Asie, Kommentar,* and *Pacific Research*. He has also contributed to the books *A House Divided* and *Ten-Year Military Terror in Indonesia*.

• PREDICTIONS •

1986

• Communist revolutionaries seize power in Thailand after a collapse of the rice market. They retain the constitutional monarchy.

1987

• Following the successful Thai revolution, the Philippine leadership (headed by Imelda Marcos) abdicates in favor of a coalition of traditional wealthy families. Bolstered by a massive U.S. and Japanese aid program, the new democratic Philippine government carries out land reform and grants regional autonomy to minorities.

1989

• In the Third India-Pakistan War, both sides will use nuclear weapons, destroying major population centers.

1991

• The elected Communist government of West Bengal will secede from India amidst the chaos caused by the Third India-Pakistan War. West Bengal—the area around Calcutta—will be the world's third-most-populous Marxist regime.

1997

• For several billion dollars, China renews the United Kingdom's lease to Hong Kong's New Territories for another 49 years (after the original 99 years). The treaty sparks massive protests within China, but the government suppresses all opposition.

1999

• The U.S. launches its first submarine aircraft carrier. The ship, the largest submarine built to date, surfaces to launch its V/STOL (vertical and short takeoff and landing) planes.

2008

• Following an unprecedented series of loan defaults by third-world nations, Western capitalist governments form a World Central Bank with authority that is superior to national legislatures.

2018

• Nuclear wastes from Asian reactors break out of their South Seas containment, contaminating most of Melanesia and Polynesia. Japan agrees to pay reparations, but other Asian nations refuse.

2020

• Indonesia invades and occupies Singapore, but the corrupt Indonesian military is incapable of operating the technocratic island republic. It turns power over to an international consortium of banks and multinational corporations.

UPHEAVALS THROUGHOUT AFRICA

Predictor ANTHONY J. HUGHES, a British-born citizen of Kenya, is editor of the bimonthly *Africa Report*. The *Report* is published by the nonprofit African-American Institute, based in New York City. Most of Mr. Hughes's professional career—as writer, media executive, and consultant—has revolved around African-related activities.

· PREDICTIONS ·

1982–1992

• International developments, changes in the Middle East, and stresses within Islam will bring about dramatic changes in the governments of North Africa. This will affect "radical" states such as Libya and Algeria, as well as "moderates" such as Egypt, Tunisia, and Morocco.
• The Horn of Africa will be the most volatile region of the continent. Expect further warfare with international involvement in Ethiopia, Somalia, Sudan, Kenya.
• The Sahelian region will suffer another serious drought. The international community, beset by political and energy problems, will not divert adequate resources to make the stricken states become viable societies.
• In West and Central Africa, violent uprisings and possible changes of government are likely in Zaire, the Central African Republic, Chad, Cameroon, Gabon, and Ghana. Nigeria will remain under civilian rule.
• Namibia will be granted independence under an "internal" South African–controlled process. SWAPO (South West Africa People's Organization) guerrillas will not succeed in dislodging the South African–backed state.
• In South Africa whites will make dramatic concessions to blacks in social and economic fields, while holding on to political and military power. Black resistance, involving urban terror, hijackings, and seizures, will increase greatly.

1993–2030

• New developments in the technology of energy and agriculture will permit the economic transformation of those African societies which have solved their sociopolitical problems. These may include Libya, Tunisia, Algeria, Nigeria, the Ivory Coast, Senegal, and Kenya.
• Revolutionary developments in South Africa will lead to Big Power intervention and ultimately to black majority rule.

SOVIET UNION RULES THE WORLD— "AMERICAN DREAM" DEAD

Predictor DAVID S. SULLIVAN has served as a strategic and Soviet foreign policy analyst for the Central Intelligence Agency, as a Marine officer in Vietnam, and as a defense consultant. He has published several books and articles on international and military affairs, including *Revolutionary War: Western Response* and *Change and the Future International System*.

• PREDICTIONS •

By 1983

• Fully within the terms of the proposed SALT II Treaty, the Soviet Union will have achieved clear-cut, unmistakable strategic nuclear superiority over the U.S. The Soviet Union will have more strategic delivery vehicles, warheads, throw-weight (payload), greater missile accuracy, and a clear first-strike counterforce capability. This strategic nuclear supremacy will checkmate or neutralize all U.S. strategic forces, seriously eroding deterrence of war at the intercontinental, theater nuclear, and conventional levels.

• The Soviet Union will also achieve theater nuclear superiority over the NATO alliance, Communist China, and Japan.

• The Soviets will add naval superiority to their long-standing superiority in conventional and ground forces. The Soviets will therefore achieve overall military superiority over all of their enemies combined.

1983—Soviet Union achieves overall military superiority.

• There will be a severe nuclear crisis somewhere in the world, perhaps precipitated by events in the Middle East. This will be a U.S.-Soviet "Cuban Missile Crisis" in reverse, with the U.S. retreating and backing down this time. There will be no nuclear attacks or even conventional fighting.

• The U.S. stock market will crash, completely destroying U.S. economic stability. The value of the dollar on international money markets will drop drastically, and the U.S. will enter an economic depression far deeper and of longer duration than the Great Depression of 1929–1936. The U.S. economy will be destroyed, and the U.S. will no longer be a superpower. The Soviets know that they can use their strategic and military superiority to attack the greatest U.S. vulnerability—the unstable psychology of the U.S. stock market and the already shaky economic prestige of the U.S.

By 1993

• The U.S. will have ceased to be a great power and will be struggling to hold itself together as a viable nation. The Soviet Union will be approaching hegemony over most of the world.
• The People's Republic of China will seek rapprochement with the U.S.S.R. NATO will have long before dissolved, and all of Europe and Japan will be dominated by the U.S.S.R.

1993–2030

• Economic crisis and chaos will persist in the U.S., due to the collapse of our military power, foreign policy, and economic prestige. The depletion of world oil reserves in the 1990s will add to the social and economic crisis in the U.S. The "American Way of Life" and the "American Dream" will not persist.
• Americans will become refugees in the world. There will be racial, economic, and civil war in the U.S., and nomadic tribes will reappear.

2000

• After a series of local wars around the world in which the U.S.S.R. continues to suppress rebellion against Soviet hegemony, the U.S.A. will finally begin to revive itself and fight back against Soviet repression.

U.S. ANNIHILATES SOVIET UNION; U.N. MOVES TO MOON

Predictor DR. MARI'ON MUSHKAT is a professor of international law and international organization at Tel-Aviv University in Israel. He also serves as chairman of the Israeli Institute for the Study of International Affairs located in Tel-Aviv, is vice-chairman of the Jerusalem Peace Research Institute, and has written several books on international affairs.

· PREDICTIONS ·

1982

· The successors of Khomeini's regime in Iran will be defeated by a coalition of Kurdish and other minorities, autonomous movements, and liberal and left-wing groupings, supported by both the U.S.S.R. and U.S. A nuclear clash between the superpowers in this area will be prevented by a renewed partition of spheres of influence and the reentry of the U.S. in large parts of the Middle East.

1983

· After a clash between Syria and the PLO on one side and Israel on the other side, the Israeli-Egyptian peace treaty will be suspended and a new international conference on the Middle East will take place. This will result in the emergence of a Palestinian moderate state encompassing the Jordanian Kingdom and the greatest part of the West Bank. Once more Soviet influence will be increased in the area as the price for Soviet agreement not to interfere militarily in the armed conflict.

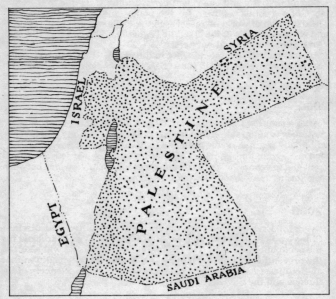

The new state of Palestine?

1985

· Production of new energy resources will be put into operation, and

Saudi Arabia and Libya will lose their wealth. Both countries will start to develop a new political democratic order.

1986

• The U.S. and all the West, together with the Soviet bloc, will agree on common steps to effectively fight hunger and underdevelopment in the third world. The first important agreement on arms control and disarmament will be signed at a special U.N. General Assembly session.

1987

• After a cruelly suppressed armed revolt of Polish dissidents, the U.S.S.R. will agree to open negotiations on federal links between the two Germanies. At one of the follow-up Helsinki conferences, a commitment will be made by all parties to implement all three baskets of the Helsinki Final Act (i.e., political, economic, and cultural cooperation).

1988

• Soviet preparations for a first-strike nuclear attack on the U.S. will be discovered. However, the Soviets plan to attack the U.S. in a way that will avoid damaging Western European industries in order to secure their use for the Warsaw Pact nations. The U.S. will strike first, and the majority of Soviet centers will be destroyed along with nearly 100,000,000 Soviet citizens. It will appear that the Soviets were late with their plan and are unwilling or incapable of a retaliatory nuclear strike. They will agree to open negotiations for a new world order.

1992

• The negotiations started after the first nuclear war four years ago will end in economic, political, and ideological convergence between the former NATO and Warsaw Pact members.

2000

• A joint East-West military observation committee will disclose China's preparation for a nuclear attack on the Soviet Union and for the occupation of Japan. The committee's admonitions will result in the prevention of a renewed nuclear clash but on the condition that all Southeast Asia will become an exclusively Chinese sphere of influence and the Soviet Far East will be demilitarized.

2010

• A federation of all Middle East countries will come into being with Jerusalem as its capital, but with a Christian enclave to which the Vatican will be moved on the decision of the then black Catholic pope, Dr. Ulusolo Mojo.

2020

• The generations-old war in South Africa will come to an end. However, the white minorities will be asked to remain, and political rights will be granted to them.

2030

• The first regular communication between the earth and the moon will be festively opened in the first atmospheric city, to which the headquarters of the U.N. will be moved and where its transformation into a transnational, federal world authority will be proclaimed.

CIVIL WAR IN THE U.S.; SOVIETS CEASE TO BE WORLD POWER

Predictor ELDON BYRD has had 20 years' experience as an engineer, scientist, and warfare analyst. Currently employed as a physical scientist at the Naval Surface Weapons Center in White Oak, Md., Mr. Byrd is the author of many publications and reports dealing with weapons, medical technology, and various other topics. His book *How Things Work* was published in 1970.

• PREDICTIONS •

1982

• A new class of signals will be discovered that may revolutionize communications, especially for military and intelligence use. These signals, traveling faster than sound but not as fast as light, will be useful only for communicating around the world, not into outer space.

1982–1990

• It should be possible to affect human behavior electronically at a distance. The method will involve the electrical entrainment of the firing rate of nerve tissue in the brain.

1982–1992

• The Soviets are investigating exotic technologies—involving, in

108

part, the use of electromagnetic signals to alter behavior—that are virtually ignored in the Western world. If they are able to perfect weapons based on these technologies, the Western world, caught by surprise, would have little in the way of countermeasures. Fortunately, if the dangers are recognized in time, some of the technologies can easily be countered.

• New scientific discoveries of *vast* military significance will be made. These include new methods of communication and new ways to build nonconventional weapons based on forms of energy transfer other than a chemical explosion or nuclear effect. The laws of physics will have to be extended and expanded into other dimensions to accommodate the discoveries. The impact on technology will be as profound as the jump from Newton's macrophysical "laws" to quantum mechanics.

• The Middle East, China, and the Soviet Union should be embroiled in wars or warlike acts (although not necessarily with each other) prior to 1993. Subsequently, most major nations of the world may become involved. Although ahead in strength presently, the Soviets will ultimately cease to be a world power.

1987–2030

• Weapons for future global-scale conflicts will include devices that tap vast supplies of energy with very little input power required. High-acceleration devices capable of catapulting masses to velocities allowing them to shoot into outer space should become operational in the late 1980s or early 1990s. Weapons other than lasers that change the energy levels of atomic particles and use the difference to provide tremendous power will become available about 1990.

1993–2030

• Economics will play a major role in future wars. As economies of the world begin to collapse, working people—who equate productivity with money—will cease to produce. Wars will ensue and temporarily alleviate economic disasters. Not until after the year 2000 will war be deemed by those surviving to be an ultimate waste of time.

• Civil war in the United States is a strong possibility in this period, if not sooner. The war will take the form of anarchy and will follow the economic collapse of the country and subsequent collapse of the central government. However, out of chaos will come order.

2000

• It should be possible to treat almost all illnesses, including battlefield trauma, electromagnetically. Cells of the body will be "fooled" into producing antibodies, coagulants, new tissue, chemicals, etc., by being exposed to certain kinds of electric and magnetic fields. This type of drugless treatment will revolutionize military as well as all other types of medicine.

POLLUTION KILLS
THOUSANDS IN MEXICO;
SAN FRANCISCO FLATTENED BY
"THE GREAT EARTHQUAKE"

Predictor JAMES CORNELL, the author of *The Great International Disaster Book*, is publications manager for the Harvard-Smithsonian Center for Astrophysics in Cambridge, Mass. A frequent contributor to such magazines and newspapers as *Smithsonian*, *Science World*, the *New York Times*, and the *Boston Globe*, Mr. Cornell is also a lecturer in science communications at Suffolk University in Boston, Mass.

• PREDICTIONS •

Early 1982

• A massive earthquake will strike northern Iran, destroying property in several major cities and taking a large toll of lives. The inability of the ruling party to deal with the crisis will lead to its eventual fall, causing further turmoil and a disruption of oil production.

Late autumn 1983

• A typhoon channeled up the Bay of Bengal will generate storm surges that sweep over the low-lying islands off Bangladesh at the mouth of the Ganges. Over 10,000 people will be killed.

Early autumn 1984

• A tropical hurricane will cross the island of Cuba, causing extensive damage to agricultural areas (and further distress to the economy) before striking the U.S. mainland at Florida. Many people will be trapped in Miami Beach, and the loss of both life and property will be high.

Winter 1985

• A series of severe winter storms will batter northwestern Europe, disrupting communications, transportation, and commerce for more than two weeks. The extreme cold will spell hardship for thousands of oil-short Europeans.

Summer 1990

• A medium-sized earthquake and a series of aftershocks will hit southern California. Although not on the scale of the 1906 San Francisco tremor, extensive damage will be done to highways, communications, and water systems; the damages could be in the billions of dollars and the loss of life in the hundreds.

Winter 1993

• A long-lasting temperature inversion over the Valley of Mexico will produce levels of pollution in Mexico City higher than any in recorded history. Thousands of people will die from respiratory complications, and as many as two million more will become seriously ill.

Fall 2000

• An earthquake centered in northern Peru will cause serious damage throughout Lima and other major coastal cities and trigger landslides and avalanches in mountainous parts of the country.

Winter 2009

• An extended period of drought in the Sahel region of Africa will cause great loss of life due to starvation and disease when crops fail and livestock dies.

Summer 2012

• The long-awaited and feared "great earthquake" will finally strike northern California, with unimaginable losses of life and property in the San Francisco Bay area.

San Francisco after the 1906 earthquake.

• An outbreak of a new, unidentified, and particularly lethal influenza virus will appear first in India and then spread rapidly throughout the overpopulated cities of that subcontinent. The disease will leapfrog to Southeast Asia and from there to Europe and the West Coast of the U.S. Untold thousands of people worldwide will succumb to the new flu strain before it finally burns out six months later. Only Argentina, Chile, and sub-Saharan Africa will be spared the ravages of this disease.

FLOODS, QUAKES, AND "UNIMAGINABLE DESTRUCTION"

Predictor DR. JEFFREY GOODMAN is the director of Archeological Research Associates, Inc., in Tucson, Ariz. A frequent lecturer on archaeology, geology, and parapsychology, Dr. Goodman recently served as a consultant for the Crime Attack Team of Montana on the use of psychics in police work. His innovative research has been featured in many books, including *We Are the Earthquake Generation: Where and When the Catastrophes Will Strike* and *American Genesis: The American Indian and the Origins of Modern Man*.

• PREDICTIONS •

1982–1992

• Several major earthquakes in California along the San Andreas Fault, or other faults, causing great destruction and death in San Diego, Los Angeles, and/or San Francisco.
• A major earthquake in Alaska (Anchorage, Fairbanks affected) comparable to the infamous 8.1-magnitude Good Friday Quake which struck in 1964.
• A large earthquake striking one of the following metropolitan areas, which all have a history of large earthquakes: Salt Lake–Ogden, Puget Sound (Seattle–Tacoma), Hawaii, St. Louis–Memphis, Buffalo, or Charleston.
• A large earthquake triggered by man's offshore drilling activity.
• A large earthquake triggered by Soviet underground nuclear testing.
• Flooding in the Great Lakes area due to accelerated glacial rebound.
• At least one out of every three winters being unusually harsh.

• Japan severely damaged by earthquakes, especially the Tokyo area.
• Several volcanic eruptions in the Caribbean. Watch Mount Pelée on Martinique.
• Food shortages in the Middle East, Italy, Greece, and Turkey.
• Archaeological discoveries proving that the American Indians have been in North America for at least 250,000 years.
• Discoveries proving that the American Indians were among the first fully modern men in the world and that they were very sophisticated and knowledgeable from the start.

1993–2030

• An ever increasing number of people having dreams of impending earthquakes and disasters for the U.S.
• Geophysicists consulting psychics for help in earthquake prediction, especially for guidance as to where to set up their monitoring equipment.
• Animals used to help in earthquake predictions. Monitoring centers utilizing catfish and farm animals set up across California.
• Earthquake preparedness programs set up for many metropolitan areas. Bolt down those gas water heaters!
• At least one violent volcanic eruption in the Pacific Northwest: possibly Mount Hood outside of Portland, Mount Baker outside of Seattle, or Mount Shasta in northern California.
• The Pacific Coast of the U.S. rocked by flurries of large-scale earthquakes. Significant sections of the Pacific coastline subsiding or breaking up and sloughing off into the sea.
• The Imperial, San Joaquin, and Sacramento valleys of California undergo extensive flooding.
• The New York City–northern New Jersey areas hit by a moderate-to-large earthquake, which also endangers the nuclear power plant at Indian Point, N.Y.
• Flurries of massive quakes rock China.
• Shifting of the Gulf Stream current.
• Large-scale flooding of the British Isles.
• Krakatoa in Indonesia explosively erupts again.
• Major earthquakes and unimaginable destruction in Hawaii and Japan.
• Scientists will use sudden changes in underground temperatures to help predict some earthquakes.
• Sudden ice buildups at both poles and accelerated movement toward a new ice age.
• The earth's rotational balance is compromised by polar ice buildups, jolts from massive earthquakes, and rare planetary phenomena requiring the earth's axis of rotation to make a sudden adjustment or shift.
• Worldwide food shortages and even famine.
• The period ends with geologic and climatic stability.
• Psychics used to make major archaeological discoveries.
• Archaeological discoveries proving that there have been lost civilizations (such as those popularly called Atlantis and Lemuria), which existed at least 40,000 years before the start of civilization in the Near East.
• Archaeological discoveries proving that some American Indian

113

groups are direct descendants of lost civilizations and that the American Indians are responsible for the appearance of fully modern man in Europe (Cro-Magnon man) and Asia.
• Archaeological discoveries proving that the first civilizations of China (Shang), North America (Olmec), and South America (Chavin) were all in communication and bound by a powerful feline religious cult.
• Recognition that civilization has risen and fallen several times in the past (as described in many American Indian myths) and that our present civilization could also fall.
• Archaeological discoveries showing that fully modern man appeared independently of all supposedly evolutionary forms such as *Homo erectus*.
• Widespread scientific research on the relationship between man's behavior and changes in the environment such as climate and earthquakes—"Biorelativity!" The power of prayer is explained in terms of the principles of physics and the Heisenberg Uncertainty principle (which states that it is impossible to specify or determine at the same time both the position and velocity of a particle with full accuracy).
• Scientific recognition of the spiritual dimension in the world.
• Renaissance in science and many new creative discoveries. For example, fantastic Buck Rogers-like applications for crystals, such as ray guns and personal healing and energy crystals.
• The use of color and music in healing.
• Limb regeneration.
• A back-to-the-land food and energy movement in the U.S.
• Resurgence of deep religious-ethical thought among all nations. Concern for the evolution of a worldwide "ethic." Ethics a course taught in all schools.

HOW ANIMALS COULD PREDICT FUTURE EARTHQUAKES

On February 4, 1975, an earthquake of 7.3 magnitude hit Haiching, China. Although half the city was destroyed, few fatalities were recorded. Fortunately, the residents had been evacuated prior to the quake because strange animal behavior had been observed in the preceding days. Snakes had left their hibernation holes only to freeze to death on top of the ice-covered ground, pandas in the city zoo were seen moving about oddly, and livestock in the nearby countryside was also disturbed. One of the most earthquake-prone countries in the world, China has long attempted to find reliable quake predictors. Evidence is mounting that animals may provide at least part of the answer. According to a pamphlet issued by the Chinese government's earthquake office, a quake may be imminent when:

1. Cattle, sheep, or horses refuse to go into their pens.
2. Rats abandon their hiding places.
3. Chickens fly into trees and pigs break out of their pens.
4. Ducks refuse to enter the water and dogs bark for no obvious reason.
5. Snakes emerge from their winter hibernation.
6. Pigeons are frightened and will not return to their nests.
7. Rabbits with their ears standing upright jump around and crash into objects.
8. Fish jump out of the water as if frightened.

How have animals fared as quake predictors in the past? In addition to the Haiching earthquake, the following animal forecasts have been recorded.

1. Talcahuano, Chile. All the dogs reportedly left town before an earthquake struck in 1835.
2. Oga Peninsula, Japan. In an unprecedented action, tuna weighing more than 30 lb. beached themselves prior to a 1939 quake. There were also reports of octopuses coming ashore and acting as if they were intoxicated.
3. Alaska, U.S. In 1964 Kodiak bears left their hibernation spots and headed for the hills before a massive 8.4 earthquake rocked Alaska.
4. Friuli, Italy. Hours before northeast Italy was shaken by a 6.5 quake in 1976, terrified animals apparently anticipated it. Dogs barked incessantly, cattle bellowed, caged birds attempted to break free, cats fled to the countryside, and deer rushed down from the mountains.

Research is continuing throughout the world to increase our understanding of how animals can help us avert future earthquake disasters.

—F.B.

14 SPECIES THAT MAY BE EXTINCT BY 2000

Headquartered in Washington, D.C., the World Wildlife Fund was founded in 1961 to support projects aimed at protecting endangered plants and animals and preserving natural habitats. DR. THOMAS LOVEJOY, program scientist for the organization, has compiled the following list of animal species headed for extinction in the near future. Dr. Lovejoy comments: "I have confined the list to vertebrates about which generally more is known, but it is important to remember that for every vertebrate species lost, a much larger number of invertebrate species will go, certainly unheralded and often unknown. Extinction is not new to the world, but extinction on a massive scale with a net reduction in species number is new. It is very hard to predict exactly which species will become extinct, because so many factors are involved, but it is predictable that vast numbers will be lost, with attendant degradation of the planet's capacity to support people."

1. JAPANESE CRESTED IBIS, *Nipponia nippon* (Japan and Korea)

Less than 10 individuals are known, including one in Korea's demilitarized zone. Possibly some may persist in China.

2. CALIFORNIA CONDOR, *Gymnogyps californianus* (U.S.)

Probably less than 30 of North America's largest bird survive.

3. MOUNTAIN GORILLA, *Gorilla gorilla beringei* (Central Africa)

Probably only 400 left. Victims of habitat destruction and poaching. This will be the closest relative modern man has driven to extinction.

4. RED WOLF, *Canis rufus* (U.S.)

It is possible that no pure red wolves are left. Habitat alteration has brought the red wolf into contact with the coyote, and it is interbreeding and being genetically swamped.

5. KOUPREY, *Bos sauveli* (Cambodia)

First discovered in 1937, this wild ox occurs only in remote areas of the Laos-Cambodia border, where conservation measures are not feasible. Numbers unknown but small.

6. LAKE ATITLAN GREBE, *Podilymbus gigas* (Guatemala)

It occurs only on this single lake, where it is threatened by habitat alteration.

7. JAVAN RHINOCEROS, *Rhinoceros sondaicus* (Java)

Perhaps only 20 individuals left, none in captivity.

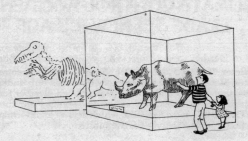

8. AYE-AYE, *Daubentonia madagascariensis* (Madagascar)

A very peculiar nocturnal lemur. Numbers not known but probably terribly rare.

9. KAKAPO (OWL PARROT), *Strigops habroptilus* (New Zealand)

The curious nocturnal parrot. Numbers probably less than 100.

10. IVORY-BILLED WOODPECKER, *Campephilis principalis principalis* (U.S.)

Most likely gone in North America from loss of old timber suitable for nests and feeding, although there are occasional rumors that some exist.

11. CARIBBEAN MONK SEAL, *Monachus tropicalus* (Caribbean)

May already be extinct.

12. BLACK-FOOTED FERRET, *Mustela nigripes* (North America)

Affected by campaigns against its prey, the prairie dog. It does persist in prairie regions of North America, but there is no effective conservation program to aid it.

13. INDRI, *Indri indri* (Madagascar)

One of the most spectacular of the lemurs of Madagascar. A victim of habitat destruction.

14. GIANT PANDA, *Ailuropoda melanoleuca* (China)

Probably fewer than 400 individuals are confined to a few small areas of bamboo forest in western China. The giant panda seems today to depend primarily on two species of bamboo which bloom and die simultaneously with highly adverse effects on the pandas.

CLIMATE-CONTROL ACCIDENT LEADS TO NEW ICE AGE

Predictor ROLAND CHAPLAIN, former acting director of the Edgbaston Meteorological Observatory (Britain's only independent urban weather-forecasting center), is an applied weather forecaster, climatologist, and futurist. He serves as secretary for the Future Studies Centre in Leeds, England, which acts as an information and contact point on alternatives for the future.

1983

• Schools begin to be replaced by centralized sports, laboratory, workshop, drama, and music centers on the one hand and on the other by home-based tuition and learning groups. The latter involve growing numbers of educated unemployed and healthy retired people who are bored with excessive unproductive leisure.

1987

• A basic social wage as a right is introduced for all people as a result of rising unemployment in Europe and North America, leading to increasing militancy, particularly amongst those with higher education qualifications. This results in the regeneration of small-scale industry, food growing, and rearing sheep, goats, and rabbits on marginal land, which, combined with increasing energy costs, threaten the economic viability of large, highly mechanized farms.

1988

• A limited nuclear attack against the U.S.S.R. by a new power group in South Africa, Israel, Pakistan, China, or some other new nuclear state takes place as part of an enormous gamble on the part of the group to seize power in their own country by creating an "enemy" who will not dare actually to retaliate. Their calculation is successful, but the main effect is to make large powers increasingly vulnerable to similar forms of blackmail in the future.

1990

• World Disarmament Referendum. This includes a choice of scenarios such as:
  1. Progressive worldwide conversion of the armaments industry to peaceful uses.
  2. Retraining of armies for famine relief, other emergencies, and assistance for special programs of aid to poor rural areas and the decaying inner zones of large cities.
The attractiveness and inherent good sense of these options produces a huge worldwide YES!

1992

• An uprising in a Warsaw Pact country is controlled by a new virus, which temporarily incapacitates people. This might never have become known but for this virus's breeding with existing strains of "flu" and producing a major epidemic with many deaths throughout Europe.

1995

• There is a sudden worldwide increase in militant environmentalist action as fast-breeder reactors and associated reprocessing facilities steadily increase in number. Such action was previously contained by surveillance and infiltration of known antinuclear organizations, but now there is a rapid growth in spontaneous revulsion as new communication techniques enable citizen groups to inform one another far more effectively.

1996

• Workers at nuclear reactors and reprocessing plants induce a series of major controlled accidents as a protest against unsafe working conditions evidenced by a massive increase in cancer deaths amongst older nuclear-power workers. This, combined with far higher costs than those previously officially forecast, results in governments' having to shift their priorities towards conservation and use of renewable sources of energy, utilization of solar energy in space, and small-scale fusion power.
• As a result of the 1990 Disarmament Referendum, plans are speeded up for introducing a system of world government designed to produce a new equilibrium in the international economic order, which would conserve natural resources, coordinate all technological developments which might endanger ecosystems, optimize the use of land, share the costs of productive space research, and bring remaining nuclear-power generators under an independent world authority.

2000–2005

• With World Government having taken away many of the reasons for which nation-states had in the past existed, there are now a series of new groupings of people. The regions of the U.K. and the component states of the U.S. and U.S.S.R. achieve autonomy in all decisions which do not conflict with World Government decision-making. Cultural and ethnic diversity is positively encouraged as a reaction against necessary uniformity.

2020

• Climate-control accident. Attempts to introduce a high-energy input into the upper levels of the atmosphere (to control surface movements of weather systems intended to bring rain to desert areas) result in unforeseen developments. The westerly wind belt shifts 15° south, bringing a broad band of easterly winds over northern Europe and North America, and there is greatly increased winter snowfall. Those involved dare not attempt to change this for fear of upsetting ozone layers and thus producing an even worse worldwide disaster. Within three years a new ice age is on its way.

CASUALTIES OF
A COMING ICE AGE

NIGEL CALDER, author of *The Weather Machine*, predicts that the next ice age is due and singles out the following 15 nations for obliteration by ice sheets. Many others will suffer extensive glaciation or drought. He puts the chances of a severe onset of the ice age during the next hundred years at "something like 10 to 1 against" but comments that that is "a very high risk indeed for an event that could easily kill two billion people by starvation."

1. Bhutan
2. Canada
3. Denmark
4. Finland
5. Greenland
6. Iceland
7. Irish Republic
8. Liechtenstein
9. Nepal
10. New Zealand
11. Norway
12. Sikkim
13. Sweden
14. Switzerland
15. United Kingdom

SOURCE: Nigel Calder, *The Weather Machine*. New York: Viking Press, 1975.

WEATHER FORECASTERS
CONTINUE TO BE WRONG

Predictor DR. STEPHEN H. SCHNEIDER is a climatologist at the National Center for Atmospheric Research in Boulder, Colo. He is the author of *The Genesis Strategy* and coauthor of *The Primordial Bond*. The editor of the journal *Climatic Change,* Dr. Schneider is also a regular contributor of scientific and popular articles on climate and its implications.

1982–2000

• Climatic variability will continue to cause episodes of world food-production fluctuations, food price spirals, and intermittent famines in poorer countries. Members of the U.N. are likely to give continuous lip service to the need for world food reserves, but little will be done to provide them.

Mid-1990s

• A return of the so-called "22-year drought cycle" is due for the Great Plains and the western U.S.

Beyond 2000

• The burning of coal, oil, and natural gas for energy production produces carbon dioxide (CO_2), which will continue to build up in the global atmosphere. Present theory suggests that this will warm the earth's climate through the so-called "greenhouse effect" mechanism. Noticeable warming is due, if the theory is correct, around 2000.

1982–2030

• Scientists, journalists, amateur meteorologists, and other climatic pundits will continue to offer conflicting speculations on both the course and causes of climatic change. Most will continue to be wrong!

NUCLEAR PLANT DISASTER

Predictor DR. BENJAMIN SPOCK wrote his bestselling book *The Common Sense Book of Baby and Child Care*—the bible of two generations of parents—in 1946. More recent books include *Dr. Spock Talks with Mothers* and *Problems of Parents*. Active politically since 1962, Dr. Spock was staunchly antiwar during the Vietnam War and is a leader in the antinuclear movement.

1982–2030

• A major disaster in a nuclear power plant will result in a panic demand that all such plants around the world be shut down. This will cause major dislocations, since the world will be much more dependent on nuclear power than it is now.

• Unless the U.S. and the U.S.S.R. can negotiate a true disarmament, there will be an increasing deterioration in living standards in the U.S., the bankruptcy of more cities, and quite possibly a nuclear disaster through brinkmanship, madness, or accident.

RADIATION WARS AND WIDESPREAD FAMINE BRING WORLD POPULATION DECLINE

Predictor DAN HALACY, a former Arizona state senator, is the author of hundreds of short stories, articles, and humorous pieces. His many books include *Feast and Famine*, *Century 21: Your Life in the Year 2001 and Beyond*, and *Census: 190 Years of Counting Americans*. He is a senior staff member at the Solar Energy Research Institute in Golden, Colo.

• PREDICTIONS •

CLIMATE

From now until 1992, world climate will be more variable than usual. We will experience frigid winters, yet have unseasonably hot weather at other times. Our concept of "normal" climate will be severely shaken.

By 2030, in spite of the much-feared "greenhouse" heating effect predicted to raise the earth's average temperature, everyone not living in the tropics will be painfully aware that we are moving into another ice age. All signs point toward frigid climate, with glaciers again beginning their icy spread down from the poles. A cooling trend has been measured for the last several decades; the last several winters have been far colder than normal; and generally accepted climate theories call for a new ice age because of the changing tilt and orbit of the earth in its journey around the sun. The historical record of several earlier ice ages supports this astronomical theory.

For all the bold talk of scientists and engineers, we will no more be able to change climate than we have changed the weather. Thus, the ice age will be a catastrophe for those at higher latitudes. Freezing cold and failing crops will drive us toward the equator. The brutal blizzards of the late 1970s will seem mild as snow and ice pile up and temperatures plunge to lows never before recorded. Fuel shortages will grow ever more serious because of the need for far more heating to stay alive through longer, colder winters.

A relative handful of humans retreated before the last ice age. The next will threaten billions, for whom flight will be difficult, if not impossible, because of our dependence on cities and their services.

EARTHQUAKES

Earthquakes, which have killed hundreds of thousands of human beings in past centuries, will be responsible for far greater casualties in the future, as population grows and the concentration of people in cities on or near faults increases.

Between now and 2030, it is inevitable that strong quakes will again rock such unstable areas as Greece, Turkey, Japan, China, Ecuador, and many others. In the U.S., California is earthquake country, and quakes will probably take many lives.

By the year 2030, one or more major quakes will have rocked the heavily populated areas of Los Angeles and San Francisco, with a toll in deaths and damage tens of times as bad as the terrible 1906 quake. Science will have found no more accurate methods of quake prevention than the Greeks and Chinese knew long before Christ's birth. Attempts to release fault pressures with small man-made quakes will fail, and no other methods will be successful either. Worst of all, even with accurate predictions, evacuation will be so difficult that thousands will still die.

THE ENVIRONMENT

Except for that resulting from war, environmental pollution in 1992 will be no worse than what we now endure.

Population increase will continue to slow; we are reducing automotive pollutants by driving more efficient vehicles; and protective measures are improving the quality of air and water or at least holding it at existing levels. But North America, Europe, China, and the U.S.S.R. will experience another and more virulent form of pollution.

Of all environmental horrors, nuclear war is the worst, and by 1992 atomic weapons again will have killed tens of thousands of humans, scarred the earth, and poisoned it and the air and water. This will result from a Soviet-American skirmish quickly brought to a halt. But between 1992 and 2030 a worse encounter will occur, using advanced weapons combining presently unknown blast, heat, and radiation effects to kill life and environment as well.

ENERGY

By 1992 (30 years after the catastrophic failure of America's first commercial breeder), the nuclear breeder reactor will have joined the Concorde SST as a dying species. Even the earlier and safer light-water reactors will be routinely phasing out their 35- to 40-year lifetimes, never to be replaced. Economics, fuel shortage, environmental considerations, and the threat of weapons proliferation will have ended the brief life of nuclear power. Fusion? It will still be in the laboratory, with new breakthroughs announced less and less frequently.

A major reorientation in energy use will be well under way; a remarkable switch from nonrenewable, polluting sources to the renewable and clean sources provided by the sun. The U.S. will be well on the way to President Carter's 1979 pledge of 20% of our energy from the sun by the year 2000.

Solar heat will supply hot water for homes and industry; space heating and cooling with solar energy will be commonplace; encouraging amounts of electric power will be generated by a variety of solar plants, including wind machines, thermal power plants, and ocean-thermal-energy-conversion (OTEC) plants. Gasohol, using alcohol from grain and other "biomass" to stretch petroleum supplies by 10%, will be standard at filling stations.

By 2030 the U.S. and most other nations will be tapping sun, wind, and water for 50% or more of their power and heating needs. The world will be moving happily toward an enhanced version of the renewable energy economy that prevailed on earth until the advent of coal as a fuel. Pollution from fuel will largely be a specter of the past, and no nation will be an energy "have-not."

HUNGER

Hunger, like the poor, is always with us. There will be the hungry and the starving in 1992, but with additional suffering caused by supply dislocations occasioned by war and its aftermath.

By 2030, broader and more devastating wars will have combined with other driving forces of starvation to bring about a decline in population for the first time in recorded history. Bitter cold and frozen crops will also add to the toll, and the long-predicted global famine will at last have caught up with us.

MIND-CONTROL DRUGS ADDED
TO WATER SUPPLY

Predictor THEODORE J. RUBIN has been a government and business economist, military systems analyst, long-range planner, and international affairs researcher. Most recently he was manager of Environmental Information Systems for General Electric and manager of the International Affairs Center in Santa Barbara, Calif. He is a researcher and consultant and an avocado rancher.

• PREDICTIONS •

1982–1992

• Intensifying terrorism against corporate, governmental, and private persons in foreign countries. Abduction and murder by members of radical movements to gain attention and ransom, to embarrass large powers (especially the U.S.), and to embarrass their own governments.
• Continuing terrorism and internal instability in Middle Eastern countries like Iran, Lebanon, Oman, and Yemen, fomented by East-West strategic competition, conflicting oil policies, Islamic resurgence, and unresolved issues between Israel and the Arab nations.
• Continuing China-Vietnam border skirmishes and confrontations over Soviet presence and influence in Southeast Asia and over disputed offshore oil resources.
• Possible punitive military action by the U.S. against one oil-producing nation to attempt to set an example against oil price gouging, to placate an outraged citizenry, and to provide the emotional climate for an austere fuel-rationing program.

1993–2030

• End of oil piracy after 2000 as alternative energy sources become operational on a large scale and as oil reservoirs diminish. Oil potentates become equivalent of deposed European aristocracy of the early 1900s. Peace, based on the resolution of indigenous issues, finally comes to the Middle East.
• Deployment of defensive high-energy weapons upsets the East-West strategic nuclear deterrence standoff and, for the first time since the end of World War II, reopens the possibility of nonnuclear military actions between major powers.
• Growing use of mind-control and behavior-control chemicals by authoritarian governments to suppress dissension and unrest. Unlike chemicals currently applied in crisis situations (e.g., tear gas for mob control), these chemicals will be applied subtly in water and food supplies.

• First example of "corporate warfare" in which giant multinational conglomerates, seeking to expand and consolidate worldwide markets, engage in organized espionage, terrorism, and acts of intimidation to discourage competitors. (The current model is international drug trafficking.)

DARK CLOUDS AHEAD

Predictor ANNE EHRLICH is a senior research associate in biology at Stanford University. With her husband, Dr. Paul Ehrlich, she has concentrated on the problems of population control and environmental protection and has written many technical articles in these fields. She is also the coauthor of several books, including *The End of Affluence: A Blueprint for Your Future* and *Ecoscience: Population, Resources, Environment*.

• PREDICTIONS •

1982–1992

• The next decade can be expected to bring increasing difficulties with raising food production to keep pace with population growth. The 1970s saw three years in which world grain production failed not only to exceed the previous year's level but even, by several percent, to match it. I would expect to see similar failures, perhaps more than three, during the 1980s, and they may be more severe.
• Birthrates in many countries may continue to decline, but the rate of world population growth will still be approaching 2% per year—unless faltering food production results in large-scale famine and a rise in death rates.
• Environmental deterioration will continue to increase, despite tightening controls on pollution—controls which will occur mainly in developed countries. The destruction of natural environments will proceed with expansion in the "blessings" of development, both in overdeveloped and less developed countries, and expansion of populations, especially in less developed countries.
• There will be increasing problems in obtaining needed resources, oil being the most obvious example. Costs of energy and materials will rise substantially, as will those of food and other commodities. The debate on the mix of future energy sources will intensify—soft-path choices (renewables such as solar, emphasis on conservation) versus hard-path choices (nuclear power and high-technology syn-fuels).

1993–2030

• During this longer period, the difficulties and trends described above can be expected to continue and intensify. Population growth will slow, but the occurrence of large-scale famines is virtually certain during this time. Death rates may temporarily rise high enough to cancel out or even reverse growth. Maintaining food production will be even more difficult; many regions may lose ground in the quantity and quality of food supplies. These problems will be reinforced by environmental deterioration, which limits agricultural production, either by bringing on deleterious climate changes or through land and soil depletion. Resource problems will become severe; competition might lead to a nuclear war. But even if that is avoided, life for the average person will not be easier or pleasanter than it is today.

"SURVIVORS ENVY THE DEAD"

Predictor DR. PAUL EHRLICH, the founder of Zero Population Growth, Inc., has made numerous ominous and controversial predictions. In his well-known book *The Population Bomb* (1968), Ehrlich stated that "if population control measures are not initiated immediately and effectively, all the technology man can bring to bear will not fend off the misery to come." A professor of population studies at Stanford University in Stanford, Calif., Dr. Ehrlich continues to warn us of the consequences of overpopulation.

• PREDICTIONS •

Early 1980s
• U.S. engaged in heated debate over immigration; Congress passes restrictive legislation.

Mid-1980s
• Increased economic problems in overdeveloped countries, with monetary inflation coupled with production depression.

Late 1980s
• Massive famines in underdeveloped countries.
• First terrorist threat by a subnational group which actually has an atomic bomb.

Early 1990s
• Nuclear fission power being phased out in most countries.

2010–2030
• Breakdown of world trade system.
• Famines continuous over much of globe.
• Life expectancies decline in overdeveloped countries.
• Thermonuclear war (if we're lucky and one doesn't break out sooner).
• Survivors envy the dead.

AN INVENTORY OF WEAPONS WHICH COULD BE USED AGAINST EARTH IN AN INTERPLANETARY WAR

1. Beam warfare—selective destruction using lasers, heat rays, etc.
2. Biological warfare—particularly the use of the deadly bacillus botulinus, which works on the nervous system. If a small amount were released, it could quickly destroy an entire population.
3. Nonlethal obscuring clouds to "blind" our air force. This could be combined with electronic jamming of radar to produce the maximum effect.
4. Fire storms of hydrogen to lay waste the planet.
5. Nuclear devices to punch "windows" in the ionosphere, thereby jamming radio communications and permitting the entry of lethal ultraviolet rays.
6. Environmental warfare—climate modification to destroy our agriculture, and the initiation of major earthquakes to destroy lives and property and disrupt communications.
7. Fission bombs and projectiles, which could spread deadly radioactive isotopes, such as a cobalt isotope, that would endure for ages.

SOURCE: John W. Macvey, *Space Weapons/Space War*. New York: Stein and Day, 1979.

4

PREDICTIONS ON YOUR HOME AND FAMILY

1982–1992

A metabolic medicine will be found that will keep you from getting fat.

1996

You will be able to buy an extra room to add onto your existing apartment via a plug-in tower.

2020

More than 65% of all married women and 75% of all married men will commit adultery during their married lives.

2030

You will be able to grow your own building by programming crystal structures.

WOMEN ON THE SUPREME COURT
AND MURDER IN OUTER SPACE

Predictor F. LEE BAILEY, in his spectacular career as a criminal lawyer, has represented some of the most controversial defendants of the last 20 years. Dr. Sam Sheppard, Albert DeSalvo (the Boston Strangler), Capt. Ernest L. Medina (of the My Lai Massacre trial), and Patty Hearst are only a few of his famous clients. Mr. Bailey is the author of *For the Defense* and *Secrets* and coauthor of *The Defense Never Rests*.

• PREDICTIONS •

1987

• Electronics will become a major part of the courtroom scene. Videotapes and television monitors will be universally used and will eliminate the need in many cases to bring parties and witnesses into court. It will not be uncommon for law firms to use vans equipped with videotape recorders so that the court can come to the witness rather than the witness to court. Live "television broadcasts from courtrooms" will be a routine procedure.

1990

• There will be a decriminalization of so-called victimless crimes. These will include drunkenness, gambling, and most soft drug use.
• Juries will be abolished in most civil cases, and judges will make all the decisions. There is a need for this because many civil cases even now are too complicated to be understood by laymen.
• A crime of passion will be committed in outer space. Most probably an astronaut will shoot and kill a crewmate. The provocation: a woman. But don't rule out the possibility of a woman astronaut doing away with a fellow crewman. The cause: another woman.

1992

• The "nine old men" of the Supreme Court will be gone. In their place will be a court made up of "nine old persons," but four or five of them will be women.

2000

• An international court will be established to determine who will qualify for transplant operations. The demand on "transplant banks" will become so great that a system will be set up that will allow lawyers to argue why their clients should be given preference for the available hearts, kidneys, or eyes.

2020

· The profession of law will have become galactic. There will be a Supreme Court for Outer Space, staffed by jurists from each of the leading space powers, and a code of law for space will cover everything from spaceship traffic violations to interplanetary "claim-jumping."

· The growing incompetence of American trial lawyers will force the U.S. to shift to the British system. In the U.S., any licensed lawyer can defend a client in court, regardless of whether he has had any training, or indeed, has any skill, in trial law. In Britain, only barristers—highly trained trial lawyers—can defend a client in court.

2030

· The resources of the world—oil, food, water, etc.—will be distributed to the third world through an allocation system operated by the major powers. Lawyers from a third-world nation will come before a court to plead for their nation's allocation, arguing that its need is greater than some competing nation's.

ENCLOSED CITIES
AND END TO OVERWEIGHT

Predictor MELVIN BELLI, one of America's foremost trial lawyers, was admitted to the bar in California in 1933. He is well known as a lecturer and has written numerous books, including *Modern Trials and Modern Damages* (6 vols.), *Life and Law in Japan*, and *The Law Revolt* (2 vols.). Author of the syndicated column *That's the Law*, Mr. Belli maintains offices in Los Angeles and San Francisco.

• PREDICTIONS •

1982–1992

• The telephone will be automatic worldwide and there will be video on it as well as audio.
• There will be revolution in Saudi Arabia. The Saudis will be overthrown and a Third World War narrowly averted.
• Gas engines will be made much more efficient and compact—50 mpg and up.
• A "cure" for cancer, the common cold, and viral ailments will be found, and there will be a similar nostrum or prophylactic for all three.
• A metabolic medicine or "antidote" will be found to prevent overweight. Then my gluttonous friends and I can eat all we want of that wonderful Italian pasta and keep model-thin!
• Trains will make a comeback in the U.S. and will be built lighter and faster.
• There will be more covered cities and parts of cities like the Houston Astrodome.

1993–2030

• An alternate source of power will be found and used universally instead of oil, gas, and electricity. It will be some sort of "atomic" power or power from the sun.
• Jury trial will be cut down and rarely offered, allowed, or used.

COMPUTER BUTLERS— AT YOUR SERVICE

Many people would like to (or at least imagine that they would like to) have a butler or chambermaid to get their day off to a comfortable start. A computer can play this role rather well. More precisely, one or more microprocessors, supported by considerable memory, programming, and peripheral devices, can play major parts of the role of a butler or a chambermaid well. The peripheral devices are certainly the most challenging. This application requires that many parts of your house be made computer peripherals, a task that is difficult, but comparatively practical, and certainly realistic for the person who would enjoy this job.

A terrific personal servant should start by planning, the night before, for your needs during the following day, considering how you will feel and what situations you will encounter. If you use your computer to keep your daily calendar for you, to print out your daily schedule of activities based on previously entered special and repetitive events, the computer has a good amount of the intelligence necessary to also start your morning off appropriately. You can enter other information the night before. Typically you might enter facts such as your being physically exhausted tonight and needing more energy in your breakfast tomorrow, and that your normal route to work is detoured so you will need to start your morning schedule 20 minutes earlier. A computer programmed with your biorhythm data can add considerable intelligence to next-day planning. Your computer can assemble all this information and prepare a schedule, activity plan, and personal "horoscope" for your review (and acceptance or modification) the night before, or you can simply elect to receive this as a set (surprise) plan the next morning.

Additional data could be accumulated during the night. A bed motion sensor (to measure how restless a night you had) might determine whether you needed an extra half hour of sleep. Weather sensors for variables such as temperature, wind speed and direction, and relative humidity could provide data to help your computer select your clothes and breakfast menu.

Come morning, your computer could really go into action. It could, if you like, select and play music you would be likely to enjoy, or music to set your mood appropriately for the day's activities. The music could be gradually made louder or changed in tempo if you didn't awake soon enough. Before time to awake, your computer could, by operating appropriate controls, turn on your bedroom heater, coffee pot, and lights, and start hot water running for your morning bath or shower. Signals could be sent to the furnace to heat up various rooms as they would be needed. By unlatching bins in your ceiling, your computer could select clothes appropriate for your scheduled activities, and the weather, and drop these clothes onto your bed or in your dressing area.

Breakfast in bed is another service you could expect. As mentioned before, your menu could be determined by the conditions you would face that day. Your computer could remember menus from prior days and also provide the desired amount of variety. Microprocessors control microwave ovens, and interfacing an oven to your home computer shouldn't be particularly difficult. Many vending machines have electrically controlled turntables to allow selection from a variety of hot and cold food. These or similar controls could be peripherals of your home computer. Construction of a simple version of a programmable food-dispensing machine shouldn't be difficult. There are several ways of transporting selected food from its preparation points to your bed. A model electric railroad is an interesting possibility. A breakfast-in-bed computer could also learn. For example, your computer might be programmed so that if you sent back 50% of your orange juice (determined by a scale sensing the weight of the returning "empty" dishes) two days in succession, your computer would give you only 75% as much juice the next day.

These computer services can continue through the day, but our explanation will stop here. The next steps in thinking about what your computer can do for you, and accomplishing these things, are up to you.

SOURCE: Reprinted from *Your Home Computer* by James White, copyright © 1977 by Dymax, P.O. Box 310, Menlo Park, Calif. 94025.

DIAL-AN-ENVIRONMENT IN YOUR ECO-HOME

Predictor ROY MASON, an architect who specializes in energy-conscious structures, is currently working on a 45-home development in Columbia, Md., called Solar Village. His pioneering efforts in energy conservation range from foam and underground structures to solar houses and home microcomputers to regulate energy use. Mr. Mason coproduced a documentary film on futures studies entitled *Toward the Future* and worked with the studio design staff on the sets of the *Star Trek* movie.

• PREDICTIONS •

1983

• There will be earth-integrated and underground residential structures in subdivisions to further energy conservation.

1984

• High-speed rapid-transit systems will have brought many cities back to life and created intown/new town megastructures where we work, live, and play in one environment.

1988

• With the development of energy-conscious technology and low-cost materials and building systems, we will begin to see the eco-home—an affordable home that is a descendant of the house trailer—which will be within the price range of the average worker.

1989

• An outgrowth of the space shuttle and space research will be manned earth stations on the moon, whose researchers live on or under its surface.

1990

• Ten percent of all homes will have some type of alternative energy system, such as solar or wind.

1992

• Forty percent of all homes will have some form of home computer (the "house brain") which will control information, entertainment, and energy-management systems. There will be telecommunication, telebanking, and teleshopping. There will be a new evolution of the cottage industry, with the office in the home.

1996

• It will be possible to buy an add-on room or a totally self-contained living unit to plug into your existing apartment in its plug-in tower.

2005

• Large-screen video TV walls will provide media texture in the home, the total video environment where you can "dial an environment" and surround yourself with the Grand Canyon, Taj Mahal, or other imagery space.

2010

• Girderlike building systems stretching between tower supports will bridge over existing cities and terrains, thus increasing available housing.

2015

• Environments will be responsive to one's mood, in terms of light, sound, and color, and through biofeedback—interfacing with flexible materials—they will change in shape and/or form.

2020

• There will be 3-D holographic environments, creating interior and exterior space mirages.

2022

• The long transportation corridors now linking U.S. cities will develop monorail-type continuous transport systems and apartment ribbons, which will have highways on their roofs, thus leaving more open land.

2025

• New enclosed environments, such as domes, will enable cities to be built on now unused land masses such as deserts and arctic regions.

2030

• Advances in our understanding of the process of plant growth and programming of crystal structures will enable us to grow buildings.

TOMORROW'S SECURITY COMMUNITY

Predictor DR. MARVIN ADELSON is a professor in the School of Architecture and Urban Planning at the University of California, Los Angeles. He teaches courses in decision making, imaging the future, architectural programming, and the group process in planning, design, and action. A founder of the Institute for the Future, Dr. Adelson is particularly interested in those aspects of the future that are at least partly designable, as opposed to those that are only predictable.

• PREDICTIONS •

1982-1992

• Architects using computers will be able to design, and try out be-
forehand, buildings which will satisfy numerous demanding performance specifications. These will include energy conservation, the
living pattern of each occupant, aesthetics, cost, and the materials,
components, and detailed construction process required. To the extent that these possibilities are actually realized in practice, architects will provide suitable, individualized buildings for human
uses of all kinds, and a much greater proportion of buildings will
reflect the benefits of an architect's participation.
• Wealthy people will tend to move toward the centers of cities. The
"slums" will move to the suburbs as run-down centers are revived.
• Some poor people will find a home in the city through programs
that provide ownership in return for rehabilitation of run-down
buildings and neighborhoods. Educational training programs, plus
advice and counsel from the building trades, will provide these "new
pioneers" with the necessary know-how.
• Mobile homes and prefabricated homes will become more acceptable, especially to those who are starting out in home ownership and
to those who have retired. Styling and livability will improve greatly.
By the end of the nineties, it is possible that vertical frames—which
hold large numbers of such units on a space-rental basis—will have
become commonplace.

1982-2000

• A good deal of the innovation in architecture and urban design will
most likely occur in areas of the world where large amounts of oil
money combine with underdevelopment to create relatively open
opportunities, and where tastes have not become as conven-
tionalized as they have in more developed areas. "World-scale"
projects for attracting tourism and investment will stagger the imagination. Unfortunately, the match between transitional architecture
and transitional social structure will not always work out well for the
people concerned.

1982-2030

• Major new urban projects will be undertaken which combine what
have heretofore, because of zoning practices, been strictly separated
functions. The nucleus for some communities may be the shopping
mall or the California-style "security community," which has its own
pool and sauna, security gate (with or without guards), entertainment
area, and other amenities. Interestingly, the occupants—whether
owners or renters—will find themselves paying "fees" to a private
organization for versions of "police," "parks and recreation," and
other services formerly provided by tax dollars, a trend which may
help keep municipalities solvent.
• A lot of people and firms will leave cold, northern cities for the sun
belt, but perhaps not as many as might have been expected. Energy
savings and physical comfort will have to be balanced against very

138

high prices for land and increased living costs. Moreover, northern cities will work very hard to remain attractive. Sensible modes of planning and development will enable the cold-climate cities to provide amenities without excessive taxation.

1993–2030

· In many areas, individual homes will generate enough energy from the sun so that they can pump electricity back through their meters into the "grid" and draw on this surplus when sunlight is inadequate. Utilities will learn to profit from this traffic, but only after some squawking.

BETTER SEX WITHOUT GUILT

Predictor DR. ALBERT ELLIS is the executive director of the Institute for Rational-Emotive Therapy in New York City, where he practices as a psychotherapist, marriage and family therapist, and sex therapist. Dr. Ellis has published over 500 articles in psychological, sociological, and popular journals and over 40 books, including *Sex without Guilt, A New Guide to Rational Living, Sex and the Liberated Man, Reason and Emotion in Psychotherapy, The Intelligent Woman's Guide to Dating and Mating,* and *Handbook of Rational-Emotive Therapy.*

· PREDICTIONS ·

1992

· Almost no males or females will be very guilty about masturbation.
· Severe guilt about premarital sex will be felt by less than 10% of the population.
· Men will learn to be better lovers and will almost always see that women are given noncoital orgasms if they desire to have them.
· Many more males will be using condoms as a VD prevention device.
· Millions of people will quit orthodox religious groups unless these groups liberalize their sex attitudes.

2000

· The majority of couples who legally marry will first live together in "sin."

2010

• The attitudes of most religious groups toward sex will be much more liberal.

2020

• More than 75% of married males and 65% of married women will commit adultery at some time during their married lives.
• More than 90% of single men and 85% of single women will have premarital sex relations.
• A virtually foolproof and harmless method of contraception will be discovered.

RELAXATION OF
SEXUAL RESTRICTIONS

Predictor DR. WARDELL POMEROY, a longtime associate of the famous Dr. Alfred C. Kinsey, is a practicing psychologist in San Francisco, Calif. In his work with Dr. Kinsey, Pomeroy interviewed thousands of Americans about their sex lives. These interviews formed the basis of the pioneering studies *Sexual Behavior in the Human Male* and *Sexual Behavior in the Human Female,* which are known worldwide as the Kinsey Reports. A founding member of the Institute for Sex Research, Dr. Pomeroy is the author of *Boys and Sex, Girls and Sex,* and *Dr. Kinsey and the Institute for Sex Research.*

• PREDICTIONS •

First I would like to make a general prediction as to where "sex" is going in the future. In the late 1960s and the early 1970s we experienced a sexual revolution in this country, not in regard to overt behavior but in terms of changing attitudes and more open discussion about sex. The women's liberation movement, legalized abortion, the gay rights movement, more open sexually explicit materials, hundreds and hundreds of new books about sex, etc., etc., were all part of this radical change. Then we experienced a backlash, thanks to a conservative Supreme Court, to Phyllis Schlafly, and to Anita Bryant (to mention only a few). Hence, in the near future (2 to 7 years), I see a continuation of this backlash, but in the more distant future (10 to 20 years), I see the revolution as being inexorable, and thus some very profound changes will occur. Now to be more specific.

Life-styles. I see an increase of persons living together without

140

marriage, more open marriages, and even more communal living. This will be gradual over the years.

The Role of Organized Religion. I see a further split between conservative and liberal religions, so that in 20 years the conservative churches will still be shaking their collective fingers at homosexuality, abortion, premarital and extramarital intercourse, etc., and the liberal churches will be more relaxed about what people do sexually.

Sexology. There will be a growing realization that sexology is a field or discipline in its own right, and there will be more and more trained sexologists in the U.S. I predict that in 5 to 10 years there will be at least one "sex expert" in most of the universities, medical schools, and teaching hospitals in the country.

Sex Therapy. This one is hard to predict. There will be, at first, an increase in sex therapy and a movement away from the medical model. Later, there may be an assimilation of sex therapy into general therapy, but on the other hand there may be a further specialization. Massage, nudity, and "hands on" therapy will be more accepted.

Sex Education in Schools. This phenomenon will remain static for the next many years. As in my second prediction above, the religious lines will be drawn in the schools, and a "standoff" will occur. Children will turn elsewhere for sex education.

Consenting Adult Laws. In 10 years all states will have laws allowing consenting adults to do in private whatever they want to do sexually.

Pornography. For the next 2 to 5 years there will be further restrictions on the dissemination of pornography. This may even be longer, depending on the makeup of the Supreme Court. In 10 to 20 years we will go in the direction of Denmark and the President's Commission on Obscenity and Pornography and will allow sexually explicit materials to be freely seen by adults. I also see a considerable increase in the quality of such materials.

Homosexuality. For the next 2 to 5 years the antihomosexual forces will continue to be heard from. More and more homosexuals will come out of the closet, and homosexuals will become a stronger political force in the country. Bisexuality will become more "fashionable." In 10 to 20 years we will wonder what all the fuss was about.

Abortion. In 2 to 4 years the pro-abortion forces will have won the battle.

Contraception. In 3 to 5 years a workable male birth-control method will have been devised.

SEXUAL INTERCOURSE ON THE DECLINE

Predictor SHERE HITE is the author and researcher of *The Hite Report: A Nationwide Study of Female Sexuality*, considered one of the definitive works on the subject. She is also the director of Hite Research International, which completed a study on male sexuality and the politics of private life in 1980. Ms. Hite was listed as one of the 25 most influential women in America by the 1978 *World Almanac*.

• PREDICTIONS •

By 2000

• Men will no longer speak of their "sex drive" as a biological phenomenon. Male sexuality will change radically from the way we know it today. Masculinity will no longer be as universally equated with intercourse, and there will be more open discussion of sex and sex roles among men.

• By this time, women will have introduced many new activities and feelings into their sexual relationships, which will be highly beneficial. Many women will be able to end in their own lives what has been a sexist definition of sex for centuries.

• Birth control will much less frequently be necessary, because intercourse (coitus) will not automatically be considered the goal of "sex." Intercourse will not be as popular as it is today; its basis as a cultural symbol will have eroded. This will allow people to enjoy it more easily, when desired. Similarly, there will begin to be a shift away from a reproductive focus in sex education, and the clitoris will be discussed.

• Women and men will enjoy life more, and love between women and men will be redefined.

• Because the definition of "sex" will be in such a profound state of transition, homosexuality versus heterosexuality will no longer be an issue.

• Before all of the above happens, there will be a very strong reaction, which will be short-lived, as the benefits of this new thinking for everyone become apparent. A feeling will grow that we can create a more humane and beautiful world.

CHANGES IN RELIGIOUS AND SEXUAL LIFE-STYLES

Predictor DR. ROBERT FRANCOEUR is the chairperson of biological and health sciences at Fairleigh Dickinson University in Rutherford, N.J. An embryologist and sexologist, Dr. Francoeur is the author of several books, including *Learning to Become a Sexual Person* and *Hot and Cool Sex: Cultures in Conflict*.

· PREDICTIONS ·

1982–1992

· Massive immigrations from the third-world countries, especially those in Latin America and Southeast Asia, will make whites a definite minority in many areas of the U.S. Unlike previous immigrant groups, these new citizens will place a high priority on their cultural integrity, insisting on their constitutional rights to a bilingual education. In the states of Florida, Texas, and California, and in New York City, Boston, Washington, D.C., Chicago, and other large cities, these new populations will wield considerable political and economic power. They will introduce a wide variety of life-styles and value systems.

· Our civil laws will have ceased trying to regulate sexual behavior and relationships between consenting adults. Homosexuals and other sexual minorities will be protected by law the same as heterosexuals. Marriage and monogamy will no longer be privileged by law. Civil contracts written by parties in alternative life-styles and new religious covenants recognized by some churches will be accepted by the law of the land as defining the relationship, mutual responsibilities, rights, and status of the participants. Civilly and religiously, our morality will be focused on persons rather than on actions and legalities. Our view of morality will be personalized but will transcend gender and genitals. Birth certificates will no longer list the sex of the newborn.

1995

· Nationwide, adult life-styles and relationships will be very diversified. Fifty percent of all Americans between ages 18 and 40 will be either single, never married, divorced, or widowed. Many of these singles will live in unmarried relationships, so that the term single is no longer accurate. Reconstituted families—couples in their second or third marriages—are the second most common life-style. Nonexclusive marriages—small groups of three to seven adults—are more common than in the 1970s. Small communities or communes, some sexually open, others more traditional in their dyadic relations, have organized around a "New Age" philosophy, advocating environmental responsibility in the practical reality of "living lightly," in tune with nature but without rejecting our technological advantages. Pressures from the third world, limited energy and resources that must be shared equally, make the "living lightly" life-style increasingly popular. An open, accepted pluralism in life-styles has replaced the nuclear monogamous family. A growing emphasis on cooperation in all areas of life and deemphasis of private property has led to synergism in human relationships and deemphasis of exclusivity and jealousy.

2000–2010

· Human reproduction has been brought under complete control, and couples now have the option of choosing the mode of conception, pregnancy, and birthing they prefer. Coital conception may still be common, but accurate diagnostic techniques will pinpoint ovulation and also allow the selection of fetal sex. Frozen eggs and sperm will be commonly available from gamete banks, along with frozen embryos for embryo transplantation; artificial insemination will be common. Embryo transplants will be a popular solution to the finally resolved dilemma of abortion, since women with unwanted pregnancies can have the fetus transplanted to a surrogate mother or artificial womb for subsequent adoption. Artificial wombs for full-term pregnancies are available at home or in pregnancy centers. There are strong possibilities that the control of conception and pregnancy will be removed somewhat from personal decision, in that males may be sterilized shortly after puberty but not before depositing a semen sample in the frozen gamete bank as a national health policy. Conception then would require approval of a state or federal committee which investigates the genetic health of the two proposed genetic parents and licenses conception.

2020

• The increasing pressures of worldwide economics, satellite communications, population, food production, equitable use of resources, and protection of the environment have created a new spirituality, a new religious awareness. This has been prompted by, and has contributed to, a convergence of all major religions in an ecumenical union that transcends past sectarian boundaries of Hindu, Muslim, Buddhist, Christian, and Jew. People have regained a sense of the spiritual and cosmic akin to the medieval faith, but without being strongly church-related. Emphasis is on the role each person and sociocultural group plays in the ongoing creation and evolution of our global tribe, earth, and cosmos. There is a new level of consciousness, a new respect for different cultures and traditions. Yet in most denominations, a small vocal minority of traditionalists tries to maintain the integrity, exclusivity, and elitism of its sect. New rituals are not parochial or even church-related. The clergy as a caste has mostly disappeared.

2030

• The average life expectancy of Americans is now between 100 and 110 years due to major advances in the prevention of the mental and physical deterioration of aging, heart attacks, stroke, and high blood pressure, along with control of viral and environmentally induced cancers. Half of the American population is over the age of 50. The birthrate is about 25% below replacement level with many childless couples, and those who do have children have only one or two. Despite the prospect of youthful vitality after the age of 100 or 120, the election of euthanasia is morally and legally accepted. Changes in our patterns of gainful employment, productive work, retirement, and leisure have been radical.

144

FUTURE FAITHS

Predictor MALCOLM BOYD, an Episcopal priest, has been at the forefront of social and religious activism since the 1950s. He was described in *The New York Times Magazine* as "a latter-day Luther or a more worldly Wesley, trying to move organized religion out of 'ghettoized' churches into the street—where the people are." This reputation comes, in part, from his bestselling *Are You Running with Me, Jesus?*, a book of prayers written in a very modern style and dealing with contemporary themes. Mr. Boyd, who has written 19 other books, lives in Sherman Oaks, Calif.

• PREDICTIONS •

1982–1992

• A woman priest will be ordained in the Roman Catholic Church in an illicit but valid ceremony.
• Christian-Jew-Muslim will replace Protestant-Catholic-Jew as the front-runner religious category.
• A small but significant number of Jews will place the development of an indigenous expression of Judaism in their adopted homelands ahead of a primary relationship to Israel.
• The underground church movement will attract more who feel alienated from establishment religion—religious singles, feminist women, gays, the elderly, and political idealists.
• Emergence of a biblically illiterate generation for whom the Bible is folkloric and irrelevant.
• Breakdown of dialogue between fundamentalistic Christians and those whose moral and political views are not based on a legalistic, literalistic approach to scripture.
• Social action eclipsed in many churches and synagogues.
• Deepening of a "people's faith." A growing gap between religious professionals and a theological elite on the one hand and the rank and file of religious-oriented people on the other.

1993–2030

• Faith will be viewed entirely differently when basic structures of society collapse, giving way to a new age and a drastically changed world view.
• There will be altogether new religions.
• A sharp increase in cults and "messiahs" utilizing electronic communications techniques to gain power. Contrapuntally, a serious, low-key, and unpublicized development of a new Christian theology will change the course of church history.
• Women will look back and laugh at old struggles for acceptance, while gays will be fully accepted.
• Black and Hispanic religious leaders will replace many white ones.

• Titanic battle between those who adhere to a narrow, enclosed, protective view of religion (via rigid dogma and theology) and those who wish to bring humanity into a "one God" concept.
• A return to religious social action as people grapple with problems of survival, energy, food, environment—and freedom.

NEW METHODS
OF BIRTH CONTROL

FOR WOMEN

1. SILASTIC IMPLANTS

Silastic (siliconized elastic) rods containing progestogen (which acts like the body's natural hormone, progesterone) have been implanted under the skin of women volunteers in Brazil and Chile. The rods slowly release the progestogen into the bloodstream, thereby interfering with ovulation and changing the cervical mucus so that sperm can't penetrate it. Tests show that the rod implant could be effective for as long as 6 to 10 years. Although the device can cause irregular menstrual bleeding, ovarian cysts, weight fluctuation, and skin irritation at the implant site, there is no chance of liver damage as in oral contraceptives, because the chemical doesn't enter the digestive system. This method is not yet as safe or effective as it could be, and extensive testing is still needed before FDA approval.

2. INTRAVAGINAL RING

This plastic ring, inserted like a diaphragm, slowly releases progestogen to prevent pregnancy. Worn by the woman between periods, the ring should be effective for six months. The greatest disadvantage is that there is an increased chance of vaginal infection because the ring is a foreign body. Intravaginal rings, now in the clinical testing stages, could be available by the mid-1980s.

3. PERIODIC HORMONE INJECTIONS

Approved in the U.S. solely for treatment of cancer of the uterine lining, the progesterone-based drug Depo-Provera is being used as a contraceptive in other nations because it is 99% effective. Administered every three months, the drug works in several ways. It inhibits ovulation, induces the cervical mucus to block sperm entry, and, if those precautions fail, makes the uterus unreceptive to the fertilized egg. But Depo-Provera can cause cervical cancer, affect menstrual regularity, and lessen menstrual flow. Animal testing has begun in the U.S., but it will be at least 1990 before the drug is marketed in America.

A more promising but less developed line of research is concerned with inhibin F, a substance that seems to inhibit FSH production. FSH is a hormone produced by the pituitary gland early in the menstrual cycle; without it, eggs do not mature and are not released by the ovary. A small dose given on day one of a woman's period could be all that's necessary for contraception that month, and because inhibin F is not a steroid, it has none of the side effects of birth-control pills. The drug has worked on rhesus monkeys, but more primate tests must be made before humans try it. Availability is at least 10 years away.

4. ONCE-A-MONTH BIRTH CONTROL

Scientists have been working on perfecting the "morning-after pills," which are already on the market but have drastic side effects. These pills employ huge doses of estrogen to disrupt the normal female reproductive system, and they cause vomiting and diarrhea. Doctors at the Worcester Foundation of Experimental Biology in Shrewsbury, Mass., are developing an alternative. They have been experimenting with F2 alpha analog, a variant of prostaglandin, a natural substance that causes uterine muscle contractions (as during labor). Taken at the end of every menstrual cycle, the pill would reduce progesterone levels in the body and bring on menstruation (without violent contractions), and also end a pregnancy. There are no known side effects, but more long-term tests for toxicity must still be carried out. If proved safe, F2 alpha analog could be marketed in 10 years. Prostaglandins in the form of vaginal suppositories that can induce abortion up to the ninth week of pregnancy may be available by the early 1980s.

Scientists at the University of Texas and the University of Maryland School of Medicine are in the process of isolating LHRBI, which might prove to be another postcoital contraceptive. LHRBI is a naturally occurring chemical that blocks the binding of LH (luteinizing hormone), essential for the growth of an already fertilized egg. It is in extremely early stages of experimentation, and it may be another 20 years before it is on the market.

Natural plant derivatives that cause strong uterine contractions are also being studied. One such plant is zoapatle *(Montanoa tomentosa)*, used for centuries by Mexican women to bring on menstrual bleeding.

5. LRH INHALER

In Sweden and in New Orleans, La., researchers looking for a way to help infertile women conceive may have found a new method of contraception. LRH analog, a variant of the natural hormone LRH, replaces the hormone and reverses its function so that ovulation is inhibited. Daily sniffs from an LRH analog inhaler showed 100% effectiveness in tests. Although menstruation is also halted during its use, the nasal spray is thought to be safer than oral contraceptives on a short-term basis, but its long-term effects must be studied before it can be widely used.

6. CONTRACEPTIVE VACCINE

Doctors have successfully used antibodies often found in infertile women to immunize test animals against conception. Since the antibodies bind with the spongy covering of an ovum, they make it impossible for the sperm to penetrate and fertilize the egg. There is no tampering with hormones, so menstruation is not affected; full fertility returns after several cycles. Due to the possibility of allergic reactions, several years of testing are still necessary.

Immunization against the production of HCG, a hormone needed to prepare a woman's body for pregnancy, has been tested on women in India and Sweden. Immunization would block HCG from reaching the ovaries when an egg has been fertilized. The process seems to be safe and reversible on laboratory animals, and it may be available by the late 1980s.

Some prostitutes are thought to be extremely infertile because of overexposure to sperm. One enzyme present on the surface of the sperm, LDH, does cause a reaction in female enzymes. When female test animals were vaccinated with a variant of LDH, they developed antibodies against the male sperm, causing an 80% reduction in fertility that was completely reversible. Though animal research has begun, its effectiveness will have to be improved if it is to be tested on humans.

7. MORE EFFECTIVE SPERMICIDES

Scientists at the University of Illinois Medical Center in Chicago have been working with NPGB, which attacks the enzyme found in sperm that enables the sperm to tunnel into and fertilize the egg. In animal tests the researchers have discovered that fewer pregnancies occur when NPGB is added to spermicide creams and even nonspermicidal lubricating jelly (such as K-Y Jelly) than with the spermicide creams or jellies alone. Adding NPGB to noncontraceptive jelly makes it 70% to 80% effective—as effective as a spermicide. NPGB must be improved before human testing can be carried out, because it can cause complications if absorbed into the bloodstream. It could be on the market by 1985.

8. COLLAGEN SPONGE DIAPHRAGM

Made of a natural spongy material pretreated with spermicide to make additional creams or foams unnecessary, the collagen sponge diaphragm both absorbs and attacks sperm. It is soft, nonirritating, and easier to use than the conventional diaphragm, but there are still some difficulties in insertion and removal, and women volunteers have complained about odor and mess. Clinical tests are now under way, and the collagen sponge diaphragm may be in the stores in five years.

9. MODIFIED CERVICAL CAP

Only about the size of a quarter, this updated version of one of the oldest forms of birth control is made of rubbery plastic. It's held in place on the cervix by a thin film of mucus, and it's fitted to the proper size for each individual woman. It is flexible enough to expand and contract with the cervix during the fluctuations of the monthly cycle. It has a one-way valve that allows the free flow of menstrual fluid out without permitting sperm in. Inexpensive, highly effective, with no adverse reactions, the improved cervical cap could be available by the mid-1980s.

10. IMPROVED RHYTHM

Both the calendar and temperature methods of rhythm offer only about 80% effectiveness, but doctors of the World Health Organization have been working on a more scientific method—based on changes in cervical mucus—to accurately determine the fertile days of each menstrual cycle. One tamponlike device, the Ovulimeter, measures chemical changes in mucus when it is briefly placed in the vagina. Do-it-yourself kits for determining "unsafe" days could be on the market by 1985.

FOR MEN

1. BIRTH-CONTROL PILL

It has been difficult to develop a male birth-control pill because suppressing sperm efficiently requires dangerously large doses of hormones, and because sperm production is an ongoing, rather than cyclical, process. But safe pills may be available by the end of the century. After Chinese doctors noticed a relationship between the consumption of cottonseed oil and increased male infertility, they were able to devise a 99.9% effective pill based on gossypol, a substance taken from cotton plants. For four years, Chinese volunteers have been taking the pill on a regular schedule (once a day for the first three months, then twice a week thereafter). They have complained of minor bloating, digestive upsets, and weight fluctuation, but the gossypol has reduced sperm production. The volunteers have not noticed any problems with impotence or lower sex drive, and the sterility is apparently reversed after the men have been off the drug for a year. The Chinese and the World Health Organization are still analyzing the data and testing the long-term effects. Tests done in the U.S. by the Population Council have shown the derivative to be highly toxic. However, if a safe synthetic form can be produced or the proper long-term dosage level determined, gossypol could be sold in stores by the mid-1980s.

The hormonal drug Danazol, recently approved by the FDA for treatment of inflammations of the uterine lining, has been shown in tests to be an effective male contraceptive after one or two months' use. When used alone, Danazol inhibits the hormones LH and FSH, affecting sperm production. But it also decreases sex drive, a condition presently being corrected with testosterone. Long-term studies are needed to determine effective dosages. A low dose doesn't reduce sperm count effectively, while a large dose can cause liver damage.

2. CONTRACEPTIVE VACCINE

After five years of research at the Harbor-UCLA Medical Center, a vaccine has been developed that neutralizes the hormone FSH, making sperm count too low for fertility. Since the process involves injecting antibodies, there is a danger of allergic reactions, but the vaccine is aimed specifically at sperm production and so should not cause other side effects. A patent has been obtained on the process, and testing has begun on male monkeys, but it could be 1990 before such a vaccine is available.

3. TESTICLE WARMER

A man's testicles hang away from the body because sperm must be stored in lower-than-body temperatures to remain fertile. Warming the testicles only a few degrees is enough to decrease fertility temporarily with no side effects. Japanese doctors are testing the efficiency of hot baths, and a heating device for the scrotum has actually been invented. The method is effective, but it is not expected to be too popular.

4. ULTRASOUND

Ultrasound waves—sound pitched above the human ability to hear it—have been proved to produce temporary sterility by reducing live sperm count when directed at the testicles shortly before intercourse. Although it seems to be perfectly harmless and completely reversible, it is not yet known whether ultrasound can be made convenient enough for general use.

—S.D.

THE DWINDLING FAMILY

Predictor DR. SUZANNE KELLER is a professor of sociology at Princeton University in Princeton, N.J. Her specialities in research and teaching include social architecture, the family, sex roles, futurism, and urban planning. A 1972 recipient of the Guggenheim Award, Dr. Keller is the author of several books, including *Beyond the Ruling Class* and *The Urban Neighborhood*.

· PREDICTIONS ·

By 1992

The Family. Current trends will accelerate. More two-bread-winner families carrying on the momentum of the 1970s to become the predominant pattern; declining fertility; rise of one-child and no-child family. A smaller percent of the population will marry, hence divorce should decrease; more sharing of household tasks and child care by couples as women have full-time jobs; more and more long-term singlehood as a respected status. The suburban mystique will give way to urbanized patterns of earning and learning.

Marriage. There will be less compulsion to marry but no real accepted alternatives. Most people will still enter into the married state, but growing minorities will not. There will be greater equality between husbands and wives and greater cooperation in all aspects of family life. Greater understanding of and preparation for marriage will make for more responsible behavior in marriage.

Sexuality. Continued advances in contraceptive technology will decrease the number of unwanted and illegitimate children; fewer abortions. A male contraceptive pill will be available. Contraceptives will be easily available at low or no cost. Along with reliable contraception, there will be ever-growing acceptance of nonnormative forms of sexual behavior. Much confusion will persist, but there will be less ignorance about the body. Greater awareness of sexuality will lead to more responsible attitudes to sex in its human aspect. Furtive sex will decline.

Sex and Gender Roles. Women will be trained toward self-reliance and jobholding, toward independence and achievement. The admired woman will be active, striving, successful, and nondeferential to men. Men will be trained away from dominance over women and learn to expect a sharing of work and domestic duties. Sex differences will be better understood. Sex expression will be accepted as normal for both sexes. Women will continue to make some headway in their attempts to equalize opportunities for education, jobs, and achievements.

2030

The Family. The family as an institution will be carried on by a minority (40%) of the population, much as a small fraction (3%) of farmers now feed the whole society. This minority will marry for life and have children they will cherish within a general context of zero population growth. They will be helped by a number of social and financial supports now missing—to guarantee adequate health, nutrition, and education; sound child-care facilities; and free parental education and marital counseling. For the majority, the family will have become a part-time institution.

Marriage. This key institution for producing children will engage the minority who choose to be parents. For the rest, relationships between men and women will resemble contemporary friendships in being voluntary and reflective of personal, not social, needs.

Sexuality. Permanent infertility will be the rule, to be positively altered only upon the thoughtful voluntary decision to bring a child into the world and assume responsibility for it. The sexual repression to which Freud applied his genius will have become a relic of history, like the dancing manias of the Middle Ages. By being more fully integrated into all aspects of one's life, sexuality will have become sensuality. The heterosexual orthodoxy will have become less stringent, which will make homosexuality, not more, but less, likely as the compulsion to take on fixed sexual identities diminishes.

Sex and Gender Roles. The categorization of individuals by gender will be far less pronounced than it is today, and gender will have ceased to be a *master* status. Men will be under far less pressure to succeed and provide because they are men, and women will take for granted that they will be self-supporting and nondependent. The polarity of men versus women will be greatly played down in favor of the similarity between men and women. Categorical discrimination of the sexes will have been abolished, and the phrase "equality of the sexes" will therefore have become a redundant phrase.

THE FUTURE FAMILY

ALVIN TOFFLER, author of *Future Shock* and *The Third Wave,* has written: "Instead of commuting to factories and offices, many parents will work in their living rooms, which will be equipped with computers, and millions of teenagers will be able to study at home, often with their own parents as teachers. Just as was true on the old farmstead years ago, kids will be expected to help with the family work chores—feeding the computer with signals, for example. The result will be a tighter family unit—a work-together-study-together unit."

SOURCE: Reprinted from *Seventeen* magazine. Copyright © 1980 by Triangle Communications Inc. All rights reserved.

CHANGING ROLES
FOR WOMEN

Predictor DR. CAROL CREALOCK is a psychologist teaching at the University of Western Ontario, Ontario, Canada. Her field of specialization is the future for women, and she teaches several courses in special education and women's issues.

1982–1992

• Two patterns of motherhood will emerge for working women. The first will see women having children between the ages of 20 and 30 and then going out to work as soon as the youngest enters school. The second will see women choosing career development between the ages of 20 and 30 and then having one or two children with some or no career disruption.

• Male dominance will be broken down, not by confrontation, but by the slow and steady involvement of women into all areas of endeavor. Today's women will be the models that will wear down the resistance of both sexes to new roles for each.

• Women will receive a greater share of the economic benefits in our society. This will come about through (a) more direct employment in present areas; (b) greater government support; and (c) a large growth in family-support employment, such as day-care, housekeeping, and baby-sitting services.

• Women will be more active in seeking out meaningful interpersonal relationships but they will lose the security of their role within traditional marriage.

• At least 50% of women will have experienced the ecstasy and the agony of a long-term relationship and its end.

• Knowledge concerning the inequities in opportunity suffered by women throughout the world will become much more available.

1993–2030

• Many more demands to redress these inequities will be made and acted upon by the concerned groups and nations.

• More time and effort will be spent addressing the issue of the roles of all persons within society. Androgyny or situation-specific rather than sex-specific roles will become a more acceptable option for both men and women.

• More women will become involved in community- and job-related politics. As their focus of interest moves from the home to the work place, concern about good conditions will influence such involvement.

• Nearly 100% of women will have experienced the growth and death of a meaningful relationship.

• Women will continue to outlive men but they will suffer more of the physical ailments associated with the stress of increased decision making in careers and personal life.

"Thus far women have been the mere echoes of men. Our laws and constitutions, our creeds and codes, and the customs of social life are all of masculine origin. The true woman is as yet a dream of the future."
—Elizabeth Cady Stanton, U.S. woman-suffrage leader, 1888

TOMORROW'S WOMAN:
THE SHAPE OF THINGS TO COME

Predictor HELEN GURLEY BROWN, writer, editor, lecturer, and television personality, first came to national attention with the publication of her book *Sex and the Single Girl*. Three related books, recordings, a newspaper column, and a television interview show followed. In 1965 Ms. Brown became editor of *Cosmopolitan* magazine. Under her leadership, the magazine has become a multi-million-dollar enterprise. Ms. Brown lives in New York City.

· PREDICTIONS ·

1982–1992

The female body of tomorrow:	Still thin.
Attitudes toward marriage:	More marriage.
Sex:	More but with fewer.
Childbearing:	Less.
Careers and jobs:	The exception will be the woman who doesn't work.
New material for clothes:	More cotton. Natural fibers (cotton, linen, wool, silk) treasured above all.
New styles:	Still bare because body will be prettier.
Feminine beauty standards:	High. More demanding than ever.

1993–2030

The female body of tomorrow:	Same as previous decade. Flabby hips and stomachs won't come back in style.
Attitudes toward marriage:	Cyclical rebellion, favoring less marriage.
Sex:	Less because of boredom with total sexual freedom.
Childbearing:	If no war has intervened, less.
Careers and jobs:	Compulsory.
New materials for clothes:	Mostly synthetic.
New styles:	Throwback to the 1970s.
Feminine beauty standards:	Far-out and spacey.

THE EMERGENCE OF A COOPERATIVE SOCIETY

Predictor THOMAS CARLETON is a cofounder and codirector of Earthrise Inc., a nonprofit organization formed to initiate independent research into the nature of Western society. The Earthrise Project includes Futures Lab, Earthrise Newsletter, and the Global Futures Game, a participatory exercise allowing players to simulate political, environmental, and social development on a global scale through the year 2020. Mr. Carleton has lectured to dozens of community and college audiences around the country and has been invited to participate in several conferences on the future.

• PREDICTIONS •

According to Carleton: "The word *prediction* is too strong; it implies an authority beyond what I believe to be humanly possible. I personally do not want a blueprint for my future, nor do I want a national or global blueprint for the future with its autocratic implications."

1990

• Futurism (or futuristics, futurology, or futures studies), which began in the 1960s, will dissipate as a movement as it is assimilated into the public consciousness, and as a particular public vision of the future emerges from those alternative visions currently projected.
• A new social paradigm struggles to emerge in North America through the 1980s, characterized as being cooperative, heterogeneous (involving women and third-world people), participatory (involving larger numbers of people in decision-making), culture-sensitive (racism is reduced), value-sensitive (the aspirations of individuals and value orientation of non-Western cultures are recognized), flexible (open to change), decentralized (economic production is smaller in scale, labor-intensive, and democratically managed), and ecologically balanced.

2000

• The majority of predictions and forecasts projected beyond the year 2000 will appear to be ridiculously shortsighted before the year 2000.

FROM CHAOS TO CLARITY

Predictor DR. ROBERT F. BUNDY is a long-range planning consultant working primarily with educational groups. His principal interests lie in helping people think imaginatively about how our world is changing and the kinds of human skills needed now to cope with the future. His clients include students, parents, teachers, school and college administrators, and professional associations. Dr. Bundy is the editor of *Images of the Future: The Twenty-first Century and Beyond*.

· PREDICTIONS ·

For most of us, the future is not an object of knowledge and therefore cannot be known in advance. To try and predict the future, then, is not even very interesting unless one is a fiction writer seeking to entertain. Thus, it is less important to ask what the future *will be* than to ask what it is we can reasonably make the future *become*.

In the process of invention, one can write many different scenarios describing both good and bad outcomes and how they might arise from the present. From the bad we learn what to avoid if we can. And from the good we explore goals and purposes—what might reasonably be accomplished with the power we have to act individually and collectively in the present.

In the following I present a scenario which, of all I have considered, seems the most likely to me at this moment in time. I present its negative aspects in the immediate years ahead, not as a prediction, but as a challenge; not as a *fait accompli*, but as a very real possibility if current values do not shift rapidly. Basic to the scenario, however, is a message of hope; a call to become attuned to the powerful energies already at work healing the excesses, ignorance, and greed that have given rise to our current condition. With all this in mind then, and if current trends continue, a likely scenario for the 1980s will be:

> A time of great unrest, uncertainty, and confusion. The continuing high cost of conventional energy and the unwillingness of energy producers to move to renewable resources; escalating inflation; rising unemployment; declining institutional services and amenities; intensified international scandal; conflict and competition; unusual weather patterns and biospheric disturbances; limited wars and frequent acts of terrorism, as well as assassination of prominent leaders; the emergence of self-appointed saviors; and a strongly eroded faith in established governments and religions in many parts of the world—all of these will cause great havoc in every nation. Many major cities and countries will come under extensive military rule. Maintaining a semblance of international commerce and governance will be a formidable challenge as totalitarian forces severely test the powers of democratic institutions.

These changes will impact formal education at every level, but the changes will be most pronounced in the industrialized nations because of the elaborate arrangements and cost of schooling. In the U.S., a large number of elementary and secondary schools will close, as well as many colleges and universities, or they will be taken over for various community projects. Strikes, layoffs, reduced working hours, and violence and vandalism in the schools that remain open will be commonplace. Expenditures for education will drop sharply, and a large percentage of young people will be pressed into service for important tasks within the community. The value of a degree will decline, and the capacity to demonstrate competence in a given area of knowledge will be essential. New types of schools, however, will emerge—schools designed to teach basic survival skills for an age of scarcity. People of all ages will attend these schools for varying lengths of time and share their knowledge. Some of these schools will also begin to teach a different literacy based on sharing, cooperation, and ecologically sound living. By the end of the 1980s, then, our current system of schooling (that largely served a superindustrial, expansionist economy, out of tune with our natural environment) may largely have been dissolved. But the foundations for a new system will already be discernible.

The 1990s through the first several decades of the 21st century will be a time of rebuilding and reorganization, and we will see the emergence of a new world order and social ethic. Certain very clear shifts on the planet will be well in progress. Holdouts for the old order will still be present but much in the minority. The basic shifts will include:

• A replacement of excessive competition—and the paranoid desire to exert selfish control over nature and other people—by one of cooperation and working together. Initially, the motivations will not be highly altruistic for most people, but will come from an awareness that even enemies have no choice but to work with each other on common concerns given our ever tightening social, economic, and psychic webs.

• A movement away from nationalism to a one-world understanding. This does not necessarily mean a one-world government within this time frame (although it does mean international nonprofit structures for arbitrating conflict and promoting social justice) but an awareness of (1) our interdependencies at every level of existence and (2) how the welfare of every part of the human family depends on the welfare of every other part.

• A change from the kind of decision-making whose outcome is short-run profits to satisfy immediate greed or need to an awareness of responsibilities for yet unborn generations.

• A transformation of our concern for bigness in our factories, institutions, and way of life to an appreciation for smallness; the appropriate use of technologies to stay ecologically in balance and prevent people from being swallowed up by huge impersonal institutions.

• An evolvement away from fragmentation in our life and thinking to a sense of wholeness and systems awareness; an understanding of how everything touches and involves everything else; an integration of rational and intuitive capacities.

• A reduction in excessive materialism in which we identify our value and our worth by the number of possessions owned to an acceptance that we have powerful inner resources for growing and actualizing ourselves.

The new world views to support these shifts will flow out of the pioneering work that has been done in plant and animal communications, demonstrating the convergencies between mysticism and modern physics, the laws of consciousness, holistic healing, life after life studies, etc. Educators will be talking about new notions of literacy that extend across a spectrum from the psycho-motor, the cognitive and affective, to the psychic and mystical. Many experimental schools will be in existence, but they will be more integrated into community life so that students will have a responsible part to play in the real joys and problems of everyday living. There will be much coming and going, exit and reentry, in formal schools. Some unusual psychic talents will be manifested, particularly in younger children. Whole new theories about human capabilities and the powers of consciousness will be evolving. Regional and cultural differences around the earth will remain, but the new literacy will have a global character to it, reflecting our changed understanding of our interdependencies and human capacities. This period will be looked back on as one of the most phenomenal shifts that has ever occurred in history. A major step forward in the evolution of human consciousness.

5

PREDICTIONS ON YOUR HEALTH

1988

Through use of nuclear transplantation, "fertilization" outside the uterus, surrogate motherhood, the first human being will be successfully cloned.

1992

The first human will be successfully resuscitated after being frozen and thawed.

2002

Every kind of cancer will be totally curable, if caught in its early stages.

2030

The average consumer will be able to trade in his or her original body or body parts for new, custom-built, improved models.

2030

The average human being will live to the age of 120 years or more.

HOW LONG CAN WE LIVE?

Life Expectancy in the Western World

Year of Birth	Years of Life
B.C.	18
A.D. 1	22
1200	33
1600	33.5
1800	35
1850	40.9
1900	49.2
1946	66.7
1960	70
1975	72.6
1980	74
2000	85
2030	120
2060	IMMORTALITY?

THE COMING DIETARY REVOLUTION

Predictor NATHAN PRITIKIN is the founder and director of the Longevity Center and the Longevity Research Institute in Santa Monica, Calif. His popular ideas on diet and exercise are found in his two bestselling books, *Live Longer Now* and *The Pritikin Program for Diet and Exercise* (with Patrick M. McGrady, Jr.).

• PREDICTIONS •

1982–1992

• This decade will witness a revolution in dietary customs in the U.S. which will infiltrate to other developed nations of the world. The changes will be toward a dietary intake limiting animal protein to a maximum of 1½ pounds with no more than 700 milligrams of cholesterol per week; fat to under 10% of total calories; and protein of any kind to less than 15% of total calories. Almost all foods will be unrefined. As people observe the dramatic effects of this kind of diet on others who previously had degenerative disease symptoms and then returned to normal functions, more and more will adopt this dietary life-style. By 1985, 50% of the country will have made at least a partial commitment to this kind of diet. By 1992 the diet program will have swept the country, and food producers and restaurants will be catering to this population as a primary market.

• As the popularity of this dietary life-style increases, there will be a simultaneous and proportional reduction in health-care costs in terms of hospital use, doctor care, and medication. Physicians will become experts in the prevention rather than in the treatment of degenerative diseases.

• There will be important economic ramifications from the change in dietary life-style as a result of the savings in food costs for individuals and families of up to 50%; the decrease in health-care costs; and the reduction in energy requirements for the nation stemming from the shift from energy-squandering animal food production to energy-thrifty plant food production needed to meet the new dietary life-style demands. Savings in energy up to 50% will decrease the national need for foreign oil and other energy sources and will resolve the energy crisis. The federal government will begin to take a role in helping food producers make the adjustments resulting from lessened need for industrial plants to refine and process foods and the drop in demand for animal food products.

1993–2030

• Longevity in our country and other Western countries will have begun to extend beyond the present average seven decades and less to well over a hundred years (centenarians will be numerous by 2030) as people start to lead healthful life-styles by means of good diet, regular exercise, and abstinence from smoking and drinking. The unhealthful diet of earlier decades with its high intake of cholesterol and fat will have long given way by the year 2000 for most people to a diet in which 80% of calories will come from complex carbohydrate foods—plant foods as grown or minimally processed—with fat comprising under 10% and protein under 15% of total calories. Concomitant with the increase in numbers of elderly people in the population as a result of these beneficial life-style changes, there will be a growing tendency on the part of young people to conceive fewer babies so as to improve the quality of life for themselves and their offspring. By 2030 these population pressures will be reflected in marked changes in the age distribution in Western countries.

• The demand for healthier food supplies will, by the year 2030, have completely transformed our food-production system. In addition to fewer growers of animal food, in the field of plant crops, many small growers will begin to supply the market demand for locally grown, field-ripened, chemical pesticide–free crops. Where climate or geography interferes, new forms of plant culture will have evolved to make possible local production of crops for local consumption by artificially extending the growing season or by growing crops under shelter in artificial substrates.

• Medical care and medical technology will by the year 2030 have an entirely different character. Physicians will conduct schools for health in which the principles of good living will be inculcated. Medical technology will be oriented toward correcting genetic or congenital failings rather than toward crisis intervention necessitated by degenerative diseases.

CLONING, CRYONICS, AND ANTI-AGING DRUGS

Predictor DR. PAUL SEGALL is the director of biological research for Trans Time, Inc., in Berkeley, Calif., and a postgraduate research physiologist at the University of California. His research speciality is the physiology of aging, and he is studying approaches to modifying the aging processes in mammals. Dr. Segall is the vice-president of the Bay Area Cryonics Society.

• PREDICTIONS •

1988

• Cloning of the first human being will occur by means of nuclear transplantation, "fertilization" outside the uterus, and surrogate motherhood (substituting either a human volunteer, an artificial uterus, a subhuman primate, or a human uterus existing in laboratory conditions).

1989

• The combination of diet and drug therapy, potent and antiviral agents, low-toxicity and anticancer drugs, and synthetic organs (such as artificial hearts) will allow many people in advanced nations to live to be 90 and 100 years old.

1990

• Research will produce pharmacological techniques which will allow for the arrest and, to some degree, the reversal of aging in laboratory animals.

1991

• An understanding of the process of dying together with advanced medical techniques (computerized scanning of internal organs, drastic lowering of the body temperature, progress in brain surgery, etc.) will extend the period of reversible death from 5 to 10 minutes. More people will recover from surgery, and the number of deaths from accidents and heart failure will diminish.

1992

• The first human will be successfully resuscitated after being frozen and thawed. Within a few more years, large numbers of terminally ill or hopelessly aged patients will be frozen prior to death and stored

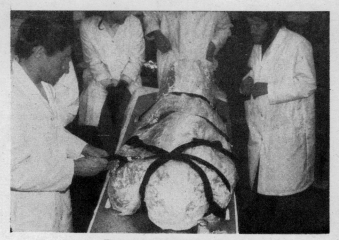
This cryonic patient, having been
encased in plastic, is about to be placed
in a cryogenic storage capsule.

for reanimation in the future, when cures are developed for their
illnesses or techniques of age reversal become available.

2002

• Human cloning will provide genetically identical organs, tissues,
and cells for aged persons or persons who have suffered serious in-
juries. Even large-scale loss of brain tissues will be repaired by the
introduction of nerve cells taken from fetuses cloned from the patients' own bodies.

2010

• Anti-aging drugs will be available on prescription to arrest and
reverse aging in humans.

2020

• The combination of cloned organs and tissues, anti-aging drugs,
artificial life-support systems, advanced techniques of resuscitation,
anticancer and antiviral agents, and highly evolved surgical technology will soon banish aging and death from modern society.

2030

• Computerized analysis of human chromosomes, followed by their
artificial construction and their subsequent introduction into human
egg cells that have been removed from the body, will allow for the

creation of human bodies according to any desired genetic program. Advanced techniques of neurosurgery will then allow the consumer to trade in his or her original body or body parts for new, custom-built, improved models.

2034

• A greater understanding of the physical workings of the brain and memory will mean many advances over the next century. This understanding together with advanced techniques in resuscitation and the use of clones will make it possible to completely reconstruct an individual (with the memory and personality intact) who has been dead for several hours or more. Refinements of these techniques will allow for the eventual reconstruction of individuals who were frozen to death with imperfect techniques in the 1970s and 1980s.

THE TRANSITION TO
A SOCIETY OF IMMORTALS

The forecasts presented here are a composite of those made by 31 graduate students enrolled in future studies at the University of Houston at Clear Lake City, Tex. These students first read and discussed reports dealing with current scientific research on immortality and then constructed scenarios depicting the effects that the discovery of an anti-aging pill might have on society.

• 1 YEAR AFTER THE INTRODUCTION OF THE ANTI-AGING PILL •

Personality. There is an extremely wide range of reactions to the anti-aging pill. Most people are happy and some are euphoric, but a sizable minority are confused and disoriented, especially those with strongly held religious beliefs.

Family Life. Divorce rates rise as couples shun spending eternity together, but so do birthrates as parents who anticipate limits on new births decide to have children now.

Education. Educators are demoralized as they recognize that their traditional clientele of children and adolescents cannot continue.

Leisure. Dangerous sports such as auto racing and boxing begin to lose participants.

Employment and the Economy. The economy threatens to destabilize. Some employees desert their positions and others hold tenaciously on to their jobs. There is little hiring going on, and unemployment rises to 8%.

National Government. The government has been quick to take over the distribution of the anti-aging pill (but not the production). Major problems have been identified, and the debates have begun already: whether or not people such as habitual criminals or the insane, or even house pets, should be given the pill; how birth limitations are to be imposed; how employment and retirement questions are to be determined.

International Affairs. There is a rapid worldwide diffusion of the pill, except in some Communist countries, where it is initially resisted.

Spiritual Matters. Traditional religions mount a campaign against the pill. After a short-lived increase in church attendance, a steady decline ensues.

• 10 YEARS AFTER THE INTRODUCTION OF THE ANTI-AGING PILL •

Personality. With virtually everyone taking the anti-aging pill by now, adults in this society resemble adolescents in the pre-pill days in that they are mercurial, introverted, uneasy, and casting about for purposes and alliances. Suicide becomes more common than ever, reaching a peak that it will never again attain.

Family Life. The divorce rate ascends, marriage becomes uncommon, and much more amorphous groupings appear. Since the number of children per family is prescribed by policy (but still not by law), the dipping number of children results in great attention and goodwill for each youngster.

Education. The educational system finds renewed purpose. Emphasis is shifting from children to adults and from degree-granting programs to courses relating to careers and leisure experiences.

Leisure. Contact sports die out, to be replaced by thrilling but not dangerous activities. Travel greatly increases.

Employment and the Economy. The economy is slowing down. Production is increasingly automated as labor becomes difficult to handle.

National Government. Public confidence in the government remains high. The major dilemma occurs in enforcing the hard decisions about who will *not* get the pill. The government has legislated away all retirement plans and in some respects is beginning to take responsibility for the job market.

International Affairs. Belligerency between nations steadily decreases. Not only does no one wish to die for his country, but the realization grows that the people here now will be together for eternity.

Spiritual Matters. Organized religions are largely disgraced and disbanded. Cults devoted to the self or the environment gain members.

• 20 YEARS AFTER THE INTRODUCTION OF THE ANTI-AGING PILL •

Personality. Low levels of discontent and distress remain, but for the most part tensions have eased. There is little competition or risk taking.

Family Life. The end of the family is in sight, since less than 25% of the population is married. Increasing in popularity are fluid groups of 12 to 30 adults. The very few children around are indulged and treasured.

Education. Continuing education is by far the commonest mode,

with courses open to all. New information and knowledge are being generated at a faster pace than ever before, since the life of a scholar is attractive to many.

Leisure. As thrill seeking becomes less common, the use of recreational drugs reaches new heights. Taboos against any form of physical intimacy have disappeared. Having an abundance of free time, people turn to travel, games, the arts, and so on, in even greater numbers.

Employment and the Economy. Gross national product is now rising at less than 1% annually. Production has become so automated that individuals spend only 10 hours a week for 8 months at a job, then have 4 months off.

National Government. The paternalistic government still enjoys wide popular support. The decision that anti-aging pills would contain birth-control medication is being successfully enforced. The administration of employment is now the government's major obligation, following the dismemberment of the Department of Defense.

International Affairs. Increased cooperation, increased travel, and greater sharing of wealth all lead toward a lessening of distinctions between nations. New supranational governmental entities are beginning to form.

Spiritual Matters. Devotion to the environment assumes near-religious proportions.

• 50 YEARS AFTER THE INTRODUCTION OF THE ANTI-AGING PILL •

Personality. While people remain safety-conscious and cautious, they are less introspective than before. They are generally acquiescent, content, and somewhat curious.

Family Life. The family has officially disappeared. Condominium life is the most common living arrangement, where relations are intense but short-lived and nonintrusive.

Education. Education is not only funded but also directly administered by the federal government. Standards of teaching and scholarship reach new heights.

Leisure. The distinctions between leisure and education, and between leisure and work, are rapidly disappearing. Most people consider all these activities to be pleasurable and instructive.

Employment and the Economy. Automation has become so sophisticated that it extends beyond production and into management. The economy is largely operated by computers. The labor force does no rote work, but generates new knowledge leading to improved performance.

National Government. With the development of computer systems that can administer government agencies, most of the government's responsibilities have become routine. Its presence is perceived to be fading.

International Affairs. A well-managed global community is now in existence.

Spiritual Matters. The environment continues to be revered, but attention is turning again to the entire universe, whose origins and evolution are finally comprehended.

SOURCE: By Jib Fowles in *The Futurist,* June 1978. Reprinted by permission of the World Future Society, 4916 St. Elmo Avenue, Washington, D.C. 20014.

PROLONGING HUMAN LIFE

Predictor DR. ALBERT ROSENFELD is the former science editor of *Life* magazine and *Saturday Review.* He has received numerous awards, including an Albert Lasker Award with a special citation for "leadership in medical journalism." A contributing editor of *Geo* and *Prime Time,* Mr. Rosenfeld is the author of *The Second Genesis: The Coming Control of Life* and *Prolongevity.*

• PREDICTIONS •

1982–1992

• The interaction of genetics and environment will be increasingly understood. We will have a better knowledge of which substances are likely to be dangerous and be able to ban them without the necessity of expensive and extensive testing.

1990s

• We will have a greater understanding of genetic susceptibilities. Many forms of cancer, heart disease, and other major ailments not formerly thought of as "genetic" will be seen to have genetic components. More and more genetic and biochemical "markers" will turn up for conditions as diverse as alcoholism and mental illness.

1992

• Prolongevity. The human life span will be extended and many of the ravages of what we now call aging will be eliminated through discovery and control of the basic mechanisms of biological aging. There will be individual drugs, remedies, and antidotes for specific kinds of aging wear and tear.
• The body's own pharmacy. Recent research has turned up many druglike substances produced by the body itself, e.g., the endorphins

[morphinelike proteins found in the brain and other tissues]; the interferons [proteins which cells produce when invaded by viruses]; and the prostaglandins [fatty acids which act like hormones]. These substances, and others, will prove clinically useful.

• The common cold will be essentially curable as soon as sufficient supplies of interferon become available. Other remedies are also likely to be available. [Interferon has received special attention recently because of its success in combating a number of viruses, including strains which produce colds and certain forms of cancer. Because it is almost prohibitively expensive to obtain interferon from human body cells, a major breakthrough was made in 1980 when the substance was produced in the laboratory.]

2000

• Good headway will be made on a new vaccinology. Instead of using live viruses, or even dead ones, to immunize the body, only the viral protein (the part of the virus which induces immunity) will be necessary. Perhaps we will need only that part of the protein molecule which contains the active "antigen"—the substance which causes antibodies to be produced. This method may result in an entirely safe multiple vaccine which will give an individual lifelong immunity against many viral diseases.

2030

• The importance of computers in medicine and pharmacology will probably be fairly well realized by this date, though their promise should have been recognized by 1992. Apart from already understood possibilities for diagnosis and therapy, it will be possible to construct new drugs in theory and simulate them on computers to see if they will work. Because drugs won't have to be routinely synthesized and tested on living creatures (though this would always have to be done at the final stages), years of work and expense in drug development will be saved.

• There will be a whole armamentarium of the body's own drugs, either synthesized or induced, so that the body can produce as much of any given drug as it requires.

• The basic aging process will be discovered and the human life span will be extended to 120 and beyond, accompanied by a large diminution in all degenerative diseases.

INTEGRAL MEDICINE— A NEW APPROACH TO HEALTH

Few would argue the unprecedented advances made by modern technological medicine. We have witnessed dramatic decreases in infant mortality, life-saving innovations in emergency medical care, and the virtual elimination of most infectious diseases that once decimated entire civilizations. Yet most Americans are not really healthier. Heart disease, cancer, stroke, arthritis, and a host of other stress-related diseases of civilization often remain unresponsive to the best therapies Western medicine can provide.

Medical specialization and a dependence on technological innovations have also led to widespread depersonalization within our health-care delivery system. As a result, the mutual trust and confidence which once characterized the doctor-patient relationship have been progressively eroded. Many consumers believe that modern medicine is designed more for the convenience of physicians than to meet the unique needs of the patient. They also resent the paternalistic manner in which doctors assume primary responsibility for diagnosis and treatment, forcing their patients to passively assume the role of "sick role."

Within the health-care community, however, a new focus has begun to emerge, characterized by a whole-person, or "holistic," approach. Holistic medicine stresses the psychosocial aspects of the healing process and focuses on the maintenance of health rather than the treatment of disease. Since the patient is given primary responsibility for his or her health, a variety of nonsomatic factors in illness are emphasized, including the inability to deal with stress, loss or change, problems in family or work environments, beliefs and expectations, self-destructive compulsive habits, and other life-style issues. Major emphasis is placed upon the prevention of illness and upon the development of educational self-care programs for health consumers. From the holistic perspective, disease is a consequence of mental, emotional, and social, as opposed to primarily physical, factors, and treatment emphasizes alternative approaches such as acupuncture, biofeedback, hypnosis, nutritional therapy, and other unconventional techniques.

Unfortunately, holistic medicine has become somewhat of a fad, and the term loses its meaning when one speaks of "holistic electroconvulsive shock therapy." Although its premise implies treating the whole person, holistic medicine is often administered in much the same way as is Western medicine—that is, the emphasis becomes technique-oriented. Instead of prescribing two pills to suppress symptoms, the holistic practitioner might recommend two biofeedback sessions. Or four acupuncture treatments. Or three massage sessions. Or 10 vitamins. What is missed is a thorough understanding of the message that symptoms convey and the needed changes in beliefs and habits that the patient will have to make. Finally, some holistic practitioners are ignorant of the significant contributions that conventional medicine has to offer, and minor problems that could easily be diagnosed and treated early in the game by standard medical approaches soon become major ones.

In the future, optimal health care will be provided when therapists are able to utilize the best of both the traditional and holistic approaches. This point of view is shared by practitioners of what is being called "integral medicine." While it emphasizes the importance of patient education, health maintenance, and disease prevention, integral medicine takes a multifaceted perspective of illness, recognizing the complex contributions of physical, mental, emotional, social, spiritual, and environmental influences. Therapies utilized may include drugs, surgery, and/or a variety of alternative techniques according to the unique needs of an individual patient/client. Exclusive responsibility for health rests with neither the doctor nor the patient, but with the health-care team, in which doctors, patients, and family members serve equally important roles. The doctor's primary role is to explore the meaning of symptoms, to establish an accurate diagnosis, to discuss the variety of treatments available, and to thoroughly explain the rationale for recommending any particular approach. In addition, the physician must be available to provide information, advice, and support during the course of treatment.

The patient's responsibility is to provide the doctor with honest information so as to make an accurate diagnosis possible. When a specific treatment is prescribed, the patient should discuss it thoroughly with his doctor to ensure that he completely understands and agrees to it. He should then follow the treatment program diligently, providing his doctor with feedback about his progress. Whenever possible, the patient should utilize available educational resources and learn self-management techniques in order to maximize his own self-healing potential.

Fred Stewart represents a typical case in point, for he has suffered for more than 10 years from excruciating facial pain. After countless visits to his internist, neurologist, orthopedist, otolaryngologist, dentist, and gnathologist, he has received drugs, shots, ointments, braces, and splints, yet no enduring relief. A few years ago, his doctors might have said, "Nothing more can be done. You'll just have to learn to live with it." But in the future he will be referred to an integral-medicine center, staffed by a multidisciplinary team of health professionals.

This team views Fred's situation, not as a problem, but as a challenge. After carefully reviewing his medical history and conducting a thorough physical examination, the team determines that Fred's problem is not primarily a medical one. In a caring and supportive way, it helps Fred to discover for himself that much of his discomfort is related to job dissatisfaction and family stress. Fred begins a course of biofeedback therapy to help him learn to relax the muscles in his face. With a vocational counselor he begins to reevaluate his work situation, and with members of his family he enrolls in a stress-management class. Several acupuncture treatments are recommended for symptomatic relief, and nutritional supplements are provided which will help him get a better night's sleep. Through guided imagery, Fred begins to appreciate the enormous power of his mind and the ways in which feelings of helplessness and hopelessness have contributed to his facial pain. Fred's prognosis is good, for in the long run, he is learning how to help himself.

John and Barbara Roth and their three children will also spend a day at an integral-medicine center in the future. Though the Roths have no medical complaints, they will be given a comprehensive series of evaluations and tests by a health team that specializes, not in treating illness, but in helping clients to maintain and improve their overall health.

The Roths are greeted by their personal health counselor, who, with the aid of a computer-based data-acquisition system, reviews the family's current health status. Each member of the family is then examined by a physician with appropriate medical skills, and, if indicated, specialized diagnostic tests (e.g., X rays, ultrasound, treadmill, etc.) are conducted.

The Roths are also seen by a nutritionist who analyzes their dietary needs and a kinesiologist who discusses their daily exercise programs. Finally, a team of mental-health specialists reviews such psychosocial issues as job/school satisfaction, stress at home, lifestyle habits, recreational drug use, and the impact of situational changes. At the end of the day, the Roths meet again with their health counselor, who summarizes their current health status, identifies any significant health risks, and recommends specific resources available to the family for improving their overall well-being.

The Roths' health-insurance carrier reimburses them for the entire cost of their evaluation, for it recognizes that catastrophic illness is easier (and less expensive) to prevent than to treat. In addition, insurance pays tuition costs for educational programs that encourage early treatment, prevention, and health maintenance.

Although the integral-medicine center of the future sounds like an idealized situation, it is not far beyond reach. At this very moment, a model program is being tested at the Center for Integral Medicine in Pacific Palisades, Calif. In the future, similar programs will undoubtedly be widespread.

—D.E.B.

PREVENTIVE MEDICINE: EXERCISE AND DIET REFORM

Predictor JIM FIXX is the award-winning author of the bestselling *Complete Book of Running*, which has sold over 1,000,000 copies in hardcover and has been translated into 12 languages. A former magazine editor, Mr. Fixx has served as articles editor of *Saturday Review*, senior editor of *Life*, and editor in chief of *McCall's*. His other books include *Games for the Superintelligent*, *Solve It!*, and *Jim Fixx's Second Book of Running*.

• PREDICTIONS •

1984

• An effort to permit women to run a full 26.2-mile marathon in the Olympic Games will be narrowly defeated.

1985–2000

• The U.S. diet will change radically, producing major economic dislocations. Use of meats will decline sharply as the correlation between meat eating and heart attacks and strokes is more convincingly documented. Use of fruits and vegetables will increase despite tastelessness induced by modern agricultural methods. Growers will experiment, unsuccessfully, with introducing artificial flavors.

1988

• Women will finally run in the Olympic marathon. The winning time will be 2:21, only 30 seconds per mile slower than the winning time for men.

1990

• Due to changes in diet and exercise, heart disease will be 37% below 1980 figures.

1995

• Preventive medicine will be a major specialty. Reliance on current ex post facto medicine will decline correspondingly. Automatic, remote diagnosis by computer, including a home computer for minor diseases, will be common.
• Physicians, acknowledging the close link between body and mind, will treat an increasing range of diseases with meditative techniques, hypnosis, and autosuggestion.

1997

• One third of American workers will bicycle, run, or roller-skate to and from work. Major American companies will install showers and locker rooms and give time off for exercise.

2000

• Exercise will routinely be used to treat drug and alcohol addiction and many psychological problems, including depression and phobias.

2005

• A woman will run a marathon in 2:17.

2010

• Cigarette smoking will be uncommon. Consumption of marijuana and alcohol will be down sharply, but use of other psychogenic chemicals, including artificial endorphins for mood enhancement, will have increased.

2030

• Jim Fixx, age 98, will compete in his 58th Boston Marathon.

EXERCISE:
SALVATION OF CIVILIZATION

Predictor JACK LALANNE is America's best-known exercise teacher. Through his numerous books, television shows, and health spas, he has spread his message of proper diet and regular exercise. Using such phrases as "ten seconds on the lips and a lifetime on the hips," Mr. LaLanne estimates that he has helped take a ton of fat off American women every day for the past 25 years.

• PREDICTIONS •

1982–1992

• I predict that for the next 10 years preventive medicine will be the thing; that 99% of the medical profession will be into proper, corrective nutrition. I also predict that there will be a tremendous decrease in the incidence of heart attacks, strokes, and cancer—about 50% in my opinion. I predict also that exercise, instead of being passive, will be vigorous and violent; you will work your muscles to the point of muscle failure during short periods of exercise. It will be a status thing that all men, women, and children will exercise vigorously three or four times a week, like training for the Olympics. I think that this will be the salvation of our civilization, ensuring that we will survive as a first-class nation. I also predict that if we get into this physical-fitness movement—nutritionwise, supplementationwise, exercisewise, and mentalfitnesswise—the country is going to be more buckled together than it has ever been in our history. We will have something in common, transcending people's color, education, and race. We'll have this common bond of being physically fit both for personal reasons and for reasons of national pride—for our own survival and for our country's.

1993–2030

• Legislation will be passed forbidding indiscriminate use of sugar, white flour, salt, artificial colorings, flavorings, and all food additives. I also think that new legislation will prevent farmers from using artificial fertilizers so widely. I predict that the life span of man will be increased by at least 10–15 years, because in the last 8 years there has been a 400% increase in the number of people who have lived to 100 years and over. It will be a progression of what is going to happen in the next 10 years and happen even more so 10 years after that—just like a snowball, it is going to gain momentum . . . gain . . . gain . . . gain. Man is going to be better than he ever has been in history—mentally, morally, spiritually, and in every way.

FIGHTING FOOD SHORTAGES

Predictor ROBERT RODALE, senior spokesman for the back-to-health movement in medicine and agriculture, has been the president of Rodale Press, Inc., since 1954. His company publishes books and magazines which focus on health, farming, food, energy, and appropriate technology. Mr. Rodale often writes articles and editorials for the various company magazines and is also the author of several books, including *The Best Health Ideas I Know* and *Sane Living in a Mad World*.

• PREDICTIONS •

1982

• Amaranth grain will be used for the first time in commercial breads, cereals, snacks, and other foods. Amaranth is a vigorous plant which yields tasty seeds with more nutritional value than other grain. Health foods will be the first to use amaranth.

1983

• Trend toward nutrition as a major force for prevention and treatment of disease will continue. High cost of regular medicine will accelerate trend, but main factor will be growing body of evidence that foods, vitamins, trace elements, and other nutritional factors have more influence on health than drugs. Foods grown organically will become the most popular for health promotion. Use of better diet plans to prevent chronic, degenerative disease will become widespread.

1984

• Rising cost of energy and other resources will limit shipment of food over long distances. Trend will be toward local and regional food production. Processing will be limited too, because of cost. Home will become a major center of food production, through gardening and other means, such as seed sprouting and even small-scale fish production. Food will be stockpiled in homes as insurance against inflation and food shortages.

1985

• Shortages and high prices of dairy products will lead to intense new interest in soybeans, which are a cheaper source of protein and have important health-promoting values. Simple processing of soybeans into milk and meatlike products—tofu and tempeh—will become very popular.

1990

• Vegetarianism will replace a meat-centered diet as the major factor in American food consciousness.

1993 and beyond

• Trying to look more than 10 years into the future is extremely risky, but it's hard to avoid making the prediction that major food shortages will be a problem as this century nears its end—if not sooner. Here are the reasons:

1. Erosion of topsoil continues at a heavy rate. In prime corn-belt areas, five to six bushels of topsoil are eroded away for every bushel of corn, beans, or grain produced. Vital topsoil reserves won't last much longer.
2. Much farmland is being lost to building, highways, and other uses.
3. Extensive irrigation is using up fossil water deposited aeons ago that is not being replaced by current rainfall. Large areas of the arid West will not have water for irrigation use much longer.
4. The energy shortage, especially the lack of oil, could put a serious crimp in farm operations.
5. Shortages of vital fertilizer nutrients, particularly phosphorus and potash, are likely to occur in a few decades. At current rates of use, concentrated stores of those nutrients will be depleted before oil supplies are exhausted.
6. Food processing and distribution is very energy intensive. Transport of food over long distances is commonplace. Unpredictable events, ranging from strikes to weather catastrophes, could cause serious strain on the system.
7. Growing world population is going to put enormous strains on food supplies. Yield of grain per acre no longer increases at rapid rates, and the outlook for great increases in the future is dim. Currently, the U.S. has to export food to get needed foreign exchange. That condition is likely to continue.
8. Continued burning of large amounts of fossil fuels could change world climate, raising the levels of the oceans and shifting prime growing areas northward, where soils are not as fertile. Buildup of carbon dioxide in the atmosphere would be the cause of that climatic change.

ALL THE FOOD NEEDED TO FEED THE WORLD (4½ BILLION PEOPLE) COULD BE PRODUCED FROM:

1. Exactly 3,767.5 million acres, using the same production techniques that are currently in use throughout the world (this is the amount of land now in use).

   or

2. About 3,000–3,250 million acres (10%–20% less than present) with the same production techniques currently in use by eliminating 70%–90% of postharvest loss.

   or

3. About 1,850 million acres by feeding all the world's cereal crops to people instead of animals and distributing these cereals efficiently (49% of present land).

   or

4. About 1,625 million acres using Chinese production techniques (43% of present land).

   or

5. About 425 million acres using North American production techniques and a vegetarian diet (11% of present land).

   or

6. The southern half of Sudan, if it were drained, the proper infrastructure developed, and the nomadic cattle raisers of the region changed to sedentary farmers (or farmers brought in from other regions).

   or

7. About 150 million acres of greenhouses using North American production techniques with three crops a year (3.9% of present land).

   or

8. About 125–250 million acres using the "bio-dynamic intensive" method of food production (3.3%–6% of present land).

   or

9. About 15 million acres using hydroponics (.4% of present land).

   or

10. About 13.5 million acres growing algae (.35% of present land).

SOURCE: *Ho Ping: Food for Everyone* by Medard Gabel. Copyright © 1979 by Medard Gabel. Reprinted by permission of Doubleday & Company, Inc.

TOMORROW'S MENUS

As the world's population increases, finding alternative foods becomes imperative. Although there are approximately 80,000 edible plants, only 20 are cultivated extensively. To free ourselves from the specter of famine in the future, we must turn to new food sources, possibly bringing into our diet the host of insect and plant species we have ignored and calling upon technology for the creation of synthetic foods.

MENU I

Slug Soup
Wasp Grubs Fried in the Comb   Termites Bantu
Moths Sautéed in Butter   New Carrots with Wireworm Sauce
Fricassee Chicken with Chrysalids
Cauliflower Garnished with Caterpillars
Slag Beetle Larvae on Toast   Chocolate Chirpies

SOURCE: Ronald L. Taylor, *Butterflies in My Stomach*. Santa Barbara, Calif.: Woodbridge Press, 1975.

RECIPE FOR CHOCOLATE CHIRPIES

2 c. sugar
2/3 c. cream
2 oz. unsweetened chocolate
⅛ tsp. salt

1 tbsp. butter
1 tsp. vanilla
½ c. dry roasted crickets, chopped

In a saucepan, mix sugar, cream, chocolate, and salt. Cook over medium heat, stirring constantly until chocolate is melted and sugar dissolved. Continue cooking, stirring occasionally, until candy thermometer reads 234°F, or until a small amount of mixture forms a ball when dropped into ice water. Remove the mixture from heat and add butter. Cool mixture to 120°F without stirring. Add vanilla and beat vigorously with a wooden spoon until candy is thick and no longer glossy—about 7 to 10 min. Stir in insects. Spread evenly in a buttered loaf pan. Cool until firm. Cut into 2-in. squares.

SOURCE: Ronald L. Taylor and Barbara J. Carter, *Entertaining with Insects*. Copyright © 1976. Used by permission of Woodbridge Press, Santa Barbara, Calif. 93111.

MENU II

Whey Sherry
Wakame (Seaweed) and Chrysanthemum Soup
Pueblo Chenopod Salad
Science Soy Bread   Peanut Flakes
Cottonburger
Lake Chad Algae   Opaque 2 Corn
Amaranth Cakes   Tofu Fruit Whip

SOURCE: Barbara Ford, *Future Food*. New York: William Morrow
and Company, 1978.

RECIPE FOR WAKAME (SEAWEED)
AND CHRYSANTHEMUM SOUP

¼ c. dried chrysanthemum flowers
1 c. water
4 c. vegetable broth flavored with sake and soy sauce
⅓ tbsp. honey
½ c. dried wakame, cut into 1-in. lengths
½ c. chopped spinach
A pinch of grated fresh ginger

Freshen chrysanthemum flowers for 10 to 15 min. until soft. Pull
the petals off the calyxes, discarding the calyxes. In a soup pot, bring
broth almost to a boil and add honey. Now add the flower petals,
soaking water, and wakame. Continue heating (but do not boil) for 2
min., then turn off heat. Add spinach and ginger.

SOURCE: By permission from Sharon Ann Rhoads, *Cooking with Sea
Vegetables*. Copyright © 1978. Autumn Press, Brookline, Mass.

MENU III

Powdered Martini or Soft Drink Gel
Artificial Caviar
Imitation Low Cal Spaghetti and Sauce with Fabricated Meatballs
Fabricated Vegetables   Extruded Onion Rings
Simulated Chocolate Pudding with Imitation Whipped Cream

FABRICATED MEATBALLS

Remove meatballs from package. Brown lightly and add to hot
imitation spaghetti sauce. Cook 1–15 min. and serve. Fabricated
meatballs are made from the following ingredients:

Textured soy protein
Water
Vegetable oils (partially hydrogenated soybean and cottonseed oil,
corn oil)
Natural and imitation flavors and spices
Lactose
Salt

Sodium caseinate
Sugar
Modified tapioca starch
Sodium phosphates
Hydrolyzed vegetable protein
Carrageenan
Niacin
U.S. certified colors
Iron
Thiamine (B$_1$)
Pyridoxine (B$_6$)
Riboflavin (B$_2$)
Cyanocobalamin (B$_{12}$)

—K.H.J.

RUTABAGAS AND PRUNE JUICE TO BECOME EXTINCT

Predictor DR. JUDITH WURTMAN is the author of *Eating Your Way through Life*. A teacher in the department of nutrition at M.I.T., she has also served as a nutrition consultant in the Newton, Mass., public school system. She has written numerous articles and currently coedits the multivolume series *Nutrition and the Brain* with her husband, Dr. Richard Wurtman.

• PREDICTIONS •

1987
• Most homes will have microwave ovens, and the food industry will concentrate on engineering foods designed for this appliance.

1992
• Families will eat together only on special occasions like birthdays and holidays or as part of a weekly ritual.
• Supermarkets will go into the catering business and sell precooked main courses, side dishes, and desserts to take out. (They will do this to survive at a time when most people will refuse to shop frequently or to cook food at home.)
• Vending machines will become ubiquitous: in apartment buildings, laundromats, libraries, shopping malls. Their contents will be expanded to provide complete meals and to represent a larger selection of ethnic, regional, and health-oriented products.

• Certain foods—like hot cereals, liver, lima beans, rutabagas, and prune juice—will become extinct because of disinterest in their consumption.

1997

• Because of continued advances in food fabrication and fortification, it will be possible to obtain a nutritionally complete diet by eating fewer than 10 foods per week. No longer will people have to eat representatives of the "four basic foods" or to take vitamin and mineral supplements to be well nourished.

2002

• Ninety-nine percent of the population will be on a reducing diet; 90% of the population will be overweight.

2023

• Scientists will discover that such food additives as caffeine, red dye #2, sugar, and sodium nitrite actually promote longevity, as does the consumption of "empty calories." There will be an enormous increase in the voluntary consumption of food additives and an aversion to so-called health foods.

CHRONOLOGY OF TOMORROW'S MEDICINE AND MACHINES

Predictor DR. JERROLD S. MAXMEN is an assistant professor of psychiatry at Albert Einstein College of Medicine in New York City. Coauthor of *Rational Hospital Psychiatry: The Reactive Environment*, Dr. Maxmen has also written *The Post-Physician Era: Medicine in the 21st Century*. In this latter book, he discusses medicine's future with special emphasis on the collaboration of medical personnel and computers. Dr. Maxmen suggests that the following predictions have a 50% probability of occurrence.

By 1985

• Wide use of videophones in hospitals.
• Intercity conference videophones for medical use.
• Establishment of national computerized organ bank for transplants.

- Three-dimensional television available for commercial use.
- Artificial heart implantation.
- Development of reliable chemical tests for psychotic disorders.
- Effective anticold vaccine.
- Chemical treatment of gallstones.
- Drugs to raise intelligence quotient (IQ) of borderline retardates by 10 to 20 points.
- Wide application of drugs directly to diseased organs rather than orally.
- Wide use of implanted chemical capsules for contraception.
- Capacity to detect many diseases in embryo.
- Some kind of continuing education for medical doctor (M.D.) re-licensure required by 50% of states.
- The "classical" lecture system ended in 40% of medical schools by teaching machines, closed-circuit television (CCTV), interactive television (IATV), and audiovisual aids.
- Five percent of M.D.'s in solo practice.
- Decriminalization of marijuana.
- 3.6 billion prescriptions filled in the U.S.
- Ninety percent of medical costs covered by national health insurance (NHI).
- Noncarcinogenic cigarette.

By 1990

- Wide use of computers for monitoring devices attached directly to patients in their homes.
- Wide use of computers to prescribe medications.
- Medical records of 80% of U.S. population stored in national medical data bank (NMDB).
- Wide use of general-purpose computers in the home.
- Some people able to have daily checkups of body functions by computer with preliminary analysis and warnings of impending illness.
- All body fluids and functions routinely analyzed and diagnostic reports and summaries prepared by machines.
- Development of artificial colon.
- Development of safe chemical means to reverse effects of arteriosclerosis.
- Chemical cure for schizophrenia.
- Development of anticancer vaccines.
- Failure to consult a computer considered grounds for malpractice suit.
- Pharmaceutical industry nationalized.

By 1995

- Invention of "pharmaceutical automat."
- Cable TV with 80 channels widely available.
- General availability of computers to conduct psychotherapy.
- Three-dimensional TV widely used for home entertainment.
- Frequent use of conference videophones for group psychotherapy.
- First experimental use of computers for all diagnostic and treatment decisions in patient care.

- Development of drugs that alter memory and learning.
- Development of synthetic blood substitute.
- General availability of physical and chemical means to modify some forms of criminal behavior.
- First human clone.
- Application of compulsory birth control in some nations without being effective.
- Virtual elimination of state mental hospitals.
- Eighty-five percent of pharmacists working in hospitals and clinics rather than in drugstores.
- Twenty percent of U.S. M.D.'s in a labor union.
- Techniques that permit useful exploitation of oceans through aquaculture farming, with the effect of producing 20% of the world's caloric intake.

By 2000

- Wristwatch TV commonly available.
- Wide availability of computers that "learn" from experience.
- Full wall-sized color 3-D IATV.
- Moderate chemical control of senility.
- Effective transplantation of all organ systems except for the central nervous system (CNS).
- Development of electronic sensors enabling blind people to "see."
- First clinic or hospital on the moon.
- Periodic polling of public on health-care issues by computer.

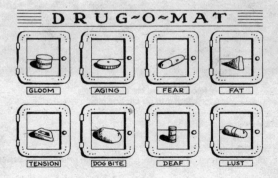

By 2005

- Wide use of "pharmaceutical automats."
- Demonstration of way to decrease time between birth and maturity.
- Development of drugs from substances originating on other planets or the moon.
- Human parthenogenesis.

Robot washing car before being
allowed to go out and play.

By 2010

• Robots with sensory feedback performing routine household chores in hospitals.
• Wide use of artificial insemination to produce genetically superior offspring.
• Use of highly complex chemical simulation models of the human body for use in drug experimentation.
• In vivo renewal of worn-out hearts by stimulating natural growth processes.
• Most forms of mental retardation are cured.

By 2015

• Use of drugs or altered prenatal conditions to raise IQ of normal individuals by 10 to 20 points.

- Laboratory demonstration of biochemical processes that stimulate growth of new organs and limbs.
- Extrauterine development of human fetus.
- Replacement of human organs with those derived from specially bred animals.
- Virtual obsolescence of the pharmacist.
- Virtual cessation of M.D.'s providing clinical services except for surgery.
- American Medical Association (AMA) disbanded.
- Average U.S. life expectancy of 95 years with commensurate prolongation of vigor.
- Effective weather control, thereby enhancing global food production.

By 2020

- Ninety-five percent of population has medical records stored in NMDB.
- Electrical control of mood disorders available.
- Demonstration of long-duration human hibernation; allows for prolonged space travel.
- Moderate use of genetic engineering in humans by chemical substitution of deoxyribonucleic acid (DNA) chains.
- Wide use of self-contained dwellings using life-support systems that recycle water and air to provide independence from external environment.

By 2025

- *In utero* genetic modification.
- First subject using cryogenic preservation "unfrozen" without success.
- Maintenance of human brain extracorporeally for one month.
- Researchers rather than surgeons (M.D.'s) conduct most operations.

SOURCE: Jerrold S. Maxmen, *The Post-Physician Era: Medicine in the 21st Century*. Copyright © 1976. Reprinted by permission of John Wiley & Sons, Inc.

ARTIFICIAL ORGANS AND SPARE PARTS

Predictor DR. PIERRE GALLETTI, professor of biology and medicine at Brown University, is one of the country's leading experts on and a proponent of the development and use of artificial organs. He is working on an artificial liver, lung, and pancreas, as well as looking for new ways to improve artificial blood vessels.

• PREDICTIONS •

1985

• Substitutive medicine, i.e., forms of treatment which rely on the replacement of defective parts of the body by implants or transplants (rather than treatment by drugs), will claim a substantial share of treatment resources and medical-care costs.

1990

• Consumer organizations focused on life-saving spare parts will exert a significant influence on the health-planning process at the local and national level.
• Persons wearing an organ substitute will be fairly common, and the public will accept the concept that patients may require several spare parts to keep their body functioning as close to normal as possible.
• An implanted, programmable pump controlled by telemetry will automatically deliver insulin to diabetics in accordance with their needs, as modulated by meals, exercise, and other life activities.
• People requiring mechanical support of the heart to pump the blood around will wear the device inside their body and carry the battery power pack on their belt.

1995

• An artificial booster lung implanted in the chest or in the abdomen will help to oxygenate the blood of patients in terminal chronic respiratory failure.
• Patients requiring kidney dialysis treatment will wear the device internally and evacuate excess water and waste products through normal channels (e.g., the urinary bladder).

2000

• People kept alive by spare parts may constitute almost 1% of the U.S. population.

2010

• There will be an open market for used and reconditioned body spare parts.

THOUGHT-ACTIVATED
ARTIFICIAL LIMBS

Predictor DR. W. ROSS ADEY is associate chief of staff for research and development at the Jerry L. Pettis Memorial Veterans' Hospital in Loma Linda, Calif. A former professor of anatomy and physiology at the University of California at Los Angeles, Dr. Adey is the author of over 370 publications on anatomical, physiological, and bioengineering research.

· PREDICTIONS ·

1990

· Personal medical-monitoring systems with radiotelemetry for those in hazardous occupations or entrusted with the lives of others (airline pilots, truck drivers, etc.) and for certain patients chronically ill at home.
· Optimization of action of therapeutic substances, including drugs, hormones, and immune substances, by combination with microwave fields pulsed at low frequencies.
· Worldwide medical consultation networks; worldwide medical data banks, including location and availability of rare therapeutic substances; and tissue- and organ-transplant banks.

1995

· Thought-controlled prostheses for limb amputees and thought-controlled personal locomotion systems for quadriplegics.
· Fully automated (pilotless) passenger aircraft, using electronic guidance systems controlled either within the aircraft or from a ground station.
· Ionospheric modification for long-range, zonal, and seasonal weather control, and local weather control by tropospheric, stratospheric, and other low-level manipulations.

2000

· Development of techniques for spinal-cord regeneration by combining hormonal growth factors with microwave fields pulsed at low frequencies.

2005

· Development of direct brain-computer interfaces as a means of extending human mental capacity. These interfaces will be based on patterns in brain waves (EEG) and other brain signals.

• Power transmission on national and international networks by microwave and laser systems from terrestrial solar generating plants.

2010

• Behavioral control through imposition of modulated microwaves and other electromagnetic fields, as in classroom environments to enhance attention, or for mood control in psychiatric patients and the mentally retarded.

BIOFEEDBACK: MEDICINE'S NEWEST CURE-ALL

How would you like to set your own blood pressure at the optimum level, without taking a pill or losing a pound? How would you like to warm up your hands without putting on gloves, or make your aching back stop hurting, or get rid of headaches, menstrual cramps, or arthritis pain at will—even coax a tumor to respond to therapy?

Absurd? Not necessarily. According to some experts, you can— right now—produce some or all of these pie-in-the-sky effects. What you need is a short course in biofeedback, an increasingly respectable learning technique that uses instrumental feedback to teach you to take unprecedented control of your own body.

It works in many ways, but here's a reasonably typical one. Let's say you want to get rid of a chronic tension headache, and all your doctor's vague instructions to "Relax!" haven't helped a bit. At a biofeedback center, a technician is more specific. He starts out by asking you to lie down and close your eyes while he (painlessly) attaches a couple of surface electrodes, coated with conducting fluid, to your forehead. You promptly hear a high-pitched whine coming from the electrodes, which are hooked up to an electromyograph (EMG), a machine that monitors muscle tension and relaxation. That, says the technician, is the sound that tells you your forehead muscles are all tensed up. If you relax them, the sound will drop in pitch. You try to make the muscles go limp. The whine continues. The technician may help you by suggesting that you think of something soothing and pleasant—a sunbath on a deserted beach, a stroll through a field of flowers. Or he may ask you to visualize your forehead muscles drooping, sagging, sinking. Perhaps he offers some key phrase: "Let it all go limp, let it all smooth out."

You keep trying—and the pitch of sound begins to change. It drops a tone, steadies, drops again to a low hum. That means you've relaxed those muscles! How? You don't really know, but it doesn't really matter, because the headache is going away and that's the whole point. If you're a good learner, after a number of training sessions in which you magically turn whines into hums, you may be able to repeat the mysterious process any time, any place, without needing the sound effects to tell you you're doing it. From that point on, you can hope to prevent, reduce, or eliminate your headaches any time they threaten you.

In short, though you don't know what you've done, how you've done it, or why it works, you have learned to control your pain by altering a physical state that accompanies it.

There is nothing very new about this, since all learning depends on feedback in one way or another. For example, when a mother hugs her baby for toddling into her arms, she is feeding back approval that tells the baby to repeat that behavior. Nor is the use of instruments to produce feedback in the form of whines, hums, bells, buzzers, or flashing colored lights a recent innovation.

What is new is the idea of clinically packaging this learning technique and applying it to all sorts of health problems in an attempt to give patients mastery over their bodily processes, including many previously considered utterly uncontrollable. Today biofeedback techniques are being used—either as standard practice or experimental medicine—all over the U.S. and Canada. While many in the medical establishment still consider the practice unproved, others cite remarkable results.

One of the most widespread uses of biofeedback is in rehabilitative medicine, where it is used to train brain-damaged patients to regain lost or damaged muscle functions. One dramatic improvement occurred at the Emory University Medical Center in Atlanta, where an 18-year-old girl was treated for "acquired cerebral palsy"—the result of brain damage caused by an auto accident when she was 10. When the girl was brought to Emory, she could not walk normally; every time she tried to bring her heels down to touch the floor, the muscles in her calves went into spasm. Her family was about to have the girl's heel tendons surgically lengthened when biofeedback training was suggested as a last preoperative resort.

At Emory, technicians attached electrodes, which terminated in an EMG, to the girl's calves. As she attempted to walk, a buzzer signaled the onset of muscle spasm. Each time she succeeded in controlling the spasm, the buzzer shut off. By the time the girl had completed three concentrated training sessions, she was able to inhibit the spasms at will, walk with her heels touching the floor, and avoid a costly, painful surgical procedure.

Stroke patients who have lost their sense of proprioception—awareness of where body parts are in space—have used biofeedback to provide "artificial" awareness. When a buzzer sounds or a light flashes, these patients know they have made a mistake in placing a head, arm, or leg, and can correct the error. Patients with twisted necks, partial paralysis, and other conditions resulting from brain damage have successfully used EMGs and electronic transducers (which register changes in joint angles, posture, movement, and pressure) to help them achieve more normal motion. In one recent study, 67% of a group of stroke patients were able to discard short leg braces after five weeks of biofeedback training. Nonetheless, experts like Dr. John Basmajian of the Chedoke Medical Center in Hamilton, Ontario, caution against expecting too much. Though some trainees, like the girl at Emory, make spectacular progress, others fail to improve at all. The typical patient makes modest to moderate progress. "Biofeedback," Dr. Basmajian explains, "depends on training the

189

residual resources after brain damage. We can train old pathways, or those pathways that are dormant. We cannot train neural pathways that have been destroyed."

Rehabilitative medicine is the discipline in which biofeedback is most acceptable to the medical establishment. But among laymen, its most popular function is to teach relaxation of the voluntary muscles, especially those connected with tension headaches, low-back pain, dysmenorrhea, arthritis, and fibrositis (inflammation of muscle sheaths). Many chronic-pain patients try biofeedback only after years of costly workups, medication, acupuncture, and other forms of therapy, when they are seriously depressed about their conditions. They may have been told by skeptical physicians that biofeedback is "just another placebo" or that "the good it does you is all in your head," but to most of them, outside opinions are irrelevant, and they require no lab tests to judge the success or failure of techniques they learn at biofeedback or pain-control centers (most of which, incidentally, are run by physicians). To the patient, success means that he can control his pain at need, without medication.

Biofeedback also is in demand for problems of the autonomic (involuntary) nervous system, especially high blood pressure and migraine headaches. Unlike tension headaches, migraines result from blood vessels swelling around the brain. Training focuses on helping patients ward off the headache before it gets started by dealing with its classical onset signal, the cold hands that indicate that blood vessels in the extremities are narrowing. In one technique called autogenic feedback training, patients learn to head the ache off at the pass by warming their hands during the onset period. The therapist offers helpful visualization cues—"warm gloves" or "sitting in front of a campfire"—while the patient attempts to raise his skin temperature. If he succeeds, the headache is usually averted. This technique, which originated at the Menninger Foundation in Topeka, Kans., has been used with considerable success.

Another anti-migraine method is employed by Dr. R. Edward Berman, a psychologist at the Center for Behavioral Psychiatry and Psychology in Birmingham, Mich. A typical patient is Sandra R., a 35-year-old housewife with a 20-year history of migraines that have been increasing in frequency and intensity. Sandra's life has been dominated—almost destroyed—by the pain and nausea caused by her headaches. Before coming to the center, she had had one full neurological workup, consultations with four physicians—all of whom regretfully told her they could find no organic problem to treat—and three months of psychotherapy, which also failed to reduce her misery. For a while, strong painkillers helped, but they have long since stopped giving her any relief.

A psychological workup shows that Sandra is a perfectionist who has difficulty relaxing. When asked to describe her symptoms, she tends to tense up as if another attack were imminent.

The first thing Sandra has to have, says Berman, "is the motivation to accept responsibility for controlling her own health. The instruments are then used to show the patient a correlation between the mind and the body." Sandra is told that an increase of perspiration indicates a rise in her anxiety level. Using a technique called galvanic skin response feedback, she is trained to control the amount of sweat her hands produce. Over the next three months, she has 11 training sessions, plus psychotherapy, and when she is discharged, she has progressed from despair to a genuine hope that she can keep her migraine attacks under control.

Equally fascinating is the biofeedback work being undertaken with cancer patients. Cancer involves not only the birth and growth of abnormal cells but a failure on the part of the host's immunological, or defense, system to destroy the invading cells. Acting on the theory that the emotions may affect the functioning of the immunological system, researchers looked for ways to fight cancer by rallying the powers of the mind against it. "At our center," says Dr. Carl Simonton, a radiation oncologist at the Cancer Counseling and Research Center in Fort Worth, Tex., "we help the patient increase his will to live and use his mind to help control his body's responses. This often helps him prolong his life and, in some instances, save it."

Dr. Simonton's staff uses relaxation and mental-imagery techniques, along with other therapies, such as radiation, but no instrumentation. The patient's feedback, they explain, comes from the remission of the disease. First, the patient is taught to relax his body. He then visualizes his tumor as, for example, a hunk of raw hamburger meat. Next he visualizes his defensive white blood cells as white fish attacking and eating up the cancerous growth. Finally, he sees the radiation therapy he receives as bullets of energy also attacking the tumor.

Remissions for patients using this system are startlingly higher than usual, as if their immunological systems have become especially effective in dealing with cancer. Four and a half years ago, Simonton's team began keeping records of biofeedback-trained cancer patients, all of them "incurable," none of them with a life expectancy of more than about one year. The group eventually numbered 159. Out of the 159, 63 were still alive in 1979, with an average survival time of over 24 months. Those who died averaged over 20 months' survival.

At Children's Hospital in Boston, under funding by the United Cerebral Palsy Research and Education Foundation, children with cerebral palsy (CP) are using biofeedback in a variety of ways. CP can produce a wide range of manifestations and disabilities in the sensory and/or neuromuscular systems. Dr. Sheldon R. Simon, director of the gait-analysis lab, finds that the best results are obtained from children over the age of six who have limited problems—confined, for example, to one limb. "We'll use biofeedback," Dr. Simon says, "when we have a good idea of the cause of the child's problem and can focus on it." Treatment, which is highly individualized, usually involves rewarding a child with music when an EMG indicates that he has done something well. When a youngster who drags one leg begins to pick it up when walking, a pressure device in the child's shoe responds, triggering a burst of congratulatory music as soon as his foot comes off the floor. As long as the foot is in the air, music plays; when the foot hits the floor, the music stops. The child is rewarded each time he picks up his leg—until, it is hoped, a good walking pattern becomes reward enough.

In general, biofeedback's future seems to be limited only by the scientific imagination. For example, since some men have been trained to raise their scrotal temperature several degrees, it seems possible that many could learn to elevate it high enough to kill sperm for contraceptive purposes. If people can regulate blood pressure, perhaps they can also direct blood circulation, enabling a cancer victim to cut off a tumor's blood supply, or a patient with an infection to channel white blood cells toward the invader with greater efficiency. If migraine patients can avert an attack by utilizing the onset signal, epileptics who also receive warning signs before seizures may be able to learn to control their brain waves, to prevent the electrical storms that trigger an attack. And patients who get good results only as long as they use feedback instruments, but fail on their own, may not always have to continue to make frequent visits to clinics. Berman says: "Our instrumentation continues to become more refined, reliable, and simplified. I envision that as the equipment becomes more available and less expensive, we will see people using biofeedback right in their own homes."

In the meantime, as the possibilities expand, the structure needed to provide expert researchers and technicians expands, too. Already there are 1,750 members of the Biofeedback Society of America, which was founded in 1968 to provide an open forum for professionals interested in the exchange of ideas, methods, and research. Basmajian is currently president of the society. Although there are no state or national licensing procedures yet, some state chapters are setting up training and certification programs.

Basmajian says, "Years ago, researchers knew that people could produce tears voluntarily. But they didn't realize the extent of the mind's ability to control these involuntary functions. With biofeedback, we can train patients to do things for themselves with their internal resources. Within certain limits, the patients can cure themselves. Perhaps half the ailments we suffer could be cured by self-regulation."

SOURCE: Linda Stern Rubin in *Family HEALTH* Magazine. Reprinted with permission of *Family HEALTH* Magazine, March, 1979.

DOCTORS, DIABETICS, AND NEW DRUGS

Predictor DR. LOUIS LASAGNA is a professor of pharmacology and toxicology at the University of Rochester School of Medicine and Dentistry in Rochester, N.Y. The author of *The Doctors' Dilemmas* and *Life, Death, and the Doctor,* Dr. Lasagna writes a regular column for *The Sciences,* a publication of the New York Academy of Sciences.

1982–1992

• Materials that are derivatives of, or relatives of, normally occurring brain peptides will be available to treat pain—especially chronic and severe pain—in better fashion than we are able to at the moment. This will imitate nature's own endogenous [internal] mechanisms for relieving pain.

• Artificial pancreases will be made practical for implantation into diabetics, especially young diabetics with essentially nonfunctioning pancreases. This should revolutionize the treatment of diabetes mellitus.

• At least one new class of effective antidepressant drugs will be discovered, utilizing theories now evolving that are broader than the ones that have held sway up until very recently.

• The life span of patients with advanced cancer will be significantly prolonged by the empirical working and reworking of various combinations of older and newer cancer drugs.

• There will be considerable increase in the use of coronary-bypass surgery, and indeed even a modest increase in the number of cardiac transplants being performed.

1993–2030

• Hypothalamic hormones or modifications of naturally occurring hormones will be used to treat at least five important human diseases, including diabetes mellitus and hyperthyroidism. There is also the possibility that this work will produce new approaches to contraception.

• Prostaglandins, much as hypothalamic hormones above, will produce benefit in the management of such things as renal [kidney-related] disease, hypertension, and asthma.

• Medical schools will be doing much less research in the years ahead than they are today, as national funds continue to shrink. Tuition will be at least $25,000 per year by 2000.

• More and more of medical practice will be performed by health professionals other than physicians.

• We will train bacteria with recombinant DNA techniques to make many biologically important substances for treating human disease.

COMBATING MAJOR DISEASES

Predictor DR. BERNARD DIXON, with an extensive background in microbiology, is the European editor of *OMNI* magazine. From 1969 to 1977, Dr. Dixon edited *New Scientist* magazine. He is also the author of several popular books, including *Magnificent Microbes*, *Invisible Allies*, and *Atoms and Humours*, as well as numerous articles in scientific and general periodicals.

• PREDICTIONS •

1982–1992

• Major breakthroughs in understanding the very powerful influence of psychosomatic factors in cancer—with potential practical significance in preventing the disease.
• First applications of recombinant DNA technology in combating hereditary disorders. [A large molecule found in the chromosomes of cells, DNA carries the genetic code and thereby determines the heredity of all living organisms. Debates have raged over the safety and ethics of recombinant DNA technology—a form of genetic surgery by which genes can be separated out from a DNA molecule and spliced together with those from an unrelated organism.]
• Development of a near-perfect immunosuppressive agent—which protects organ transplants but does not interfere with normal immunological defenses—that has positive implications for organ-transplant surgery.
• Marked reduction in the prevalence of coronary disease and a fall in coronary mortality in most Western countries, following wider adoption of preventive measures.
• Widespread use of computer diagnosis at the primary health-care level, with enormous dividends in early detection of serious illnesses.

1993–2030

• Introduction of the first wide-spectrum antiviral drugs, highly active against such illnesses as influenza and the common cold.
• Total elimination of poliomyelitis in most Western countries.
• Real understanding of the distinction between normal and malignant cells, leading to methods of either preventing the emergence of malignancy or inducing cancer cells to revert to normal.
• Major reductions in the incidence of many forms of cancer, following considerable progress in the control of environmental carcinogens.

LASERS FIGHT TOOTH DECAY

Lasers may "cap" teeth in a way that makes them permanently decay-resistant.

Capping molars with plastic is a common preventive procedure today, but the plastic chips or cracks, and the tooth usually has to be recapped at least once a year. The laser, which can accurately direct a tremendous amount of energy to a particular spot, would fuse a cap of toothlike material on the molar.

The problem is that the ceramic material expected to be used for this process will fuse at a temperature of 600°F—but if the temperature of the whole tooth is raised by only 10° the tooth will die.

The developer, Dr. R. F. Boehm, professor of mechanical engineering at the University of Utah, plans to direct a laser pulse of 1,000,000 watts at a tooth for less than a millionth of a second. In experiments on extracted molars, he has raised the surface temperature of a tooth to 270°F, while the temperature near the root area was raised by only 1°. Soon he expects to be able to reach the desired surface temperature while keeping the root area of the tooth well within the safety zone of 10°.

Dr. Boehm, an expert in thermal processes, says of this procedure, "It's actually safer than the high-speed drills in use today." He envisions special clinics staffed by dentists trained in the use of lasers. Soon we may be able to go all through life with our own teeth.

SOURCE: *Future Facts*, copyright © 1976 by Stephen Rosen. Reprinted by permission of Simon & Schuster, a Division of Gulf + Western Corporation.

LASER DENTISTRY

Predictor DR. R. F. BOEHM is a professor of mechanical engineering at the University of Utah in Salt Lake City. An expert in thermal processes and dentistry, Dr. Boehm is developing a method in which lasers are used to cap teeth so that they are permanently decay-resistant. (See also previous article.)

• PREDICTIONS •

1982–1992

• A great deal of fundamental knowledge regarding the precise causes of tooth decay will be gained. Both heredity and environmental factors will be shown to have critical impact.
• Some serums will be demonstrated to be partially effective for tooth-decay prevention in large-scale clinical evaluations.
• Caps made of materials just like tooth enamel will be successfully attached to live teeth in the dental clinics by use of lasers. This will

lead the way to successful, permanent, preventive treatment of the critical "pit and fissure" decay problem.
• Simple techniques will be demonstrated for enhancing the fluoride uptake of human teeth, along with a significant increase in effectiveness of fluoride treatments.

1993–2020

• Tooth decay will be eliminated in 95% of all people who avail themselves of the combined pre-decay treatments mentioned above. Students will take part in preventive treatment after permanent teeth come in, much as they now receive immunizations.

AN END TO CAVITIES

Predictor DR. ISRAEL KLEINBERG, chairman of the Department of Oral Biology and Pathology at the State University of New York at Stony Brook, recently discovered sialin, a component of saliva that neutralizes tooth-decaying acids. He hopes that synthetic sialin can be added to toothpaste, candy, and soft drinks to offset the negative effects of sugar. The author of over 180 scientific papers, Dr. Kleinberg has also acted as a consultant to various industries and universities and to the U.S. government.

• PREDICTIONS •

By 1990

• Dental researchers will know how to manipulate the microbial populations in the mouth, and this will provide important answers for the control of bacterial populations in other parts of the human body and in animals and plants. This information will have great importance both in the control of disease and in the control of industrial processes involving bacteria.
• Dental research will provide new clues that will lead to the control of tumor growth.
• A new antibiotic, as important as penicillin, will be discovered in saliva.
• A new blood coagulant and a new substance for the treatment of peptic and duodenal ulcers will be found in saliva.

Before 1992

• A recently developed fluid meter that measures the minute volumes of fluid in the gingival crevice (the space between the gums and the teeth) will become a common instrument in dentists' offices. Presence of excess levels of this fluid is the earliest sign of disease of the gums and eventually pyorrhea or periodontal disease. This disease generally develops very slowly and is responsible for most tooth loss in middle and older age groups. Individuals will be as conscious of their gingival fluid flow levels as they are now of their blood pressures.

By 2000

• The practice of dentistry will have undergone drastic change because dental caries (cavities) and periodontitis (pyorrhea)—two of the most prevalent diseases in man and presently responsible for the loss of about 95% of all teeth—will be under control.

• The use of saliva in diagnosis of oral and medical conditions will be as routine as blood analyses are today.

• The composition of gingival crevicular fluid will be analyzed routinely by specially developed microanalytical techniques and used along with saliva as a diagnostic fluid for many medical conditions.

• Despite their high price, silver and gold will still be used for the repair and replacement of missing teeth, the number of which should be much smaller than it is today.

• Major new industries will have emerged, based on research discoveries in dentistry. One of these will be in the area of odor control.

6

PREDICTIONS ON
YOUR INCOME

1982–1989

Welfare and food stamps will come to an end as
the U.S. government forces private corporations
to hire all chronic unemployables.

1982–1992

Labor shortages in repair and service jobs.
Openings for mechanics, gardeners, plumbers,
electricians, electronics repairmen.

1993–2030

Inflation will cease.

REMEMBER
THE GOOD OLD DAYS?

In the 10 years between 1969 and 1979, consumer prices—overall—rose 95%. Here's a look at what prices could look like in 1989:

Item	1969	1979	1989
Single family house	$28,000.00	$68,300.00	$158,748.00
Paperback novel	1.25	2.60	4.88
First-run movie ticket	2.50	3.00	4.93
Maximum annual Social Security deduction	374.40	1,404.00	3,561.00[1]
Gallon of regular gas	.33	1.00	3.02
Loaf of white bread	.23	.42	.84
Quart of milk	.31	.51	.93
First-class postage stamp	.06	.15	.34
Newspaper	.10	.20	.48
Apples per pound	.15	.44	1.02
6-pack of American beer	1.16	1.81	2.82
Tube of toothpaste	.95	1.45	2.21
Pound of coffee	.76	3.27	14.07
Hospital room for one day	46.10	131.38	374.43
Carton of cigarettes	3.13	5.41	9.35
Car tune-up	25.61	52.09	105.74
Hershey® bar	.05	.25	.70
Mustang 2-door sedan (FOB)[2]	2,982.00	4,793.00	7,669.00
Can of dog food	.18	.29	.47
Pack of Wrigley's® gum	.05	.20	.80
Comic book	.15	.40	1.06
Record album	3.99	5.98	8.97
Toilet paper	.15	.20	.27
Man's necktie	3.00	7.50	18.75
Brassiere	4.00	6.00	9.00
Box of regular Tampax®	1.19	2.19	3.29
TV Guide	.15	.35	.80

1. If proposed changes within the Social Security system become law, the maximum tax in 1989 will be considerably less than this.
2. FOB (free on board) means that this price does not include transportation costs, taxes, or any dealer's handling charges.

—D.B.S. and L.S.

JAPANESE IN THE SOUTH BRONX; BOOM TIME IN WYOMING

Predictor LEONARD A. LECHT is director of special projects research at the Conference Board, a nonprofit business and economic research organization located in New York City. He has a Ph.D. in economics from Columbia University and has directed research for the National Science Foundation, the U.S. Office of Education, and the U.S. Department of Labor. Dr. Lecht is the author of *Goals, Priorities, and Dollars* and *Dollars for National Goals—Planning for the 1980s*.

• PREDICTIONS •

1982–1992

• Inflation will continue as a serious problem, and wages and salaries, like savings accounts, will come to be annually adjusted upward to match increases in the cost of living. The cost of living will shoot up again after each economywide readjusting.
• Continuing inflation will reverse the trend for men to retire before age 65, and compulsory retirement at any age will be outlawed by 1990. "Joe College" in the late 1980s will as frequently be a 65-year-old preparing for a new career as an 18-year-old freshman trying to decide on a major.
• Energy shortages and changes in life-styles will revive the large central cities as places to work and live and will shift the problems of urban decay to the suburbs. Real estate prices will fall sharply in many suburbs and correspondingly increase in the renewed urban centers.
• Declining birthrates in the late 1960s and 1970s will transform the labor market for teenagers and young adults in the 1980s from a condition of chronic shortages of jobs to one of shortages of job-seekers for many entry-level positions.
• Changing attitudes toward work and authority together with government regulation will make the personnel field a high-growth area in the 1980s for college graduates, with career opportunities comparable to those for engineers, programmers, or health professionals a decade or two earlier.

1993–2030

• Japanese investments in the U.S. in branch-plant manufacturing facilities come to provide an important source of jobs for many persons in formerly depressed areas such as the South Bronx.
• A new class of affluent employees will develop, made up of persons who can repair electrical automobiles and install and service solar

and geothermal home-energy units or the modular homes that have become common by 2010.

• Rapid productivity growth after 1990 will make it feasible for most employees to enjoy sabbaticals every three years like those now taken by teachers every seven years. Sabbaticals will be used to travel, to develop hobbies, to rest, or to prepare for second careers.

• The arrival of low-cost computers, automated word-processing, and linking of telephones with two-way television will enable most white-collar workers to work regularly at home rather than commuting to an office. People who choose to work at a central office will do so on the basis of their preference to relate to a work group rather than on the basis of the greater efficiency of working in an office.

• Wyoming and Colorado become major boom areas for people seeking better jobs as new technology makes it cheaper by the year 2000 to obtain oil from shale rock than to import oil from Saudi Arabia or Venezuela. A barrel of oil sells for 40 (1979) dollars by 2000.

15 MOST COMMON JOBS FOR 1990
(1978 Rankings in Parentheses)

	No. Employed
1. Secretaries and stenographers (1)	5,357,000
2. Retail trade sales workers (2)	3,785,000
3. Building custodians (3)	2,740,000
4. Cashiers (7)	2,100,000
5. Bookkeeping workers (4)	2,045,000
6. Local truck drivers (5)	2,040,000
7. Blue-collar worker supervisors (6)	1,925,000
8. Industrial assemblers (12)	1,662,000
9. Kindergarten and elementary school teachers (9)	1,652,000
10. Waiters and waitresses (8)	1,635,000
11. Nursing aides, orderlies, and attendants (18)	1,575,000
12. Registered nurses (16)	1,570,000
13. Cooks and chefs (11)	1,564,000
14. Engineers (14)	1,441,000
15. Carpenters (10)	1,390,000

SOURCE: Occupational Projections and Training Data, Bureau of Labor Statistics Bulletin 2058, 1980.

15 FASTEST-GROWING JOBS
1978–1990

		Percent Change in Job Openings
1.	Occupational therapists	100.0
2.	Computer service technicians	92.5
3.	Speech pathologists and audiologists	87.5
4.	Dental hygienists	85.7
5.	Homemaker and home health aides	70.0
6.	Industrial machinery repairers	66.0
7.	Dining room attendants and dishwashers	62.8
8.	Licensed practical nurses	62.2
8.	Travel agents	62.2
10.	Lithographers	61.1
11.	Mining engineers	58.3
12.	Health services administrators	57.1
13.	Flight attendants	56.2
14.	Business machine repairers	56.0
15.	Respiratory therapy workers	55.0

SOURCE: Occupational Projections and Training Data, Bureau of Labor Statistics Bulletin 2058, 1980.

15 SHRINKING PROFESSIONS
1978–1990

		Percent Change in Job Openings
1.	Railroad station agents	−59.6
2.	Merchant Marine sailors	−36.9
3.	Blacksmiths	−36.4
4.	Railroad telegraphers, telephoners, and tower operators	−30.2
5.	Private household workers	−23.2
6.	Secondary school teachers	−20.8
7.	Postal clerks	−19.0

8. Telephone central office equipment installers	−15.9
9. Compositors (printing)	−12.8
10. College and university faculty	− 9.2
11. Meatcutters	− 8.3
12. Telephone operators	− 6.8
13. Railroad shop trades	− 6.7
14. Photoengravers	− 6.3
15. Gasoline service station attendants	− 5.6

SOURCE: Occupational Projections and Training Data, Bureau of Labor Statistics Bulletin 2058, 1980.

CHANGES IN THE WORKPLACE

Predictor JAMES O'TOOLE is the director of the Twenty Year Forecast project at the University of Southern California in Los Angeles, where he is an associate professor of management in the Graduate School of Business. He served as chairman of "Work in America," a task force set up by the U.S. Department of Health, Education, and Welfare. Dr. O'Toole is the author of five books, including *Work in America* and *Energy and Social Change*.

According to O'Toole: "We futurists know only one thing for certain about the future: It cannot be predicted. Therefore, we leave predictions to fortune-tellers, horserace touts, fools, and economists! Having said that, it is nevertheless the case that it is often useful to make *probabilistic* statements about the occurrence of future events. That is, while self-respecting futurists would not make the forecast that there will be a rapprochement between China and Russia in 1985, we might say that there is a 20% probability of such an event. The purpose of making such a forecast is *not* to predict an event, but to get policymakers to think about what might happen should the event occur. In this spirit, I make the following forecasts about work."

Probability of Occurrence Before the Year 1990

Possible Event
Flextime (workers set the time they will come to

	Probability of Occurrence Before the Year 1990
work and leave work) becomes the norm in large U.S. corporations.	45%
Most full-time workers now paid on an hourly basis will be paid annual salaries by large U.S. corporations.	65%
In most large U.S. corporations there will be an equal number of men and women employed in managerial positions.	35%
All forms of constitutional protection (e.g., civil rights and due process) are extended to the workplace.	60%
Paternity leaves become a legal right for all male employees.	40%
Private pensions become fully portable from employer to employer.	30%

Possible Event	Probability of Occurrence Before the Year 2000
Federal government mandates that workers be represented on the boards of large corporations.	25%
Workers own the majority of the shares of the companies in which they work in at least a third of *Fortune*'s 500 companies.	20%
Organized labor breaks with the Democratic party and forms a political party modeled after the British Labour party.	30%
Pay raises of workers are determined by a vote of the employees themselves.	45%
Paid educational sabbaticals become the norm in large corporations.	60%
Private corporations become the "employer of the last resort"; that is, government forces corporations to hire chronic unemployables and eliminates all welfare, food stamps, etc.	65%

HERE COMES FLEXTIME

Time glides.

A system of flexible working hours allows employees to determine the number of hours they will work in any day. Begun in Germany in 1967 as the "Gleitzeit," it has seriously challenged the nine-to-five, five-day workweek in both Europe and Japan; and it presents an alternative to the four-day workweek which has been more popular in the U.S. Here, the concept of flexible hours is known as "Flextime."

Under flexible working hours, a workday contains a number of fixed hours, arranged around the middle of the day, during which all employees must be present. Hours before and after this "core period" are voluntary, and employees can come and go as they please. An employee is required to put in a certain minimal number of hours during a time period the organization chooses—usually a week or a month. Generally, supervisors and employees decide together how many people are necessary to do the job during the flexible time period. They themselves split up the work load, but without imposing fixed, staggered hours.

The entire workday is thought of as a "bandwidth," and a typical bandwidth is from 8:30 A.M. to 5:30 P.M. Flexibility can be extended by broadening the bandwidth and thus give workers a wider range of choice in when to work. And when to eat lunch.

A "credit" and "debit" system permits employees to accumulate time off or owe time to be worked later. If the employee puts in more than the requisite number of hours, the extra hours are carried over as a bonus to the next time period. If he puts in fewer hours, it's a deficit which must be made up at a later time. The most flexible (but rare) form of Flextime is the variable-hours system—where there's no core period and employees work whenever they choose, including evenings and weekends.

The Hengstler Company of Germany, a large manufacturer of electromechanical counters and controls, developed the concept of Flextime. It experimented with the concept on its own 1,500 employees and later set up a special division to counsel other organizations considering flexible hours. As of 1973, more than 5,000 organizations in Europe were operating on Flextime. During the same year Hengstler formed a U.S. subsidiary, Flextime Corporation, to introduce this work concept into the U.S. and to counsel organizations here.

Standard time clocks can be used under Flextime to record employee hours, but Hengstler provides special automatic equipment to companies. Employees themselves can adjust their hours, and the

Santa Claus goes on Flextime.

205

equipment gives instantaneous totals of accumulated hours during any accounting period. It provides feedback to employees and record-keeping information to supervisors and management.

Studies in Europe and Canada have shown that lateness and short-term absenteeism drop sharply with a flexible-hours system. Productivity increases, but without the necessity of overtime. There is less turnover on jobs, and morale of workers improves.

According to the Flextime Corporation, "Using the flexibility allowed them, employees adjusted work schedules to their own personal rhythms and generally applied their most productive hours to the job. Flextime can help man maintain his individuality in this age of modernization, mechanization, and automation."

SOURCE: *Future Facts*, copyright © 1976 by Stephen Rosen. Reprinted by permission of Simon & Schuster, a Division of Gulf + Western Corporation.

LESSENING LABOR PAINS

Predictor PAUL DICKSON is a 40-year-old Washington-based author who has written extensively on the future. His books include *The Future File*, *Think Tanks*, *The Electronic Battlefield*, and *The Future of the Workplace*.

• PREDICTIONS •

1982–1983

• The discovery is made that the long-term trend away from self-employment has significantly reversed itself—a countertrend much like the recent discovery that large numbers of Americans were beginning to move back into rural areas.
• In the face of a continuing decline in American worker productivity, work practices in America come under broad scrutiny. "Work content" becomes a major topic.

1985

• The "quality of work"—meaningful, challenging, productive, and lightly supervised jobs—becomes a matter for collective bargaining in a number of industries.

1985–1990

• New time and schedule arrangements become dominant in most areas of employment. Novelties of the 1970s—flextime, 4-day work-weeks, worker sabbaticals, and the like—have become part of the American way of work.

• For the first time in decades a sizable percentage of the American work force works at home. A number of pressures—ranging from energy conservation to the trend away from strict supervision on the job—have brought this about.

1995–2000

• With a growing number of Americans deciding to start second careers and with life expectancy increasing, the average retirement age begins to drift toward the late 60s. Increasing numbers of middle-aged Americans are in school preparing for second careers.

2000

• The typical work patterns which were solidly in place as late as 1970 have changed in the light of a host of new options in terms of time, schedules, benefit packages, education, and retirement. For instance, individuals now put together their own benefit packages tailored to their needs (up to a certain limit), pensions are universally portable, and most employees will select their own working hours from week to week.

CORPORATIONS
SUPPLANT EVERYTHING
—CORPORATE UTOPIA

Predictor DR. WILLIAM OUCHI is a professor of management in the Graduate School of Management at the University of California in Los Angeles. The recipient of numerous grants to study work organization and control, Dr. Ouchi is writing a book describing his research in these areas. He also serves on the editorial boards of *Administrative Science Quarterly* and *The Academy of Management Journal*.

• PREDICTIONS •

1993–2030

• What I foresee is a series of fundamental changes in the organization of places of work. These changes will arise as our society matures and either develops a sense of wholeness and solidarity or else decomposes into a mutually suspicious set of subgroups who hold each other at arm's length.

1. OCCUPATIONAL COMMUNITIES

Where we work will increasingly become where we live, in the sense that friendship ties will center around occupational ties. Geographical mobility is a long-term fact of American life, and this mobility has permanently disrupted our traditional sources of emotional support as well as of self-discipline. These used to come from the primary relationships developed in the extended family, church, neighborhood, club, and childhood friendships. As these traditional sources have been eroded, our society has gone adrift, without a sense of communal obligation or support. Over the next 50 years, many companies and government agencies will come to accept their role as a primary social force and will encourage the lifetime employment that is common in Japanese companies today and which permits people to develop strong bonds in at least that one domain of their lives.

2. A NEW INDIVIDUALISM

The present American emphasis on self-reliance will take on a new coloration, or else we will see a continuing drop in productivity and in our capacity to act as a nation. The kind of self-reliance that stems from the ethos of the draftsman and the farmer is out of place in an industrial society. It rejects dependence on others, it demands clear individual responsibility, and it requires reward for individual performance. However, industrialism succeeds only to the extent that people cooperate together in complex and interdependent processes of manufacture and of service. If we can develop an understanding of the individual strength that derives from being part of a team, and if we can learn to trust others sufficiently to be dependent on them, then we will be better able to cope with the increasingly interdependent demands of modern technology.

3. INCREASED LEGISLATIVE PROTECTION OF EMPLOYEE WELFARE

The move towards occupational community will be hastened by new laws which will increasingly protect the welfare of employees in broad ways. The voters will come to realize that, just as some profit-seeking firms polluted the air and water with impunity until they were made to pay a price for doing so, they will continue to pollute people until they are made to pay the costs of rehabilitation. Research initiated by Professor Chris Argyris of Harvard University has shown that people who have a very alienating work experience suffer from a generally diminished ability to function in all spheres of life. The company does not bear these costs; at most it bears the cost of reduced productivity until it fires such an employee. A company that grossly mistreats employees in this way will gain a bad reputation over time and thus suffer through a diminished ability to hire new employees, but less obvious offenders in our mass society can escape detection for a very long time. The voters will seek governmental control of such offenses.

4. THE RISE OF HUMAN TECHNOLOGIES

There will be a dramatic shift towards the organization of manual and clerical work in which workers are placed in teams or groups which operate most of the time without supervision. Workers can be encouraged to decide among themselves who should run which machine, how the work flow should be arranged, and which job applicant should be hired into their group. The consequences are greatly increased control by workers over their own time and activities, increased morale, and increased productivity.

These technologies will move from the experimental to the implementation stage quite rapidly. Gains in our wealth will no longer come mostly from new technological inventions which increase capital investment and thereby raise productivity. Instead, the emphasis in the future will be on understanding the technology of organizing and of managing people, who have far more impact on productivity than do machines. American productivity will rebound from its recent decline only if our people technology improves significantly.

5. MORE PEOPLE EMPLOYED IN FEWER BUT BIGGER COMPANIES

The trend towards large companies will continue and may, in fact, accelerate. Again, the great success of the postwar Japanese economy is instructive. In Japan, the government encourages companies to become large and to form close ties with other companies. This concentration of industry has been a factor in the success of the Japanese economy.

The U.S. Department of Justice, through its antitrust activities, has prevented such concentration whenever possible in America, on the theory that such concentration, by making it difficult for new firms to compete, promotes inefficiency and leaves us paying more for our goods and services from big, inefficient producers who aren't really trying anymore.

However, two new arguments may change that Justice Department position dramatically. First is evidence that only four or five competitors are necessary to produce fierce competition of the sort that drives prices down and quality and innovation up; having more competitors does not usually improve the situation. Second is research pioneered by Professor Oliver Williamson of the University of Pennsylvania, which demonstrates that often a single company which owns two divisions can operate them more efficiently than they would operate if each division were a separate company. What this means is that a competitive economy is made more effective when mergers are permitted, when smaller firms are taken over by larger firms. The result of the current research may be a major shift in U.S. antitrust policy to favor rather than to resist the growth of huge firms.

If this shift occurs, then everyone—managers, professionals, and manual workers—will want to be in the large firms. Every major industrial sector will be dominated by a few large firms competing against each other. Small firms will be limited to those marginal businesses in which employment is unstable and wages are low. Gaining employment in these large firms will be very difficult, and entry will be based primarily on the educational background of applicants. These firms will tend to hire only at bottom-level jobs and promote from within, so that people who begin their careers in small firms will have no later opportunity to move to big firms. Such a shift would also greatly change higher education as we know it. If we have an economy dominated by large firms, each of which is committed to lifetime employment, then these firms will provide their own technical and postbaccalaureate employee training, which will be tailored to their needs. Most firms today rely on us to pay for our own training before being hired, both because economically they are too small to provide their own tailored training and because employees can easily leave for a better job after the company has invested in their education. But if all major firms hire only at the bottom, then a trained employee cannot leave one employer to join another large firm (since they will not hire an experienced person), and thus we will see education shift from schools to firms.

CORPORATION REVENUES

The following is a chart of the total revenues of seven of the largest corporations in the U.S. for the years 1969 and 1979. The 1989 revenues have been projected based on the same percentage increase as occurred in the 10-year period between 1969 and 1979.

Corporation	Total Revenue 1969 ($)	Total Revenue 1979 ($)	Projected Revenue 1989 ($)
American Telephone & Telegraph Co.	15,684,000,000	45,400,000,000	131,418,000,000
Coca-Cola Co.	1,365,000,000	4,961,402,000	18,033,340,000
Exxon Corp.	14,930,000,000	84,350,000,000	476,552,060,000
Ford Motor Co.	14,756,000,000	43,513,700,000	128,316,750,000
General Electric Corp.	8,448,000,000	22,460,000,000	59,712,546,000
General Motors Corp.	24,295,000,000	66,311,200,000	180,990,940,000
International Business Machines Corp.	7,197,000,000	22,863,000,000	72,629,800,000

—J.A.D.

THE TOP 20 NATIONS IN GROSS NATIONAL PRODUCT IN 2020

For over 20 years French-trained industrial economist Felix Fremont has followed the economic statistics for every country for which valid growth data are available. These statistics exist in the form of gross national product (GNP), which is the total market value of goods and services produced by a nation in a given period. From these figures, Fremont has made the following predictions. (Numbers in parentheses represent the country's standing in 1978.)

1. United States (1)
2. Soviet Union (2)
3. Japan (3)
4. West Germany (4)
5. People's Republic of China (6)
6. France (5)
7. United Kingdom (7)
8. India (12)
9. Italy (8)
10. Mexico (18)
11. Canada (9)
12. Spain (14)
13. Brazil (10)
14. Iran (17)
15. Turkey (34)
16. Romania (22)
17. Poland (11)
18. Ivory Coast (70)
19. Korea (33)
20. Australia (13)

SOURCE: Felix Fremont, *World Markets of Tomorrow*. London: Harper and Row, 1973.

THE NEW LIBERTY

Predictor DR. MURRAY ROTHBARD is a professor of economics at the Polytechnic Institute of New York. A member of the Libertarian party's platform committee, he is also editor of the *Journal of Libertarian Studies* and of *Libertarian Forum*. Dr. Rothbard's numerous books include *For a New Liberty*, *Conceived in Liberty* (4 vols.), and *Man, Economy, and State* (2 vols.).

• PREDICTIONS •

1982–1992

• Accelerating inflation, punctuated by recessions; increasing flight from the dollar; ever higher gold prices; permanently stagnating stock market.

• Higher taxes, crippled productivity and savings. Accelerated decay in the urban centers of the Northeast. A return to rent control with resulting shortage of apartments and decay in the quality of housing.

• Accelerated increase in military spending, with ever greater and more frequent alarms of tyranny all over the globe, and increasingly ineffective attempts by the U.S. to police and mold the entire world according to its heart's desire.

• Establishment of national health insurance, with consequent great increase in taxes, spending, and inflation, and a shortage of medical care and decline in its quality.

• Slow deregulation of businesses, to the accompaniment of a great deal of squawking by the cartelized industries being regulated (in the case of FCC, CAB, ICC, etc.) and squawking by environmentalists and liberals (OSHA, environmental protection, etc.).

• Tighter controls on energy, in the form of price controls, import quotas, and taxes, bringing about higher prices and shortages.

1993–2030

• By the early 1990s a "backlash" by the public, by intellectuals, and by the media will take place, against the statism that has governed America since the 1930s (more precisely, since 1900). There will be a triumph of libertarian ideologies, institutions, and policies on every front in American life. Specifically:

1. Inflation will be ended by the separation of government from money; by the abolition of the Federal Reserve System; and by the return to a gold standard fully backing the dollar. This will be followed by a return to the gold standard by all the world's governments, bringing the chaotic nature of the international monetary system to an end. Taxes will be cut drastically across the board, on the federal, state, and local levels, and we will return to the idea that individuals, groups, and organizations should take care of their own affairs or voluntarily help each other. A huge number of government "services," now performed badly if at all, will be returned to the private sector, there to be performed much more efficiently and cheaply and with much greater attention to consumer needs. As a result, there will be a great burst of creative energies by the American people and in the American economy, with a large number of new products, industries, and technological marvels.

2. Industries will be deregulated rapidly and across the board. Energy will be freed at last and will become cheaper and more abundant, and government land, hoarded off the market, will be opened up to production.

3. We will finally realize that attempting to police the globe is harmful and counterproductive, and we will finally concentrate once again on our own defense, which will require enormously smaller military outlays. And we will finally abandon the remnants of the Prohibitionist mentality and stop trying to outlaw goods and services that other people find enjoyable. In short, the 1990s will bring freedom and therefore peace, prosperity, and creativity.

FROM COMPETITIVE
TO COOPERATIVE VALUES

Predictor HAZEL HENDERSON is an independent futurist and a contributor to such magazines as *The Nation*, the *Saturday Review*, and the *Harvard Business Review*. Mrs. Henderson is also the author of *Creating Alternative Futures* and *The Politics of Re-Conceptualization*. She serves as the only female appointee to the advisory council of the U.S. Congressional Office of Technology Assessment.

• PREDICTIONS •

1985–1990

• New political parties will emerge in the mature industrial societies (U.S., Canada, West Europe, Japan, Australia, New Zealand) leading to viable coalition governments promoting policies for ecologically and humanly compatible, sustainable production systems, based on renewable resources.

• Today's North-South dialogue between the so-called "developed" and "developing" countries will transcend the 19th-century struggles between the competing ideologies of capitalism and communism. Both will come to be viewed as "cargo cults," concerned mainly with material production, rather than as holistic systems equally concerned with cultural and ecological resources and the human search for higher purposes and meanings.

• The 300-year split between scientific endeavor and religious concern will converge in a more reverent approach to nature and to viewing humans as embedded within the natural order, not dominating it. At the same time, the acceptance of a humbler view of our material selves will permit a soaring of spiritual striving and a new flowering of philosophies and life-styles based on the complementarity of the old dichotomies of mind/matter, body/soul, physical/metaphysical, and all other artificial boundaries and schematizations.

1980s–2030 and beyond

• Tendencies counter to the previously described evolutionary path for the human species will continue to strive to retain their dominance. Even though the competitive, patriarchal, nation-state system with all its institutional forms of hierarchy, dominance/submission, and "machismo" technologies and its aggression-based values can no longer be maintained, leaders will continue to try to shore up these social systems. As these leaders try to maintain control, they will continually propose dangerous policies of confrontation and violence, risking nuclear proliferation and war, rather than admitting that the value systems by which they rose to power were viable only in the expansionary phase of human evolution, but cannot be perpetuated as boundary conditions are reached in a finite planetary ecosystem. In the new phase of global human interdependence, only a switch from competitive to cooperative value systems can assure the continuation of human development and avoid extinction.

7

PREDICTIONS ON SCIENCE AND TRANSPORTATION

1982

Pleasure driving in privately owned vehicles will be banned, and gas rationing will be introduced everywhere.

1985

Gasohol will replace gasoline.

1985

The U.S. government will nationalize all energy distribution systems, including pipelines and gasoline stations.

AUTOMATED HIGHWAYS
AND HONEYMOONS
ON THE MOON

Predictor JOHN P. THOMAS is the director of tourism studies at the Hudson Institute, a nonprofit policy-research organization. In addition, Mr. Thomas has participated in a number of studies relating to national defense, economic development, and transportation.

• PREDICTIONS •

1982–1992

1. AIR

More efficient subsonic jets carrying 500 passengers by 1982–1985. Second-generation supersonic jets by 1990 or thereabouts, carrying 300 passengers and traveling 2,000 mph. Million-pound subsonic aircraft carrying 500–1,000 passengers up to 10,000 mi. (Peking to London, for example) by 1990. Vertical/short takeoff and landing (V/STOL) aircraft, such as helicopters, that do not require airports, will be used for urban-suburban and intercity commuting by the late 1980s.

2. AUTOMOBILES

Lighter and slightly smaller than at present. Although we will continue to use principally spark ignition and diesel engines, they will become more efficient with the development of electronic ignition and fuel systems and better transmissions, tires, brakes, etc. Costs growing due to more expensive materials, electronics, and government-mandated safety devices (the latter—air bags, etc.—will add $2,000 to $3,000 to car prices by 1985). Electric city-cars probable by 1985–1986.

3. FUELS

Gasohol in widespread use by 1985. Alcohol in limited use for farm machinery and other special equipment by 1985. Synfuels (from oil shale, coal, etc.) in limited use by 1990 or so. Electricity in limited use in cities. Hydrogen in use experimentally in the 1980s.

4. HIGHWAYS

Experimental automated highways by 1990. Central control of all vehicles using them, making possible much greater traffic density and speeds.

5. PUBLIC TRANSPORT

Flywheel-electric buses for urban use. Flywheel spun to high speeds (10,000 rpm) and energy used to move buses. Braking puts energy back into flywheel. Wheels brought back up to speed every 3 mi. or so by electricity from power pole; 60–90 sec. needed to re-charge. Pollution eliminated from bus operations, ca. 1990. High-speed (200 mph) trains in Northeast Corridor of the U.S.; other such areas using upgraded road beds, ca. 1985.

6. TRAVEL

One-stop reservations for all aspects of trip, including aircraft, rental car, hotel, etc., by 1982. Home computer reservations for all aspects of trip by 1985–1990. Tickets become obsolete. On arrival at airport, baggage checked at curb; credit card in slot gains admission to boarding area. Seats assigned when reservations made. Baggage delivered to hotel destination and placed in reserved room. Traveling will be very simple, much less troublesome. International travel much more pleasant due to streamlining or elimination of customs procedures and expedited passenger and baggage handling.

2000 on

1. AIR

Third-generation supersonic jets carrying 500 passengers at 2,500–3,000 mph for 10,000-mile ranges. Hypersonic transports appear, carrying 200 passengers at 6,000 mph, ca. 2020. Personal V/STOL aircraft come into widespread use ca. 2000 to supplement automobiles; may largely replace them by 2020. Costs and other considerations may end private ownership of vehicles by year 2000. Leasing may be the standard by the end of this century.

2. FUELS

Hydrogen becomes principal fuel for most surface and air vehicles which don't use electricity. Inexhaustible and clean-burning, its use will solve energy shortages and eliminate much pollution. Also widely used for electric-power generation.

3. TRAVEL

Space travel to the moon, space stations, and other planets may become commonplace in latter-day space shuttles. Honeymoons on the moon or at space spas may be the in thing in the early years of the next century, say ca. 2020.

4. PUBLIC TRANSPORT

Transcontinental and intercontinental subways capable of very high volume (200 passengers per minute) and very high speeds (to 14,000 mph) may appear. Operating in evacuated tunnels and pro-pelled, suspended, and braked electromagnetically, such systems would permit transcontinental and intercontinental commuting at little expense.

5. HIGHWAYS

Automated highways come into widespread use. Cars and other vehicles using them enter approach ramp, enter destination into central highway computer, are automatically fed into traffic stream, routed to exit ramp nearest destination, where driver takes over. Power supplied to vehicles by highway. Present-day traffic jams should be eliminated since such highways can handle much more traffic and move it at much higher speeds. Auto accidents eliminated on such highways. In urban and suburban corridors, especially useful for commuting.

AUTOMOBILES AND FUELS
OF THE FUTURE

• AUTOMOBILES •

1. TYPE: GAS TURBINE

Advantages: The smooth continuity of rotary motion—as opposed to the reciprocating, or up-and-down, motion of the standard auto engine—gives the gas turbine smoother, longer-lasting, practically maintenance-free operation. It is also a simpler device with far fewer moving parts, is lighter and less polluting, and potentially can improve mileage by a third. It can run on a variety of fuels other than gasoline—from perfume to peanut oil, according to one auto executive.

Story Behind It: The principle of the turbine, a vaned wheel spun by an impinging stream of gas or liquid, has been known for centuries. In 1791, John Barber of England patented a gas-turbine engine utilizing heated, expanding gases, but successful commercial devices had to wait for mid-20th-century technology to produce a material able to take the high, continuous heat involved—some 1,750°F. Over the past few decades, a number of demonstration trucks, buses, and cars have been built and tested.

Current Status: In the early 1960s, Chrysler Corporation produced 50 gas-turbine cars and turned them over to the public for test driving. Though driver response was positive, the high hopes for production were dimmed by problems that defied solution at the time, and still do. The device is most efficient at high speed, while cars are often driven at low speed, leading to increased fuel consumption; inherently high noise level and very hot exhaust can be handled but add to cost; and, most important, the continuous high temperature of operation presently calls for extremely expensive materials, raising the cost of manufacturing. New developments in high temperature/low cost ceramics may help the gas turbine fulfill its long promise.

When: 1985–1995.

2. TYPE: STEAM CAR

Advantages: Because the fuel in a steam car is burned in a separate combustion chamber ("external-combustion engine"), almost any kind can be burned—including even solid fuels such as coal or wood if absolutely necessary. The fuel is burned continuously and at atmospheric pressure, resulting in more efficient burning and, hence, less pollution. A highly developed, well-tuned steam engine would emit mostly water vapor, which is harmless, and carbon dioxide, which is not a problem now but may be in the future. The steam car is powerful at low speeds, which eliminates the need for clutch and transmission, and when idling or decelerating it uses almost no fuel. The ride is smooth and silent.

Story Behind It: The first self-propelled, horseless carriage appears to have been powered by steam. In 1769 a French military captain, N. J. Cugnot, designed and built a steam-driven vehicle that could carry four passengers at the grand speed of 2¼ mph. For over a hundred years steam reigned as the major power source in railroads and ships. From the turn of this century through about the mid-1920s, steam-powered cars and buses were running neck and neck with gasoline and electric vehicles in a race for supremacy. In 1906 the Stanley steam car was the fastest automobile in the world, having reached a top speed of 127.66 mph. But the steam and electric types lost out to the internal-combustion engine's lower cost and greater reliability. Current problems with oil supply and air pollution have revived interest in these and other alternative approaches to powering autos.

Current Status: Many pilot models have been built over the years but, consisting of a number of separate units, they are complex and expensive, and they have numerous operational problems, including poor fuel economy, which remain to be overcome.

When: 1990–2000.

3. TYPE: ELECTRIC VEHICLE (EV)

Advantages: The EV uses stored electricity as motive power, which permits instant start; quiet, reliable operation and long life; and no use of power when the car is stopped. This approach is also attractive because batteries can be charged from energy sources which currently cannot otherwise be used in transportation, such as nuclear and solar energy and hydroelectricity. The EV is said to be nonpolluting. This is true for the actual vehicle. The question is whether the environmental problems are merely being transferred to the site of electrical generation.

Story Behind It: The electric car was the first to travel at a mile a minute. Its origins go back to 1800, when Volta invented the first device capable of producing a steady flow of electric current; this was his voltaic pile, predecessor to the wet-cell, fully rechargeable storage battery we know today. The first EV was built by a Scotsman, Robert Anderson, way back in 1839, half a century before the equivalent gasoline-powered car was developed. Toward the end of the 19th century, and well into the 20th, thousands of EVs were built and used. But, as with the steam car, the EV lost ground rapidly to the gasoline-powered cars.

Current Status: The EV was in limbo from 1930 to 1960. Two crises brought it back to life—pollution in the 1960s and fuel shortages in the 1970s. Currently, some two dozen manufacturers are putting out both complete EVs and conversion kits that will permit travel for perhaps 50 to 70 mi. at some 30 to 50 mph (higher speed = shorter range), after which the EV is out of commission for 6 to 8 hr. while its batteries are recharged. (Rapid exchange of the complete set for a charged set is a likely development at some station of the future, assuming no way is found to perform a satisfactory 10-min. charge.) Current designs have as much as half their weight taken up by the one to two dozen lead-acid batteries required to do the job. Most EVs are small and light and, unhappily, cannot mix safely with present-day cars in fast traffic. In sum, current approaches give less performance at higher cost; in addition, the batteries must be replaced every two or three years at a cost of over $500. Still, the EV's unique advantages continue to generate great interest. The federal government is backing a large development program and plans to put thousands of EVs on the road in the next few years for testing

Electric auto charge stations replace gas stations.

and demonstration. New batteries now in the experimental stage promise to more than double the speed and range of current EVs.

When: 1985–2000. Federal officials estimate three to four million EVs could be on the road by the end of the century.

• FUELS OF THE FUTURE •

Background: No one can say when we will run out of petroleum-based fuels. It won't happen fast and it won't happen all at once—but the day will come. Clearly we should be preparing for it. Even the steam car and gas turbine will require some sort of burnable fuel. Currently, the only nonpetroleum fuel available is ethanol, a kind of alcohol that can be made from renewable sources such as grains, sugar crops, and almost any starchy plant, as well as potentially from coal, of which we have ample reserves. Current research suggests a number of other possibilities.

1. TYPE: SYNFUELS

Conversion of coal and midwestern oil shale (a kind of rock) into a synthetic crude oil is one of the most promising possibilities because the resources are abundant and there is already technology for the conversion. Another reason is that syncrude is similar to natural crude (though it can be made cleaner), which simplifies its distribution and handling. But the extraction process is expensive, requires massive facilities, and poses serious environmental problems of its own. Every barrel of oil from shale, for example, requires the mining and processing of 1.5 tons of rock, plus large amounts of water, not easy to come by in the thirsty western states. Several demonstration plants have been built in the U.S., and a program for further development along these lines is part of the federal energy program. Perhaps new extraction processes can be developed that will have less environmental impact.

When: 1985–1995.

2. TYPE: METHANE

Another fuel that can be made from coal is methane, a gas. Although it burns cleaner and has a higher energy density than that of gasoline on a mass basis, it suffers, like other gaseous fuels, from problems of on-board storage and limited power output, which tend to restrict its automotive application. But there is a precedent for use of gaseous fuels; natural gas and propane have been used for years in some limited automotive applications. Also, methane is available as a waste material in some coal mines, and it can be manufactured from various agricultural and other wastes.

When: 1990–2000.

3. TYPE: HYDROGEN

Finally, there is hydrogen, another gas that may turn out to be the ultimate fuel. In liquid form it has 2½ times the energy density of gasoline and produces mainly water as a by-product. But storing it, especially on board the auto, poses tremendous problems. Some gases, like propane, liquefy easily under compression. To liquefy hydrogen requires a temperature of −423°F. For each 30 lb. of this material, storage currently requires a heavy thermos-bottle-type tank weighing 50 lb. An alternative now under development is storage of the hydrogen as a metal hydride. This takes place in a sort of spongy metal box that in itself weighs some 300 lb. and needs 50% more space than a gas tank with equivalent fuel-storage capability. Perhaps some better method can be found. In its gaseous form, hydrogen can be distributed through the present natural-gas pipeline system when that fuel runs out. But perhaps most important, the raw material for hydrogen is water, of which the world supply is virtually unlimited. Energy sources such as nuclear or solar power might supply the needed high energy for breaking up the water into its constituent oxygen and hydrogen. Or perhaps some form of photosynthetic process can be developed to do the job easily and cheaply.

When: 2000 and beyond.

BUT . . . by that time we may also have cars that are directly powered by solar or nuclear energy, or black holes, or antimatter, or . . .

—H.H.

THE PLANETRAN EXPRESS

Shortly before 2000 A.D., transcontinental travel time between New York City and Los Angeles will be reduced to 54 min. if the Planetran system is operational. Should problems related to the negative effect of acceleration on passengers (i.e., feeling 40% heavier in weight) be resolved, the journey may be even faster—an astounding 21 min. Less than two decades later, the mass-transportation system conceived by Dr. Robert Salter, a physicist at Rand Corporation in Santa Monica, Calif., could be extended into South America, Asia, Europe, and Africa.

The tremendous speeds envisioned (up to 14,000 mph) are made possible by electromagnetically propelling cars through evacuated tubes in underground tunnels. The cars will "float" one foot above guideways which directionally control a powerful magnetic field triggered by either a pulse-forming electrical source or a traveling electrical wave oscillated continuously by an alternating-current power supply. Each car will contain its own "superconducting" cable loop producing a high magnetic dipole field in opposition to the guideway field. The repelling action between the two magnetic fields will continuously accelerate the car until its field is reversed at the journey's midpoint. The reversal will decelerate, or "brake," the vehicle for the arrival at the terminal.

The main line will utilize Dallas, Tex., as its midpoint. Each leg will be exactly 1,360 mi. long, to provide equal acceleration and deceleration phases for the cars. This line will service the Eastern, Central, and Pacific Southwest states, with a second main tunnel between Dallas and New York City using Chicago as a midpoint. The latter route will service the Midwest region, providing access for Little Rock, St. Louis, Toledo, and Cleveland. Other linkups will in-

Boarding the Planetran Express—
New York to L.A. in 54 minutes.

clude Boston, San Francisco, and Washington, D.C. States that do not generate sufficient passenger revenue to justify Planetran terminals will be given over exclusively to the airlines, which will also serve to feed travelers into the mainline network.

Because of the tremendous speeds and gravitational forces involved, the tunnels will be bored through solid rock wherever possible, at depths of several hundred feet, following the general curvature of the earth. Each main tunnel will be 40 ft. in diameter and capable of housing four tubes. Two will be used for transporting the Planetran "rocket" cars and the other two will be set up to carry high-speed rail traffic moving freight. The tubes will be evacuated to an atmospheric pressure equivalent to that of 170,000 ft. above sea level and they will be constructed of prestressed concrete capable of withstanding pressures of 10,000 lb. per sq. in. The concrete surface will also be coated by plastic or a glaze, to assist in retaining the high-vacuum state inside the tube. Joints consisting of sleeve clamps fastened over "O-ring" packing will allow critical alignment for the prefabricated concrete sections. Should the tunnel alignment be threatened by earthquake or other disruptive stresses, sensor-controlled jacks—installed between the tubes and the wall of the tunnel—will be able to react almost instantly by means of their roller mountings.

Precise control of any lateral deviation by the car as it races along the guideways is a design "must," to eliminate potentially disastrous physical effects on the passengers. Thanks to recent advances in the state of the art of microelectronic technology, microprocessor computers can now be supplied to monitor this transverse movement. Any errors in the path that are allowing the car to approach the maximum sideways deviation will be continuously detected and corrected by computer signals.

The cars in this system will resemble jet-aircraft cabins of the 1980s. All seats will be gimbal-mounted, rotating forward or backward about a horizontal axis to reduce unpleasant effects of acceleration or deceleration on the travelers. A liquid-helium environment will be designed for the current-carrying cable in the car's bottom, to reduce the temperature to nearly absolute zero ($-459.67°F$). This extremely low temperature is essential for the cable to acquire the superconduction properties necessary for the high-speed operation.

To keep the transit tube at operational vacuum, the sections near the loading terminals will include a series of air locks, designed to bring the car back into normal-atmosphere conditions while passengers are being boarded. Giant "guillotine" doors, operating at microsecond speeds, will open and close to control the increasing (or decreasing) air pressure within each lock as the car passes through. Air bags, partially inflated and placed forward and aft of the vehicle will also help to control the longitudinal flow of air within the tube in addition to doubling for use on emergency stops.

Basic fares will be set at $1 per min. of tube travel. Thus, for a New York City to Los Angeles trip of 54 min., the ticket cost will be $54. Initially, 200-passenger cars, traveling one minute apart in each direction, are being contemplated, to produce revenues of about $96 billion dollars annually. If demand evolves, 500-passenger cars, spaced on 10-sec. "headways," may be substituted.

The total cost for Planetran is estimated to be about $250 billion. Nearly one half ($122 billion) will go for construction of subterranean tunnels and aboveground terminals. Another $63 billion is slated for the evacuated tubes, which will require "roughing pumps" (two to the mile, rated at 2,600 cu. ft. per min.) to produce the vacuum. The remaining $65 billion will be allocated for the system's hardware (cars, computer controls, etc.).

This staggering cost is justified by the urgent need to conserve world energy supplies. Current studies predict that the capital investment needed for energy purposes in 2020 A.D. will reach a mind-boggling $40 trillion ($40,000,000,000,000). The funds that will be available, if present trends continue, will be only one fourth of that amount, prophesying a "Doomsday" situation unless radical savings are effected. The shortfall can be partially met by installation of the Planetran system, which would reduce world energy consumption by 12%. By design, the energy for the system is almost totally used for kinetic movement of the cars. With equal numbers of accelerating and decelerating cars in transit at any given point, energy extracted from the system by accelerating cars is returned by the decelerating vehicles, producing an efficiency of almost 98%.

The new tunnels will have supplemental uses as well. For U.S. defense, there will be 21,000 mi. of underground tubes capable of housing military installations or dispersed command posts, should the need arise. But the tunnels can also be used to carry pipelines for movement of oil, gas, water, and waste materials, affording fast transport at lower cost. Communication networks can be interspersed along the tubes, and slurried, bulk materials can be moved as well.

With worldwide completion of the Planetran concept, no two points on the face of the earth will be more than a few hours apart.

—W.K.

HYDROGEN POWER

Predictor GABRIEL BOULADON is an engineer and inventor who specializes in new systems of transportation and energy. He has done work on the electric car and invented both an accelerated moving pavement and a pneumatic-tube train. The author of numerous articles in French and English on transportation, Mr. Bouladon lives and works in Grenoble, France.

· PREDICTIONS ·

1988

· One-thousand-seat aircraft.
· More than 50% of external body for commercial aircraft of reinforced plastic.

1990

• Synthetic fuel from coal available at gas stations at competitive price with natural sources of gasoline.

1995

• Automatic guiding system for traffic in large cities by means of a small on-board car computer.

2000

• Automatic freight trains with 10 or 20 trains running at the same speed, thus increasing by 100% the capacity of a rail track as it is presently operated.

2010

• First commercial hydrogen car.

2020

• First commercial hydrogen aircraft.
• Large hydrogen production from water via solar energy.

FUSION REACTOR BECOMES MAJOR ENERGY SOURCE

Predictor DR. BRUNO COPPI has been a professor of physics at the Massachusetts Institute of Technology in Cambridge since 1969. His special areas of expertise include nuclear-fusion research, theoretical plasma physics, and space and astrophysics. Dr. Coppi has developed the Alcator program, which has brought us significantly closer to the realization of a fusion reactor.

• PREDICTIONS •

1982–1992

• The scientific feasibility of a fusion reactor employing isotopes of hydrogen as fuel should be demonstrated. The experimental principle adopted is that of using intense magnetic fields to confine high-temperature plasmas (fully ionized gases at about 10 million degrees). In view of their attractive features (availability of fuels, lack of radioactive reaction products, possibility of evolving efficient and "clean" systems), fusion reactors can be expected to become one of the major energy sources in the future.

1993–2030

• Fusion reactors will evolve from the stage of physics experiments devoted to proving their scientific feasibility to the stage of power stations. The types of fuels that will be adopted will gradually improve so as to minimize the activation of the materials employed in the reactor, the degree of thermal pollution, etc. Thus tritium—a radioactive isotope of hydrogen—will be gradually phased out as a fuel, and only deuterium or a mixture of deuterium and helium-three (a rare isotope of helium) will be used. The development of fusion reactors for propulsion will be undertaken.

EARTHQUAKE PREVENTION

Predictor DR. WILLARD LIBBY is a chemist, professor, and writer who received the 1960 Nobel Prize in chemistry for his work in developing the "atomic time clock," a method of radiocarbon dating. Other awards for his pioneering work include a gold medal from the American Institute of Chemists and the Albert Einstein Award. Dr. Libby, a longtime staff member at the University of Chicago and the University of California, is the author of *Radiocarbon Dating* and *Environmental Geology*.

• PREDICTIONS •

1985

• Jewel-quality synthetic diamonds will be developed.
• Economical diamond transistors will be available.
• The history of the earth in the first billion years, forming the continental masses, will finally be learned.

1990

• The origin of the earth's magnetic field will be discovered.
• Long-range weather prediction will be accurate.
• There will be economical chemical synthesis in factories in outer space.

- The mining of the seas and desalinization of seawater will be economically feasible.
- The origin of life will be discovered and understood.

2000

- A reliable method of earthquake prediction will be developed.
- A cure for cancer will be discovered.
- There will be local control of weather conditions.
- Widespread colonization of desert land will begin.
- There will be nuclear-powered space travel and transport.
- We will use nuclear power to make hydrogen from water. Automobiles and aircraft will be propelled by hydrogen.

2010

- Practical and controlled thermonuclear-fusion energy will be a reality.
- Intercontinental travel will be done in rockets which fly outside the earth's atmosphere.
- There will be a manned laboratory on the moon.

2020

- We will be able to prevent earthquakes by injecting water into wells along faults in the earth.

ROBOTICS

Predictor ALAN THOMPSON is the editor of *Robotics Age* magazine, a quarterly publication devoted to the science of robotics. A native of Virginia, he holds degrees in physics and mathematics from the Massachusetts Institute of Technology. Before founding *Robotics Age,* Mr. Thompson was a member of the NASA Robotics Research Program at the California Institute of Technology's Jet Propulsion Laboratory, and he continues to serve as a robotics consultant for JPL and other organizations.

• PREDICTIONS •

It is extremely difficult to tie technological developments to any particular date, since there are so many variables that influence such progress. The amount of available research funding, changing economic pressures, and especially the random occurrence of insight on the part of individual researchers are all strong factors in any breakthrough. Therefore, where noted, I will base my comments on an assumption about the level of research effort needed to realize the particular result.

One prediction easy to make is that the early 1980s will see major growth in robots as a hobby. As a direct consequence of the current microcomputer revolution, people will discover that experimenting with robots is far more rewarding than just playing computer games, and their interests will be served by an increasing number of robot kits and related products, as well as a transfer of technical knowledge from the professional researcher to the amateur, as has occurred for microcomputers.

Although these hobbyist robots will begin largely as toys, new technical results will be rapidly assimilated, leading to increasingly sophisticated capabilities in home robots. Prize competitions for intelligent robots (such as those offered by the International Robot Foundation) will stimulate development of robots performing practical household chores. By the mid-1980s, home-built robots could be emptying wastebaskets and doing some of the vacuuming, etc. However, the availability of mass-produced robot appliances for the nontechnical consumer will probably come a good deal later.

The mid-1980s will be a productive time for professional researchers in robotics and "artificial intelligence." Computer programs that are specialists in particular areas will be routinely used by the medical, legal, and other professions, conversing with their users in typed English or other human languages. With continued effort, developments in specialized techniques and computer hardware could result in research robots with a sense of sight adequate for performing a variety of industrial and domestic tasks that were previously not feasible to automate. It is likely that by the late 1980s, robots will be able to converse with their owners by means of normally spoken sentences (no pauses between words).

On the industrial front, robots will continue to take the place of humans in dangerous, tedious, or otherwise unwanted jobs. By the late 1980s, most repetitive manufacturing and assembly will be performed by robots. The increased productivity made possible by robots will grow to be a significant anti-inflationary element in the economy. Contrary to conventional ideas, however, increased automation through the use of robots will probably not result in unemployment. Decreased production costs will permit continued expansion in many areas and an increase in the standard of living (assuming that the economy is free to respond to these changes).

The period from the mid-1990s through the turn of the century will perhaps bring the maturation of the robot as a consumer appliance. In addition to functioning as a servant, the domestic or personal robot will eventually serve as a competent librarian and adviser, through its access to other computers with vast information-processing resources.

The development of space as a resource and habitable environment will be made practical through the use of robots. Orbital facilities built largely by robots will provide countless new industrial opportunities, as well as making virtually unlimited solar power available on earth. Ultimately, "self-replicating" robot factories could be sent to other planets to create a self-sustaining economy before the first human settlers ever arrive. These systems would include robots that reproduce themselves as well as build those that produce the materials and habitats needed to support human life—all using materials obtained from the planet itself.

The prospect of machines with intelligence invariably brings to mind the popular science-fiction theme of the human creators losing control of their bright mechanical progeny with predictably disastrous results. To be sure, no hypothetical "laws of robotics" can prevent the threat of robots intentionally programmed as weapons. (The cruise missile is a prime example.) It is important to point out, however, that if or when a robot or computer attains creative intelligence comparable to that of a human (instead of merely reproducing programmed behavior that mimics aspects of human intelligence), as a nonliving entity such a machine would have no basis for choosing values apart from those intrinsic in its programming. Short of being explicitly told to do so, an intelligent machine could have no reason either to harm or to protect humans. However, the potential for abuse is quite real, and appropriate safeguards must necessarily be constructed.

COMPUTER NOMINATED FOR NOBEL PRIZE

Predictor MALCOLM PELTU, editor of the British publications *Computer Weekly* and *Dataweek,* is also computer consultant to *New Scientist* magazine. A former employee of the British computer manufacturer ICL, Mr. Peltu specializes in interpreting the way information technology (computers, microelectronics, telecommunications, etc.) affects personal, social, and working life-styles.

• PREDICTIONS •

1982–1984

• Computers accepted as expert professional consultants; for example, as medical diagnosticians, tax advisers, oil-exploration specialists, and chemical analysts.

1984–1986

• Computers widely used as automatic translators of texts by international bodies.

1985–1987

• Computer program beats world chess champion.

1986–1988

• Traditional office desk and filing cabinet largely replaced by an electronic, computer-controlled "work station" which handles all voice, text, and pictorial information storage and processing.

1986–1989

• Traditional mail services largely replaced by the use of digital electronic transmissions; for example, between word processors (computerized typewriters) in the office, and between home computers.

1988–1990

• Computer program makes original scientific discovery that is considered worthy of a Nobel Prize.

1990–1992

• Opening of first full-production, commercial, automated factory in which there is no human intervention between the receipt of an order and the dispatch of goods.
• Keyboard ceases to be main method of communicating between a person and a computer, and is replaced by direct-speech communication (including automatic typewriter, which accepts speech input and then produces the typed version); visual recognition of text, pictures, and objects by the computer; and pictorial and animated displays.

1993–1996

• Traditional classroom-based teaching largely replaced by the widespread use of computer-assisted learning devices, including lectures and activities recorded on video discs; these devices will be located mainly at home, in community centers, etc., rather than in buildings devoted solely to education.
• Widespread use of computer programs written by computers, i.e., self-programming computers.

1995–1998

• Fully mobile robots that can recognize objects and respond to human speech; widespread use of such robots in dangerous environments; for example, undersea exploration and maintenance of oil rigs.

1997–2000

• Medical, commercial, and military use of techniques that directly link human brain to computer or microprocessor; for example, to control artificial limbs and overcome blindness and other physical disabilities, or to control aircraft and missile launchers where split-second timing is vital.

2010

· Robot that can cross busy highway without being hit.

2020

· Robot developed with a measurable IQ of over 100.

2030

· Computers and robots become more intelligent than humans and make major economic, social, and technical decisions using reasoning that is beyond human comprehension.

SMART MACHINES

Predictor EARL C. JOSEPH is a staff futurist working on research and long-range planning for the Sperry Univac Division of Sperry Corporation. He is also director of the Minnesota Futurists as well as futurist in residence at the Science Museum of Minnesota. Mr. Joseph has published over 90 papers and contributed to numerous books.

· PREDICTIONS ·

1. SMART MACHINES

Office, factory, home, transportation, and leisure/sport machines which incorporate microcomputers, sensors, and/or actuators for making commonly used machines considerably more functional, versatile, safer, friendlier, easier to use, and capable—that is, for making machines smart. Predicted for initial use by 1983 ± three years; predicted for common use by 1990 ± five years.

2. PEOPLE AMPLIFIERS

Future calculatorlike portable devices which assist an average person to perform as a pseudoexpert; for example, microcomputer appliances like a smart management implement, smart doctor implement, smart auditor implement, smart teacher implement, smart politician implement, smart lawyer implement, etc. Predicted initiation date by 1985 ± five years; predicted for common use by 1990 ± five years.

3. SMART AGRICULTURE MACHINE

A single energy pass (over the land) machine for tilling and conditioning the soil, planting seeds, applying fertilizer, pesticide, fungicide, some moisture inhibitors and plant-growth controls via real-time soil sensing and conditioning, microcomputers, and biodegradable encapsulated (pill) techniques. This will allow farming to become less energy and capital equipment intensive. Predicted initiation date by 1986 ± four years; predicted for common use by 1990 ± five years.

4. SMART AUTOMOBILE—COLLISION-AVOIDANCE TYPE

An automobile made smart through the incorporation (imbedding) of microcomputers, sensors, and control actuator electronics, which is virtually accidentless throughout its life. Predicted initiation date by 1988 ± five years; predicted for common use by 1990 ± five years.

5. SCHOOL ON A WAFER

A portable (carried or worn) communications-linked appliance cast on a piece of semiconductor silicon which gives a person access via a machine to all school-related activities that now occur in a physical school building—thus saving considerable energy (now spent on traveling to/from schools; heating, cooling, maintaining, and erecting schools). Predicted initiation date by 1990 ± five years; predicted for common use by 2000 ± 10 years.

6. COMPUTERS ON A WAFER

A multiple set of computers, memory, hard wired programs, sensors and/or communications circuits all integrated onto a single wafer of silicon—e.g., a component-computer-system-on-a-wafer for imbedding into other devices and machines. Predicted initiation by 1988 ± five years; predicted in common use by 1995 ± 10 years.

7. OFFICE OF THE FUTURE ON A WAFER

A portable (carried or worn) electronic communications-linked appliance, cast onto a piece of highly circuit-integrated silicon, which gives to an individual via a machine access to office-related information activities that now require going to a physical office building. Predicted initiation date by 1988 ± five years; predicted for common use by 2000 ± 10 years.

8. SMART AUTOMOBILE—DRIVERLESS TYPE

An automobile with imbedded microcomputer, sensor, and control actuators for self-operation via voice command which also incorporates collision-avoidance electronic hardware. Predicted initiation date by 1990 ± five years; predicted for common use by 2000 ± 10 years.

9. ETHNOTRONICS

Future smart people amplifier computer appliances which are portable (carried or worn) and which are far more capable than present-day calculators that allow an individual to have access to

societies' knowledge for real-time application to assist and amplify an individual in whatever he/she is doing. Predicted to start by 1990 ± five years; predicted for common use by 2000 ± 10 years.

10. MICROMINIATURIZED MOBILE FARM FACTORY

A single energy pass agriculture factory machine for converting mature harvest into final packaged and palletized products—e.g., cookies, corn flakes, canned or frozen peas, dresses, etc. That is, a microminiaturized and microcomputerized machine that harvests a field of "cookies" (e.g., multicropped and intermixed rows of wheat, oats, sugar beets, spices, and a crop convertible into packaging material). An energy crisis forced new direction. Predicted date of initiation by 1988 ± five years; predicted for common use by 1995 ± 10 years.

11. NON-THROW-AWAY SOCIETY

An energy and material crisis imposed future in which things (clothes, machines, autos, buildings, etc.) are designed and manufactured to last at least 10 times as long as they do today. Predicted to start by 1995 ± 10 years; predicted to be common by 2000 ± 10 years.

12. ALL-WIN POSTINDUSTRIAL AGE

A future in which we use our present knowledge for making systems (machines, government, business, things in general, etc.) which are designed to last 10 times as long as they do now. This develops a society which is less energy/material/labor/capital intensive in their manufacture. Society wins by making (freeing up) energy/materials/labor/capital so that the society enjoys a higher quality of life. Such systems are designed for self-repairability and self-adaptability, are fail-safe and fault-tolerant (don't make errors), have piecemeal updatability (allow innovations to be added), and are convivial (easy to use and friendly)—thus allowing individuals and society to win with more symbiotic surroundings. Since systems last longer and use less resources in their implementation, this would allow them to be both less costly for individuals (users) and at the same time more profitable for business—thus both individuals and business win. Predicted

The Cookie Farm.

to start by 1990 ± five years; predicted for common use by 2010 ± 15 years.

EINSTEIN'S THEORY NEEDS REVISION

Predictor DR. JAMES TREFIL, a professor of physics at the University of Virginia, specializes in elementary-particle physics, fluid mechanics, and cancer therapy. He is the author of two physics textbooks and more than 100 articles, which have appeared in both professional journals and such popular magazines as *Science Digest*, *Saturday Review*, and *Popular Science*.

· PREDICTIONS ·

1985

· Experiments now being built will show that the basic particles that make up all matter are unstable, but that they will be around long enough to last until the end of the solar system.

1987

· New generations of experiments will show that Einstein's theory of general relativity is wrong in some predictions and has to be modified.

1990

• Particles capable of traveling faster than the speed of light will be discovered.

1992

• Despite massive efforts, the process of fusion will still not be demonstrated in a laboratory. The energy burden in the U.S. will be carried by coal and nuclear reactors.

2010

• Satellites high above the earth will collect sunlight, convert it to microwaves, and beam the power to earth. In this year the first energy from extraterrestrial sources will arrive at a receiving station in Arizona.

2015

• The first permanent colony on the moon will open. Its primary function will be mining material for satellites.

2020

• Work will begin on the first space colony—a doughnut-shaped ring capable of housing 10,000 people.

2030

• By the end of the period, in spite of a great deal of searching, we will still have received no messages from extraterrestrials. We will start to get used to the idea that we are alone in the universe.

DEATH NO LONGER PERMANENT

Predictor F. M. ESFANDIARY is a futurist, writer, lecturer, designer, and consultant. He has worked with the U.N. and taught at both the New School for Social Research in New York and at the University of California in Los Angeles. A frequent contributor to *The New York Times*, Mr. Esfandiary is the author of *Optimism One*, *Up-Wingers*, and *Telespheres*.

1982–1992

• Accelerated breakdown of industrial-age systems. Rapid shift to postindustrial decentralized telespheres: teleducation, electronic mail, telebanking and electronic funds transfer, teleshopping, teleconferencing, automated and robotic manufacture, telemedicine, teleconomics, decision making via rapid referendums and direct initiatives, electronic communities, etc.
• Continued breakdown of kinship, family, marriage and exclusivity. Rapid spread of new life-styles: singlehood, nonexclusive couplings and triads, nonparenthood and shared parenthood, mobilias (fluid group arrangements), and global networks of friendships.
• Continued shift from nationalism to transnationals, common markets, subcontinental blocs, continentalism, international infrastructures, world economy, global mobility, and global consciousness.
• Continued decline in the relative powers of the U.S. and the U.S.S.R. Accelerated spread of wealth, power, and information across the planet.
• Continued slowdown of world population growth.
• Steady introduction of private rapid transit (PRT)—monocabs, monorails, horizontal movers, ultrarapid magnetic trains, and automated guideways. Accelerated air travel. The beginning of freefly via jetpacks or rocket belts.
• Extensive mapping of the human brain.
• Extensive mapping of genes. More and more diseases and disabilities treated through genetics.

1990s

• Self-control of pain and moods and continuous telemonitoring of vital body functions via implanted electrodes.
• Beginning of head-to-head communication via implanted microtransceivers.
• Beginning of new Age of Limitless Abundance.

1995–2010

• Procreation via ova and sperm selection from sex cell banks (telegenesis). Fertilization and gestation entirely out of the body (in vitro). Gender distinctions increasingly irrelevant. Each new life totally planned, totally monitored, totally wanted. Children brought up by many parenting figures.
• Significant improvement of humanity's gene pool. Significant heightening of everyone's intelligence.

2000

• Indefinite life expectancy. Significant slowdown of aging. Tens of millions over 100 years old and going strong. Death mainly accidental, but not permanent. Burial and cremation rapidly giving way to deep-freeze suspension.

2000–2020

• Superabundant resources, ultraintelligent machines, global life, accelerated space colonization, and hyperliberated values (the new psychology of abundance and nonexclusivity) all coalesce and help phase out money economics, profit motive, retail merchandising, taxation, employment for livelihood, and global imbalances in wealth.

2000–2030

• Popular travel options: orbital cruises, satellite hopping, grand tours of solar system.
• Rapid emergence of posthumans—a new species arising from the coalescence of humans and ultraintelligent machines.

2010

• Most above projections considered absurdly modest. These and many other advances will have interfaced to accelerate growth and create marvel-filled worlds difficult to project today.

2010–2030

• Planet Earth on a 24-hour "day." All services available via telespheres day and night. Solar satellites cancel out day/night cycles. Communities regulate desired light inflow.

NO CURE FOR CANCER, NO CONTROL OF WEATHER, NO SPACE COLONIES

Predictor DR. HULEN B. WILLIAMS, chemist and educator, is dean of the College of Chemistry and Physics at Louisiana State University in Baton Rouge. He is the author of several textbooks in physical chemistry for the life sciences and is a frequent contributor to professional journals dealing with chemical education, geochemistry, and organic chemistry.

• PREDICTIONS •

1982–1992

CHEMISTRY

The most significant advances will be made in the area of biochemistry and microbiology.

Many virus diseases will come under control because of increased knowledge about their biochemistry and structure.

The major problems associated with arteriosclerosis will be solved in this time span, and the metabolic diseases now known that result from the absence of certain enzymes will be controlled or cured, although new diseases will be discovered.

Important new advances will be made in genetic engineering and will continue far into the 21st century. The production of specific peptides and proteins of great biological significance will be engineered.

New technology (techniques and equipment) will lead to a great unfolding of the details of biochemical activity (molecular biological processes) going on within the living cell.

COMMUNICATIONS

There will be two-way and probably portable TV/radio/telephone service for a substantial fraction of the population, perhaps with Social Security numbers as "telephone" numbers. This subscription or pay service will provide merchandising opportunities in many forms: catalog information, opinion polling, educational services, banking services, tax paying, etc.

COMPUTERS AND COMPUTING

By 1990 the price/performance ratio of computers will be about one sixteenth of its current value. As a result, the cost of the hardware portion of a computer system will be almost negligible, and in many cases computer hardware will be free to customers who buy the software for the system.

Software development is a labor-intensive effort, and custom-designed systems will be very expensive. This problem will be exacerbated by an extreme shortage of computer specialists, particularly those with postgraduate training, since the job market will continue to make it economically unfeasible to go to graduate school. The problem will feed on itself inasmuch as most of those who go to graduate school will go into industry after graduation, thereby reducing the supply of teachers of computer specialists.

More visible to the general public will be the continued automation of performance and problem diagnosis of automobiles, and there will be home computers for games, education, message exchange, appliances, energy systems, security systems, "mail," etc.

ECONOMICS

The role of the individual will continue to diminish. Industry will become more socialized. There will be increasing reliance on pension funds for industrial capital. Nationalization will occur for some or all railroads, natural resources, health services, and international trade. "Make-work," or subsidized employment, will increase markedly.

HOUSING

Cluster/condominium housing will become the norm, with subscription access to amusements (pool, game rooms, films, entertainment space) and food service (growing and preparing). Company housing of this nature will develop as a part of employment arrangements, with such facilities integral with company-sponsored home-to-work transportation.

1993–2030

During this period there will come on the scene:
1. Reasonably self-sufficient and enclosed farmlands.
2. Major advancement in the management of the world's fresh water.
3. Effective management of pollution and waste.
4. Earthquake management through lubrication of faults.
5. Alternate explanation(s) of the "red shift."
6. Cures for some forms of cancer.
7. Continuing, though perhaps now unimagined, developments in genetic engineering.
8. Almost total control of viruses and viral diseases.
9. With particular regard to computers and computing, foundations have been laid for an interesting phenomenon, the onset of which will probably occur early in this period. Computer hardware will be so complex and so powerful that we will rely increasingly upon computer systems to "program themselves." Research in natural language processing, using the computer's power to develop and test its own programs under human guidance, will begin to become practical. The long-term result will be that by the year 2020, individual users, armed with three or four orders of magnitude more computing power than previously available, will have simple procedures to follow to get the computers to solve their specific problems. The picture of a single manager operating a large bank in this way is not farfetched. The societal impact of this possibility is difficult to imagine.

Some wished-for developments that will *not* occur by 2030:
1. Practical fusion power.
2. Practical microwave energy relays in space.
3. Space colonies.
4. Controlled weather.
5. Demonstrated existence of gravity waves.
6. A universal cure for cancer.
7. "Seeing" *inside* the atom.

8

PREDICTIONS ON
YOUR LEISURE

1987

You will enjoy laser holography via your TV set. Projected figures and objects will be fully rounded out in three dimensions.

1989–1992

In basketball, the baskets will be raised from 10 feet to 12 feet.

1998

Built into your clothing will be electronic gadgets that enable you to change the color, pattern, and shape of the suit or dress you are wearing.

COMING ATTRACTIONS

Predictor ARTHUR KNIGHT is a film critic and author who is chairman of the history and criticism program at the University of Southern California Division of Cinema. The film critic for *Hollywood Reporter* and *Westways*, he has been a guest lecturer at many U.S. universities and a juror at most international film festivals. Mr. Knight is the author of *The Liveliest Art*, *The Hollywood Style*, and *The History of Sex in the Movies*.

· PREDICTIONS ·

1983

· Video discs will be in full competition with the present cassettes for home viewing of feature films on TV receivers. They will be sold like phonograph records, but the stylus will be a laser beam.

1983–2030

· Boy will still meet girl, but their costumes will be different from those worn today. And despite computer efforts to anticipate audience tastes, films will still come in cycles, and many will fail.

1984

· The major studios of today will have withdrawn completely from

production but will handle the financing and distribution of movies made by so-called independent companies, which will dominate the field.

1985

· Video tape will replace celluloid film.
· Satellites will provide at least 300 channels of programming to home video viewers.

1986

· Large-screen TV will replace film in theaters, with theater chains serviced by cable from a single TV center.

1987

· Complete computerization of all special effects and matte process shots.
· Laser cinematography (or holography)—a true 3-D without glasses.
· A laser-created "theater in the round," where life-sized figures will be perceived as on a stage.

1988

· Aldous Huxley's "Feelies" will finally arrive—but they won't last. [Feelies are movies where the spectators hold on to knobs attached to their seats and feel the sensations being acted out on the screen.]

TV VIEWING
BECOMES CREATIVE

Predictor NICHOLAS JOHNSON is the chairman of the National Citizens Communications Lobby in Washington, D.C. Prior to holding that post, he served on the Federal Communications Commission for seven years. The youngest person ever appointed to the FCC, Mr. Johnson was a controversial figure because he advocated reform. Mr. Johnson is also the author of several books, including *How to Talk Back to Your Television Set*, *Life before Death in the Corporate State*, and *Broadcasting in America*.

1982–2030

• Diversity and range of choice. The trend toward increased diversity and range of choice for the consumer of radio and television product will continue. This is represented by an increase in the number of stations, alternative networks, cable television, pay broadcasting, superstations via cable, and proposals for direct satellite-to-home-earth-station distribution.

• Time binding. Viewer choice over radio and television product will increasingly provide audience control over the time when programming is received. This practice radically alters the relationship between the broadcaster-advertiser combine and the audience. Material will continue increasingly to be available at the time a member of the audience wants it rather than at the time the broadcaster wishes to distribute it—as through the audio-taping and video-taping facilities already available in the market.

• Consumer as editor. We have already seen the beginnings of the substitution of editing by readers for editing by publishers in written material available to subscribers of electronic data bases through key-word searches. Related technologies will make it possible for the audience to search audio and video material according to their own dictates as well. Thus, with sufficient video material available for ready access on-line, a potential viewer could search through the data base for his or her favorite politicians, actors, or musicians and put together his or her own variety show.

• Audience creation. There will continue to be an increase in the quantity of audio and video material created by the audience (as well as edited by them). This is already true of home audio and video taping.

• Related but alternative uses of time and technology. An automobile commuter may have the radio turned on but be using a citizens band transmitter rather than an AM radio receiver. Someone in a home or office may be watching a television screen but be seeing displayed upon it a response to his or her computer programming rather than the product of television program producers. The principal competition for the ABC television network is increasingly Radio Shack rather than CBS. The three networks can no longer count on 100 million Americans watching their output every evening, like the blind following the bland.

A NEW CHAPTER IN PUBLISHING

Predictor JOHN GARDNER, one of America's most gifted and original authors, has written short stories, novels, biography, criticism, poetry, and children's books. He first gained national attention with the publication of *The Wreckage of Agathon* in 1970. Other novels *(The Sunlight Dialogues* and *Nickel Mountain)* and a collection of short stories followed, and in 1976 he won the National Book Critics' award for fiction for *October Light*. In 1978 he wrote *On Moral Fiction*, in which he investigates the state of contemporary writing.

People have been predicting the death of the novel, and of fiction in general, for years, claiming the art of fiction will be beaten out by TV and so on. It's not true. There will always be people who especially like music, others who especially like the visual arts, others who like bowling. And since TV and film are completely different from fiction on the page—they work differently and give different pleasures—fiction will remain strong as long as there are human beings. What certainly *will* happen within the next generation is that people who would rather watch TV or film than read a book will have far richer opportunities to watch TV or film. There will be TV cassettes which enable people to collect TV-film libraries the way they now collect long-playing records. Within the 80s the video-disc and cassette industry will open wide, and the publishing industry will be forced to develop its true and natural audience, readers, hunting them out in ways it has never thought of doing before and reaching them by new techniques.

One result, I think, will be a boom in children's literature by children. There have always been a great many child writers in America—the winners of the National Scholastic contest alone would fill a high-quality library. In the 80s, those writers will begin to find publishers, and though their main readership will be other children, their work will begin to be taken seriously by adults as well. The large field of scholars who study children's literature will recognize that child writers have their own kind of genius and are worth serious study not just as interesting children but as full-fledged writers; thus children will begin to be liberated as people, and their ideas and gripes will become a part of the total social concern.

The present boom in women's literature will continue, and publishers' interest in minorities will increase significantly. With so many kinds of new writing coming out, publishing will become increasingly local; that is, New York will continue to be the main home of publishing, but regional publishing will become the starting point for new writers. And as more and more small presses start up, the emphasis on graphics—too costly for the big publishers who cannot survive without large distribution—will increase. We can look for books with more photographs and illustrations, but because those books will come from all over America, we will have to look harder for the particular book we want. New kinds of book clubs will help here: book clubs which promote not just best-sellers but books of all kinds—often books sold by subscription. (Instead of printing one huge edition and paying warehouse costs, publishers will make plates for a printing, sell subscriptions through magazines and so on, and print to order by computerized processes. Result: a richer field to draw on.)

There is also a gloomy side to all this. As more and more books are printed regionally, increasing the competition with those publishers interested only in making money, the commercially oriented publishers will turn out more and more fake books, i.e., books written to order by groups of specialists responding to marketing research. Thus as the music industry invented fake rock groups like the Monkees to compete with real groups like the Beatles, book publishers will create more fake writers, that is, committee books of no enduring worth. By the year 2000, that enterprise will fail completely. The fake books will be beaten out by TV and film, because they're not for real readers in the first place, and though real readers may be fooled for a while, they will eventually rebel.

The biggest boom in the publishing industry, between now and 2000, will be in the area of science fiction or speculative fiction—science, fantasy, etc. Children, women, and minorities will play a large part in this, but the main change will be in the respectability of the field. At present there are a number of absolutely serious artists, not just hacks, working in the area of speculative fiction; but they are still considered relatively second-class. But the tendency of fiction in America has always been a transformation of low-class forms into high-class forms. (Consider how, analogously, jazz began as a low-class form and has now come to dominate serious composing in America.)

The fundamental principle of all this is that large publishers cannot make a go of works of fiction which do not sell in at least the area of 10,000 copies per edition, whereas small presses can make a profit with only 3,000 to 10,000 copies. (Less warehouse expense, among other things.) Thus the small publishers are fit to survive, as Darwin might say, in our increasingly changing world, while large publishers are more and more weighted down by their own inertia. Small publishers' best writers will reach the big publishers and get vast distribution, but the kinds of commercial concern which make big publishers choose one kind of writing instead of another will no longer be operative. The choices will be made by small publishers, to a large extent, and fiction will be better for it.

THE ARTISTIC EXPLOSION

Predictor RICHARD KOSTELANETZ, born in New York City in 1940, has evaluated the future of art not only in several critical books, including *The End of Intelligent Writing: Literary Politics in America,* but also in several anthologies of art, literature, and criticism. His articles are included in *The New American Arts, Beyond Left and Right,* and *Future's Fiction.*

The future of the arts will be determined by two different kinds of developments—first, changes within the society of art, and second, new technological developments. It is common to speak of the former as "short-term" and the latter as "long-term," but an invention that is rapidly disseminated can have immediate effects upon an art. Consider what the typewriter did to literature or what cheap photocopying is doing to publishing or what acrylics have done to painting.

In every art, we are presently witnessing the hypercommercialization of the established art industry, because of both increased production expenses and absentee (conglomerate) ownership. The obverse of increased profits is a declining interest in new works that are perceived to be less immediately profitable. Thus, in every art, especially in America, we see the growth of alternative, less commercial enterprises, which produce and distribute art less for money than for love. In the theater, these enterprises have been called "off-Broadway" and, when off-Broadway became too commercialized, "off-off-Broadway." The analogue in literature is alternative publishing; in the visual arts, it is the network of publicly funded "alternative spaces" that have recently sprung up across the country.

One reason for this continuing shift is the increasing number of Americans who consider creative art to be their primary activity. In the past two decades, the number of serious poets in the U.S. has doubled, the number of painters has tripled, and the number of people seriously pursuing modern dance has quadrupled; and this artistic population will predictably increase. As long as the established art industries remain so closed to new work, the most talented young people are more likely to work in alternative institutions, and these will surely become the principal repositories of emerging excellence in every art.

In part because of this commercialism, poets and fiction writers, for instance, will be exploring alternative means of publication—of making their works publicly known. We have already seen the beginnings of this development in the popularization of the "poetry reading," in which a work is read aloud to an audience, often before it appears in print. There will be more interest in the broadcasting media, such as audio and video, not only for the transmission of such readings, but also as "paper" on which the literary artist may work directly, creating works of literature that will exist exclusively within the new media.

Technological inventions are easier to imagine than predict, in part because few of us are intimately aware of the procedures leading to their development. Will there be better paints than the new acrylics? Will there be a new sculptural material with the solidity of steel and the light weight of balsa wood? Could humanized anthropomorphic machines execute spectacular choreography better than live dancers? Could a single electronic instrument imitate the richly various sounds of a symphony orchestra? Could a typewriter be developed that would type out words as they are spoken? Could a television system reproduce images that are present only in one's head? Can psychotropic chemicals increase memory or other mental powers? Could computerized information retrieval give the writer of this essay immediate access to a far larger and more systemized library than he can keep in his office? Indeed, could an essay like this one be written by a machine that is far more intelligent, in the human sense, than any we have so far seen? My own prediction is that most, if not all, of these technologies will exist by my 90th birthday, which will occur in 2030.

NOTES FOR THE FUTURE

Predictor JON APPLETON is a music professor at Dartmouth College in Hanover, N.H., who specializes in electronic music. He is one of three inventors of the Synclavier, a minicomputerized synthesizer capable of duplicating the sounds of 25 musical instruments individually and putting them together to create a full orchestra.

· PREDICTIONS ·

1985

· If you can play one instrument, you can play any instrument. Inexpensive digital synthesizers can be connected to your guitar, piano, or wind or brass instrument. When you play your instrument, the sound coming from the loudspeakers will be that of any instrument you select.

1990

· Digital recording will enable amateur musicians to play along with prerecorded professionals in a truly interactive expansion of "Music Minus One" (a record firm that produces recordings leaving out one instrument, so that the amateur musician can play along with his own instrument). The amateur instrumentalist will be able to control the tempo of the performance as well as start and stop at any point in the music.

1995

· The music lover, through an extension of home high-fidelity equipment, will be able to "lead" or "conduct" his or her favorite performing ensemble, past or present, through the use of a sensing device like an electrified baton. The sensing device will control the tempo, loudness, or location of the music in the room.

2000

· As Max Mathews at the Bell Telephone Laboratories has pointed out, playing the correct notes of a composition is a skill which can be done by a computer, leaving the human performer free to concentrate on those aspects which make one performance different from another. New musical instruments will then appear which make this kind of performing activity possible.

2030

· Our musical preferences will be stored in a computer data bank. A "phonograph" will be a pocket-sized transmitter connected directly to one's brain. The transmitter will sense our "musical preference moods" and communicate this information directly to the computer data bank, where an original piece of music will be composed to suit our needs and taste at the particular moment. This music will appear to be an old favorite or an exciting new musical concept.

FUTURE POP

Predictor CHARLIE GILLETT is the author of *The Sound of the City*, a history of pop music from 1950 to 1970. He is codirector of Oval Records, a small record label based in South London.

· PREDICTIONS ·

1982–1992

The decline and fall of the major record companies will accelerate, making space for a loose network of small, localized labels which will reflect the tastes and inspiration of their owners. In particular, these smaller companies will find the music which interests and excites a teenaged audience, as punk and new-wave music did in Britain in the late 1970s. Currently, such labels and bands are blocked by conservative radio programmers, and the newcomers will have to bypass that medium by making videos which can be shown on cable TV and bought by kids whose parents have video playback equipment.

With video as the main outlet for new music, a different kind of performer will come into music, with backgrounds in art, theater, mime, and graphic design, who will take advantage of keyboard synthesizers and rhythm machines which require forethought but no great dexterity. The guitar, which came into prominence in the mid 1950s and dominated the arena-playing bands of the 1970s, will recede as the archetypal instrument of pop music, giving way to the slightly robotic but very melodic sound of keyboard synthesizers.

By tradition, the greatest breakthroughs in pop music are made by artists who were previously unknown, so it is crazy to attempt to name the stars of five years from now; but already it can be seen that certain performers made an early move towards Future Pop, notably Sly Stone (as far back as 1967), David Bowie, and Donna Summer's producer, Giorgio Moroder. By 1980 Britain had become the workshop where experimental bands had the best chance to survive commercially while forging new styles, and among the leaders were Gary Numan (who topped the charts with *Are Friends Electric?* and *Cars*), the Buggles (whose *Video Killed the Radio Star* expressed the spirit of this writer's concept of the future with far more flair and fun than this typed-out prediction can achieve), and New Musik (*Living by Numbers* was another keen comment on how we will live). Waiting in the wings are Orchestral Maneuvres in the Dark, the Human League, and Ed Sirrs, each with promising records already out. There are surely many more still at work on home tape recorders, whose flexibility is an important element in Future Pop; no longer is it necessary to incur huge debts in making records and then look for a large record company to bail out the artist.

But in the end we must admit that Doris Day already said it back in 1956: Whatever will be, will be.

1993–2030

The days of buying records are already numbered; the current process is inefficient, cumbersome, and expensive, with musicians transferring their noises onto tape, somebody else transferring the tape to disc (or video disc), and then the whole complicated mess of distributing and selling records, shipping unwanted returns back to the warehouse . . .

We know that the future promises that most households will have an information/communication center, plugged into libraries of information, video material, TV, and telephone systems. For musicians, the prospect is mouthwatering: having made a tape (sound or video), the artist will pay a fee to place the digital recording in a music library (the fee will escalate, depending on whether the musician wants to make the tape available locally, nationally, or internationally).

At home, the consumer has no need of radio or records, but has access to every recording ever made, each coded and available upon pressing the right combination of numbers (which costs a fee, some of which is paid as a royalty to the performer and writer of the music). Given this almost limitless choice, the consumer does need help and advice, and there will be a new kind of program consultant, who will make suggested sequences of songs available to consumers—for a fee, of course. It will be the task of every musician who adds a new song to the library to somehow arouse the interest of a program consultant in the new work: far from being eliminated, payola may be as big a part of Future Pop as it has been in the past.

In this new world, where much new music will be conceived and recorded in conjunction with a video, will there be a place for live concert performance? The question is unanswerable in isolation. Will there be theaters, dance clubs, or any kind of public performance? Or will society finally have retreated into isolated home entertainment, scared by street violence from ever venturing out at night?

If Western civilization does degenerate into this kind of self-centered paranoia, the future for music will more likely be based elsewhere, most likely in the third world, where music plays a more fundamental role in public rituals, and where rhythm must be good for at least another 50 years.

DIAL-A-DRUG, MARIJUANAHOL,
AND CHEMICAL RELIGIONS

Predictor MICHAEL ALDRICH is the curator of the Fitz Hugh Ludlow Library in San Francisco, Calif. The Ludlow Library's collection of books, journals, and artifacts on drugs—over 10,000 items—is among the country's best. Dr. Aldrich, who holds a Ph.D. in English, has studied at the Harvard Botanical Museum, worked as a Fulbright tutor in India, and conducted workshops for the Esalen Institute.

• PREDICTIONS •

1982–1992

• Predictions will be understood to be fantasies based on the most profound of human senses, déjà vu.

• Marijuana cultivation will be legalized in many states and nations out of economic desperation, providing not only drugs but a multipurpose industry of hemp products such as paper, oil, and cloth. Gasohol from hemp pulp could replace gasoline overnight. Chemists will discover new means of extracting resources from plant wastes.

• People will use drugs more, not less. A complex pharmaceutical technology will begin to be matched by sophisticated, though at first self-taught, techniques of using drugs precisely. Medicine cabinets will be stocked with mood-altering substances selected for specific effects, leading perhaps—once home computers are linked to planetary information libraries—to dial-a-drug systems for medicine and recreation. Semiautomatic drug delivery systems, inserted subcutaneously and provided with adjustable time-dose mechanisms, will replace pills and needles. "Organic" delivery systems (e.g., smoking grass) will never be replaced but will be regarded as old-fashioned, if not downright anachronistic.

• The intimate and important relationship among drugs, vitamins, and neurotransmitters will be revealed, with drastic effects on how we view medicine and psychology. The distinction between foods and drugs will become progressively blurred until we realize they are the same thing. Forgotten botanicals will be revived for new therapeutic purposes. Holistic psychopharmacology and nondrug neuronal manipulation will begin to replace allopathic medicine as the basis of human health care, as geriatrics, immunology, and embryology become major sciences. Prenatal and postnatal manipulation and cloning will become common. This will signal the beginning of human adaptation to quite different circumstances in space, such as learning to live in low-gravity and high-energy fields. The human psyche will be profoundly deepened as we learn that space exploration means chemical transformation as much as physical travel.

• Research into chemical evolution on this planet will show that life began as a drug—probably one of the amino acids, which can be

251

produced abiotically under primitive earth conditions (a chemical "soup" consisting of hydrogen, methane, ammonia, water, and rocks), and are the basis of protein as well as the source of most alkaloids. The oldest molecules in the human brain will prove to be natural opiates called endorphins, complex polypeptides built up from amino acids.

1993–2030 (and beyond)

• As our best and brightest head into space, most of the present adult population of the planet will die of so-called "natural" causes, e.g., disappointment, cancer, radiation poisoning, stress, and old age. These will be seen to be mostly man-made, as the chemical causes of disease and aging are discovered. Once the chemical basis of life is understood, time travel becomes possible. The aging process will become obsolete and we will have to figure out how to accommodate (at least some chemical form of) eternal life. The religions of the future will be based on chemistry.

• Investigation of the origins of life on this and other planets will lead to the "artificial" creation of chemical life forms—some sentient, some not—which will prove to be invaluable in colonizing space. "Oh, yes, that's our cocainedroid. We send her out to repair the hull when the damn meteors get too close."

• If, as is now thought, the universe beyond this planet is a predominantly reducing (hydrogen) environment, the life forms we encounter out there will be chemically extraordinary. Drugs may turn out to be the best devices we have for communicating with beings of vastly different chemical structure.

• Free oxygen, on which earth life depends, is rarer than gold in outer space and may become the economic basis of our colonies there, i.e., oxygen is money. Gardens of photosynthetic plants and aquariums of oxygen-producing chemicals will be regarded as life banks. Other life forms will similarly have biocurrencies based on their chemistry. Things we regard as worthless on earth could become important items of interplanetary trade. Chemical imperialism, removing elements from their environments (mining asteroids, for instance), could well become a capital crime and the cause of intergalactic wars. On the cosmic scale, the idea of "private" as opposed to communal property will have to be abandoned.

• This planet is seed. Chemical exploration of spacetime will result in the next evolutionary transformation of the earthling race. We will evolve into different beings. We may even learn to use our brains.

THE PHARMACY OF THE FUTURE—7 WONDER DRUGS THAT ARE ON THE WAY

1. ENDORPHINS: "NATURAL" MORPHINE?

The word *endorphin* is derived from the words *endogenous* and *morphine*—endogenous meaning "within the body." The discovery of endorphins in 1975 may prove to have been the greatest medical breakthrough since antibiotics. Endorphins are hormones produced by the pituitary gland, located at the base of the brain. Some are capable of relieving pain and producing euphoria, while others have the opposite effect. Interestingly, fetuses in the womb live in an environment of highly concentrated endorphins. The synthesizing of the pain-killing endorphins may lead to a true miracle drug—a nonaddictive opiate. Sandoz laboratory has tested one such drug—FK-33824—and Eli Lilly is also working on one, LY-127623. Unfortunately, these drugs are somewhat habit-forming, though less so than morphine. DTA, a painkiller which may be completely nonaddictive, has been discovered by Dr. Seymour Ehrenpreis of the Chicago Medical School. Rather than being a synthetic endorphin, DTA works to gently stimulate the endorphin supply that is already in the body, and seems to produce no tolerance problem. Gamma-endorphins, the class of endorphins which *heighten* sensitivity to pain, are oddly enough being used with considerable success to treat schizophrenia at the Rudolph Magnus Institute in Holland.

2. ACTH—MEMORY DRUG AS "NATURAL" COCAINE?

ACTH (adrenocorticotrophic hormone) is another pituitary product, but with highly stimulating effects, closely resembling those of cocaine. In addition to producing euphoria and increased motivation, it also improves memory to the point of curing amnesia, and it increases the attention span. A synthetic copy of ACTH is being marketed in Europe by the Dutch pharmaceutical firm Organon, but it has not yet been approved by the FDA for use in the U.S.

3. VASOPRESSIN—ALL THIS AND MORE

Vasopressin, another pituitary hormone, performs many of the same functions as ACTH, particularly memory enhancement. But it has another added attraction: regular users may find themselves having long and intensified orgasms. Looking for a way to avoid the drug's more unpleasant side effects, Dutch researcher David DeWeid discovered that vasopressin can be best used in a nasal spray form. Presently, vasopressin is being tested in America for use as a memory enhancer for senile patients.

4. LRH—THE SUPER APHRODISIAC

Yet another pituitary substance, LRH, seems to possess remarkable properties. It appears to elevate sperm count and restore virility to men. It is now being further tested on men in Britain and may soon be available as a treatment for impotence.

5. NOOTROPYL—THE CREATIVITY DRUG

Nootropyl is an intelligence booster made in Europe. It is believed to enhance the flow of information between the left and right sides of the brain—respectively, the "rational" and the "intuitive." Thus far, it has only been tested on rats and mice, but in humans the right brain/left brain communication seems to be what causes flashes of creativity.

6. DOET—THE NONALCOHOLIC MARTINI

Dr. Alexander Shulgin, the inventor of STP and MDA, has come up with a new one—DOET. He may have at last realized his quest for a short-acting drug that will place the user in "the magic moment," or "the one-and-a-half-martini stage" for an hour or two, without causing undue intoxication and confusion. "At first," says Dr. Shulgin, "you really can't say what's happening after you ingest these substances. Then suddenly everything is a little brighter, conversation is a bit more relaxed, the music is just right, and you slowly begin fitting into the new environment. It's a fabulous feeling."

7. THE BETA BLOCKER—A CONFIDENCE PILL

A cure for stage fright? For fear of flying? And even relief for stammerers? All these effects are in the province of "beta-blocking" drugs—drugs which suppress the flow of adrenaline by turning down the volume on the "beta" receptors in our body. These are the receptors which produce all the physical symptoms of anxiety, such as rapid pulse and heartbeat as well as sweaty palms. Generally prescribed for heart ailments, some of the beta blockers—in tiny doses—are being used more and more for anxiety. Oxprenolol is taken by nervous musicians in London; and Inderal, manufactured by Ayerst Laboratories, is used in the U.S. Tom Brantigan, a music teacher at the University of Nebraska, conducted a study in which he gave Inderal to musicians. He claims the results were "spectacular." Brantigan speculated that this drug is currently used by players in every major symphony orchestra in America. Beta blockers have also been used to treat patients exposed to civil strife in Northern Ireland, but they have been banned from the Olympics. Moreover, there do seem to be some side effects caused by the drugs, and many doctors are wary of prescribing them for stress.

—A.W.

COCAINE LEGALIZED, SOLD IN LIQUOR STORES

Predictor SHELLEY LEVITT is the editor of *High Times*, the most popular magazine of the drug culture. She is also a delegate to the International Cannabis Alliance for Reform, a worldwide organization working toward the legalization of marijuana.

1984

· The California Marijuana Initiative is passed, decriminalizing the private possession, transportation, and cultivation of grass for personal use by adults and creating a commission to study the economic and tax-revenue benefits to be reaped by the marijuana market. For the past five years, marijuana has been the biggest cash crop in California, which is the nation's leading agricultural state. Thus, the road is clear for the legal mass industrialization of an extremely lucrative commodity. Other states quickly follow with similar initiatives—New Mexico, Arkansas, Florida, Hawaii, and Kentucky. Kentucky, in particular, welcomes the opportunity to return to growing marijuana for hemp, which was the state's leading cash crop before the Marijuana Tax Act of 1937.

1985

· Colombia legalizes marijuana to prevent the country's economy from degenerating into black-market chaos. Years ago marijuana had surpassed coffee as the country's main source of income. The legalization movement was spearheaded by the National Association of Financial Institutions. Other Latin American nations begin considering legalization and market regulation of marijuana and/or cocaine. Within the next 10 years legalization will pass in Venezuela, Mexico, Peru, Bolivia, and Brazil and also Jamaica.

1986

• Pharmacologists have successfully developed several noneuphoric strains of THC, and the medical world is now fully ready to embrace its therapeutic benefits in the treatment of cancer, glaucoma, and multiple sclerosis. Also, serious investigators begin looking into the use of cocaine as a cure for arthritis.

1987

• The U.S. legalizes marijuana to bolster a worsening economy and in response to the growing acceptance of grass both as a medical tool and a relatively harmless recreational intoxicant. Within months there are hundreds of brands of marijuana on the market, available both prerolled and loose. On the shelves of tobacco and liquor shops and in cigarette machines, one can purchase such brands as Connoisseur Colombian, Santa Marta Gold, Primo Mexican, and California Sinsemilla.

2000

• The U.S. legalizes cocaine. The government has fully enjoyed a windfall of revenue from the sale of marijuana and recognizes the ability of adults to use recreational drugs intelligently. Dozens of dope magazines have been urging the legalization of cocaine for the past 10 years in their widely read editorials. It is sold in beautiful snuffboxes in liquor shops under names such as Peruvian Flake and Bolivian Rock.

2005

• Huge advances have been made in the study of endorphins and enkephalins, opiates produced by the brain. Doctors have determined how to tap into the brain's opiate-producing sites, and now all forms of surgery are performed without any form of anesthesia. Surgeons employ methods resembling acupuncture, successfully releasing the body's own painkillers without any negative side effects.

2010

• Dozens of new drugs have been synthesized, including memory and intelligence enhancers, drugs to prevent stage fright, control obesity, encourage assertive behavior, and control extreme mood swings without dulling effects. The world of psychiatrists has changed drastically, aided as they are by a vast array of drugs having very specific effects. Psychiatrists rely less on methods of psychotherapy and more on psychotropic drugs; they have become programmers, trying to achieve the most positive balance between the drugs synthesized by one's brain and the refined drugs now synthesized by chemists.

2025

• Breakthroughs have been made in the area of life-extension drugs, and now human life can be extended 50–100 years. This ability has presented humanity with the greatest ethical problem ever: has life become a commodity that can be bought and sold? A moratorium on life-extension research is being encouraged until the issue of how to distribute these drugs is resolved.

THE THREE-MINUTE MILE, ROBOT FOOTBALL TEAMS, AND CRICKET IN YANKEE STADIUM

Predictor MARTIN ABRAMSON is a former sports and feature writer for the *New York Herald Tribune*. He has also done numerous articles on sports and other subjects for *Playboy, Reader's Digest, Cosmopolitan,* and *Esquire*. Mr. Abramson is the author of seven books, including *Monkey on My Back* (the story of fighter Barney Ross) and *Baseball Umpire*.

• PREDICTIONS •

1981–1992

• Soccer will lose some of the popularity it has enjoyed in recent years, but another sport, the age-old English sport of cricket, will become popular in the U.S. The game will be speeded up for American purposes, but it will retain some of the leisurely, homespun character that has been identified with it in England and British Commonwealth countries down through the centuries.
• A major international cricket match will be held in Yankee Stadium in the fall of 1981. It will be so successful that the first professional cricket league will be formed in this country in 1982.
• Boxing will enjoy a comeback, with more white fighters competing because of the large sums offered and because a national depression will make it hard for many young people to find decent jobs.
• Few pitchers will win 20 games per season, because the trend toward using relief pitchers and part-game pitchers will continue.
• The Mets will become New York's favorite baseball team again.

1986

• Women's basketball will continue to gain in popularity, but it will not match the appeal of the male game. For the first time, a woman player will be allowed to compete for an entire season on a male basketball team.

1988

· The record for the mile run will go down to 3 min. and 32 sec.

1989

· Professional basketball will decline in popularity because a sizable percentage of fans will not want to support all-black teams composed of giants who can amass large scores by stuffing balls in the basket instead of shooting. To try and minimize the "stuffed shots," new legislation will raise the baskets by two feet. This will make it a little more difficult to score at will.
· For the first time a woman runner will break 4 min. in running the mile.
· Someone will hit 63 home runs over the course of a season in major-league baseball, breaking the Maris record of 61.

1993–2030

· As electronic games featuring sports become ever more sophisticated and advanced, professional leagues will be formed. Their members will play games at home, competing with others who also play in their homes, via electronic and cable connections. Since games of this type do not require physical skill, but rather mental agility and dexterity, there will arise a new breed of sports performer who will not have to be physically strong or require constant training.

· Robots will become so advanced in their physical characteristics and their ability to perform as "Hessians" that football teams will be made up of these robots. They will be directed from the bench by the coach.
· The mile will be run in 3 min. flat by a male.
· A female mark of 3 min. 40 sec. will be set.
· Tennis tournaments will be won by 13- and 14-year-olds (defeating competitors twice their age).
· A series of revolts against the corruption in college sports will finally bring an end to the "professionalized" system of college athletics. Institutions of learning will go back to their original concept of using sports as a recreational activity for bona fide students.
· The record for lifetime passes caught in the NFL will be broken. The new total will be 789.

- Fran Tarkenton's record of yardage gained passing over a lifetime career will be broken. The new record will be 50,115.
- The record price for a yearling racehorse in the U.S. will be $4.5 million.
- A 3,000-lb. fish will be caught in Alaska, the largest fish ever caught by a human using a rod.
- Wilt Chamberlain's record of 31,419 points scored in a lifetime in basketball will be broken. The new record will be 37,125 points.
- The Indianapolis 500 race will be won in 2 hr. and 20 sec.
- Hank Aaron's lifetime home-run total (755) will be broken. The new record will be 807.

LEGALIZED GAMBLING, RUGBY IN AMERICA, AND NEW RULES FOR BASEBALL

Predictor W. C. HEINZ was a general reporter, war correspondent, and sports writer for the *New York Sun*. He is a five-time winner of the E. P. Dutton Award for the best magazine sports article of the year. He is also the author of five books, three involving sports: *Run to Daylight!* (with Vince Lombardi); *The Professional*, considered by many to be the finest novel about boxing ever written; and *Once They Heard the Cheers*, a reminiscent revisit with sports heroes of the years 1945–1965.

• PREDICTIONS •

1982–1992

- Boxing, as the most socially significant of all the sporting art forms, will remain, as it has always been, a refuge for the underprivileged. With the decline of prejudice and the advancement of social legislation in this country, however, most world-class boxers, and thus the champions, will emerge from the less economically secure and less socially oriented nations.
- As Homo sapiens continues to grow in height, and college and professional basketball scores mount commensurably, the basket will be raised from 10 ft. to 10 ft. 6 in. Games will still be won in the last two seconds, but with such comparatively modest scores as 98–97.
- As more secondary schools are unable to meet the rising costs of equipping football squads, and as clavicle cracking, ligament tearing, cartilage slipping, and spinal disk displacements arouse increas-

259

ing parental concern, soccer will become the primary scholastic sport. The rest shall follow until the game becomes the national, as it is the world, team sport.

• With the decline of American football, its progenitor, English rugby, involving as it does running with the ball, passing, kicking, and tackling with less expense to budgets and bodies, will take new root in this country.

1993–2030

• As television continues to provide instant gratification at the expense of contemplative enjoyment, the leisurely pace of baseball as we have always known it will be reflected in falling ratings and ballpark attendance. The rule changes that follow, in the attempt to inject added excitement, will include the manager's prerogative of rearranging his team's batter order as the game progresses. Any player—for example, the team's leading hitter—may be sent to bat at any time that he is not on base, up to four extra times during a nine-inning game but not more than twice in an inning, and for a total of not more than four more times in an extra-inning game.

• Nations, like individuals, age. As they do they lean less toward labor and more toward luck. To mark the beginnings of the 21st century and the last gasp of the puritan work ethic, the U.S., ostensibly as a social measure, will nationalize legalized gambling on sporting events.

BASEBALL RECORDS SHATTERED

Predictor LAWRENCE RITTER is the author of two well-known books on baseball, *The Glory of Their Times* and *The Image of Their Greatness*, the latter coauthored with Donald Honig. Ritter is also a professor of finance and economics at the School of Business, New York University, New York, N.Y.

• PREDICTIONS •

1982–2000

• I would expect, with a high degree of probability, that by the turn of the century or shortly thereafter virtually every major baseball record now in the books will fall by the wayside. These include:

1. Roger Maris's season home-run record of 61 (someone will hit 70).
2. Henry Aaron's lifetime home-run record of 755 (someone will reach 800).

3. Lou Brock's season stolen-base record of 118 (someone will steal 130).
4. Brock's 900-plus lifetime stolen bases (someone will reach 1,000).
5. Nolan Ryan's season strikeout record of 383 (someone will strike out 400).
6. Walter Johnson's lifetime strikeout total of 3,508.
7. Ty Cobb's lifetime record of 4,191 hits will be broken (by Pete Rose in 1985). The only big-league record that will withstand assault—indeed, it won't even be challenged—is Ty Cobb's lifetime batting average of .367.

1982–2030

• With respect to the economy, inflation will continue unabated, so that by 1992 the average secretary will be earning over $25,000 a year, and by the year 2030 over $600,000 a year. But prices will rise just as rapidly; by the year 2030, $10 bills will be considered small change, barely enough to buy a cup of coffee.

The coffee shop of the future.

THE 21ST-CENTURY GLADIATORS

Predictor DR. HARRY EDWARDS is the author of three books, including *Sociology of Sports,* and more than fifty articles in the fields of sport sociology, the family, and race relations. He has lectured at more than 300 colleges and universities and has traveled abroad extensively, including two trips to the People's Republic of China. In 1968 he organized the Olympic Project for Human Rights, which advocated a black boycott of the Olympic Games in Mexico City. Dr. Edwards teaches in the department of sociology at the University of California at Berkeley.

• PREDICTIONS •

1982–1992

• There will be tremendous increases in the role of technology in sport. Particularly in socialist bloc and developed Western nations, chemical and computer technology combined with advances in training methods will result in mostly gradual, but sometimes spectacular, improvements in most sport standards involving time, distance, weight, or height.

• In the race for international sports dominance, developed Western nations will fall farther behind socialist bloc countries overall and will become less and less competitive with emerging third-world nations in particular events, e.g., middle-distance and distance races and certain team sports such as basketball and volleyball.

• The most spectacular improvements in athlete performance will occur in women's sports. We can look for a closing of the gap between men's and women's performances in individual and team sports events, with women in Western nations improving their national standards dramatically in virtually all events.

• Sport within the U.S. will be dominated sociopolitically during this period by the "crisis of the black athlete." This will be a "transitional era," wherein the American sports establishment will take steps to reduce the black presence, preeminence, and/or visibility in major professional sports, while maintaining limited black access to such sports as tennis, golf, automobile racing, and horse racing in order to cope with the inevitable increase in cultural, political, and economic liabilities associated with increasing black domination of the sports institution in America—a predominantly white and *white-dominated* society. Thus, between 1982 and 1992 we can look for the continued decline in the mass-media coverage and visibility given such black-dominated professional sports as basketball and boxing, a diminished and diminishing presence and prominence of blacks in such sports as professional baseball and football, and relatively elevated levels of visibility and mass-media attention being given such sports as tennis, golf, auto racing, horse racing, swimming, and gymnastics.

By 1993

• The mass media will be the primary conduit of sports entertainment. There will be television schedules presenting nothing but sports events, sports personalities, sports news, sports training techniques, sports equipment, sports medicine—the total sports television network.

1993–2030

• Judicial rulings and legislative regulations will play a greater role in the control and governance of domestic U.S. sport at all levels. Legislation and judicial edicts dealing with such concerns as sports violence, amateurism, antitrust issues, and collegiate sport recruitment, participation, and rewards will have accumulated to the point of severely limiting the discretionary powers of such organizations as the AAU and the NCAA, as well as the offices of the commissioners of professional baseball, football, basketball, and other professional sports.
• Women's sports will begin showing fully developed symptoms of maladies long afflicting men's sports—overemphasis upon winning, athletic recruitment, and support violations in amateur sport; inflated salaries and egos in professional sport; and a generally disastrous economic philosophy—i.e., that a bigger league is a better league, that a bigger pavilion is a better pavilion, etc.
• Major corporations not principally in the sports entertainment business will own a substantial proportion of professional sports organizations and the industry as a whole, and will own or control virtually all amateur sports training facilities and amateur athlete support systems not directly affiliated with, or under the control of, educational institutions.
• Toward the end of this period there will have emerged either a radically altered or completely new World Sports Order over which the private multinational corporations of the West and the socialist Eastern bloc governments will wield direct and dominant power. In the all-out push for international sports dominance, athletes on both sides will be reduced to little more than "21st-century gladiators," foot soldiers and front-line troops in a global social, cultural, and ideological struggle camouflaged under the pageantry of international sports competition.

3-D TV AND PLEASURE ISLANDS

Predictor IAN MILES is a psychologist and social researcher who prepares future scenarios based upon unfolding tendencies and patterns within contemporary society. The author of *The Poverty of Prediction* and the editor of *World Futures: The Great Debate,* Mr. Miles teaches and works at the University of Sussex in the United Kingdom.

• PREDICTIONS •

Mid–1980s

• More efficient transport beats energy shortages, and tourism continues to expand to more regions of the world. Africa and central and southern Asia develop major tourist industries. Due to problems of cultural impact, recipient countries effectively set up "tourist enclaves" with facilities devised so as to discourage tourists from entering developing or unstable areas.

• Erotic clothing fashions among youth and some affluent groups. Use of body paint, dyed hair, and overt sexual symbolism in attire not exactly widespread, but noticeable in most large cities. Late in the century, clothing could contain built-in electronic gadgets to change color, pattern, and flexible shaping at will according to mood.

• Static holograms—three-dimensional pictures—common as wall, table, and desk decorations, advertisements, etc. Moving holograms will mean 3-D television in the 1990s, but the range of programs broadcast in this way will remain very limited for a long time, so the system will not be widely used.

Late 1980s

• Nostalgia emphasized in leisure sites and vacation resorts, along the lines of restored "Wild West" towns; areas are devoted to replicating 20th-century scenes and symbols. For instance, trips could be offered into the Al Capone era, famous wartime victories, 1960s hippie life, etc.

• Pocket-sized electronic books introduced. Small cassettes containing large quantities of information can be inserted into a calculator-shaped instrument whose face will display "pages." These could be linked up to the domestic computer systems—diffused toward the end of the century—for printing out and editing passages; for "personalizing" novels to make the reader the hero, or, in the case of nonfiction, the person spoken to; and for reading the text by voice synthesizers.

Early 1990s

• Widespread use of video equipment leads to questions being raised over invasion of privacy, over pornographic video cassettes, and over use of equipment by gangs, political activists, and deviant groups to record, promote, and publicize activities found offensive or threatening.

Mid–1990s

• Innovations in underwater sports: "jets" to propel swimmers, cheap submarines for short ventures, complexes established—perhaps on offshore "pleasure islands"—for training and club activities.

Mid–1990s on

• Biofeedback training used in preparation for sports—teaching athletes to recognize and extend limits of capacities. Also employed in pleasure-seeking (e.g., as a substitute for narcotics and in learning to enhance appreciation of music) and in improving memory and learning.

Late 1990s–early 2000s

• Widespread diffusion of home computers as "entertainment centers," with household heat and lighting, wall decorations, and music all centrally programmed. Customized systems allow modification of music, TV, etc., to own tastes and household environment. "Communication centers" linking home to music, video, and conventional libraries established in some urban centers.

2010–on

• It becomes noticeable that focus of cultural innovations has shifted from English-speaking to other parts of the world. English language modified by other cultural influences. Meanwhile, improved translation equipment and dubbing technology makes for much greater acceptance of cultural diversity in films, TV, books, music.

THE GROWING WORLD OF LEISURE

Predictor ARNOLD BROWN is president of the firm of Weiner, Edrich, Brown, Inc., consultants in strategic planning and the management of change. Along with Ian Wilson of General Electric, he founded and cochairs an "invisible college" consisting of some of the leading long-range planners and futurists in the U.S., who represent organizations such as AT&T, General Motors, Exxon, Coca-Cola, and the Federal Reserve Board.

• PREDICTIONS •

Mid–1980s

• Leisure expenditures will exceed $300 billion (in 1978 dollars).

• Great increase in home food gardening as inflation and serious recessions hit the middle class hard.

• Growth of "eco-leisure" phenomenon—leisure activities based on conservation, preserving the environment, etc.

• Severe and recurring energy shortages will have great negative impacts on highway-dependent leisure services, such as motels, fast-food chains, etc.

• Continued growth of adult education as a leisure activity, with greater participation by retirees as they become more financially secure.

• Growth of science-related hobbies, such as astronomy.

• Any object from before 1945 will be a potential collectible.

• Availability of home entertainment/information/shopping centers including: interactive TV, pay TV, electronic games, holographic images, video recorders and discs, minicameras, household computers, central data-bank links, electronic catalogues, plus links to commercial banks and major department and food stores.

• Spread of issue/interest/values-oriented leisure activities—e.g., package tours to marathon sites for runners, recreational centers for evangelical Christians, and so on.

• Increasing emphasis on health and physical fitness (and looking good) through diet and exercise.

• Risk and danger become more popular. Millions take up hang-gliding, glacier-skiing, shark hunting (underwater), etc.

• Abundant energy supplies by second or third decade of next century.

• Widespread adoption of maternal and paternal leaves for working parents; also shortened workday an option for parents of young children.

• No more encyclopedias; great fall-off in dictionary and thesaurus sales (and of other reference works, such as *The Book of Predictions*) because homes and schools have computer linkups to great central libraries. Book publishing of all kinds will be in severe decline as electronic books become available; same for newspapers and magazines.

• Much shorter workweek—perhaps averaging below 30 hours—as part of effort to reduce unemployment by sharing work and jobs more widely.

• Automated, computer-controlled automobiles that will do everything but decide where to stop for lunch.

• Hispanics will be by far the largest minority, and aspects of their culture—such as music and dance—will displace much of the black music in popularity. Also, the country will be, if not officially, at least semiofficially, bilingual.

• Virtually every home will have a complete home entertainment/information/shopping center, which was first available in the 1982–1992 period.

• Breakthroughs in prolonging life by the year 2000 will result in a great increase in the percentage of aged in the population by 2030. As a consequence, there will be no mandatory retirement; Social Security will be financed out of general revenues; there will be more part-time work, and there will be a huge industry focused on leisure products and services for older people.

FUTURE RECREATION
ENVIRONMENTS

In 1974 the U.S. Department of Agriculture asked 405 experts on the environment, ecology, and pollution to offer their forecasts for the future of the earth. Utilizing the "Delphi technique," which transforms a multitude of opinions into a single group consensus, the department drew the following predictions from the study.

1985

• Economic incentives encourage private landowners to open part or all of their land for public recreation.
• Cable TV available at most campgrounds.
• Companies will consult employees about what sort of recreation activities would be best for their physical and mental health.
• Most people work a 4-day, 32-hour week.

1990

• Consumers accept major costs of pollution control.
• Public schools open year-round with staggered vacations.
• Most homes have videotape systems.
• Small private aircraft excluded from metropolitan airports.

1995

• Commercial products packaged in nonpolluting containers.

2000

• Remote sensing devices used to monitor park use.
• Animal migrations monitored by satellite.
• Nonpolluting propulsion methods, such as electric power, replace internal-combustion engines in recreational vehicles.
• Utility lines within sight of recreation areas placed underground.
• Wildlife resources are used primarily for photography and observation.
• Small private recreational submarines used as commonly as snowmobiles are used today.
• Extensive areas in arid regions irrigated to enhance recreational opportunities.
• Only biodegradable chemicals may be discharged directly into the enviroment.
• Five hundred miles is a reasonable one-way distance to travel for a weekend.
• Average retirement age is 50 years.
• "Weekends" distributed throughout the week.
• Attempt to control population through tax incentives.

- Cemetery land and other open land in urban areas used for recreation.
- Only nonpolluting vehicles allowed in urban areas.
- Green space preserved between most metropolitan areas.
- Some city parks—or parts of parks—enclosed in all-weather protective bubbles.

2020

- Most metropolitan areas provide adequate outdoor-recreation opportunities so that urban residents do not feel the need to go to the country for recreation.

2030

- Most middle-income families own their own vacation home.

THE GROWTH OF TOURISM

Predictor C. R. GOELDNER is a professor of marketing and director of the business research division at the University of Colorado in Boulder. He serves as the editor of the *Journal of Travel Research* and as secretary of the U.S. Travel Data Center. Mr. Goeldner is past president of the Travel Research Association and the author of numerous studies on tourism and recreation.

• PREDICTIONS •

1982–1992

- Jobs in travel and tourism will continue to increase at twice the rate of other jobs in our society, as has been the case for the past two decades.
- The automobile will remain the major mode of transportation for the family vacation during the next decade; however, there will be a steady shift from large automobiles to small ones, accompanied by dramatic decreases (67% to 90%) in fuel consumption.
- Air travel will continue to increase. There will be a small diversion from auto travel, but it will result in an incredible increase in air travel.

1982–2000

- Tourism will continue to grow at an average annual rate of around

10% a year into the foreseeable future. This growth will be driven by contemporary socioeconomic forces such as the need for psychological escapism, an increase in young adults, an increase in household formation, smaller and delayed families, working women, and higher levels of income per capita.
• This growth rate will make tourism one of the world's largest industries.
• The women's movement will impact the travel industry in a major way. Women will be a dominant force in the industry both as consumers and producers.

1982-2030

• Attitudes in the U.S. will shift from a work ethic to a leisure ethic.
• As society becomes more technical and complex, consumer attitudes will change to the point where travel, tourism, and vacations will be viewed as a necessity. Consumers will insist on vacations and will even sacrifice other items in order to have vacations.
• The amount of leisure time available to the average person will continue to increase. The workweek will shorten to 35 hours, flextime and alternative scheduling will become more popular, and the number of paid vacations and holidays will continue to increase.
• Time-sharing (of condominiums and other property) will become the hottest item in the leisure industry.

FUTURE TRENDS IN TOURISM

This chart, compiled by staff members of the Hudson Institute, reviews the development of tourism and outlines its possible future. Foreseeing travel that is faster, cheaper, and easier, the researchers believe that their quantitative data are "quite reasonable" and that their qualitative data are in all cases "reliable." The information in the chart is derived from an article by Herman Kahn that appeared in the 50th-anniversary issue of *Travel Trade*.

	Present	1989	2009	2029
Travel modes	747; various wide-bodied craft; limited Concorde service. Rail, bus declining relatively; some technological & comfort improvements. Cars (temporarily?) held to nominal 55 mph.	Extended Concorde routes, but few aircraft. Second generation SST and million-lb. plane possible. Many subsonic jets. New general aviation. Fast rail (100 mph). Cars (80 mph).	Hypersonic transport (HST), possibly fueled by hydrogen. Personal vertical/short takeoff and landing aircraft. Limited commercial & governmental space travel & accommodations. Various guided "rail" (200–400 mph).	Many HSTs; still much subsonic travel. Suborbital travel. Private space travel & tourist accommodations. Revolutionary new modes of travel, e.g., "transplanetary tunnel." Various fast automated private vehicles.
Approximate maximum travel speeds in miles per hour (mph)	500–1300 mph	500–1300 (2000?) mph	500–3000 mph	500–6000 mph

Time needed from New York to:	Car	Rail	Air	Hours	Car	Rail	Air	Hours	Hours	Hours
Wash., DC (200 mi.)	4½	3½	1		3	2	1		1 hour	½ hour
Chicago (700 mi.)	15	13	2		12	12	2		1 hour	1 hour
LA (2,500 mi.)	70	—	5		50	—	4		2 hours	1 hour
London (3,500 mi.)				4 hours				4 hours	3 hours	2 hours
Moscow (4,700 mi.)				9 hours				6 hours	4 hours	2 hours
Sydney (10,000 mi.)				1 day				15 hours	8 hours	3 hours
Time spent working	Av. workweek—38 hours				Av. workweek—35 hours				Individual workweek reflects choices; could be about 20 hours.	Work time largely a matter of individual choice; could be slight; very many choices.

SOURCE: *The Futurist*, published by the World Future Society, 4916 St. Elmo Ave., Washington, D.C. 20014, August, 1979.

PUBLISHERS PHASED OUT—
AUTHORS FREE AT LAST

Predictor HENRY B. FREEDMAN is director of research at Policy Studies Reports, a consulting firm that provides long-range planning and technical evaluation for the graphic arts and communications industry. He is also a research associate for the Program of Policy Studies in Science and Technology, a project started by NASA in Washington, D.C.

• PREDICTIONS •

1988

• One hundred books of 200 pages, mainly text, will be transmitted by computer in a one-second time span. The books will then be stored on 2 sq. in. of film, glass, or other surface and read by a computer looking for specific concepts or sentences at a rate of over 1,000 pages per second. Any information received from this digital storage can be reproduced on paper of "printed book" quality.

2000

• The introduction of advanced computer technologies in printing—"printing on demand"—will bring about many changes in publishing, research, and printing, including the following:

1. Research on a subject will be done through a computer search using content selection. The materials found can be duplicated in whatever format (type font, paper size and kind—even Braille) desired. The material will then be bound into a single volume. Every user will be his or her own Gutenberg.
2. Printing-on-demand modular units—located in offices, libraries, shops, government facilities, and many other distribution sites—will provide a "Library of Congress" to all those who desire one, regardless of geographical location.
3. Authors will have complete control over the publication process, from editing to printing to distribution of the finished work, thus ending the relationship between author and publisher in many instances. For example, the reader, through a computer, will be a printer per se, so the publishers' role of coordinating with printers will end.

1990–2030

• Computers will shift away from digital processing as we currently use it and will return to analog processing, whereby light waves are used to compute by altering their phase relationships. This computer will be able to solve many complex problems simultaneously by being able to divide its computing ability over a very wide span of information. This way maximum efficiency of the "natural" resource of knowledge will be achieved.

L'ENVOI

Predictor GEORGES SIMENON, best known as the creator of Inspector Maigret, has written more than 200 novels under 17 pseudonyms. Eighty of these feature the French detective Maigret. Fifty of Mr. Simenon's novels have been made into films. Born in Liège, Belgium, in 1903, Mr. Simenon lives in Lausanne, Switzerland.

• PREDICTIONS •

• I am nothing of a Nostradamus, nor of a futurologist, but there are chances for the world to live the years to come as ever before: hills and valleys, wars and peaces.
• I passed through two wars, and I wouldn't be surprised to go through a third.
• High-ranking military leaders, politicians, and international business people all over the world are in the right place to answer your questions. They don't care about the opinion of the little man. So little men don't have to worry any more about the years ahead than do cattle in the green pastures, who don't know when they will be hanged on the hooks of the butcher. It is the same for me: I prefer not to know, not to worry, and live my life day by day.
• All chances are that I shall not live in 1993, all the more so in 2020. Why worry, then?

Part II

THE SEERS

9

THE PSYCHICS
LOOK AHEAD

1982

A naturally derived tranquilizer, nonaddictive and nonharmful, will be on the market. Dosage will be adjusted to tranquilize, create a high, remove tension and pain, or induce sleep.

1996

A spaceship staffed by humans will fail to return from a voyage.

2000

People will be able to walk across the Atlantic Ocean. There will be many cities on the sea, linked by flexible bridges.

WORLD EVENTS:
WHAT 7 SEERS PREDICT

• PREDICTOR: BERTIE CATCHINGS •

On her first day at a new job in 1969, Texas seeress Bertie Catchings gave a psychic reading to a co-worker. Her predictions came true that night. She began making psychic forecasts in local newspapers and on radio, achieving a consistently high degree of accuracy that propelled her into the national spotlight. She writes several columns on psychic phenomena and is organizing a statewide "psychic detective squad" in Texas. Her son, John Catchings, is also a psychic.

• PREDICTIONS •

1982–1983

• Libya will pose a threat to France as well as English-speaking nations in Africa. Armed with Soviet weapons, Libya's leader, Muammar el-Qaddafi, will lead his country into several major conflicts. He will give the Soviets a naval base on the Mediterranean.
• Argentina and Chile will dispute ownership of several small islands. Peru and Bolivia will side with Argentina.

1984

• New energy sources will be discovered when scientists learn to convert electricity into ultrahigh-frequency magnetic forces for space travel.
• Iraq and Iran will declare war on each other.

1985

• Norway and Finland will exchange fire in the Barents Sea over fishing rights.
• A bloody conflict will erupt between India and Pakistan.
• Syria and Israel will continue to be military hot spots, but Israel and the PLO will achieve peace.
• Road maps will actually be computers, built into the dashboard of your car. If you get lost in a city, you'll punch your present cross streets and destination. The map will light up in large, bright letters and lines, giving directions even a child could follow.

1986

• An extra television channel will be used to give computer information that outdoes the Yellow Pages. If you need to find a mechanic near your home or hotel, all you have to do is feed the question into the computer, and your television screen will light up with the addresses and telephone numbers of shops in your area.

• Space stations will be in orbit, and the people who live there will begin to manufacture prefabricated space cities.

1990

• Everyone will have a portable telephone that can be carried in a purse or pocket. The telephone book will be a minicomputer.

• Near the Arctic Circle, a lost tribe will be found. Its members will know of a secret passage through the ice to a place deep within the earth where beautiful gardens flourish. Though few in number, these people have lived comfortably for many centuries.

• The *Titanic*—salvaged from the North Atlantic and restored—will be made into a museum.

1992

• An underground railroad tunnel will be constructed in the U.S. between Chicago and Dallas. "Bullet" trains traveling over 100 mph will carry passengers as well as freight.

• In the Aleutians, on the island of Adak, a cave will be found filled with gold. A young boy with curly blond hair will find it and claim he is the reincarnation of the person who put it there.

• Several satellite stations, floating above major cities, will convert solar energy into microwaves which will be beamed back to earth. Here the waves will be converted into conventional electrical energy.

1995

• Space miners from earth—searching for iron, nickel, lead, and other metals—will discover instruments and mining tools left not only on the moon but on several asteroids. They were abandoned by space miners from other worlds.

• A presently unknown hybrid plant similar to rice will be grown in seawater. It will be rich in nutrients and become a staple food popular around the world.

• A dam will be built across the Bering Strait between Alaska and the Soviet Union.

1996

• In a desert area of southern California, a ship will be unearthed that holds a great store of pearls.

1998

• A shiny armor resembling that worn in battle long ago will again be used by soldiers. It will give them 10 times their normal strength. This armor will be equipped with laser weapons that can be discharged by merely lifting an arm or pointing a finger. It will also have built-in laser deflectors to protect against attack.

2000

• People will be living up to 150 years. By this time, we will be only a decade away from finding a cure for every known illness of the 20th century.

• You will be able to walk across the Atlantic Ocean. There will be many cities on this ocean, linked by flexible bridges.

• Parents will no longer worry when their children get lost in public places. Each child will wear a tag—resembling a watch or bracelet—which is tuned in to the parents' matching tag. Either the child can be signaled to return or the parent can tune in and see as well as hear what the child is doing. People who let their pets out of the yard will have a similar device to keep them from getting lost or stolen.

• Space cities will be built. They will be complete with trees, houses, lakes, and mountains. Independent of earth, they will be supplied by mines on the moon and nearby asteroids, and they will support themselves by selling solar energy, unique manufactured goods, scientific information, and astronomical photographs.

• I do not foresee disarmament. War weapons will continue to proliferate. The fear of nuclear war will always be present, but such a war will never actually come to pass.

• Wars of the distant future will be fought largely by robots, on electronic battlefields, hopefully far away from the planet Earth.

• PREDICTOR: DENNIS CONKIN •

Born in 1952, Dennis Conkin is a talented psychic who lives in San Francisco, Calif., where he lectures and teaches.

• PREDICTIONS •

1982

• A woman will begin rising to a position of great power in China. She will play an influential role in China's relationship with developing nonaligned countries. Her skill and her contributions will affect positively China's stature as a superpower—and will help shape China's foreign policy throughout the decade.

• There will be great turmoil in France. The domestic political situation will be very volatile, and major changes will occur in the president's domestic cabinet.

• A scandal will involve the top echelons of the U.S. military and defense establishment. An important official will be compromised by an aide. The aide will be discovered releasing information to persons whose interests and sympathies do not lie with the U.S.

• There will be an incident involving Israel and the atom bomb. Israel will either publicly test an atomic bomb or admit having one.

1983

- Inflation stabilizes at 23%.
- Unemployment holds at 12%.
- The economy continues to suffer. Medium-sized businesses face severe difficulties due to rising costs and decreasing production. One company—a household name—bites the dust.
- The U.S.S.R. and China are engaged in a fierce border battle. The Soviets, no match for the swift Chinese, are stung by a quick defeat.
- A devastating explosion wracks Chicago. Many fatalities result.
- The leader of an established religious denomination resigns, red-faced, when revelations about his unusual and very kinky sex life surface.
- There is continued revolution and the threat of full-scale war in Central America, particularly Guatemala. Mexico offers troops, and so does Cuba. America is vilified and asked to stay out.
- Author Jane Roberts has a book on *The New York Times* best-seller list.

1984

- Phyllis Schlafly runs for Congress.

• PREDICTOR: ANN FISHER •

At age 23, Ann Fisher attended a spiritualist church meeting and was singled out as she sat in the audience. She was told that she was destined to work in the psychic field. Now a resident of Albany, N.Y., Fisher specializes in psychic counseling and hypnosis. She holds bachelor's and master's degrees in education and psychology.

• PREDICTIONS •

1982

- All nine planets in our solar system will move into alignment. Their gravitational pull will cause great storms on the sun, altering solar wind direction on earth and reducing the speed of our planet's rotation. This will trigger some very destructive earthquakes.

1983–1985

- A disaster may strike one of the Rocky Mountain States. I see an experimental nuclear breeder chain-reacting and exploding. Many lives will be lost, and some of the best scientific minds in America will also perish. This tragedy can be prevented.

1989

• There will be a revival of moats like those around medieval castles. They will be used to provide security for new government buildings and for the homes of the wealthy.

Tomorrow's security system.

1995

• In the far south of Egypt, where the Nile River is fast-moving, through a series of clifflike gorges will be found a series of rectangular rooms. Ancient records of metals, medicine, and technology will be discovered. It will be a British find. This complex provided a refuge when those in power sought to escape war and famine.

2000

• The cap stone of the Great Pyramid of Giza will be accidentally discovered by sophisticated electronic satellites, which are presently used for spying.
• Clothing will follow more of a unisex trend. Garments of tomorrow will be woven with metal fibers. These will remain cool in the summer and retain body heat in winter. Clothes will be flash-cleaned by ultrasonic or electrostatic charges, which will be quicker and more efficient than conventional soap and water.
• The secrets of Atlantis, which are buried between the Great Pyramid and the Sphinx in Egypt, will be found and revealed to the world. They are in a sealed room that is a time capsule containing objects used by the Atlanteans, as well as records of their history and destruction. We will then learn why the Great Pyramid of Giza was built and what it was used for.
• We will witness an underground revolution, with skyscraper-type buildings placed deep in the earth and sealed against water. This type of architecture will create a new industry with vast job markets, as such complexes will be constructed worldwide.

• PREDICTOR: BEVERLY JAEGERS •

Having changed from a skeptic and debunker to a confirmed advocate of psychic methods in 1960, Beverly Jaegers describes herself as someone who has experienced "no fall on the head," has "no special powers," but is "just a person who tried and found that she could do it." Her predictions and articles on psychic subjects have appeared in numerous magazines. She is director of the U.S. Psi Squad, the only licensed psychic detective agency in America, and is herself a licensed St. Louis County private investigator.

• PREDICTIONS •

1982

• Laser surgery will replace the scalpel and revolutionize the field of dermatology, and then general surgery.
• A naturally derived tranquilizer will be marketed. It will be nonaddictive and nonharmful. Dosage will be adjusted to create a natural "high," remove pain and tension, or induce sleep.
• Both speech and thought will become predictable through computer sensors, and because of this persons with aphasia, stroke, or speech problems can be helped to learn or relearn to speak and understand. This will be extended eventually to the teaching of second and third languages by the creation of proper brain-wave programs during sleep.
• It will be discovered that a psionic weapon has already been developed and tested by the Soviets, and a prototype may soon be placed in orbit around the earth.

1982–1985

• The educational burden will revert more and more to the home, with the advent of special TV "school channels" which young people will watch for daily education. Small consoles attached to each set will allow students to ask and answer questions and take tests electronically.

1982–1989

• Single-family housing will become less and less common in the coming years. The rising cost of construction and repair, plus interest rates on loans, will put these dwellings beyond the reach of most wage earners.

1983

• New waste-treatment innovations will replace refuse dumps and incinerators, reducing all refuse to reusable, nonpolluting fertilizers, mulch, and other useful items.

• An implant device will replace the injection of insulin and insulin-stimulating drugs by triggering the body's production of natural insulin. Diabetes will be detected and the device implanted in the newborn, and it will also be used for older diabetics.
• Liver transplants will become feasible during the mid-1980s, and a new substance will be found to prevent tissue-rejection problems once and for all.

1983–1984

• For a time, New York and two other large U.S. cities will become armed wastelands with inner-city warfare and strife. Parts of these cities will be barricaded off by the National Guard.

1984

• Whole-eye transplants will become a reality by this time and common by 1986. A "bionic" eye will also enable most blind persons to regain full vision.
• Parapsychology will become an accepted subject at all major universities. Psi labs will be set up in leading cities to combat the threat of Soviet psionics, which will be in the world's headlines in the 1980s, and to explore this newest evolution of man and his mind.

1984–1986

• Virtually all cancers will be instantly arrested, cured, and eventually eliminated through a reprogramming of DNA in the individual body cells. This technique will be perfected by the late 1980s.

1985

• Student enrollment in colleges will hit a new low, and many of the top colleges and universities will compete for enrollees, offering new concepts in education, low tuition, and easy grading.
• Most present medications will be outmoded. Tiny devices, implanted in body or brain, will replace prescription drugs. Natural body secretions, hormones, and secretions of presently unknown types will be utilized as natural "drugs," eliminating the need for chemicals.

1989

• It will be discovered that for some persons it is possible to stimulate cells and grow a new body organ through a process that will be called " electronic biostimulation." Eventually, new bone structures and even entire new limbs will be grown by using this process.

1993

• "Single-cell" diagnosis centers will be installed in many cities. These will look much like a large telephone booth. People will enter and place an epidermal cell from a finger or the tongue in a receptacle. A series of several dozen instant diagnostic tests will be performed, and within 60 seconds a central computer will flash the results of the physical checkup on a viewer.

1999

• The wastelands of Utah and other seemingly barren areas will be reclaimed through the discovery of heretofore unknown water sources for irrigation.

• PREDICTOR: ANDREW REISS •

A lifelong devotee of stargazing, Andrew Reiss was fascinated by astronomy at age 4 but turned to astrology at 13, where his interest has remained. Since entering the field as a professional psychic in 1954, his forecasts have appeared in diverse publications. He is a regional advisor to the International Psychic Registry.

• PREDICTIONS •

1985

• We will benefit from a satellite security system in space that will maintain vigilance over radioactivity and other accumulations of pollutants in the air and water on our planet.
• The U.S. will change its political structure radically in the years ahead. There will be many bloody uprisings, and this country will suffer great upheaval during the next 20 years.

1989

• Nuclear weapons will be used in the late 1980s or early 1990s. Soon afterward, a group of scientists will discover a way to neutralize all atomic warheads by molecular frequency disassociation.
• Neutron rays will be harnessed to save lives rather than decimate the population. New ways will be found to neutralize neutron-ray weapons, and an electronic barrier will act as a shield around cities to defend them against air and land attacks by enemy troops. ·

1990

• Most jobs entailing assembly or mass production by humans will be eliminated. Factories will be closed, and a new technology will arise from the use of laser and light energies.

1991

• I see electronic master-robots running future work operations, and many past occupational duties will become obsolete by this time.

Most of us will live to see a huge technological empire of electronic wizardry and ultrasonic generators to power future industry.

1991–2010

• Plans will be announced to carry out mass evacuations around the world to escape air and water pollution, which has become so serious by this time that human life can no longer exist on the earth's surface. Safety will be found deep in the interior of the planet, where cities of the future will be built.

Pollution forces British citizens underground.

• PREDICTOR: FRANCIE STEIGER •

Internationally known psychic Francie Steiger is one of the few psychics who has had her claims tested by Psychological Stress Evaluator (PSE) instrumentation. Steiger is based in Arizona. Her predictions appear regularly in books and magazines.

• PREDICTIONS •

1982

• Freak weather and high energy costs will shut down factories in the eastern U.S. and send thousands fleeing for their lives. Unused, apparently valueless desert land in the Southwest will increase in value almost 100 times in the 1980s as a result of this mass migration.

1983

• A new technique to kill cancerous tissue will be developed based on the discovery that cancer cells cannot adjust to extreme temperature changes. In this treatment, the cancer and area immediately surrounding it will be chemically frozen and immediately reheated. Normal body tissue will have the ability to adjust to these rapid temperature changes, so it will not be affected. Only the defective cancer cells will die.

• Garbage will be converted into fuel when an economical process is developed to transform trash into natural gas for everyday use. It will be used first in factories, then in homes. Recycling will become a natural way of life for us.

1984

• Most businesses will adopt a 4-day workweek (10 hours a day) to conserve energy.

• Aspirin and other pain relievers will become a memory. Acupinching and acurubbing of specific areas will be proved to be superior pain relievers with no adverse side effects. Even relief from the pain of arthritis and various diseases will be afforded by these methods.

• Cars will float on cushions of air and will make present asphalt highways almost obsolete. Tree-lined grassy lanes will replace many roads and freeways. Air-supported golf carts will be invented first.

1986

• Vitamin therapy by injection will be found to be highly effective in combating disease. We will, through a staplerlike device that barely punctures the skin, inject ourselves at home.

1987

• A by-product of NASA research will be a clear insulating material that can be sprayed over both the interior and exterior of our homes to render them completely weatherproof.

1988

• Medical researchers will discover that the balancing of our glandular secretions, first chemically and later through the brain's subconscious mechanism, creates a natural resistance to viruses, germs, and disease. Hypnosis will be seen as a powerful preventative tool in altering glandular secretions and programming the body more positively.

• Fruit will become the main ingredient of cosmetics. Dangerous additives and chemicals in lotions, creams, and cosmetics of all types will be exposed and eliminated.

• The U.S. Supreme Court will allow a school prayer that is neither addressed to any particular deity nor an admission that one exists.

287

1990

• Homes and large buildings will be built underground; whole cities will exist underground. The atmosphere will be medically controlled, providing what we need and eliminating pollution. Weather will also be controlled, and particular areas will offer a range of temperatures for the individual's body-comfort needs. Outdoor, aboveground playgrounds will be created for naturalists who wish to "brave" the dangers, both natural and man-made.

1991

• Families will soon be watching "holovision" instead of TV. Life-size, three-dimensional pictures will take the place of today's picture tube in the home.

1992

• Pollution will be a thing of the past because laws will force industry to use only clean energy (solar and electromagnetic), thus eliminating waste and noxious emissions from our environment and future.

1993

• Auto repairs will virtually be eliminated when "memory metal" is invented. Dents, bent fenders, even major wrecks will be restored simply by applying extreme heat to the car's surface. This new metal will snap back into its original molded shape.
• Tiny bubbles of plastic and other buoyant materials will be sealed into the lining of children's swimsuits and other playwear. The lives of countless little tots will be saved each year by these unsinkable garments.

1994

• The average human life-span will be extended to 120 years through improved dietary habits, computer blood checks, and a miraculous meditation technique which eliminates stress and keeps the body chemically balanced. Lab-grown body parts and cell stimulants will repair and replace those not properly functioning.

1995

• Vegetarianism will be adopted on a worldwide basis, and meat eating will come to be considered as regressive behavior. Also, consumption of excess protein will be recognized as a major culprit in the body's inability to ward off disease.

1996

• All major diseases, including cancer and heart disease, will be eliminated when the mind is recognized as being the controller of the body's immunological defense against various germs and bacteria.

288

Weekly computer checks, in which a drop of blood is analyzed, will enable us to detect chemical imbalances and correct them before they lead to disorders of the system which cause disease. This will be done by computer card in the privacy of one's home.

1999

• A worldwide famine—triggered by a combination of freak weather conditions, crop diseases, and pestilence—will cause the major nations of the world to work together on agricultural advances. New strains of rapidly maturing vegetables and grains resistant to disease will be developed to solve the world's food crisis.

2000

• Zero-gravity space vehicles will totally change present-day air travel as electromagnetic energies are understood and harnessed, creating a pollution-free and inexhaustible source of fuel. This invention will come directly from mental contact between aliens and earthlings.
• Faced with the seemingly omniscient presence of alien beings of superior technology, the superpowers of our world will shift their energies from war to peace. Nations will agree to disarmament, and nuclear weapons will be dismantled.

2001

• Earth will be admitted to the Interstellar Federation. We will receive the aliens' assistance in developing new technologies and mental abilities, ushering in a Golden Age for humanity.
• Homes will become fully automated. At the touch of a button, everything from cooking to cleaning will be done automatically as computers take over household chores. Dust and dirt will be dispersed through sound waves. Cloth will be manufactured that will resist stains, soil, and grease and yet be disposable and inexpensive.

Earth admitted to Interstellar Federation.

• PREDICTOR: ALAN VAUGHAN •

Alan Vaughan has been called the most accurate predictor available today, reflecting his top-scoring prophetic "hits" with the Central Premonitions Registry (see article at the end of this chapter). Vaughan has worked for over a decade as a laboratory psychic (at the Maimonides Dream Lab in Brooklyn, N.Y.; Stanford Research Institute in Palo Alto, Calif.; and the City College of New York) and holds an honorary doctorate in parapsychology. His books include *Incredible Coincidence* and *Patterns of Prophecy*.

• PREDICTIONS •

By mid-1982

• The inflation rate in the U.S. will subside to 8%.

1982–1994

• There will be a series of small, conventional wars and skirmishes in the Near East, bringing into being a new country comprised of Sunni Muslims. The Shiite Muslim population will be confined to part of what is now Iran.

1984

• The U.S. will introduce an International World Games in Los Angeles to replace the Olympics. Selected teams from around the world will compete. Unlike the Olympics, the sports competitors will be professionals.
• The U.S. will start a massively funded program in psychic research in an attempt to catch up with Soviet advances. Like the Soviet program, the American psychic program will be developed by the military.

1987

• Holographic television will be introduced on a limited basis. These large-scale projections will be featured in nightclubs, with entertainers recorded live from Las Vegas.
• Genetic engineering will develop a gas-producing sea organism to provide enormous amounts of methane for energy production. Animal farming will develop into a new technology from these experiments.

By 1989

• Nuclear weapons will be outlawed. U.S. and U.S.S.R. stockpiles will be disarmed. A world nuclear regulatory agency will oversee the disarmament and will maintain a small nuclear stockpile to enforce the ban.

1990

• There will be a drastic devaluation of U.S. currency overnight, with ten old dollars being equal to one new dollar. New currency will be printed.
• A prototype electrosolar satellite will collect energy from the sun and beam it to earth.

1991

• Gas-powered automobiles will be banned from metropolitan areas in the U.S., Europe, and Japan. Battery-powered autos will become standard in city areas.

1992

• The first manned flight to Mars will benefit from a vastly improved propulsion system based on antigravity principles. The spacecraft will be able to rise from the earth slowly, without subjecting passengers to gravity forces.

By 1993

• Electrosolar satellites will have a large impact on energy problems.

INSIDE THE CENTRAL PREMONITION REGISTRY

PHILIPPINES TURNS COMMUNIST AND BECOMES ANOTHER IRAN
Francella 8716 12-31-79

A NEW BREED OF DOG BECOMES POPULAR BECAUSE OF ITS RESEMBLANCE TO OUR NEW PRESIDENT
Hoyes 8751 1-12-80

TRUMAN CAPOTE STUCK IN ELEVATOR
5–7 FLOOR
Kleinfeld 8805 1-24-80

These are examples chosen from the thousands of predictions which arrive each year at the post-office box of the Central Premonition Registry at Times Square Station in New York City. Every day at lunch hour, Robert Nelson, promotions manager of *The New York*

Times and director of the registry, heads for the post office to see what's arrived. And each weekend, he and his wife Nanci go through the hundred or so letters, sorting out the ones that are useless or merely request information and entering the rest in headline form. (The prediction is followed by the sender's last name and the letter's registered number and its date of arrival.) Sometimes a headline that has been entered in the registry matches up with a headline in one of the five newspapers Nelson reads each day. Then, as Nelson puts it, he has a "hit."

The Central Premonition Registry began in 1968 as a nationwide and international talent hunt for people who can demonstrate precognition. It was conceived while Nelson was working as a volunteer at the Dream Laboratory of Maimonides Medical Center in Brooklyn, under the directorship of Dr. Stanley Krippner. Nelson's job was to try to transmit images of pictures telepathically to someone asleep in the next room. He and Krippner began to notice that while the dreamer usually did not pick up on the image that they were transmitting at the time, he or she often described the exact picture that would be chosen at random by a computer the following week. The two men felt that precognition was being demonstrated in their laboratory. As word of the laboratory got around, they began receiving dozens of letters from people who believed that they had premonitions in their dreams. Nelson had heard about Dr. John Barker, who had begun a premonition registry in London in 1966, after the Aberfan disaster in which 31 schoolchildren lost their lives when a coal slag slid down a mountain and demolished a schoolhouse. Many people had predicted that event, and Barker speculated that if there had been a registry for their predictions at the time, the tragedy might have been prevented. Then Nelson heard that Alan Vaughan, a West Coast psychic, had predicted Robert Kennedy's assassination exactly 10 weeks before it happened. There was an obvious need to create a clearinghouse for the predictions of people like Vaughan and the many already writing in to the laboratory. A few months later, the Central Premonition Registry was born.

Nelson is not a psychic himself, and though he does receive premonitions in his dreams, they are always in a personal, not a newsmaking, vein. His own rather peculiar background served as a good preparation for running a premonition registry. He has an identical twin brother, Bill. As children their hobby was to do magic shows, a hobby Nelson continues today. They experimented with sleight of hand and hypnosis. Then, in high school, Bill quite suddenly developed into a trans-medium. Four or five different spirits began speaking through him. The brothers held weekly sessions with Bill's spirits throughout college, Nelson acting as the trance inducer and note taker for his brother. After graduating with a degree in psychology, Nelson went to New York to study law, but soon abandoned both fields in favor of the newspaper world. To continue his longtime interest in the occult, he joined the American Society for Psychic Research and was told about the need for volunteers at the Dream Laboratory. When the idea for the registry came up, Nelson was in the best position to direct it because of the easy access to news events that his *Times* job provides. Eventually funding ran out for the laboratory, and Nelson moved the address of the registry to New York City and its offices to the basement of his home in Connecticut.

People send in their premonitions, whether they come from dreams, tarot cards, the *I Ching,* tea leaves, or an induced trance state. Nelson registers them and files them in one of 14 categories. Until recently, he was receiving from 45 to 70 letters a week, but his TV appearances have increased the weekly number to nearly 150. About half of these contain a registerable prediction. Many have past predictions, which aren't registered, and about one fifth come from people seeking information, such as the whereabouts of a lost spouse or missing child. Among the rest, it's not always easy to tell the daydreamers and phonies from those with worthwhile predictions. For example, an uneducated woman named Arlene Handy has been writing to the registry for all 12 years of its existence. It takes Nelson a long time to figure out what her predictions are because she can't spell. Two spirits predict events to her in her dreams, and for the past 12 years they have predicted wrong—except once. About five years ago, she sent in a letter describing a vision of white-clad figures with turbans who were scaling a white, six-foot fence and predicted death to an American ambassador. Two weeks later an American ambassador was killed in Khartoum in Sudan. A picture in *The New York Times* showed a six-foot white fence. Because that "hit" was so good, Nelson says, he will read anything Ms. Handy writes, including this year's prediction that "silly putty will turn out to be carcinogenic." "I try not to rebel against the masses of crazy stuff that come in," says Nelson, "because there just might be something I would miss."

The registry also receives a lot of mail from people whom Nelson describes as "religious kooks." "If the letter starts out with a quote from the Bible, I don't read much further. Some of these go on to 20 handwritten pages, both sides, telling me how I'm an agent of the devil, and that I'll boil in oil in hell." Apparently there is a whole school of theology that believes the only justifiable place for a prediction is in the Bible, and that Nelson's work tampers with fate and could even interfere with predestination. "I don't believe in predestination," says Nelson. "The Book of Life hasn't already been written." Tampering with the future, however, happens to be one of his goals.

Of the 5,000 or so predictions that Nelson has received, 49 have turned out to be on target, and half of those came from five people. Nelson feels that with a larger percentage of predictors, he will have a larger percentage of "hits." In time, he hopes to be able to set up something like an early-warning disaster system—to use the registry as a means of preventing disaster. He feels that this is especially possible with murder, which is often premeditated. In addition to Vaughan's Kennedy prediction, there was, for example, a Bronx housewife who foresaw the assassination attempt on George Wallace. Several months before the attempt occurred, she sent Nelson a newspaper clipping with a picture of Wallace and wrote: "Last night I dreamed Governor Wallace walked out on a stage. There was a large crowd with colored banners and the governor had on a brown suit. I woke up—my voice said Governor Wallace will be shot."

At that time Nelson hadn't developed the idea for the early-warning disaster system, an idea which is still in its formative stage. Without the help of a computer, which could process all his letters into categories and match them up with news events, and without subsidization (Nelson funds the registry solely from the proceeds of lectures he gives on parapsychology—he's willing to lecture anywhere—and from his own pocket), it's difficult to imagine how far he can go with it. "But," says Nelson, "if I ever receive two premonitions of the same event from different people, I will try to do something to prevent that event—whether it be contacting a politician's aides, the administration of an airline, or whatever." The only interest the government has shown came from the U.S. Geological Survey, which recently requested that Nelson cooperate with them on earthquake predictions. "They're returning to what they call the 'lunatic fringe,'" says Nelson. "Human seismographs."

Most of the people who send in their predictions are not professional psychics who have a career at stake if their predictions go wrong, but rather housewives, librarians, handymen—you name it. "There's no pattern," says Nelson, "which is what makes me think that it can happen to anyone." When people write in for the first time, they receive a letter explaining that their prediction has been registered and a two-page confidential questionnaire. The questionnaire was designed either to confirm or disprove the theories of Dr. Larry Lashan, whom Nelson considers one of the brightest psychologists in the field of parapsychology today. Lashan believes that paranormal states have the same qualities as those that were known by the great mystics of the past—a sense of timelessness, of universality, and an identification with all living things. Nelson's questionnaire is designed to discover whether the people from all walks of life who have precognitive experiences sense any of these qualities while they are in that state. He has also designed a pamphlet, "The Art of Catching Dreams," which he says is "an instruction sheet culled from five or six books on dream research which tries to teach people how to develop the habit of catching dreams."

Besides creating the possibility of preventing future disasters, the registry provides an outlet for the many people who quite suddenly become recipients of strange forebodings of disaster, which are often very disturbing. Having a place to send predictions helps to validate the predictors' experiences and assures them that they are not going crazy. On the other end, reading all those letters which come in from France, Spain, the Philippines, the U.S.S.R., and all over America is often not the most soothing way to spend free time. "After reading my 18th prediction in one night of something happening to Teddy Kennedy or about Jimmy Carter getting mangled in a machine, it gets a little depressing. There have been so many times when I was ready to throw in the towel. Once in a while, though, I get a little help from my correspondents. They'll say, 'You know this is really heavy stuff. I hope you're prepared for it.' It's almost all bad news." One might wonder, then, what would motivate Nelson to take on all the work, responsibility and bad news that running a registry entails. Nelson's own answer: "Just out of an unshakable conviction that somewhere out there, in a little shack in Michigan or wherever, there's someone who can make predictions. I want to find that person. It's one more thing to get up for in the morning."

—J.H.

10

WHAT WILL HAPPEN TO THESE FAMOUS PEOPLE?

1983

Jacqueline Onassis will marry a man in the communications media.

1984

Henry Kissinger will be elected senator from New York.

1984

Bob Dylan will marry a beautiful young nurse who cared for him while he was in a hospital.

WHAT WILL HAPPEN
TO THESE FAMOUS PEOPLE?

Thirteen renowned psychics peer ahead—from today until the year 2000—to predict highlights in the lives of 15 internationally prominent persons. The psychics who participated in these forecasts are listed below. They will be identified by their initials in the predictions that follow.

A.F. ANN FISHER (See biography in previous chapter.)

A.R. ANDREW REISS (See biography in previous chapter.)

B.C. BERTIE CATCHINGS (See biography in previous chapter.)

E.H. ED HELIN is a noted psychic astrologer from California. Formerly a social worker, he teaches a course on astrology at California State University in Northridge, writes an astrological column, and is an astrological consultant to major corporations.

F.D. FREDRICK DAVIES. A psychic consultant to show-business celebrities and musicians in both Europe and the U.S., Davies, a London-based seer, specializes in astrology and predictions by tarot cards. Davies has founded astrology institutes in Washington, D.C., London, New York City, and Raleigh, N.C.

I.H. IRENE HUGHES. An internationally known author and psychic, Irene Hughes hosts a TV program in Canada and a syndicated radio show aired in the U.S.

J.C. JOHN CATCHINGS. Catchings co-publishes a monthly newsletter, *Psychic Views*, and he hosted his own talk show for over a year on radio stations in Dallas, Texas.

J.P. JOSEPH PINKSTON. A graduate of Eastern Baptist Institute, Joseph Pinkston earned a Doctor of Divinity degree in 1947. During a three-year stay in India, he developed his psychic abilities. He hosts his own radio program in Evanston, Ill.

K.S. KATHY SOTKA. A practicing psychic since 1974, Kathy Sotka of Sioux Falls, S.D., began developing her prophetic powers when she accurately foretold the death of a close relative. Her specialties include psychic consultations on marriage, career, and financial subjects, and future predictions.

L.B. LAURIE BRADY. One of America's best-known psychic astrologers, Laurie Brady first discovered her prophetic abilities as a child. Today she uses her psychic gifts in financial, spiritual, and marriage counseling.

M.D. MARIS DE LONG. A psychic who was consulted by Marilyn Monroe, Ms. De Long has been active as a professional seer since 1925. She is a member of the National Council of Spiritualist Ministers.

S.M. SANDRA MCNEIL. Psychic since childhood, Sandra McNeil lectures and conducts seminars on mind power across the U.S. and Canada, and has appeared on CBS News. Her psychic talents have been tested by the Edgar Cayce Foundation.

JACQUELINE ONASSIS

Widow of U.S. President John F. Kennedy and Greek tycoon Aristotle Onassis

1982 She and a well-known male writer will coauthor a book on food, fashions, and customs around the world. (B.C.)

1983 She will announce her engagement to a wealthy American. (B.C.)

By 1984 I predict she will marry (most likely in 1983) a man involved in the communications media or publishing world. (I.H.)

Before 1985 She will marry a man who is presently a statesman. (M.D.)

By 1985 She will author a best-selling book about life in the White House as seen from an intimate point of view. (M.D.)

1986 She will not remarry until this year. She will move to France a few years after she marries. (J.C.)

In the 1980s She will become increasingly reclusive and eccentric. She will remarry twice more and be widowed both times. (K.S.)

By 2000 She will become a partner in a publishing enterprise and after two years will rise to the top. (J.C.)

• She will get actively involved in politics and become a champion of deprived people and minorities. She will live abroad for a few years and remarry twice more, choosing a European and an American. (F.D.)

• She will continue to be the unhappy wanderer. Any marriage that she enters into before 1987 will not be successful. She will ride the coattails of her son, who one day will become president of the U.S. (E.H.)

MUHAMMAD ALI

Heavyweight boxing champion of the world

By 1982 His present wife will divorce him, and he will marry twice again in the 1980s. (M.D.)

1982 He will become a boxing manager. (J.C.)

1984 He will enjoy great prosperity in a field other than boxing. He will be grossly overweight at the time. (L.B.)

1987–1990 He will sponsor a young black boxer who will also become a champion. (B.C.)

Late 1980s He will consider running for public office. (S.M.)

By 2000 He will always have a cloud over his domestic life and will have an unsettled state of finances. (L.B.)

• He will experience health problems involving his kidneys. (J.C.)

• He will achieve great success as an actor and will do a Broadway show. He will be appointed goodwill ambassador to Africa. (F.D.)

• He will make a fortune in oil deals with the Arabs. He will become a vocal supporter and spokesman for the third world. (F.D.)

• He will become a voice in the film industry as he invests in his own

production company and achieves greater fame as a serious actor.
(S.M.)
• He will end up living in England. He will become a fight referee for
the International Boxing Association. (J.P.)
• He will become a much quieter, more serious person, devoted to
philanthropic endeavors. This new life will bring him even greater
renown than his boxing career. (K.S.)
• A child of his will gain public recognition in a very unusual way.
(K.S.)

FIDEL CASTRO

Cuban political leader

Early 1980s He will be in the headlines concerning a marriage, and
someone will try to poison him. He will be attracted to a new kind of
revolutionary philosophy that will drastically change his present
views and may cause him to break with the Russians. (L.B.)
1982–1985 He will marry. (I.H.)
1984 He will be in an accident while traveling in a foreign land. I see

Here's Fidel—Castro hosting his popular TV series.

an airplane in flames near mountains. While there will be many casualties, Castro will miraculously survive. (B.C.)

1985 He will be rushed to the hospital for a serious condition that will cause him to forget about politics permanently. (I.H.)

1986 News of a romance will surprise the world. (B.C.)

1993 A heart ailment will confine Castro to a hospital. (B.C.)

By 2000 He will die in an airplane crash over a Latin American country, possibly Honduras. Strange circumstances surrounding the crash will be reported. (J.C.)

• He will break major ties with Russia and concentrate on helping third-world nations. His form of government will launch a new political philosophy the same way Lenin, Marx, and Stalin influenced the Eastern world. (F.D.)

• He will host a world syndicated TV series. (F.D.)

• He will be assassinated by a Cuban insurgent. Cuba will become a more democratic country in future years. (A.F.)

• He will continue to juggle the U.S. and Soviet Union against each other. His downfall will come from a struggle within his own country. I sense a brother involved. (E.H.)

• He will take on a more popular image as he gains publicity for uncovering the truth related to international oil payoffs and nuclear arms. (S.M.)

• He will move to South America and become dictator of Chile. (J.P.)

• His end will come through the actions of those closest to him. One of the chief conspirators will be his brother. (K.S.)

RICHARD NIXON

Former president of the U.S.

1980–1989 He will surprise the world with three major announcements:

1. He will accept a government post.
2. He will join a prestigious university in a teaching capacity.
3. He will become involved with a television network on a series of programs to educate the public on politics in general. (S.M.)

1981–1984 He will do a great deal of writing and will be involved in his own radio show. (I.H.)

1982 He will take a trip around the world, with the highlight being a visit to China, but will be fortunate in leaving before a great earthquake rocks the area. (B.C.)

1982–1983 He will be very much in the news. He will return to power when the government needs help with America's China policy. (L.B.)

1985 He will suffer serious health problems from a new affliction. (M.D.)

1987–1988 He will be faced with another Watergate-type scandal. The American people will again take him to task, but he will have learned his lesson from past experience and will resolve the situation in his favor. (L.B.)

By 2000 He will be appointed to a political committee dealing with peace among nations. (M.D.)

• He will have a serious problem with his eyes. (J.C.)

- Soon after his death, a man who is now very close to him will make disclosures about Watergate that will reopen the investigation of that incident. (J.C.)
- He will regain tremendous support from the Republican party and be persuaded to run again for political office in the U.S. He will have great sway in the events of the next 20 years. (F.D.)
- He will become ambassador to China. (F.D.)
- He will be elected to the U.S. Senate and will serve as chief spokesman for Republicans in the Senate. (J.P.)

Born
Yorba Linda, Cal.
Jan. 9, 1913

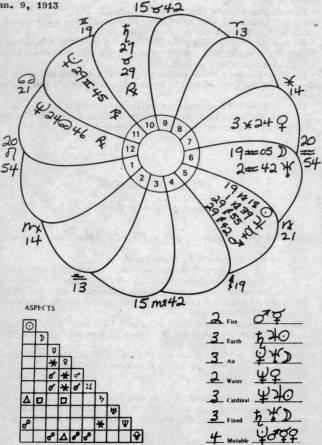

Richard M. Nixon's astrological chart.

YASIR ARAFAT

Political leader of the
Palestine Liberation Organization (PLO)

1982 He will meet secretly with Israel's Yitzhak Shamir. (B.C.)
1983 A jealous and ambitious member of the PLO will plot to assassinate Yasir Arafat, but the conspiracy will be discovered and the would-be assassin will be shot. (B.C.)
1984 There will be danger for him near motorcycles during the summer. (B.C.)

No summer cruising for Yasir Arafat.

1997 He will be forced into exile from his land. (S.M.)

1990s He will be ousted from his position as leader of the PLO. (S.M.)

By 2000 He will be assassinated by a younger relative who is also a member of the PLO. (J.C.)

• He will become president of the State of Palestine. His relationship with the Arab world and Israel will remain cool. Terrorist attacks will end and peace will reign in the Middle East. (F.D.)

• There is treachery around this man. He will die by fire in the month of May. A conspiracy headed by a close associate will be uncovered. (K.S.)

HENRY KISSINGER

Former U.S. secretary of state

1982 The summer will see tension from an impending assassination attempt that will be different from all others because it will occur within the walls of the White House. Also at this time he will be linked to a scandal involving the Chase Manhattan Bank. (L.B.)

1983–1984 He will be confined to a hospital for surgery on his digestive tract. (M.D.)

By 2000 He will be elected as a senator from a north-central state, possibly Michigan. (J.C.)

• He will be offered the office of secretary of state by a future president but will decline. (J.C.)

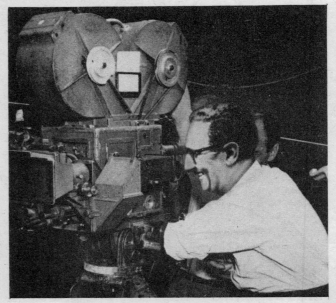

Cecil B. Kissinger.

- He will become very involved with labor and industry and later head one of the major TV networks. (F.D.)
- He will become an important filmmaker, giving up politics, but his opinions will still have a strong influence on the world. (F.D.)
- He will not be in the limelight much after 1981. (M.D.)
- He and his wife, Nancy, will adopt two children. His destiny lies with Richard Nixon. (K.S.)

MOSHE DAYAN

Israeli statesman

1983 He will receive a high award for peacemaking efforts. (B.C.)
1985 He will again hold an important leadership post in the Israeli government. (L.B.)
By 2000 He will try to rise to the rank of prime minister of Israel, but he will not succeed. (J.C.)
- He will become prime minister of Israel and will be the first leader of his nation to try working side by side with the new State of Palestine. (F.D.)
- He will gradually fade from the political scene, reemerging later on as an artist. Marital strife or a tumultuous involvement with a woman will take a toll on his health. (K.S.)

BILLY GRAHAM

U.S. evangelical leader

1984 His name will be linked with both Ted Kennedy and John Connally. (B.C.)
1985 There will be an attack on his reputation in May. (L.B.)
1980s His image will change drastically as he begins discussing such concepts as reincarnation, cosmic energy, and the possibility of life on other planets. Controversy will surround this man of God when he is caught up in a scandal over accounting for funds donated to his cause. (S.M.)
- He will announce political ambition on a local government level. (A.R.)
By 2000 There will be a significant change in his stand on gays and gay rights. (J.C.)
- He will be honored for his work by the pope, the queen of Great Britain, and the president of the U.S., all in a single year. (F.D.)
- A famous school or institution will be named for him. (A.R.)

MARCELLO MASTROIANNI

Italian actor

1984 He will make his last movie. (B.C.)
1987 He will be in a hotel or entertainment place at the time of a great fire. (B.C.)

By 2000 He will make headlines in connection with a kidnapping in Italy by using his charm and renown to rescue hostages from their kidnappers. (F.D.)

• A happy life is in store for him, and numerous extramarital affairs. (A.R.)

BRIGITTE BARDOT

French actress

1985 She will marry a wealthy gentleman from South America. (B.C.)

1980s She will marry twice. (M.D.)

By 2000 She will go in for plastic surgery but not be pleased with the outcome. (L.B.)

• She will move to Hollywood, which will become her home base. (F.D.)

• She will turn to screenwriting, and her son will become a superstar. (F.D.)

• She will not return to the screen. She will retire gracefully and enjoy the second half of her life happily married. (A.F.)

• She is in a downward cycle and will be talked into taking roles that are not good for her. There will be much wasted energy and enormous frustrations. After these experiences, she will write an exposé book that will be stormy and contain lots of sex. (E.H.)

• She'll become a voice in the field of women's fashion. (S.M.)

• She will become so conservative as to be unrecognizable. She'll be appointed to a post in the French government. Her fans will see her wearing glasses, hair swept tightly back in a granny bun, and she will be the happiest person in the world. (K.S.)

Bardot turns conservative.

BOB DYLAN

U.S. rock star

1984 He will marry a beautiful young nurse who cared for him while he was in a hospital. (B.C.)

1986 He will be the proud father of a baby girl. (B.C.)

1988 He will write a book about happiness. (B.C.)

By 2000 He will have a major TV series based on his writings and songs. (F.D.)

- He'll be rescued from a plane in a real-life drama when it makes a forced landing due to weather conditions. No one will be hurt, and a film will be made about the adventure. (F.D.)
- His life will become more and more spiritual, and he will be the founder of a religious sect. (K.S.)
- In love, Dylan's happiness lies with a tall Chinese woman. (K.S.)

JOHNNY CARSON

U.S. talk-show host and celebrity

1980s I see his name on a line of toys or games. (A.R.)
By 2000 He will purchase a string of television stations and go into syndicated programming. (J.C.)
- He will become chairman of the board of NBC. (F.D.)
- He will establish himself in prime-time TV specials with a complete change of format. These will appear no more than four times a year and will be highly successful. (A.F.)

JEANE DIXON

U.S. psychic

1980–2000 She will devote more of her time to a line of how-to books on various aspects of the psychic. She is entering a 10-year cycle of distractions and sudden change, and she may suffer the consequences of nervous exhaustion. (S.M.)
1983–1990 She will receive a gift of jewelry made from a substance from another planet. (B.C.)
1980s Her predictions and horoscopes will continue to be widely read around the world, but it will be discovered that these prophecies are being written by a team of writers familiar with the Dixon style. (A.F.)
By 2000 A line of health foods will be marketed with her name. (A.R.)
- She will establish an organization for the protection of animals. (K.S.)
- She'll be caught up in an intrigue involving foreign investments, which she does not want to be made public. (K.S.)

WILLIAM MASTERS AND VIRGINIA JOHNSON

U.S. sex therapists

1982–1986 They will write a best-selling book on sex for the senior citizen. (B.C.)
1983–1985 They will publish one of the most comprehensive books on human sexuality ever written and it will win a Nobel Prize. (A.F.)
1986 They will split and pursue separate fields or theories. (M.D.)
1980s These pioneers in sex research will write an astounding book

on the mind and psychic blocks which can create physical problems. (S.M.)

By 2000 They will host a syndicated TV talk show. (S.M.)

• Their next major area of focus will be the effects of space travel on sex. (K.S.)

• They will write musicals for the stage and make some recordings. (A.R.)

11

SCIENCE FICTION'S WORLDS

1993–2003

It is believed that God or the deathless spirit is signaling human beings. A systematic search for these signals will be made, and computer studies will resolve the mystery at last.

2000

An interplanetary ship will bring back to Earth an alien virus that will kill a tenth of Earth's population. Space colonies on the moon and Mars will not be harmed.

2010

The Soviet Union will attempt to change its past with scientific information carried by tachyons, particles that move backward in time.

PREDICTIONS FROM SCIENCE FICTION

• PREDICTOR: HUGO GERNSBACK (1884–1967) •

As a youth, Gernsback emigrated from Luxembourg to America, where he quickly became interested in the possibilities of electronics and radio technology. After designing the first home radio set in history, he put out a promotional catalog which developed into the magazine *Modern Electrics* in 1908. In this he began running, in addition to technical articles, science-fiction stories like his own "Ralph 124C 41+" (1911–1912), a classic of predictive science fiction. Gernsback founded *Amazing Stories*, the first magazine devoted exclusively to science fiction, in 1926; he lost control of the publication in 1928, but went on to found a half dozen other publications in the field. The major SF award, the Hugo, is named after him.

The Book: *Ultimate World* (written in 1959, but not published until 1971)

Gernsback's fiction reflects his personal interest in technology and social development (one of his many periodicals was the highly successful *Sexology*), with almost no attention to plot or character development. Both his first book, *Ralph,* published in book form in 1925, and this posthumously published novel are filled with technological wonders of all kinds and show a particularly vivid imagination at work. Many of the predictions from *Ralph* have since come to pass.

• PREDICTIONS •

• An alien invasion by the Xenos, who impregnate Earth women; the hybrid offspring look human but are superior mentally and physically.
• Acceleration of the natural biological cycle: embryos are brought to term in three months. Similarly, the aliens are capable of other genetic tinkering with the human species; the children grow at an accelerated rate and are able to pass their superhuman traits on to the next generation.
• Conversion of large asteroids into interstellar spacecraft.
• Interstellar war between two alien species; advanced ray weapons of an unknown nature are used.
• By the year 1996, temperature-controlled couches are developed which may be heated or cooled to any level. Similarly, rooms are heated and cooled by electronic-glass-paned air conditioners.
• Invisible energy-force fields to keep out intruders.

• Transmission of physical objects over long distances by radio. (This is much like the "transporter" in the *Star Trek* series.)
• Viewing devices that can see through walls.
• In emergencies, ordinary objects within houses can be made to resonate, acting as receivers for universal broadcasts warning of danger or disaster; in effect, a chair, for example, can become a one-way radio receiver temporarily.
• Gravitational propulsion systems are used for transportation and hauling.
• Synthesis of superheavy atomic elements.
• Newspapers are printed on synthetic paper substitutes through home receivers, the text being broadcast from various local transmitters.
• Amplifiers that can pick up sounds inside buildings 20 mi. distant.
• Humans conquer nearby space, with regular manned flights to the planets, systematic patrols to eliminate space junk in Earth orbit, mining of lunar resources, and the use of X rays and atomic power to propel spaceships.
• Watches register the time beamed from central stations. Three-dimensional TV images are projected six feet in front of the receiver.
• Telepathic hypnosis and the blotting out of harmful memories through ultrasound.
• Regeneration of amputated human limbs from cancer cells. The use of atomic flash-ray lamps to photograph minute internal parts of the human body.
• The aliens increase human intelligence with artificial brain implants.
• Radar cloaking devices and radioactive radio waves.
• Lightning employed as a weapon. Sound bombs.
• Planetwide weather control is achieved.
• Computers that can translate into 10 languages simultaneously and accurately.
• Atomic-powered lights make dim cities a thing of the past.

• PREDICTOR: GEORGE ORWELL (1903–1950) •

Eric Blair, the author of *1984*, used "George Orwell" as a pen name for all of his writings. Born in India, Orwell was sent to boarding school in England during W.W. I; after several years at Eton College, he joined the Indian Imperial Police in Burma in 1922, resigning five years later. He fought in the Spanish Civil War during the 1930s, was wounded, and later was literary editor of *The Tribune* in London during W.W. II. One of his most famous novels was *Animal Farm*. Ill with tuberculosis, Orwell retired to an island off the Scottish coast after the war to work on his last great novel. He died shortly after it was published.

The Book: *1984* (1949)

Orwell's novel was a logical outgrowth of the author's wartime experiences with governmental bureaucracy, party politics, communism and socialism in Spain and Britain, and postwar rationing. Orwell was also greatly concerned with the continual debasement of the English language, particularly in the political arena. A movie version of *1984* was released in 1956.

• PREDICTIONS •

• In 1984 the world is divided into three spheres of influence: Oceania, comprising England, the Americas, Australia, and South Africa; Eurasia, comprising Russia, Europe, and Siberia; and Eastasia, comprising China, Japan, Mongolia, and Southeast Asia.

Edmund O'Brien, in the film *1984*.

• The three superpowers are virtually indistinguishable in terms of political structure, social organization, and aims. All three are repressive totalitarian states with godlike figurehead rulers (Big Brother rules Oceania); an elite party core that makes all policy decisions; and a pervasive philosophical structure that relies on systematic falsification of records, public contradictions, and lies. Continual warfare is waged between the three states, using conventional weapons (although atomic weapons are available) to fight over pieces of Africa and India. The purpose of this warfare is to gain control over the millions of potential work slaves living in these regions, and also to

consume enough resources to keep the living standards of such populations perpetually reduced to subsistence level.
• Political alliances shift constantly, with two states ganging up against the third in a purposely unending war.
• History is systematically and retroactively changed by altering published records to reflect current political realities whenever alliances shift or Party leaders are deposed.
• Oceania is made up of three distinct social classes: the Proles, the mindless workers who comprise 85% of the population; the Outer Party, the 13% who carry out the directives of the state and serve as an impoverished middle class; and the Inner Elite, the 2% at the top who actually make the decisions and control the state.
• All citizens, particularly those in a position of power, are kept under constant surveillance. Two-way TV sets, placed in every room, must be kept turned on at all times; these are monitored irregularly. Citizens, especially children, are encouraged to spy on each other.
• Sexual activity and love are discouraged, particularly among Party members. Sex exists only for procreation. Antisex leagues abound among female members of the Party.
• Individualism is sufficient ground for execution or brainwashing: The Party demands unthinking devotion to its slogans, all of which are essentially meaningless or even contradictory.
• Language is deliberately debased and manipulated by the Party. One of the Party's principal aims is to warp the language in such a way that unorthodox thoughts cannot be voiced or even considered by the average citizen. This artificially created tongue is called Newspeak.
• The Party is sole arbiter of truth in all spheres. Its basic principle is "doublethink," the ability to believe two contradictory statements simultaneously without perceiving the illogic inherent in such a position. Party slogans (i.e., "War Is Peace," "Freedom Is Slavery," "Ignorance Is Strength") reflect the essential nature of the state.

• PREDICTOR: ARTHUR C. CLARKE (1917–) •

A native of Somerset, England, Arthur Clarke sold his first story to *Tales of Wonder* in 1938, when he was 21. He turned to writing full time in 1950. Among his successes are *Against the Fall of Night* (1953), *Childhood's End* (1953), and *Rendezvous with Rama* (1973), which won a Hugo Award and a Nebula for best science-fiction novel of the year. Clarke has lived in Sri Lanka (formerly Ceylon) since 1956.

The Work: *2001: A Space Odyssey* (movie version: Metro-Goldwyn-Mayer, 1968; book version: 1968)
Stanley Kubrick's great film classic was the first big-budget science-fiction film, and the first that could be regarded as a blockbuster in terms of box-office receipts. Adapted from the script by Clarke, which in turn was loosely based on Clarke's earlier short story "The Sentinel," the novel *2001* is a mystical tale of man encountering alien. Based upon material not used in the film, the book is not really a novelization of the movie so much as a completely new and

311

Space rescue attempt from the film *2001*.

different work; however, the book and film share some common ground.

• PREDICTIONS •

• Superior life forms which exist in outer space have taken—and will continue to take—an active interest in humankind's development. Specifically, these aliens were instrumental in instilling into prehistoric people a sense of curiosity and they now push the human race toward its next stage of development.
• By the year 2001, human beings have established a permanent base on the moon.
• A permanent space station orbits Earth, with constant shuttle service between the station and the human colony on the moon, as well as between the station and Earth.
• Advanced computer technology results in the completion of the HAL-9000, which not only communicates verbally with its human creators but can monitor a large spaceship on a continual basis and take the initiative without consulting the ship's crew.
• There is interplanetary space travel. Humans send an expedition to investigate the source of mysterious radio signals emanating from Jupiter.
• Cryogenics has advanced to the point where people can be stored in suspended animation for long periods of time and then be revived at will.
• Human beings ultimately achieve a transcendent state, another stage of reality, discarding their technology; once again children, they presumably will be shepherded by the unseen aliens to another stage in their development.

· PREDICTOR: RAY BRADBURY
(1920–) ·

One of the few writers able to transcend the limitations of the science-fiction and fantasy genre, Bradbury was born in Illinois but moved to Los Angeles as a young man. One of his first professional sales was a joke to George Burns and Gracie Allen for their radio program of the late 1930s. His best-known work is *The Martian Chronicles.*

The Book: *Fahrenheit 451* (1953)
First published in 1950 in shorter form as "The Fireman," *Fahrenheit 451* is a typical Bradburian statement on the evils of technology and the joys of culture, here represented by books and reading. This dystopian novel of a future Earth is the psychological odyssey of Montag, a sensitive and intelligent man, as he changes from a representative of a totalitarian state into a violent rebel, and from a passive, dissatisfied man into a vital, growing human being.

· PREDICTIONS ·

· The human race survives two atomic wars through the beginning of the 21st century. A third, seemingly interminable, struggle with unidentified enemies results in sporadic bombings of Earth's cities and industry. To maintain control in this chaotic situation, a repressive government systematically regulates all facets of human existence.
· Books are banned as corruptive and disruptive; to enforce its decree, the government creates a group called the Firemen, who exist

A book-burning scene from the film *Farenheit 451.*

solely to ferret out and burn contraband material, especially books and magazines.
• Children are taught exclusively through the use of giant wall television sets; TV programming is also used to control the adult population. The emphasis in both cases is on passive participation in inane and meaningless soap operas; questions are discouraged.
• Juveniles are encouraged to take out their frustrations by racing about town in high-speed jet cars, riding the air-cushioned subway systems, visiting "fun parks," breaking windows, wrecking automobiles, and shooting one another.
• Billboards are constructed 200 ft. long in order to gain the attention of the jaded populace.
• The citizens of this future society are encouraged to report suspected violations of the social rules to the authorities, who then send the Firemen out on sweeps. Punishment for harboring books is death.
• Assisting the Firemen in tracking down lawbreakers are the mechanical Hounds, robot tracking devices which can be keyed to the specific chemical scent of the victim.
• Society's malcontents collect together in the countryside, the only place of refuge; they avoid detection by memorizing books and then destroying them, each person "becoming" one particular book.
• A third atomic war destroys the last vestiges of the corrupt and decayed civilization of the cities. The surviving renegades in the countryside return to the towns to rebuild a new and vital community.

• PREDICTOR: GENE RODDENBERRY
(1921–   ) •

Roddenberry is a native Texan, born in El Paso. He attended a series of universities in New York, Los Angeles, and Miami, served in the Army Air Force during W.W. II, became a professional pilot for Pan American, survived a plane crash in the Syrian desert in which most of the passengers were killed, and then went to Hollywood to become a television writer. When he couldn't find other work he joined the Los Angeles Police Department, rose to the rank of sergeant, became a speech writer for the chief of police, and finally sold several TV scripts written at night and on weekends. As a full-time TV writer and producer, he worked on *Have Gun, Will Travel* before creating *The Lieutenant* and *Star Trek*.

The Work: *Star Trek* (television series: 1966–1969; animated series: 1973–1974; motion picture: 1979)
Star Trek did not fare well in the ratings when it was first shown, but it gradually gained ground in syndication to become one of the most popular television series ever made; it is still shown daily or weekly in all the major television markets in the U.S. Roddenberry constantly hammered home a message of hope: Our technological future is bright only if we can get along with ourselves and those around us, human or alien. The time is the 23rd or 24th century A.D.

• PREDICTIONS •

• Earth survives its present planetary troubles (and others which will occur during the late 20th and early 21st centuries) to unite under one planetary government. Humans continue space exploration and join with other planetary systems of humans, semihumans, and aliens to form the United Federation of Planets.

• Faster-than-light spaceships and communicators make the UFP and other competing empires feasible.

• Since the many intelligent life forms in the galaxy represent all levels of development, humankind will inevitably meet an alien race that has evolved further than humanity. This race may be forced to intercede in the human race's squabbles with its enemies.

• To protect themselves, humans make huge battleships to patrol the outer reaches of the space they control. The commanders of these ships have the power and autonomy to make policy decisions on the spot when necessary.

• The spaceships are powered by matter/antimatter propulsion systems.

• Matter transmitters ("transporters") enable the ships to transfer crews from ship to ship, or from ship to planet surface, quickly and efficiently.

• Advanced weaponry includes photon torpedoes and phasers (laser weapons), both as handguns and cannons.

• Vulcans, as well as other alien races, have certain mental powers,

Spock and Captain Kirk, ready for action.

including telepathy; during its travels the *Enterprise* encounters forms of telekinesis and teleportation.
• Universal translators are common personal equipment for Starfleet personnel, providing instant translations of the most esoteric forms of communication. Food synthesizers on spacecraft greatly extend their range and versatility.
• All spacecraft are equipped with sensors which can take mass, speed, energy, and life-form readings; they are also fitted with force fields for defense.
• In several episodes in the series, the *Enterprise* and its crew are able to travel through time by entering a time portal or by warping around neutron stars.
• Several of the alien entities the *Enterprise* crew encounters are immortal.
• Highly sophisticated robots are developed; computer systems are small, portable, and capable in many instances of containing all human knowledge and experience. Some computers shown in the series have the capability of independent thought or initiative. Androids (amalgamations of man and machine) are also depicted.
• The theory is established that alternate universes exist parallel to our own.
• Humans eliminate most physical and mental illnesses, employing humane treatment. Portable medical computers (tricorders) provide instant analysis, even on field missions. Medical beds aboard the *Enterprise* are equipped with constant computer monitoring sensors. The possibility of physical brain transplants is explored in one episode.
• Intelligent life based on the element silicon, instead of carbon, is discovered. The resulting life form has the appearance of a mobile rock.
• Human beings are enjoined in the Prime Directive not to interfere with the development of primitive alien cultures.
• Computer teaching devices permit accelerated learning. Books are "read" on screens; few books printed on paper survive.
• Precognition, mind exchanges, empathetic communication (the ability to read another being's emotions mentally)—all are encountered by the crew of the *Enterprise*.
• Beings of pure energy, beings which can change their body shapes at will, and beings which "eat" emotions are encountered.
• The Romulans develop an invisibility screen in several episodes of the series.
• Doomsday machines threaten to destroy all civilized life.
• Split personalities are actually realized in the flesh. In one episode, Kirk becomes two entities, each reflecting one part of his character.
• A file on every known person in the galaxy exists in the *Enterprise*'s banks, and is presumably repeated in every other computer bank elsewhere.

• PREDICTOR: JAMES BLISH
(1921–1975) •

Born in New Jersey, Blish published his first science-fiction story, "Emergency Refueling," in March, 1940. Among his works are

A Case of Conscience, winner of the Hugo Award for best science-fiction novel of 1958; the *After Such Knowledge* tetralogy; and numerous books derived from the popular television series *Star Trek*. Better remembered for his ideas than for his characters, Blish emigrated to England in 1968 and died there of lung cancer on July 30, 1975.

The Work: *Cities in Flight* (1950–1962)

Blish's epic work is a loosely connected series of novels and short stories, some of which were rewritten after their original magazine appearance to fit into the overall saga. In 1970 the four books which came to comprise the series were integrated into a single volume under the title *Cities in Flight*.

• PREDICTIONS •

• By the end of the 20th century, humans have conquered and investigated their own solar system, establishing the first space station in 1981; and they have sent manned expeditions to all the planets near Earth. A 10th planet of the solar system (which Blish calls Proserpine) is discovered about the year 2000.

• By the beginning of the 21st century, the totalitarian states have circled the globe, stifling the masses, eliminating progress and change, and fashioning an elite upper class. The sole purpose of these regimes is to perpetuate themselves in power.

• With the rise of totalitarianism, the masses are swept by new religious fervor and increased conservatism, encouraged by their governments. Robot evangelists seduce the ignorant with promises of salvation.

• By the mid-21st century, human beings have made great technological advances, but real scientific development has virtually ceased. Governments use the technology of electronics to help control their citizens. Infectious diseases have disappeared except in laboratories, and most degenerative diseases, such as cancer, are fully under control.

• Governments become increasingly similar in outlook, tactics, and philosophy, seeking to establish absolute control over their citizens. Civil and political liberties vanish.

• Medical engineers discover a life-lengthening drug while researching a cure for cancer. The sociological implications of this discovery do not become evident until much later.

• Discovery of the Dillon-Wagonner gravitronpolarity generator, nicknamed the "spindizzy." The practical aspects of this antigravity device are not explored until long after its initial development in the early 21st century.

• First interstellar expedition and first colonization of a nearby star system (2021 A.D.).

• Soviet conquest of the Western world (2027).

• The world government bans all space flight in 2039, seeking to prevent unauthorized emigration of its citizens. The Soviets also suppress many technological and scientific advances; other advances are lost in the resulting political chaos that spreads throughout the world.

• Around 2105, a new Dark Age sweeps the world. The spindizzy and immortality drugs are lost, along with many other discoveries. The world economy collapses.
• Earthlings' first contact with an alien race, the Vegans (2289). The first interstellar war (2310).
• Rediscovery of the spindizzy on Earth (2375). Entire cities now leave the home planet in search of greener economic pastures. By 2522, most of the population has left Earth, whose natural resources have been so depleted over the centuries that it can no longer support advanced technology.
• Rediscovery of the drugs which allow men to stretch their lives over hundreds of years.
• The rising interstellar empire of the Earth colonies is bolstered by the arrival of the free cities; these cities join with the colonies to defeat the decaying empire of the Vegans.
• Admiral Hrunta proclaims himself emperor of the colonies; he is assassinated in 3089 after 725 years of personal rule.
• Science flourishes during this period, with the development of frictionless bearings, interstellar communication, giant ray guns, and invisibility machines.
• Between 3089 and c. 4000 A.D., the peak of Okie civilization is reached, in which the free city-states offer their services to the highest bidder; some of the cities settle on small planets or asteroids.
• The collapse of the galactic economy occurs, followed by the rise of a new alien civilization, the Web of Hercules. The Earthmen retreat to the Greater Magellanic Cloud, the galaxy nearest to our Milky Way.
• This new cycle of decline/revitalization is interrupted by the catastrophic end of the universe, as time itself winds down. The universe is destroyed (and a new one created) on June 2, 4104 A.D.

• PREDICTOR: PATRICK McGOOHAN (1928–) •

Born on Long Island, N.Y., McGoohan later settled in England, where he made his acting debut in the play *Serious Charge* (1954). His first television break was the series *Danger Man* (1960–1966)—called *Secret Agent* in the U.S.—in which he played a suave spy for the British government. It was at this time that he first began to write and direct scripts as well as act in them. Since moving to California in the 1970s, he has continued to be active in both television and the movies, appearing in *Rafferty*, *The Man in the Iron Mask*, and *Columbo* (several episodes of which he also wrote and directed).

The Work: *The Prisoner* (17-episode television series: 1968)
This series was McGoohan's follow-up to *Secret Agent*, created with the help of producer David Tomblin and script editor George Markstein. McGoohan wrote and directed several of the episodes, including the conclusion, and starred in the lead role as an unnamed spy who decides he's had enough of secret-service work and tries to resign. Unfortunately, one side or the other in the cold war regards the information in his brain as too valuable to release, and McGoohan is shanghaied to the Village, an idyllic resort filled with

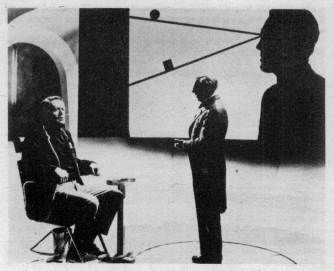

Patrick McGoohan in the TV series, *The Prisoner*.

ex-admirals, ex-generals, ex-government officials, and ex-spies. He spends the rest of the series trying to escape from this paradisiacal prison.

• PREDICTIONS •

• The Village uses the Rovers as its last line of defense against possible escapees. These are animate, man-sized balloons which pursue the renegades by land or sea, smothering them if they resist too long, dragging them back if they become docile. The balloons appear to be released and partially controlled from a central surveillance unit.
• All aspects of Village life are monitored electronically with miniature TV transmitters, radio and voice transmitters, and other sophisticated spying devices. Some of these transmitters seem to have the capability of spying through walls.
• Brainwashing devices, hidden in ordinary lamps, are used at night to empty the prisoners' thoughts of subversive ideas.
• The Prisoner is subjected to a dream projector, which can project his dreams onto a screen and then insert elements (faces of fellow spies, for example) into them while recording his uninhibited reactions.
• The Prisoner's mind is transferred to another body, and he is forced to find the inventor of the technique to effect the switch back to his own body.
• The Prisoner must repel the advances of a woman whose emotional responses are manipulated by radio transmissions.

319

• The Village uses extremely sophisticated psychological harassment, drugs, brainwashing techniques, and subtle peer pressure in ways that seem beyond the bounds of present-day science.

• PREDICTOR: JOHN BOORMAN
(1933–) •

Born in England on January 18, 1933, Boorman was educated at Salesian College in Chertsey, Surrey. He began writing film criticism at the age of 17, served in the British army, and later joined the Independent Television News in England as a film editor. His experience in producing and directing documentaries led to his appointment as director of the BBC documentary film unit. His first motion picture assignment was *Catch Us If You Can*. He achieved fame with *Deliverance* (1972), which won numerous awards.

The Movie: *Zardoz* (Twentieth Century–Fox, 1974)

Boorman wrote, directed, and produced this picture, and even coauthored the novelization with Bill Stair (1974). *Zardoz* was not a great commercial success when it first appeared, but it has since attained a cult following among science-fiction and movie buffs. The film is set in the year 2293, with the world divided into three distinct communities: the Eternals, the elite group which controls the world; the Brutals, poverty-stricken peons scratching out a living under distinctly medieval conditions; and the Exterminators, a group of barbarians trained by the Eternals to restrict the numbers of the Brutals through savage killings and slavery.

The giant stone god, Zardoz.

• PREDICTIONS •

• Civilization as we know it will be destroyed in a third world war, probably occurring about the year 2000.
• Practical immortality. Through constant computer monitoring of the human body, the natural deterioration of the genetic code can be completely stopped.
• Cloning. Individuals who are accidently destroyed can be regrown in vats of nutrients. Since the computer which controls the Vortexes (small areas where the Eternals dwell) contains the memory patterns of each citizen, these clones are for all practical purposes identical to the originals, completely reproducing their memories and feelings.
• The computer itself is a crystal a few inches in diameter, containing innumerable internal facets, which can store all human knowledge. It also appears capable of independent thought.
• Antigravity enables the Eternals to float a giant stone head (christened Zardoz by Boorman) over the barbarous sections of the world, providing a very real god with which to keep the Exterminators—and through them the Brutals—in thrall.
• An invisible force-field keeps the unsavory Brutals and Exterminators from intruding into the idyllic life of the Vortexes.
• Advanced psychological and genetic techniques provide a renegade Eternal with the means to develop over a period of generations a mutant Exterminator, Zed, who has the intelligence to see through the lies of the Eternals and the initiative to destroy their way of life.
• Although humans may achieve a technological utopia, such a culture will inevitably decay into boredom, fatuousness, and sterility without the pressure of change and possibility of growth. Hence the world of the Vortexes, although outwardly flourishing, is inwardly barren and must be destroyed if a new, revitalized civilization is to arise.
• Instant democracy is achieved. Citizens may demand an immediate vote on any subject, with the tally rendered mentally by a computer. Anyone accused of transgressing the rules of society is promptly judged by similar means. He may argue his case directly to all via the common mind-link. Punishment for crimes against society consists of physical aging of the individual for specified lengths of time (one month, one year, ten years, etc.). Since the individual cannot die, renegades ultimately are aged into permanent senility, and thereby removed from active life in the community.
• Zed, the "new man" created by the Eternals, destroys their world but helps give rise to a better world.

• PREDICTOR: GEORGE LUCAS
(1944–   ) •

Lucas attended the University of Southern California School of Cinematography, where before graduating he made a short film called *THX 1138: 4EB*, which featured a chase scene with metal-faced cops on motorcycles. He worked with Francis Ford Coppola at Warner Brothers, and Coppola served as executive producer on

Lucas's first full-length feature film, *THX 1138* (1971), an expanded version of his student short. His second film, *American Graffiti*, achieved great success, but it was his third work, *Star Wars* (1977), which made his reputation and set box-office records. This was followed by a successful sequel, *The Empire Strikes Back*.

The Movie: *Star Wars* (1977)

Set in a mythical universe, *Star Wars* is a fast, fun adventure in an outer-space setting. Lucas borrowed elements from swashbucklers, westerns, war films, serials, suspense thrillers, and fairy tales. The novelization (1976) appeared under Lucas's name, but was actually written by Alan Dean Foster.

· PREDICTIONS ·

· Interstellar spaceflight. Humans conquer the stars, spreading throughout the galaxy in faster-than-light spacecraft.

A scene from *Star Wars*.

• Commerce and communication with alien races. It is clear from the bar scene, for example, that the galaxy is full of bizarre but intelligent aliens who are on a comparable technological level with humans.
• Intelligent, functioning robots and androids of all types. Some of these are capable of speech, initiative, or even humor, although humans remain clearly in charge.
• The world changes from a loose galactic federation, apparently democratic in nature, to a totalitarian empire ruled by a hereditary monarch and policed by storm troopers as sinister as those of Hitler. Miscellaneous groups of freedom-seeking rebels, some well-organized and armed, are fighting the central government, presumably to restore the old order.
• Ritualistic fighting with lightswords (lasers-on-a-stick).
• Construction of an artificial fighting fort, the Death Star, as large as an asteroid and powerful enough to destroy whole planets with its laserlike weapons.
• Dogfights in space between one- and two-person fighter spacecraft.
• Interstellar war on a vast scale.
• Development of superhuman psychic powers which utilize the "Force," a mysterious gathering of the energy fields of all intelligent beings.
• Land jetcars which can travel at high speeds over flat terrain.
• Systematic mining and farming of marginal planets, using robots and other automated equipment to work sparsely populated regions.
• Holographically projected chess pieces, messages, and images.
• Antigravity devices.

—R.R.

PREDICTIONS FROM SCIENCE FICTION WRITERS:
Exclusive for
The Book of Predictions

• POUL ANDERSON •

One of science fiction's most prolific authors, Poul Anderson has more than 60 books and 200 short works to his credit. Although he is best known in the science fiction field, he has written several historical and conventional novels as well. The winner of six Hugo Awards and two Nebula Awards for science fiction, Mr. Anderson's books include *No World of Their Own*, *The Ancient Gods*, and *Trader to the Stars*.

HIS PREDICTIONS

1982

• Inflation in the U.S. goes out of control, resulting in panic, economic chaos, and widespread suffering. The U.S.S.R. gets effective control of Near Eastern oil and supply lines.

1982–1984

• "Finlandization" of Western Europe and Japan by the U.S.S.R. Growth of Communist and other "left" regimes throughout Central and South America. Public reaction in the U.S. sweeps into office a conservative government which gives itself broad emergency powers.

1984–1993

• U.S.-China entente. Concentration on rebuilding military and economic strength. Massive revival of U.S. effort in space. Aid to whatever friends we have left in the world. Soviet interference minimized by the threat of total nuclear war, as well as by increasing unrest throughout the Soviet empire, which finally leads to widespread revolts. Although theoretically still in existence, the U.N. hardly ever meets, and nobody pays any attention when it does.
• Though militarily neutered, Western Europe—drawing ever closer to the satellite countries in Eastern Europe—and Japan enjoy a modest prosperity which allows them to commence commercial development of extraterrestrial resources. This is largely in private hands, and it helps keep alive a wish for liberty among Americans even though they mostly accept that their own regimentation is necessary. Currency and tax reforms help stimulate U.S. productivity, and it begins to rise again.
• Scientific and technological developments in this period:

1. Fusion-power and solar-power satellites are developed and begin to come into use about 1993.
2. Recombinant DNA techniques start to become important for the production of many chemicals. They also lead to highly specific pesticide diseases which, for example, practically exterminate the rat and thus save millions of tons of food annually.
3. A start is made in really effective treatment of neurochemical disorders and some hereditary illnesses. Vaccines for several kinds of cancer appear.
4. The Second Industrial Revolution—the computer revolution—proceeds apace, and the Third—the industrialization of space—makes a vigorous beginning.
5. Early experiments with direct human-computer interfaces are conducted, adapting techniques used for communication with apes and cetaceans.
6. Cosmology is completely revolutionized by discoveries made by space-borne instruments, and this in turn leads to reexamination of the foundations of physics.

• Little or nothing of lasting value is done in the arts. Americans abandon hedonism for austerity, patriotism, and service to society. There is a period of outright persecution of liberals, environmentalists, and others "who got us into this mess." There is a strong religious revival.

1993–1995

• The international crisis peaks as the Soviet empire begins to come apart and its leaders grow desperate. Brief Soviet-Chinese war, in which some nuclear weapons are employed, is settled by negotiations under strong U.S. pressure, while the world recoils in horror at seeing the results of even so limited a nuclear conflict. A palace revolution in the Kremlin puts moderate men—old-fashioned Russian patriots and the managerial "new class"—in power there.

1996–1998

• Worldwide chaos, with frequent fighting and much suffering, as numerous regimes and hegemonies disintegrate or are dismembered and grope toward new alignments. For the sake of stability, the U.S. and China help the Russian government keep control over the core of the empire.

1999

• The "Peace of Stabilization," also known as the "Peace of Exhaustion," negotiated by the great powers (which now include Japan and the newly formed European Union) and imposed by them on the lesser powers. Like the Congress of Vienna, this conference sets up a system which can hang together for some generations to come, giving mankind a breathing spell.

2000

• The new U.S. president-elect announces that while emergency powers must be kept in reserve, most official control over the lives of citizens will be terminated "to free our energies for meeting the challenges of the new century."

2001

• Military surplus spacecraft and other equipment made available to civilians. Numerous enterprises planned. They include using a good deal of the immense material wealth that will come in from space to help the unfortunate majority of mankind return from barbarism and rise out of poverty. This will have subtle long-range effects as such societies become influential; but otherwise, for the rest of this century political developments will matter much less than scientific and technological ones.

2005

• First large civilian colony in earth orbit. Expansion of lunar settlements and industry. First asteroid brought to earth orbit for mining. Interplanetary explorations.

2010

• Cytological basis of aging understood. Prospect of halting it, leading to virtual immortality. Computer consciousness; man-computer linkages perfected.

2020

• Activity throughout the solar system. First interstellar probes launched.

2030

• Something that changes our whole concept of reality and man's place in it has been discovered by now. I don't know what it is, I just feel reasonably sure that it will come about!

Mr. Anderson adds: "The only prediction I feel any confidence in making is that any predictions I make are sure to prove wrong."

• L. SPRAGUE DE CAMP •

A patents engineer and editor turned writer, L. Sprague de Camp has authored historical works, fantasies, and science fiction novels. He produced the Johnny Black series that appeared in *Astounding Science Fiction* in the 1930s, and penned new versions of Robert E. Howard's Conan stories. His many other works, written both solo and in collaboration with others, include *Divide and Rule, The Carnelian Tube,* and *The Science-Fiction Handbook.*

HIS PREDICTIONS

Since it is easier to see long-term trends than to predict the rates at which they will operate, I shall confine my predictions to probable developments by 2030. Also, such predictions must be qualified by assuming no major unpredictable catastrophes like nuclear war, collision with a planetoid, runaway greenhouse effect, etc.

The factors that seem to be the most nearly inevitable are the increase in the earth's population to nearly double its present number before leveling off; the exhaustion of more and more natural resources; and the continuing advance of science and technology.

The combination of growing population and the desertification of large, marginally arable lands means that we may expect more and more mass famines, like that of the Sahel a few years ago, on an ever-increasing scale. As a reaction to these mass deaths, we can expect governments, especially authoritarian governments (which means a large majority of the world's governments) to adopt compulsory methods of population control, including forcible sterilization, like the measures that led to the temporary fall of Indira Gandhi.

The growth of population and of economic interdependence will, I think, result in ever-increasing governmental intervention and regulation. Life will become more highly organized, complex, and regimented, with more and more red tape, forms to fill out, reports to file. The differences between socialistic and capitalistic economies will diminish to some degree as capitalistic governments regulate private industry more severely, while socialistic and communistic governments experiment in a gingerly fashion with profit motives, each all the while insisting that it practices its kind of economy in pure form and that the differences remain as great as ever.

The progress of science and technology will bring about an older population as more people live into their eighties and nineties. (Indefinite extension of life seems unlikely because of the nature of cellular reproduction.) This will probably mean a more conservative population. The mechanization of agriculture will accelerate urbanization as displaced farm laborers all over the world flock to the cities, as they did in the U.S. between the Civil War and the Second World War. Increasing urbanization means more crime, and we may anticipate a reversal of the trend of the last century towards rehabilitation and humane treatment of criminals. We may see a revival of burning at the stake, etc., for serious offenses.

Petroleum is likely to be more or less exhausted in 30 years. This is likely to result in severe curtailing of the use of private automobiles and of air travel. Substitutes will be used, within limitations. A general shift to alcohol would cut severely into the world's food-grain supply. Hydrogenation of coal will furnish some liquid fuel, but at much higher cost than present-day petroleum products. One sure casualty of the petroleum shortage is likely to be recreational vehicles (motorboats, dune buggies, etc.) and powered lawn mowers. We may see liquid fuels reserved for official vehicles like fire engines and ambulances.

While cheap air travel may disappear, international travel is likely to continue, if need be on the surface. We may even see the steam locomotive revived, burning coal. International contact is likely to continue the present process of the homogenizing of the world's cultures, so that everywhere people dress much alike and go about their business in the same ways, reserving native costumes for special occasions and the entertainment of tourists.

The separation of sexual intercourse from reproduction is likely to continue the trend toward sexual promiscuity and a return to something like the wife-lending customs of many primitives. This in turn, however, is likely further to increase the instability of marriage, which in turn may cause increasing problems in the control of adolescents, until such time as a new equilibrium is reached. The sexual revolution is likely in the next half-century to bring about changes in Catholic Church doctrines, e.g., dropping opposition to contraception and permitting priests to marry.

The advance of science is likely to bring a further decline in the status of the traditional religions and an increasing growth of magical and pseudoscientific cults.

• PHILIP K. DICK •

Philip K. Dick is a science fiction novelist whose wide variety of work includes numerous time-travel stories (*Dr. Futurity, Now Wait for Last Year*) and tales featuring the "awareness of reality" theme (*Time Out of Joint*). His "alternative history" novel, *The Man in the High Castle,* won the 1963 Hugo Award for its treatment of a premise in which the U.S. is defeated by the Axis powers during World War II. Other notable works by Dick include *Do Androids Dream of Electric Sleep?, Galactic Pot-Healer,* and *Solar Lottery.*

HIS PREDICTIONS

1983

• The Soviet Union will develop an operational particle-beam accelerator, making missile attack against that country impossible. At the same time the U.S.S.R. will deploy this weapon as a satellite killer. The U.S. will turn, then, to nerve gas.

1984

• The U.S. will perfect a system by which hydrogen, stored in metal hydrides, will serve as a fuel source, eliminating the need for oil.

1985

• By or before this date there will be a titanic nuclear accident either in the U.S.S.R. or in the U.S., resulting in a shutting down of all nuclear power plants.

1986

• Such satellites as HEAO-2 will uncover vast, unsuspected high-energy phenomena in the universe, indicating that there is sufficient mass to collapse the universe back when it has reached its expansion limit.

1989

• The U.S. and the Soviet Union will agree to set up one vast metacomputer as a central source for information available to the entire world; this will be essential due to the huge amount of information coming into existence.

1993

• An artificial life form will be created in a lab, probably in the U.S.S.R., thus reducing our interest in locating life forms on other planets.

1995

• Computer use by ordinary citizens (already available in 1980) will transform the public from passive viewers of TV into mentally alert, highly trained, information-processing experts.

1997

• The first closed-dome colonies will be successfully established on Luna and on Mars. Through DNA modification, quasi-mutant humans will be created who can survive under non-Terran conditions, i.e., alien environments.

1998

• The Soviet Union will test a propulsion drive that moves a starship at the velocity of light; a pilot ship will set out for Proxima Centaurus, soon to be followed by an American ship.

2000

• An alien virus, brought back by an interplanetary ship, will decimate the population of Earth, but leave the colonies on Luna and Mars intact.

2010

• Using tachyons (particles that move backward in time) as a carrier, the Soviet Union will attempt to alter the past with scientific information.

• JOE HALDEMAN •

A Vietnam veteran, Joe Haldeman gained popular recognition with the publication of *The Forever War*. This book won the Hugo, the Nebula, and the Ditmar awards for the best science fiction novel of 1975. *Mindbridge* followed in 1976 and was also highly acclaimed, winning the Galaxy Award of 1978. Mr. Haldeman is currently working on a science fiction trilogy. The first volume—entitled *Worlds*—will be published in 1981.

HIS PREDICTIONS

1982–1992

One technological development that may come to pass before 1992 will change the world forever: the perfection of a reliable defense system against ICBMs. If the Soviets get it first, it will probably be a ground-based particle beam weapon; if the Americans beat them, it may be an orbiting laser weapon.

In either case, there are two possible futures. Unfortunately, the more likely is for the power that first develops the weapon to use it, launching a preemptive nuclear strike under some political pretext. You can write your own scenario for what happens after that.

Less likely, but infinitely more desirable, would be for the existence of this defense to force unilateral, universal, orderly destruction of nuclear weapons—of all countries, not just us and them. The nuclear materials might be put to use for the generation of electrical power, or for ambitious engineering projects, such as the industrialization of space, as detailed below.

1993–2030

If there is a nuclear war, it seems likely that the "winning" side will ultimately also lose, in the sense that previously existing social systems will deteriorate. This is a hunch, probably based on an instinct that sinners must suffer. Within a year after the war, world order systems such as the U.N., NATO, and the Warsaw Pact will collapse. The governments of most countries will follow, either becoming strict police states or degenerating into collections of small localized organizations, mutually uncooperative. It may be that the third-world countries of Africa and South America will survive with their governments and economies relatively intact, and the ultimate destiny of the race will be in their hands. The joker in the deck is Australia, which may be the only country to enter the 21st century with a technologically advanced society organized along traditional "European" lines.

If we reach this period without experiencing a nuclear war, we face the problem of coping with expanding material progress. Even if the world's population were stabilized, and even if our various political and economic systems would allow such a thing, it is simply not possible for all four billion of us to attain a standard of living as comfortable as the middle classes of America and Europe now enjoy—not if the energy and industry supporting that standard come from conventional sources. The second law of thermodynamics will not be repealed: Every process that does useful work produces waste heat. If everybody lived as well as Americans do, the earth's surface

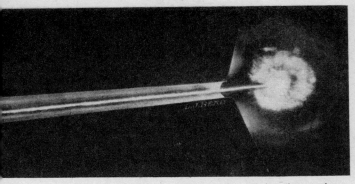

Breakthrough electron-beam defensive weapon may halt nuclear attacks.

temperature would rapidly increase to a level that would precipitate catastrophic climatic change.

A conservative scenario dealing with this would involve a downward adjustment of the standard of living in "have" countries. It's possible that this could be done noncatastrophically, people changing their attitudes toward desirable levels of physical comfort and the accumulation of possessions. This would *not* require a complete regression to primitive styles of life. Relatively little waste heat is generated by communication and cybernetic processes. It's possible to see a future where people live quite simply in terms of material wealth, yet can routinely communicate with anyone in the world, and can punch up a central library and instantly have a copy of any book ever published or any TV show ever perpetrated.

No scenario that predicts continued material progress can ignore space industrialization. It is absolutely necessary that heavy industry and power generation eventually be largely relocated off the earth's surface, so that waste heat and pollution can be harmlessly dissipated into space. The *only* alternative to space industrialization is permanent reversal of economic growth, more or less catastrophic. An interesting specific scenario, perhaps possible by 2030, would be to use the nuclear weapons stockpiled by the world's armies to capture asteroids, bringing them into orbit around the earth, where they could be used as raw materials for space industrialization. An asteroid of the nickel/iron persuasion comprises quadrillions of tons of high-quality steel, ready-made.

With the Office of Management and Budget and Congress treating NASA like a poor relation, it seems unlikely that the U.S. will take the initiative in space industrialization, even though the space shuttle would be a perfect first step. The Soviets may do it, if they manage to keep their act together into the 21st century. Some multinational corporations might have the industrial and economic capability, but they're unlikely to get involved in a project that will take 20 years to pay back a huge initial investment. Japan is a possibility; so is Germany. Perhaps the OPEC nations will see that the only way they can perpetuate their stranglehold on the world's energy resources is to move their money into space, creating a monopoly on solar-power satellites.

A remote possibility is that the U.S.—its government and its people—will pull its collective head out of the sand and look up, toward the stars.

• HARRY HARRISON •

Science fiction writer Harry Harrison is best known for his creation of the Stainless Steel Rat series, which features Slippery Jim diGriz, a space-hopping master criminal. Other humorous projects include *Bill, the Galactic Hero* and *The Technicolor Time Machine*. His anti-utopian novel *Make Room! Make Room!* was filmed as *Soylent Green* in 1973 and won the Nebula Award the same year. Mr. Harrison currently lives in Ireland.

HIS PREDICTIONS

1982-1992

• A microcomputer in every car. The continuing reduction of chip costs and expansion of cheap memory capacity will enable the mass production of this device. It will control engine fuel and air supply for maximum efficiency, monitor oil pressure, water temperature, tire pressure, etc., and instantly give warning of any variations from the norm; give a continuing readout of speed, remaining fuel, number of miles before refilling at current speed, and many other functions. This device will cost approximately $5—therefore every car will have one.

• There will no longer be any gasoline available for private motoring. At first cars will be adapted for natural gas, since this is still plentiful. As soon as this runs out, other fuels such as plant alcohol will be used. Later fuels will be much more expensive and use of the private car will be more and more restricted until eventually it will be driven only by the very rich.

• The improvement of public transportation will coincide with the decline of the private motorcar.

• A breakthrough in battery design will eliminate the lead-acid battery once and for all. The new battery will contain approximately 10 times the energy of the old batteries in the same volume. This will make the electric car a viable proposition and mark the end of the internal-combustion engine in highway vehicles.

• In India and Africa continued crop failures due to world climatic changes will coincide with population growth. The result will be mass starvation and food riots. Deaths will be counted in the hundreds of thousands, then the millions. Relief measures will be only a drop in the bucket. It will appear to the developed countries that the situation is insoluble.

• Plague and other diseases will reappear in the third world and be transmitted to all of the other countries. To survive, a military organization based upon the World Health Organization will physically as well as medically fight to control these diseases.

• As petroleum resources shrink, there will be a battle for allocation

of the three most important petrochemical products: fuel for transportation, chemical feedstocks, and fertilizers. The price of all of them will climb dramatically, and only the military will obtain a sufficient supply of fuel.
• Controlled bacterial and plant mutations will begin to supply the chemical needs formerly supplied by petroleum. Plant-generated alcohol will be used first; later, bacterial products.

1993–2030

• The world crisis in energy supply will finally be relieved by the satellite generation of electricity in space. A gigantic mirror satellite will focus the sun's energy to generate electricity. This will be transformed to shortwave energy and beamed to Earth, where it will be changed back to electricity again. After the first satellite is built, all of the others will be financed by the sale of electricity produced this way.
• The endless supply of low-priced, solar-generated electricity will generate the stable, nonpolluting, and cheap hydrogen economy. Electricity will separate water to supply the oxygen to be reoxidized to generate power.
• Railroad transportation will be revolutionized by the development of superconductors that work at ambient temperatures. This will mean that frictionless linear motors will be developed which suspend the trains magnetically above the tracks, thus permitting very great speeds.
• The continuing rapid development of silicon-chip technology will finally produce a chip with more than 10 to the twelfth memory. This is greater than the capacity of the human brain. These tiny devices will be implanted and surgically linked to the brain, giving mankind a totally new order of development.
• A number of new and positive methods of fertility and birth control will be developed. The need for world birth control will be so important that the Catholic Church will finally drop all opposition to its use.
• The final application of foolproof birth-control techniques will stabilize third-world population at a viable replacement level. There will be no starvation, no shortages, no uncontrolled plagues. Mankind will be united under a world government without losing the values of different languages and cultures. The future of the future could then be a peaceful and happy one for all.

• A. E. VAN VOGT •

A. E. van Vogt first established himself as a leading author of speculative and science fiction with his many contributions to *Astounding Science Fiction* in the 1930s and 1940s. His novel *Slan*, which deals with the "persecution of mutants," is considered by many to be his best work. Other notable books include *The Weapon Makers* (a 1946 story set within an oppressive society), *The World of Null-A*, *The House That Stood Still*, *The Beast*, and *Children of Tomorrow*.

HIS PREDICTIONS

1982–on

• *Inflation*. Inflation is in the mind of the beholder—meaning that, as long observed in economics, the more people have the more they want. During the Great Depression of the 1930s, which was the nadir of the 20th century for the West, milk was 10¢ a quart, bread 10¢ for a small loaf, eggs 25¢ a dozen, and butter 25¢ a pound. Today, the comparable prices are only 38¢, 40¢, 95¢, and $1.90—only four to eight times as high. As a comparison, in 1935 a medium-high white-collar worker earned $1,200 to $1,500 a year. Today, medium-high white-collar employees make $16,000 to $20,000. This is about 15 times as much. In addition, because of technology, everybody owns 30 to 100 times as much now as they did then. Because of technology, I predict this level of having more will expand geometrically. But because of that law of economics, people will continue to be dissatisfied and will be outraged by an inflation that does not, in truth, exist.

• *Psychology*. Freud and his successors established beyond reasonable doubt that early conditioning and trauma, as well as illnesses, profoundly influence the individual's adult behavior. Yet during the years since Freud first began to announce the results of his investigations, the individual by and large has principally responded to urban renewal, technological environment, and mass education, and has shown no sign of taking into account the effect on him of specific trauma or conditioning. I predict that such automatic behavior will continue into the foreseeable future. And so man will remain fundamentally the same, with only here and there a great man or woman behaving like an aware person.

1982–1992

• *Benefits from space*. When the sun goes behind the horizon, it presently takes the daylight with it. But it is still shining out there, quite able to do its job a lot longer. Our problem is to transport into space large sheets of aluminum foil. From a height of several hundred miles the reflecting surfaces of the foil can be arranged so as to send back the sun's rays to Los Angeles, Houston, Chicago, New York, Philadelphia—or to any city that will pay the small cost involved. No electricity needed. Brilliant reflected sunlight will shine down on one great metropolitan area after another until midnight or later, 365 days a year. I predict that such a program will begin as soon as the shuttles start regular routine flights.

• *Exercise*. It has been sadly observed that some athletes suffer from hidden problems. And so a superjogger falls dead of a heart attack at age 44. A combination of psychotherapy (which will de-intensify deadly, hidden weaknesses) and exercise will—this is my prediction—progressively prevent such personal disasters, and we may expect to see psychiatrists jogging with a number of patients, watching and questioning, not on the couch, but on the run.

• *Real estate values*. The entire West Coast from the Mexican border to British Columbia, Canada, has the potentiality of becoming Paradise U.S.A. As the winters of the East become harder to deal with indoors (due to the shortsighted slowdown of the space program), I predict that the huge corporations will progressively transfer their headquarters to, particularly, California. The consequent real estate boom will make current property prices appear minuscule by comparison.

1982–1993

• *War.* A major war—meaning a direct confrontation—between the U.S.S.R. and the U.S. would destroy the planet. So that's a possibility we cannot consider, and we can hope that no one in power in either of those countries will consider it either. I predict that war in the future will continue to be a sad regional disaster for small countries. In all of these interactions between small countries, or inside small countries, the great powers will have their equally small confrontations. The Soviet Union will meddle, with the purpose of expanding communism, and the U.S. will do what it can to fend off takeovers. Throughout, the former great powers of Europe—Germany, France, Italy, and Great Britain—will remain frozen in outward neutrality since each could be wiped out with one hydrogen bomb. But, since they have much at stake, I predict they will learn to influence events by a technique of secret terrorism.

1993–2030

• *Prolongation of life.* After a person has become terminally ill, close friends and relatives—looking back—often report that they noticed a significant change in the individual several months, or even a few years, earlier. It could be that there are signals of change for the worse in each decade of a person's life. I predict that this is an area that will engage the attention of gerontologists, and that it will provide them with decisive information about such deteriorations at the time they happen. And that because of early observation, this will be one of the techniques leading to prolongation of life in ever larger groups of people.

• *Religion.* A by-product of the U.S. venture into space was the reaction of some of the astronauts when they saw Earth as a misty ball in the great dark. The strange, wondrous sight evoked a variety of feelings, among which was an almost mystical sense of God and religion. So, as man moves into the solar system and then out to the far stars, I predict a whole series of born-again revivals. Out there in space God is not dead. If there is a deathless spirit—a soul—"it" is undoubtedly signaling its presence in thousands of ways. But because of conditioning which begins at birth, maybe even before birth, such signals (if there are any) have never been systematically searched for. I predict that computer studies will resolve this mystery to the satisfaction of intelligent people.

1993–?

• *Benefits from space.* In ancient days, villages were at the mercy of nature. Food and water shortages could destroy—or at least make a nightmare out of—human existence. The growth of large towns and larger cities automatically solved many of the problems of the previously isolated village community, because intercommunication on the town and city level provided a feedback of goods and other aid from areas where there was no shortage. In much the same way,

Village Earth is subject to the problems of an isolated (in space) planet: Village Earth thinking, with the consequent political and race divisiveness. I predict that as man establishes space communities and colonizes other planets of the solar system and other stars, there will be feedback leading to consciousness expansion that will automatically solve the mundane problems of Village Earth.

2031–on

• *Population growth*. Earth can be overpopulated, but not space. All those bright brains inside the heads of people now sleeping on the streets in the cities of India, or marking time uselessly in refugee camps, would have no problems in the future space age. I predict that in the long run the High Frontier will need hundreds of billions of human beings.

Part III

LOOKING
BACKWARD—
AND FORWARD

12

THE 18 GREATEST PREDICTORS OF ALL TIME

When Nostradamus died in 1566, he secretly had a metal plaque placed in his grave. When his grave was opened in 1700, the metal plaque was found lying on his skeleton. It read: "1700."

Hunchback Homer Lea, who lived in Los Angeles and became Dr. Sun Yat-sen's chief of staff in China, in 1912 predicted the 1980 Russian invasion of Afghanistan.

Count Louis Hamon (known as Cheiro) read Mata Hari's palm and became her lover. When he and Rasputin tried to hypnotize each other, it ended in a draw. Hamon predicted that one day Russian planes would obliterate London.

Edgar Cayce, the 9th grade dropout who became a famous mystic and predicted the Wall Street crash, made a forecast that World War III would begin in 1999.

THE GREAT PYRAMID OF CHEOPS
(c. 2650 B.C.)

Besides being a marvel of architecture and masonry, the massive pyramid across the Nile from Cairo is believed by some to tell the story of human history from 4000 B.C. to 2001 A.D. According to pyramidologists, the stone structure mutely predicted World War I, the Great Depression, and, for the dawn of the 21st century, the beginning of a glorious new age for humankind.

The Great Pyramid near Giza was a monument to the Pharaoh Cheops, founder of the Fourth Dynasty. Without benefit of the wheel, some 100,000 workers hewed, hauled, and mortared 2.3 million stone blocks, averaging 2.5 tons each, into a pyramid standing 481 ft. high and occupying 13 acres. Although the designers lacked scientific instruments of measure, the structure is almost perfectly proportioned. Its base is off-square by a matter of inches.

Inside the pyramid run passageways leading to the royal burial chambers. It is these passageways that hold the key to the pyramid's prophecies. There are no flat predictions written or depicted here—no dates chiseled in stone, no events spelled out. In fact, no markings of any kind can be found on the walls of the pyramid. The theory that the stones speak to us across the ages, indeed tell the future, was first given prominence by Charles Piazzi Smyth, a royal astronomer of Scotland, who in 1864 carefully measured the pyramid's passageways and saw in the numbers a unique perpetual calendar, a chronology of world history covering six millennia. Smyth's base of measure was what he called the "pyramid inch," equal to 1.001 standard inches. He measured the distance from the pyramid entrance to beyond the King's Chamber and reckoned that each pyramid inch represented one calendar year. Thus, from the pyramid's lowest point, representing 4000 B.C., to beyond the King's Chamber, a point denoting 2001 A.D., the intervening years can be calibrated by the pyramid inch. The condition of the passageway at any given point along the way determines the type of event occurring in that year.

For example, the entrance corridor runs downhill to a point corresponding to 1486 B.C., about the time the Israelites followed Moses in Exodus. The path then turns sharply upward to a fork, leading to the left to the Queen's Chamber, and to the right to the King's Chamber. The fork in the pathway corresponds precisely to the time of Christ. Proceeding to the right and upward, pyramid-inch by pyramid-inch and thus year by year, one walks along the Grand Gallery, which with its high ceiling represents the spiritual enlightenment of the next 1900 years.

After "centuries" of climbing along the roomy gallery of time, one begins to walk along a horizontal passage in which the time scale changes. Instead of the previous equivalency of an inch to a year, from 1909 to 1953 an inch corresponds to a 30-day month. At the point representing August 5, 1914, the passageway becomes so low-ceilinged that visitors must crawl through it. This confining tunnel opens to a more spacious anteroom at the point representing November 11, 1918. In what pyramidologists have interpreted as a

Inside the Great Pyramid.

deadly accurate forecast of World War I, the crawl space thus begins during the week that the European powers declared war on each other and ends on the exact day of the Armistice.

The anteroom allows a man to stand straight and relax for the next 10 years before entering another crawl space. Indeed, the decade following World War I was relatively prosperous for much of the world. The second low passage begins in May, 1928, on the eve of the Great Depression, and opens onto the King's Chamber at the inch representing September, 1936, the year France and other countries went off the gold standard.

The King's Chamber occupies the period from 1936 to 1953. During this time, the Armageddon (World War II) was to effect a "cleansing of nations." And the Israelites would return to their homeland. (Israel was created in 1948.) It was a time of preparation, a Second Advent, in anticipation of the Second Coming.

From 1953 to September 17, 2001, the pyramid indicates a time of reconstruction, pyramidologists say. Wars will break out here and there, but man is definitely on the road to a lasting peace. A "Builders' Rest," a sabbath, will begin in 2001. It will be a new age, better than any man has yet seen.

Of course, not everyone has accepted as valid this walk through history. H.G. Wells, for one, pronounced the pyramids "unmeaning sepulchral piles." And the interpretations of the measurements have not always hit the mark. For example, it was predicted, wrongly, that constitutional crises would rock both the U.S. and Great Britain in September, 1936. Some pyramidologists read the stones and forecast the Second Coming for 1881, then pushed the date forward to 1936, and finally settled on 1953. But most would agree that the inauguration of Dwight Eisenhower did not quite constitute the Second Coming.

Still, many of the predictions relating to the 20th century, especially those that indicated World War I, are remarkable. But how did the ancients come by such information? Pyramidologists speculate that God may have revealed the future course of history to a chosen people and that they, in turn, constructed an ingenious record of it in the pyramid, one durable enough to survive until its term of prediction had run out.

—W.A.D.

THE ORACLE AT DELPHI
(c. 700 B.C.–362 A.D.)

Crouched on a tripod set over a fissure that emitted intoxicating fumes in a subterranean chamber, the priestesses of Delphi—in a frenzied trance—muttered prophecies that, interpreted and cast in ambiguous prose or hexameter verse by priests, profoundly influenced events in the ancient world. Rulers of empires puzzled over and reinterpreted Delphic prophecies before making decisions about war and colonizing. Delphi became incredibly wealthy thanks to its nervous and grateful clients, whose tributes include marble and gold statues (Nero stole 500 of them), paintings, jewels, and other treasure. Visited each year by thousands of people who regarded it as a "prophecy center," the town became a complex of stone temples and bulging treasure houses, and it also boasted an amphitheater.

According to legend, it all began with a fume-crazed goat who had wandered too close to the Delphic fissure. The "mephitic gases" the goat breathed emanated from the rotting body of the dragon Python, killed and hurled into the gorge by Apollo in order to gain entrance to the cavern inhabited by the earth goddess Gaea. Shepherds also became intoxicated and muttered incoherently, and far too many of them—dizzied by the fumes—fell into the crevice. Therefore the priests appointed one priestess, the Pythia, as the human agency for the transmittal of what was clearly the wisdom of Apollo, the god of eloquence, and perhaps of Dionysus, who also had a cult there.

The original temple at Delphi was a simple structure of woven branches, beeswax, and bird feathers. At first, the priestesses were beautiful virgins of noble birth, raised by peasants so that they would not defile Apollo's pronouncements with worldly ideas of their own. Later, after the Thessalian Echecrates abducted and raped one of the young priestesses, only women over 50 were chosen for the job.

In the beginning, one day a year—the seventh of Bysios, Apollo's birth—was set aside for prophecies, but as the power of Delphi grew, prophecies were made on the seventh of every month. At the height of Delphi's popularity, three Pythias were on duty at one time. Once a year, a Pythia made prophecies for the masses from the temple steps.

The Pythia's ritual began with a bath in the Castalian spring. Then she donned an ornate robe, placed a laurel crown on her head, and proceeded to the *omphalos* ("sacred navel," an egg-shaped rock or meteor, symbolic of the center of the earth) in the temple's inner sanctuary. Seating herself on a tripod above the fissure, she chewed narcotic laurel leaves as the air filled with the smell of burning bay leaves and incense.

Meanwhile, after sacrificing a sheep or goat in front of the temple, the supplicant walked past a huge gold statue of Apollo into the inner sanctuary. There he stood behind a screen while one of the attendant priests put his question to the Pythia. Upon hearing the question the Pythia fell into a trance, during which she provided an answer. According to Apollonius of Tyana (1st century A.D.), "Her eyes flashed, she foamed at the mouth, her hair stood on end."

After the priests had transcribed her utterances, they gave one copy to the client and put another, recorded on a stone tablet, in the Delphic archives. Plutarch, who served as a priest at Delphi in the first century A.D., felt that the ambiguity of these transcriptions was necessary: "For it was not just a question of some individual person consulting the oracle about the purchase of a slave or some other private matter, but of very powerful cities, kings, and tyrants with mighty ambitions, seeking the gods' advice on important issues. To anger or annoy such men by harsh truths that conflicted with their desires would have had its disadvantages for the priests of the oracle. . . . As for the answers given to ordinary people, it was also sometimes advisable that these should be concealed from their oppressors or hidden from their enemies. Thus these too were wrapped up in circumlocution and equivocation so that the meaning of the oracle, while hidden from others, could always be grasped by those whom it concerned if they applied themselves to unraveling it."

It also meant that the oracle was always right. When Croesus, the Lydian king famed for his wealth, asked whether he should wage war against Cyrus of Persia, in 550 B.C., the oracle told him, "After crossing the Halys [a river], Croesus will destroy a great empire." For this advice, Croesus paid a fortune worth well over a billion dollars today: 117 bricks of precious metals, a gold lion weighing 570 lb., a 4½-ft.-high gold statue of his pastry cook, and assorted other treasures. He went to war happily, expecting to win. He didn't, but the oracle was still correct—only the empire Croesus destroyed was his own.

The Pythias did not always tell the whole story. One Pythia warned the wealthy Siphnians of an "ambush of wood" (pirate ships) which came a few days after she spoke, but she failed to mention that their gold and silver mines would be destroyed by floods.

At other times the Pythias gave an answer unrelated to the question. For example, when a Greek named Battus sought a cure for his stammer, the Pythia responded that he would establish a city in North Africa. Battus went on to fulfill the prophecy by founding the city of Cyrene in Lybia—but he never overcame his speech impediment.

In 480 B.C., threatened by an invasion of Persian forces led by Xerxes, Athenian leaders consulted the Pythia Aristonice, who after telling them all would be destroyed, relented with a softer prophecy: ". . . all-seeing Zeus grants Athene's prayer that the wooden walls not only shall not fail, but will aid you and your children. . . . Divine Salamis, you will bring death to women's sons." The general Themistocles interpreted this to mean that the Athenians would win (otherwise why so kindly call the island of Salamis divine?) and would win with wooden ships ("wooden walls"). Others disputed this, but Themistocles won the argument and the battle—a naval fight that routed the Persians.

Though she had her detractors, Euripides among them, the oracle was revered, even by such skeptical philosophers as Plato and Socrates. Later, the Roman Cicero said, "Never could the oracle of Delphi have been so overwhelmed with so many important offerings from monarchs and nations if all the ages had not proved the truth of its oracles."

By Roman times, the oracle was losing power. Plutarch, when serving as high priest, said, "The oracle is no longer concerned with complicated or secret matters. The questions she is asked have to do with people's everyday concerns."

The Pythia was not always treated well by the Romans. For instance Nero, after his mother was assassinated at his command, went to Delphi to hear the following prophecy: "Your presence outrages the god you seek. Go back, matricide. The number 73 marks the hour of your downfall." Though Nero thought the 73 referred to the age at which he would die—and he was then only 30—he was still not happy with the Pythia. He had her buried alive with the bodies of her priests, whose hands and feet had been cut off. The number 73, it turned out, was the age of Nero's successor Galba, who became emperor in 68 A.D., the year Nero died—at 31.

To Emperor Julian's physician, in 362 A.D., the oracle plaintively issued a final pronouncement: "Tell your master that the curiously built temple has fallen to the ground, that bright Apollo no longer has a roof over his head, a prophetic laurel, or a babbling spring. Yes, even the murmuring water has dried up." Julian had the temple restored and the Castalian spring unblocked. But Delphi's days were numbered.

In the 1890s, French archaeologists excavated Delphi to find that the famous temple had been destroyed more than once and that there was no fissure from which "mephitic gases" could have arisen, although it is possible they were closed by earth tremors. Still, seeing the temple ruins set in those awesome, spectacular crags high above the plains of olive groves with the Gulf of Corinth far below—a place where eagles wheel and thunderbolts strike—one can believe that once, in Delphi, a god spoke through trance-crazed maidens.

—A.E.

ROGER BACON (1214?–1294)

Roger Bacon, the Franciscan friar who tried to lead Western civilization from the Middle Ages into the Renaissance, had an imagination unfettered by tradition, Church dogma, or peer pressure. He predicted most modern transportation systems and emphasized the value of scientific experimentation.

Born into a well-to-do English family, Bacon was a precocious youth who received a solid education at Oxford and the University of Paris. Soon, however, his interest shifted from dry theory to outright experimentation. He probed into every aspect of medieval science —alchemy, astrology, astronomy, optics, and mathematics—and poured his time, energy, and money into acquiring esoteric books and building scientific instruments. In an age when theologians dictated the nature of the universe, Bacon dared to suggest that long-held beliefs should be subjected to rational, objective scientific inquiry. From his work in optics he concluded, "Instruments can be designed so that enormous things will appear very small, and contrariwise," and thereby anticipated the microscope and provided the scientific foundation for the telescope. He also described eyeglasses.

However, many of Bacon's scientific predictions sprang less from

Roger Bacon.

his lab work than from his visionary genius. While admitting that he had conducted no experiments to confirm his theories, Bacon in his *Epistola de Secretis* (c. 1268) predicted modern land, sea, and air transportation. Centuries before Gottlieb Daimler and Henry Ford, he foresaw "chariots . . . that will move with incredible rapidity without the help of animals." Even limited vertical transportation was possible according to Bacon, with "an engine . . . whereby a man may ascend or descend any walls"—the first theoretical description of an elevator. And the bulky bridges of old would give way, Bacon correctly predicted, to spans "without pillars or any buttress." He thought that "Vessels might be made to move without oars or rowers, so that ships of great size might move on sea or on river, at the governance of a single man, more swiftly than if they were strongly manned." He forecast the submarine when he wrote of a machine which would "enable man to walk at the bottom of the sea." And, although the Wright brothers later improved upon his idea, Bacon looked forward to "instruments of flying . . . in which a man, sitting at his ease and meditating on any subject, may beat the air with his artificial wings after the manner of birds."

Bacon was long thought to have invented gunpowder. Although Chinese explosives clearly predate his efforts, Bacon was the first to foresee the massive and instantaneous destruction of modern warfare. "Sounds like thunder can be made in the air," he wrote, "but more terrifying than those which occur in nature; for an appropriate material in moderate quantity, as big as a man's thumb, makes a horrible noise and shows a violent flash; and this can be done in many ways by which a whole town or army may be destroyed."

In some ways, Bacon was necessarily a product of his age. For example, he shared the alchemist's belief in the existence of the philosopher's stone which would convert base metals to gold, and the elixir of life which would make human beings essentially immortal. He also believed in the power of astrology, though he considered it a very inexact science.

Ironically, although Bacon's visions of the future were remarkably astute, it is one of his mistaken beliefs that may have had the greatest impact on history. In Columbus's correspondence with Ferdinand and Isabella, he remarked that his momentous 1492 voyage was in part inspired by Bacon's statement that "the sea between the end of Spain on the west and the beginning of India on the east is navigable in a very few days if the wind is favorable."

Friar Bacon's search for truth in a tradition-bound age, his churlish disposition, and his utter contempt for those unmoved by Baconian science inevitably brought down the wrath of his superiors, who placed him in virtual solitary confinement in Paris. But Bacon went over the heads of the Franciscans to plead his case to Pope Clement IV. In his correspondence with the pontiff, he argued that scientific experimentation, conducted objectively, would undoubtedly confirm long-held religious beliefs and ultimately benefit the Church.

His interest aroused, Clement ordered Bacon to send him secretly the scientific proposals alluded to in his letters—unaware that the treatises existed only in Bacon's mind. Undaunted, the friar immediately set forth on the work, concealing his efforts as best he could from the watchful eyes of his Franciscan brothers. In an amazingly brief time he prepared the scientific compendiums which were to make him famous: *Opus Majus, Opus Minus,* and *Opus Tertium.* Unfortunately, the pope died less than a year after receiving the manuscripts, and Bacon again was thrown back on the mercy of an unenlightened clergy. Nonetheless, supremely confident of his own genius, he continued to lash out at his detractors and to attack the core institutions of medieval society. As a result he was arrested in 1278 on the vague charges of teaching "suspected novelties." His books were burned and he was imprisoned for 14 years. Released in 1292, he died soon afterward.

During the ensuing centuries Bacon's reputation reached almost mythic proportions, particularly after dramatist Robert Greene portrayed the good friar as a great magician in his popular play *Friar Bacon and Friar Bungay* (1594). Although Bacon's contributions have been subjected to harsher judgments in more recent years, he still shines forth as a major light of his times, well deserving the epithet which has followed him down through the ages: *doctor mirabilis* ("wonderful teacher").

—W.A.D.

ROBERT NIXON (1467–1485)

English seer Robert Nixon possessed a weird mental duality which led to his apparently contradictory nicknames: He was known as both "the Cheshire Prophet" and "the Cheshire Idiot." By all accounts, Nixon was an illiterate plowboy who was so retarded mentally that he was verbally incoherent most of the time. Yet in his lucid moments, he spoke with absolute certainty of things to come. His predictions ranged from his own place and time—including local storms, fires, floods—to future historical occurrences. Nixon accurately foretold such events as the British Civil War (1642) and London's great fire (1666) well over a century before they took place. Among his predictions which as yet are unfulfilled is one that states: "Foreign nations shall invade England with snow on their helmets and shall bring plague, famine, and murder in the skirts of their garments."

Robert Nixon was the only child born to a poor farm couple in Cheshire County, near an ancient estate belonging to the Cholmondeley family. Since it was generally conceded, even by his parents, that he was too dim-witted to learn anything, he was put to work in the fields as soon as he was tall enough to grasp the handles of a plow. Nixon had no apparent desire to communicate with others, and he usually reacted to questions with a silent, vacant stare. If he responded at all, he grunted or stammered out a "yes" or "no." When he did try to speak, which was seldom, he drooled. On top of all this, according to one man who knew him, he was an unnervingly ugly boy with a disproportionately large head and "goggle eyes." The only subject that animated him was food. If allowed to, he would single-handedly put away a whole leg of mutton at one sitting.

When he correctly predicted the death of an ox belonging to a farmer named Crowton, Nixon attracted the attention of a Cheshire

County squire. Lord Cholmondeley sent for the boy and briefly kept him at his own estate, Vale Royal, believing that Nixon would learn to read and write in this new environment. The squire was wrong. When his exasperated teachers gave up, Nixon was sent back to the plow; his prediction about the ox was written off as a lucky fluke.

Nixon distinguished himself on the job mainly by the trouble he caused; he would put in his time at the plow only when his food allotment was threatened. Nixon's co-workers thought he had considerably less intelligence than the animal pulling the plow, and made him the butt of much crude humor; he developed a reputation as the classic village idiot. Nixon ignored—or was oblivious to—this, but he sometimes ranted at the neighborhood children who followed him around and made fun of him.

One day, not long after the failed educational experiment at Vale Royal, Nixon suddenly stopped plowing and stared up into the sky. He ignored other workers who spoke to him. The overseer came over and ordered him back to work. Getting no response, he struck Nixon. His blows had no more effect than his words. Nixon stood still for an hour, then resumed plowing as suddenly as he had stopped. When asked about his behavior later, he answered with—for him—unusual clarity: "I have seen things I cannot tell you, and which man never saw before."

There were apparently some things he could tell. On one occasion Nixon gave his audience a two-hour crash course in European history—but it was history which had not yet happened. He described the British Civil War, the defeat and beheading of Charles I, the Restoration, the reign of William of Orange, the French Revolution in the 18th century, the Peninsular War between France and Great Britain, and the subsequent victory and international prosperity of the British nation.

Nixon predicted the abdication of James II in 1688 in the following terms: "When a raven shall build [its nest] in a stone lion's mouth on top of a church in Cheshire, a king of England shall be driven out of his kingdom and return nevermore. . . . As token of the truth of this, a wall of Mr. Cholmondeley's shall fall. . . ." Lord Cholmondeley examined the wall Nixon indicated and remarked to his bailiff, "Nixon was out [i.e., 'off'] here. That wall will never fall down."

But fall it did, the very next day, and a thorough inspection produced no logical explanation of its collapse. According to local history in Cheshire County, Nixon's raven did build a nest in the place described when James II was deposed; and his predictions that a mill at Luddington would be moved and Ridley Pool would be drained dry later were proved right. Nixon also said that a Cholmondeley heir would be born "on a cold snowy day, when an eagle perched on top of the house." This occurred in 1684, at a time when the Cholmondeley family line was in danger of dying out, two centuries after Nixon's death.

On August 22, 1485, Nixon was plowing when, once again, he stopped in his tracks. The overseer and other workers, well acquainted with Nixon's quirky behavior by now, ignored him—for a moment. Then Nixon started dancing around the field, screaming and foaming at the mouth. Brandishing his whip like a sword, he whooped, "There Richard! There! Now! Up, Henry! Up with all arms! Over the ditch, Henry . . . over the ditch and the battle is won!" A strange smile appeared on his face. Seeming to notice the crowd which had gathered, Nixon said indifferently: "The battle is over.

Henry has won." Then he went back to work as though nothing had happened.

Cheshire got the news—and an explanation for Nixon's dramatic pantomime—two days later. Hard-riding messengers spread the word that, on August 22 at Bosworth, the evil hunchback king, Richard III, died fighting the Earl of Richmond. The earl was now Henry VII, King of England. Even as word of Nixon's prophecy spread, he gave the local folk something new to talk about. Running from house to house, he begged fearfully for a hiding place from the king's men who were coming for him. If he were taken to the royal palace, Nixon insisted, he would end up "clammed," or starved to death. This was double idiocy to the villagers. First, the king was not apt to ask for an audience with the town loony; and even if he did, how could anyone *starve* in a king's palace?

The king's men came for Nixon a few days later. Henry had heard of the Cheshire idiot-genius who foresaw the future, and wanted to know more about him. The king assigned one of his scribes to accompany Nixon at all times and record any prophetic utterances. Nixon obliged the king with many predictions, including the one about an invasion of soldiers "with snow on their helmets" (usually interpreted as a vision of war between Russia and England). Nixon became one of the king's favorites and enjoyed the run of the palace, a situation which caused endless aggravation for the servants in the royal kitchen. Always hungry, Nixon often stole food they had painstakingly prepared for the king's table.

When Henry went off on a hunting trip, his long-suffering cooks ignored the strict instructions left concerning Nixon's care. They locked the pesky boy in a closet and forgot about him. Henry returned two weeks later and immediately asked for his court prophet. Robert Nixon was finally found in the closet—dead of starvation and dehydration.

—M.S.S.

URSULA SOUTHIEL
(MOTHER SHIPTON) (1488–1561)

The trail backwards through time to the "real" Mother Shipton is littered with forgeries attributed to her by 19th-century charlatans, strained interpretations of her vague verses that cynics snicker at, and legends about her life that challenge credulity. Was there a Mother Shipton at all? Probably yes. Janet Ursula, the daughter of Agatha Southiel (or Southill), was born in July of 1488, in a small town in Yorkshire.

Legend has it that Agatha was impregnated by a being of awesome, superhuman origin, who rewarded her for her sexual generosity by giving her powers similar to his own. The birth of the future

Mother Shipton.

Mother Shipton was, according to an old Scottish tale, accompanied by "various wonderful presages," including a croaking raven and a thunderstorm. "It was also observed," the tale goes on, "that as soon as she was born, she fell a-grinning and laughing, after a jeering manner, and immediately the tempest ceased." The thunder heralded the coming into this world of an extremely ugly child—"the devil's child," the neighbors said. And her 18th-century biographer, S. Baker, writing over a distance of about 300 years, said: "Her stature was larger than common, her body crooked, her face frightful; but her understanding extraordinary."

In spite of all her alleged carryings-on with the devil or his cohorts, Agatha Southiel retired to a convent, where she died. Little Ursula was given to a nurse to raise and, in time, she trudged off to school, where she did well scholastically but was teased about her appearance by the other children. She got even by exercising some of her powers—supposedly inherited. The children who plagued her were pinched, bitten, and knocked down by unseen presences. Eventually, Ursula quit school, a preteen dropout.

At 24 she married a carpenter, Tobias Shipton, and went to live with him in the village of Skipton, near York. She became known for her ability to foretell the future. Her predictions, typical of those of the time, were presented in riddles, often in verse. Her first histori-cally important prophecy concerned Henry VIII's invasion of north-ern France in 1513: "When the English Lion [Henry] shall set his feet on the Gallic shores, then shall the Lillies [French] begin to droop for fear.... The princely Eagle [Maximilian] shall join the Lion to tread down all that shall oppose them, and though many Saggataries [French cavalry] shall appear in defense of the Lillies, yet shall they not prevail because the dull animal of the north [English cavalry] shall put them all to confusion; and though it be against his will [the attack was unplanned], yet shall he cause great shame unto them."

In 1530 she made a prediction concerning Cardinal Thomas Wolsey, still powerful though his relationship with Henry VIII was shaky. A lover of pomp, he traveled with a splendid retinue of 800 people and was the possessor of several wealth-producing titles. She foresaw that he intended to hide out from trouble by going to York: "The Mitred Peacock [Wolsey] shall now begin to plume himself, and his train shall make a great show in the world. . . . He shall want to live at York, and shall see it, but shall never come thither." When he heard of this (who knows how), Wolsey decided to investigate Mother Shipton. According to one version of the story, he sent Thomas Cromwell to see her, but the most quoted version (and the most colorful) has it that he sent three men in disguise—perhaps the Duke of Suffolk, Lord Darcy, and Lord Percy—with a local man, named Beasley, who acted as their guide.

When the four appeared at Mother Shipton's door, she said, "Come in, Mr. Beasley, and the three noble Lords with you." As she gave them oatcakes and ale, the lords asked her if she had indeed claimed Wolsey would never see York. "No," she replied. "I said he might see it, but never enter it."

"When he comes, he'll surely burn thee," they warned.

Mother Shipton dramatically threw a linen handkerchief on the fire. "If this burn, so shall I," she pronounced. When she retrieved the handkerchief 15 minutes later it was untouched by the flames.

Impressed, the nobles asked her to tell their fortunes. To the Duke of Suffolk she said, "My love, the time will come when you will be as low as I am, and that's a low one indeed." (He was beheaded in 1554.) To Percy: "Shooe your Horse in the Quicke, and you shall doe well, but your body will bee buried in Yorke pavement and your head shall be stolen from the barre and carried into France." (A Lord Thomas Percy *was* beheaded in 1572 and his head set on a pole over the Michlegate Bar (gate) at York and later taken to France; however, *that* Lord Percy was only two years old when Mother Shipton supposedly had this conversation with him. If a Lord Percy did go to see Mother Shipton, it was more likely to have been young Thomas's uncle.) To Darcy: "You have made a great Gun, shoot if off, for it will doe you no good, you are going to warre, you will paine many a man, but you will kill none."

Wolsey did travel toward York and managed to reach Cawood, from which he could see York, 8 mi. away. It was at Cawood that Lord Northampton caught him on a stairway and presented him with a warrant for his arrest. Wolsey was forced to turn back to London, destined for the Tower and probably eventual execution, but he died on the road.

William Lilly, a 17th-century London astrologer, records in his *Collections of Prophecies* (1646) 18 of Mother Shipton's predictions, collected by her neighbor Beasley. Lilly claimed that 16—mostly having to do with famines, wars, fashions, and minor events of the time—were fulfilled by the time he wrote his book. Other interpreters claim she also predicted the London fire of 1666; the defeat of the Spanish Armada ("The Western monarch's Wooden Horses / Shall be destroyed by the Drake's forces."); the reigns of certain British kings and queens; and additional historical events.

The waters were muddied further by shenanigans in 1880, when this famous quotation was attributed to her: "Carriages without horses shall go [automobiles], / And accidents fill the world with woe. / Around the earth thoughts shall fly [telegraph] / In the twinkling of an eye; / The world upside down shall be, / And gold found at the root of a tree. / Through hills man shall ride / And no horse be at his side [railroad] / Under water men shall walk, / Shall ride, shall sleep, shall talk [submarine]. / In the air men shall be seen / In white, in black, in green [airplane]; / Iron in the water shall float, / As easily as a wooden boat [steamship]. . . . The world to an end shall come / In eighteen hundred and eighty-one." In 1862 Charles Hindley, a British editor, admitted that he was responsible for these "prophecies," a reality at the time—for example, the ironclad ships *Monitor* and *Virginia* battled at the onset of the Civil War.

Other predictions by Hindley that were attributed to Mother Shipton include: Sir Walter Raleigh's importation of tobacco from the New World, the Australian gold rush, London's Crystal Palace, World War II ("In 1936 and . . . shall mighty wars be planned . . .").

The 16th-century seeress, like many other psychics, including the most recent, did foresee a Middle East Armageddon: "Then shall come the Son of Man, having a fierce beast in his arms, which kingdom lies in the Land of the Moon [Middle East], which is dreadful throughout the whole world; with a number of people shall he pass many waters and shall come to the land of the Lyon; look for help of the Beast of his country, and an Eagle [the U.S.] shall destroy castles of the Thames, and there shall be a battle among many kingdoms . . . and therewith shall be crowned the Son of Man, and the fourth year shall be many battles for the faith and the Son of Man, with the Eagles shall be preferred, and there shall be peace over the world, and there shall be plenty of fruit, and then shall he go to the land of the Cross [The U.S. will defeat the Arabs in a religious war lasting four years]."

Mother Shipton died in bed at 73. On a monument in Clifton, just outside York, is inscribed her epitaph: "There lies she who never ly'd, / Whose skill often has been try'd, / Her prophecies shall still survive / And even keep her name alive." But if Mother Shipton "never ly'd," those who profited by using her name did.

—A.E.

NOSTRADAMUS (1503–1566)

In his own day Nostradamus was acknowledged as the greatest seer alive, and even today he is often labeled as the most important prophet of European civilization. Many of his predictions, made public in the 1550s, appear to have come true. But what really sets Nostradamus apart is the specificity of his forecasts. He named names. Pasteur, Napoleon, Hitler, Franco—all were mentioned in his writings centuries before their births.

Born December 13, 1503, at St. Rémy, France, Michel de Nostredame (he later Latinized his name to Nostradamus) was the son of a well-to-do notary public. He learned astrology from his grandfathers, both of whom claimed occasional rare visions of the future.

Nostradamus became a devout Catholic and at 21 enrolled as a

Nostradamus.

medical student at the prestigious University of Montpellier. Two
years later the Black Plague ravaged southern France, prompting
Nostradamus to quit medical school to treat victims of the epidemic.
His highly successful work in arresting the plague won him national
fame. He then returned to school, earned a medical degree, and in
1529 set up practice in Agen, France.

Nostradamus might have quietly spun out his years as a physician had it not been for the sudden death of his wife and two infant
sons. Heartbroken and blaming himself for the loss of his family, he
drifted aimlessly from city to city for the next 10 years, occasionally
practicing medicine and consulting with philosophers and astrologers. During this period, he increasingly experienced visions of the
future and made predictions to amuse friends. While in Italy, he spotted a young Franciscan friar named Felice Peretti and abruptly knelt
before him, saying, "I must kneel before His Holiness." In 1585, 19
years after Nostradamus's death, Peretti was elected Pope Sixtus V.

After spending some time in the Abbey of Orval contemplating
his psychic powers, Nostradamus went to Marseilles, again to combat a plague epidemic, and in 1544 settled in Salon, France, where he
practiced medicine and astrology. He is said to have caught glimpses
of the future while staring for hours nightly into a brass bowl filled
with water and mounted on a tripod. He soon began to record these
visions and in 1555 published *Centuries*, a book of prophecy set in
verse. In it, he deliberately wrote in cryptic phrases and used puns,

anagrams, and scientific jargon to obscure his meaning, supposedly because he considered it dangerous to give people too clear a picture of the future and because he did not want to offend church authorities.

But for all its seemingly nonsensical verse, *Centuries* refers so specifically to certain people and events that it has piqued the interest of even the most skeptical critics of the occult. Take the rise and fall of Napoleon, for instance. Nostradamus wrote, "An Emperor shall be born near Italy / Who shall cost the Empire dear / When it is seen with whom he allies himself / He shall be found less a prince than a butcher." Elsewhere he names him "Pau. nay. loron," an anagram for Napaulon Roy. He further predicted, "The man with cropped hair shall assume authority / In a maritime city held by the enemy. / He will expel the vile men who oppose him / And for 14 years will rule with absolute power." Napoleon, unlike previous French kings who wore long hair or a wig, cropped his hair short and first gained national fame in 1793 by recapturing Toulon, a port on the Mediterranean, from the British. He then expelled the Directory and ruled France from November, 1799, to April, 1814. Nostradamus further prophesied that Napoleon would prove a fearsome ruler, "causing to tremble Italy, Spain, and the English." But, he continued, France "will have chosen badly in the cropped one / Its strength will be sapped by him," and indeed the flower of French youth fell on the road to Napoleonic glory. The prophet continued with uncanny accuracy to predict Napoleon's exile, escape, ultimate defeat at Waterloo, and lonely death on St. Helena: "The captive prince, conquered, to Elba. / He will pass the Gulf of Genoa by sea to Marseilles / He is completely conquered by a great effort of foreign forces.... Will end his life far from where he was born / Among 5,000 people of strange customs and language / On a chalky island in the sea."

Nostradamus's reference to the most famous chemist of the 19th century was brief but to the point. "Pasteur will be celebrated as a godlike figure."

The first of Nostradamus's great predictions to come true was the death of Henry II of France: "The young lion shall overcome the old one / In martial field by a single duel. / In a golden cage he shall put out his eye, / Two wounds from one, then shall die he a cruel death." In 1559 Henry II was mortally wounded simultaneously in the eye and throat during a friendly joust with a young Scots Guard, whose lance accidentally penetrated the visor of the king's golden helmet.

The next century bore out Nostradamus's prediction that London was to be "Burnt by the fire of 3 times 20 and 6," that is, in 1666. "The ancient dame shall fall from her high place, / Of the same sect many shall be killed." The Virgin's statue on St. Paul's toppled, and many other churches were destroyed in the Great Fire.

Several of his forecasts came true in the 20th century. "In the mountains of Austria near the Rhine," he wrote, "There will be born of simple parents / A man who will claim to defend Poland and Hungary / And whose fate will never be certain." He described him as "A bold, black, base-born, iniquitous man" named "Hister." With allowances for the slight misspelling, the reference to the Nazi dictator is unmistakable. And considering the number who believe that Hitler escaped Berlin in 1945 to hide out in South America all these years, his fate is indeed uncertain. Nostradamus also predicted Hitler's ultimate defeat.

The role of Spain's late dictator was set forth in these terms: "The assembly will go out from the castle of Franco, / The ambassador not satisfied will make a schism. / Those of the Riviera will be involved, / And they will deny the entry to the great gulf." This is said to refer to a meeting between Spain and the Axis powers held in 1941 on the Riviera during which Gen. Francisco Franco denied Germany access to Gibraltar via Spain.

Nostradamus also anticipated the love story of the century, the abdication of Great Britain's Edward VIII (later the Duke of Windsor) in 1936, and the succession of his brother George VI, a reluctant monarch: "For being unwilling to consent to divorce / Which later shall be recognized as unworthy / The King of the Isles shall be expelled by force / And replaced by one whose nature will not be that of King."

Although he died decades before the Pilgrims landed at Plymouth Rock, Nostradamus referred specifically to an American government and linked it to Great Britain long before British claims to the Western Hemisphere were established. He predicted America would one day be "free from British Isles / Not satisfied, sad rebellion." In one interesting forecast that has not yet come to pass, he foretold a reunion between the two nations: "There will be a head of London from the government of America."

In other predictions yet to be borne out, Nostradamus foresaw a "third Antichrist" (after Napoleon and Hitler), this one an Arab, "a strong master of Mohammedan law," who will conquer much of Europe and lock horns with the West. Then, "A Germanic heart will be born of Trojan blood / . . . He will drive out the foreign Arabian people, / Restoring the Church to its pristine preeminence." For late 1999, he predicted the long-awaited Armageddon, as "Plague, Famine, Death by the military hand, / The Century approaches renewal." Good ultimately is to triumph over evil, and the world is to enter a tranquil 21st century, wrote the seer.

Although much of his prophecy was proved right long after his death, Nostradamus's reputation had been secured with the forecast of Henry II's accidental death while jousting. Deeply interested in the occult, Queen Catherine de Médicis, Henry II's widow, brought Nostradamus to the royal court at Paris, where he served as her friend, adviser, and—possibly—lover. Most of Parisian society hailed him as a divinely inspired genius, while the remainder pronounced him a fake or, even worse, a sorcerer. His predictions influenced politics, for rulers and diplomats combed them for hints of coming events. After several years in Paris, Nostradamus was forced to return home to Salon because of gout.

On the night of July 1, 1566, a pupil named Chavigny bid his teacher Nostradamus good night, to which the old man replied, "Tomorrow at sunrise I shall not be here." The next morning he was found dead at his workbench. He was entombed in the chapel of St. Martha in Salon in an upright position, because he did not want anyone to walk on his bones, and a marble tombstone asked posterity not to disturb his rest. Secretly, Nostradamus had arranged to have a metal plaque buried with him. In 1700, when his coffin was opened in order to move his remains to a newly built tomb, the metal plaque was discovered resting on his skeleton. On it was inscribed the date 1700.

—W.A.D. and R.J.F.

WILLIAM LILLY (1602–1681)

Of humble origins, William Lilly began his career as a servant to a London couple and ended up the most famous astrologer in England. King Charles I sought his advice, then ignored it to his own peril. Lilly's most spectacular forecast, one that provoked a summons from Parliament, was his prediction of the Great Fire and Great Plague that swept London in the 1660s.

Born of yeoman stock in Diseworth, south of Derby on May 1, 1602, William Lilly received a better-than-average education grounded in the classics. His hopes of attending Cambridge were shattered when hard times drove his father to debtors' prison. With a few shillings in his pocket, 18-year-old Lilly left his hometown and headed for London. There he found work as a houseboy to Gilbert Wright, a fairly wealthy man with some political influence. It was to be a very profitable association. In 1624 Wright's second wife died of breast cancer and left Lilly £5 for having nursed her through her fatal illness. A short while later his master gave him a £20 life annuity, remarried for a third time, and in 1626 died. Lilly then married his master's widow, and when she passed away in 1633, Lilly inherited £1,000.

Now financially secure, Lilly had time to dabble in other things—like astrology. "I was curious to discover," he wrote, "whether there was any verity in the art or not." Convinced that astrology was indeed a sound enterprise, he studied under a man named John Evans who, although a debauchee, was a competent astrologer. By 1640 Lilly was ready to strike out for himself, and he began doing a bit of professional forecasting. Four years later he published his first almanac, crammed with predictions, called *Merlinus Anglicus Junior*. That same year his third publication, *A Prophecy of the White King*, sold out its entire printing of 1,800 copies in three days. Annual books of predictions followed regularly until his death.

With the British Civil War under way, Lilly studied Charles I's chart and pronounced 1645 a bad year for the king. The very day Lilly's ominous portent appeared in *The Starry Messenger*, Cromwell's forces crushed the Royalists at Naseby. Two years later Charles, still hopeful of a return to power, asked Lilly through an intermediary where he could best hide out to be safe from recapture. Lilly advised him to seek refuge in Essex and was paid £20 for the consultation. Instead, Charles fled to the Isle of Wight and was apprehended and confined by the local governor. When he appealed to Lilly a second time for advice, the astrologer told him to sign certain propositions put before him and to accompany the commissioners to London, where public distaste for the army might work to his advantage. Again, the king ignored Lilly's counsel. In short order Charles was tried, and then beheaded for treason on January 30, 1649. If only he had listened, Lilly later wrote with regret, England would have been spared such a sorry spectacle.

Lilly's growing reputation was met with increasing hostility, both from fellow astrologers envious of his fame and from Parliamentarians who felt that astrology smacked of the devil's work. Lilly's almanacs also aroused ire because they were seen by many as

William Lilly.

mere vehicles for his political views. When he dared to call for prompt pay for Parliamentary soldiers, he was arrested for overstepping his bounds. Although charges were dropped, he was again arrested—and briefly imprisoned—in 1651 after predicting that "Parliament stood upon a tottering foundation and the commonalty and soldiery would join together against them." (Parliament was in fact dissolved two years later.) In 1655 he was brought to trial once more, this time on trumped-up charges of witchcraft, but the case was quickly dismissed.

With the restoration of the monarchy in 1660, which he also predicted, Lilly's enemies launched a full-scale attack on him, circulating a pamphlet which declared him guilty of "several treasons, blasphemies, and misdemeanors acted, spoken, and published against God, the late King, his present Majesty." Only through a combination of influential friends and well-placed bribes did Lilly manage to escape the hangman.

A few years later, events were to bear out a dire and, unfortunately, accurate prediction Lilly had made many years before. In 1648 Lilly had forecast "a strange catastrophe of human affairs in the commonwealth, monarchy, and Kingdom of England. . . ." What was to be the cause of this disaster? "Sundry fires and a consuming plague," Lilly flatly predicted. As for the time of the event, the astrologer was less sure. As near as he could tell, the twin catastrophies would strike sometime between the mid-1650s and the mid-1660s.

In the summer and fall of 1665, the Great Plague decimated England. In September, 1666, the Great Fire consumed hundreds of acres of London.

Some suspected that Lilly, perhaps more interested in his own reputation as a seer than in the safety of his countrymen, might have had a hand in the fire, or, at the very least, had learned of an arson conspiracy. Thus a committee of the House of Commons summoned the astrologer for questioning. Treated with respect and civility, Lilly answered all queries put to him. No, he did not know who or what touched off the fire. The culprit, he believed, was "the finger of God only; but what instruments He used thereunto I am ignorant." Lilly was released.

Meanwhile, the aging astrologer had retired to his country house at Hersham, where from 1670 on he combined astrology with medicine and tended to the needs of the sick, usually without fee. Within a few years his vision grew dim and he fell prey to a variety of ailments. Finally, on June 5, 1681, he succumbed to a severe paralytic attack.

Though Lilly had been scoffed at by Samuel Pepys and caricatured by Samuel Butler, his advice had been earnestly sought after and believed by people from all strata of society. More important, his reputation stood the test of time. His most famous astrological work, *Christian Astrology*, became a classic and was reprinted for nearly 200 years after his death.

—W.A.D.

A FORGOTTEN AMERICAN ORACLE: DAVID GOODMAN CROLY (1829–1889)

Born in Ireland but reared in New York City, Croly was a distinguished journalist who worked for both the New York *Evening Post* and the *Herald* and who served as managing editor of the *World* from 1862 to 1872. He married Jane Cunningham, one of the first female reporters in the U.S. and a leading women's rights advocate. Croly became known as a financial prophet after he foretold the Panic of

1873 two years before it happened. He even named the first bank to
fail (Jay Cooke & Company) and the first railroad to fold (the Northern Pacific). When ill health curtailed his career in the 1870s, he
began writing a column for the *Real Estate Record and Builder's
Guide*. Billed as "Sir Oracle," Croly dealt primarily with the possible
future of business and politics. He set the column up in a question-
and-answer format and supplied both sides of the dialogue. Selec-
tions from these columns—expanded upon, reorganized, and
intended "to be read now and judged in the year 2000"—were reprinted in his *Glimpses of the Future* (1888).

CROLY'S 1888 PREDICTIONS
WHICH HAVE ALREADY COME TRUE

1. WORLD WAR I

A war will break out which will involve all the leading nations of
the earth. It will be instigated by Germany.

2. INDIA'S INDEPENDENCE

England will lose India before 1950. [India became independent
in 1947 and established itself as a republic in 1950.]

3. U.S.S.R.

Russia will become the dominant power in Europe and will exert
its influence in Asia, but it will not subdue China. The only country
to rival Russia as the leading world power will be the U.S.

4. MARRIAGE

Marriage will no longer be considered a religious rite. It will be a
civil contract which will allow a change of partners whenever the
contracting couple mutually agrees to separate.

5. FEMALE EMANCIPATION

Women throughout the world will enjoy increased opportunities
and privileges. Along with this new freedom will come social tolerance of sexual conduct formerly condoned only in men. In addition,
because of the greater availability of jobs, more women will choose
not to have children.

6. MEGACORPORATIONS

The business world will be in the hands of a few great firms which
will control the wealth of many nations.

7. PHOTOELECTRONIC PRESSES

Printing will be revolutionized. The compositor or typesetter will
be replaced by a process through which texts and illustrations will
be photographed and reproduced.

8. MOTION PICTURES

Novels will be transformed into a new kind of entertainment.

Instead of employing real actors, as in a play, voices and visual images will be projected onto a stage, creating the illusion of reality.

9. MASS ART

Techniques to reproduce the great masters will be perfected so that most people will be able to afford their own gallery of fine art.

10. NEW YORK CITY

New York will continue to expand as a major commercial center. Brooklyn and the surrounding towns will form an integral part of the metropolis, which will be characterized by enormously high buildings. A subway will whisk people from one part of the city to another in a matter of minutes.

11. AIR TRAVEL

Navigation of the air will be the most momentous event in history. It will do away with all uncharted regions on the earth and it will enable people to be highly mobile, spending summers in one place and winters in another.

12. NEW FORMS OF ENERGY

Steam energy will be replaced by electricity and/or other power sources.

CROLY'S 1888 PREDICTIONS
WHICH HAVE NOT YET COME TRUE

1. MORE STATES

New states will be carved out of Texas and California. The population surrounding New York bay—including the Jersey shore—may decide to form a separate state.

2. NEW U.S. CONSTITUTION

Because our constitution is so inflexible, we will not be able to reform it. Instead, under the pressure of radical changes and perhaps a social war, we will adopt a new constitution.

3. U.S. EXPANSION

The U.S. will absorb Canada, Mexico, Central America, and the West Indies.

4. EUGENICS

Legal measures will be instituted to prevent the criminal, the insane, and the diseased from bearing children.

5. ART AS RELIGION

Because Christianity and the other major religions are not compatible with scientific knowledge, man will satisfy his emotional/spiritual cravings with art.

6. CENSORSHIP

A body of censors will be created who will be responsible for policing the U.S. legislature at all levels.

7. DOME LIVING

People will live beneath domes which will provide temperature-controlled environments and will filter harmful substances out of the air.

8. ENHANCED SLEEP

Compounds will be discovered which will have all the virtues and none of the defects of opium. They will enable us to experience magnificent visions while we sleep.

9. FLEXI-HOURS

People will work no more than six hours at a time, and this will be in staggered shifts. A whole range of goods and services will be available during the nighttime hours.

10. A NEW LOOK IN LITERATURE

Printing will be done in the colors of nature—blues, greens, browns, etc. Permanent literature will be printed in the most easily perceived color combination—yellow ink on a dark blue background. [Croly's short-lived magazine, *The Modern Thinker,* used a rainbow of inks and papers. The only colors excluded were black and white.]

11. A NATIONAL CONSERVATION POLICY

The federal government will reforest all waste areas and the headwaters of all major rivers. Anyone who cuts down a tree will be legally responsible for planting another one in its place. We will also have a national policy for flood and pest control and for irrigation.

12. MIRACLES OF SCIENCE

Soil will be stimulated into maximum productivity, and the entire range of plants formerly considered weeds will be utilized for food or for clothing. These breakthroughs will enable the earth to support comfortably 50 billion people.

—F.B.

ANTON JOHANSON (1858–1929)

Obscure in his own day and in ours, Anton Johanson—the "Christian seer of the Finnmark"—accurately prophesied not only World War I but also many of the social and political upheavals that followed it. A robust, sturdy man, he lived far north of the Arctic Circle in the Norwegian province of Finnmark.

The most striking of his predictions consisted of one great series of events revealed to him in the course of a single night in November, 1907, when he saw, heard, and felt events that were to take place in two periods, from 1914 to 1921 and from 1947 to 1953. Among the events he witnessed that night were the outbreak of World War I, the Russian advance on the eastern front in 1914, the trench warfare on the western front, the great naval battle of Jutland in 1916, the worldwide influenza epidemic that claimed over 20 million victims in 1918–1919, and the political and social turmoil of Germany in the early 1920s. Making repeated trips to Stockholm and Oslo throughout the war, Johanson contacted various Norwegian and Swedish officials, including the brother of the king of Sweden, to warn them of the perilous times ahead. A number of his visions had been reported in the Scandinavian press as early as 1913, and after the war many remarked on their accuracy.

Born May 24, 1858, to a poor farmer and woodsman in Tarna parish, near the Swedish Lapmark, Johanson had learned to read by the age of six. Largely self-taught, he worked as shepherd, teacher, fisherman, and surveyor. Enduring great hardship in the course of many mapping expeditions in the Finnmark, he greatly impressed his co-workers with his courage, intelligence, integrity, and even disposition. Although he did not identify himself with any particular sect, he remained deeply religious throughout his life and attributed his remarkable visions to the power of God.

Prior to the great visions of 1907, Johanson had numerous experiences of prescience, all religious in nature. His first vision came to him on Good Friday in 1884, when—in a trance—he saw two of his brothers on the bottom of a rocky inlet in a lake about 25 mi. from his home. Johanson later learned that his brothers, while out fishing, had drowned at precisely the place and time he had foreseen in his trance.

His second premonition came a few years later, when he was struck by a blinding light and a voice spoke to him while he was attending a church service. The voice, which he described as pleasant, told him to pray for a young couple who were members of the congregation. A week later the newlyweds were drowned in a boating accident. This experience convinced Johanson that these revelations were coming directly from God, and immediately afterwards such premonitions began to visit him more frequently.

Johanson's visions almost always took one of three possible forms. Some events he literally saw, often viewing them as if from an airplane or high tower. Others were verbal accounts related by the now familiar voice, which he had come to accept as that of Jesus himself. Yet others were merely a feeling—a certainty, deeply and wordlessly held, that some event was about to happen. The great visions of 1907 were exceptional even by these standards, for they took all three forms simultaneously, almost overwhelming Johanson with their immediacy and detail.

At first pertaining only to relatives and neighbors, his early visions were not concerned with the larger world and gave little hint of what was to come. By the turn of the century, however, he began to foresee calamities such as the great volcanic eruption in 1902 that destroyed St. Pierre, a city of 30,000 on the Caribbean island of Martinique; the 1906 San Francisco earthquake; and the violent Messina earthquake of 1908, which utterly devastated that Italian city. He even predicted the *Titanic* disaster, not only giving the name of the ship but also noting that an eminent member of the famous Astor family would perish. And indeed, just as Johanson had seen in his vision, John Jacob Astor IV—the builder of the Astoria wing at the famed Waldorf-Astoria Hotel—was numbered among those lost.

Shortly after midnight on November 14, 1907, Johanson was awakened from a sound, dreamless sleep by the voice and the blinding light. Soon he found himself taken through an "illuminated space" to many locations to witness many events. He saw the very first flames of the great war in Austria-Hungary and Serbia, the collapse of Germany just after its greatest success, the abdication of the kaiser and his exile in Holland, revolution—with an enormous loss of life—in Russia, and violence and revolution in Germany even after the war. All these things he saw in great detail and all came to pass just as he had predicted: the assassination of the Austrian Archduke Francis Ferdinand led to Austria-Hungary's ultimatum to Serbia, which touched off World War I; Germany's military fortunes collapsed in 1918 only months after its success against Russia; Kaiser Wilhelm II was forced to abdicate and fled into exile in Holland; the Russian Revolution and subsequent civil war took lives in numbers uncounted to this day; and postwar Germany was gripped by years of political violence.

As striking as this accuracy appears, both Johanson and his visions went completely unheeded and almost as completely unreported. Moreover, his predictions for the second period—1947 to 1953—lacked some of the accuracy of those for the first. He saw a great war pitting Sweden and Norway against the Soviet Union and France, for example. He prophesied a series of worldwide storms and natural catastrophes that would do great damage especially in North America. He saw New York City's skyscrapers in ruins.

Anton Johanson died peacefully on January 3, 1928, in Oslo, Norway, without seeing that second period. Yet perhaps he would have found much that seemed familiar, for scattered among those generally less accurate predictions we find a number that it is impossible to call coincidental—an eruption of Vesuvius in 1953, a great storm on the North Sea devastating Holland in that same year, the rise of a Jewish state in Palestine—all just as the old seer of the Finnmark had foreseen.

—J.B.S.

EVANGELINE ADAMS (1865–1932)

Known as "America's female Nostradamus," Evangeline Adams transformed astrology from a disreputable con game into a respectable science. By the time she had reached her mid-30s, she was well on the way to achieving her goal of becoming the most famous astrologer in America, if not the world.

363

Evangeline Adams.

Born into an influential New England family, Evangeline and her three brothers were raised in the conservative religious atmosphere of Andover Hill, Mass. Although her father died when she was 15 months old, Evangeline enjoyed a happy childhood and evidenced her willfulness and determination at an early age.

While still a young woman living at home, she was stricken by a serious illness which was to result in a fateful association. During Evangeline's long recovery, her family physician came to know her well and was intrigued by her "unusual ideas." He suggested that she see his colleague, Dr. J. Heber Smith, a prominent diagnostician who practiced astrology in connection with his medical work. After charting Evangeline's horoscope, Dr. Smith told her that she was a born astrologer.

Thus encouraged, Evangeline persuaded the doctor to share his knowledge with her. Also a student of Sanskrit and Eastern religion, he taught her his philosophical as well as mathematical approach to astrology. She soon shocked her family's well-bred Boston friends by opening an office in the Hotel Copley, where she practiced until 1899, when her horoscope indicated she should move to New York City.

On her first night in New York, she settled into the Windsor Hotel on 8th Avenue and provided proprietor Warren E. Leland with a reading. Evangeline hesitated momentarily before telling him that she saw the next day—Friday, March 17—as a day of imminent danger for him. Leland did not take Evangeline's warning seriously, but on Friday during the annual St. Patrick's Day parade, the Windsor Hotel burned to the ground. Although Evangeline lost most of her possessions in the fire, her prediction received so much publicity that she was able to set up a successful practice in a Carnegie Hall studio, where she worked for the rest of her life.

Evangeline again made the headlines in 1914 when she was accused of being in violation of a New York statute that prohibited "acrobatic performers, circus riders, men who desert their wives, and people who tend to tell fortunes." No doubt the judge was surprised when, instead of a gypsy with a crystal ball, a stout, strong-jawed, homely woman who looked and dressed like a practical, successful businesswoman walked into his courtroom.

Evangeline was determined to see astrology vindicated. Even as the judge attempted to dismiss the case, Evangeline briskly insisted that the trial proceed, and, in her own defense, she proposed to chart the horoscope of a person totally unknown to her. Consulting her charts and performing some mathematical calculations, she gave an analysis of the judge's son which so impressed the presiding justice that he declared, "The defendant raises astrology to the dignity of an exact science." From that time on, the practice of astrology was no longer prohibited in the state of New York.

By the 1920s, Evangeline had become a very wealthy woman from her clients' fees. She read millionaire J. P. Morgan's horoscope many times and provided him with a monthly service illustrating the probable effects that changing planetary positions would have on politics, business, and the stock market. He came to take her advice seriously, as did the great American naturalist John Burroughs and motion picture actress Mary Pickford. In 1930 Evangeline gained additional fame when she launched a series of radio broadcasts in which she offered advice and predictions to millions of listeners.

Perhaps because she was a descendant of U.S. President John Quincy Adams, Evangeline never failed to scrutinize the race for the White House. In 1920 she predicted that Herbert Hoover, the leading candidate for the Republican presidential nomination, would not be chosen. Although politicians took the prediction with a grain of salt, Evangeline held firm, insisting that the nomination would go to a man whose horoscope she hadn't read. Sure enough, a little-known senator from Ohio rose up to win the Republican nomination. His name was Warren G. Harding and he was elected to the presidency by one of the largest landslides in history.

One of Evangeline's most famous predictions was made in 1931, when she prophesied that the U.S. would be involved in a war in 11 years. But her political interests were not limited to the U.S. She clearly foresaw the fate of Edward VIII, a bachelor who ruled as king of Great Britain and Ireland for barely a year. In 1931, while Edward was Prince of Wales, Evangeline wrote a book, *Astrology for Everyone,* in which she stated that Edward's chart indicated he had a strong interest in married women who could never share his throne. Five years later her prophecy was proved right. In 1931 Edward had met Wallis Warfield Simpson, an American "commoner" who eventually divorced her second husband so that she could marry the new king. In 1936, facing a constitutional crisis, Edward abdicated in order to wed Mrs. Simpson.

Perhaps the most unerring predictions revealed to her by her charts concerned death. The famed opera singer Enrico Caruso became so ill the winter before he died that a priest prepared to deliver the last rites. But when Evangeline was consulted, she insisted that Caruso would not die from that illness. In the summer of 1921, the tenor was again taken ill, and this time Evangeline warned, "He may die any time." Two weeks later, the great Caruso's voice was forever silenced.

Evangeline also accurately predicted the death of England's King Edward VII in 1910, and she foresaw her own end as well. In 1932 she announced that she would not live out the year. True to her astrological forecast, Evangeline Adams died in her Carnegie Hall studio on November 10, 1932, a victim of heart disease.

—A.K.

COUNT LOUIS HAMON (CHEIRO)
(1866–1936)

British clairvoyant Count Louis Hamon—known professionally as Cheiro (from the Greek word for "hand")—won fame throughout Europe and the U.S. during the late 19th and early 20th centuries because of his uncanny ability to predict the future by employing palmistry, astrology, and numerology. In 1900 Hamon was awarded the Order of the Lion and the Sun by the grateful shah of Persia, whose life he had saved several months earlier in Paris. Because of a premonition, Hamon had warned the shah's grand vizier that an assassin would strike while the shah visited the Paris Exposition. Extra guards were assigned and security was tightened, thus foiling an attempt on the shah's life a few days later. In June, 1911, Hamon wrote to another client, the English author and editor William Stead, and warned him not to travel by water during April of 1912. Nine months later, Stead ignored Hamon's forecast of doom and boarded the *Titanic*. On April 14, 1912, he drowned in the North Atlantic.

Born William John Warner in a village outside Dublin, Ireland, in 1866, Hamon later changed his name and added the spurious title of count when he went into business as a palmist. The son of a conservative English businessman and his attractive French wife, Hamon was introduced to the occult by his mother, a firm believer in astrology. When, at the age of 10, Hamon wrote his first essay on palmistry, his enraged father shipped him off to school with the intent that he should eventually become a clergyman. In his late teens Hamon left school and ran away to Bombay, India—but not before reading the palm of Irish nationalist Charles Stewart Parnell and correctly predicting that his political future would be ruined by a romantic entanglement. In India he made friends with Brahmin priests who were

366

also students of palmistry. Following three years of training with a Hindu guru, Hamon left India. Then after journeying through Egypt's Valley of the Tombs of the Kings, where he was given a mummified hand which he carried with him for years, he returned to England.

In London, at the age of 24, Hamon began his practice as a palm reader. The tall, broad-shouldered, handsome seer was an immediate success, partly due to the accolades of statesman Arthur James Balfour, whom Hamon foresaw as the prime minister of Britain. Another early client was playwright Oscar Wilde, who was warned by Hamon that he would be ruined seven years later unless he reformed himself. After seven years had passed, Wilde was convicted and imprisoned for having homosexual relations.

In 1893 Hamon read over 6,000 sets of palms, driving himself until he became seriously ill and had to spend three months in a nursing home. After his recovery, he visited the U.S. and lectured throughout the country on the arts of palmistry and astrology. His fame reached new heights when he visited convicted murderer Henry Meyer in his prison cell and assured him that he would not be electrocuted. The day before the scheduled execution, Meyer's sentence was commuted to life imprisonment. Among the many notables who consulted Hamon were Mark Twain and President Grover Cleveland, whose palms indicated that he would not serve a third term in office. A Civil War hero and renowned New York lawyer, Col. Robert Ingersoll, remarked at the time, "I may not believe in God, man, or the devil—but I believe in Cheiro."

Returning to Europe, Hamon became more successful than ever. In 1894 he was called to the British War Office in Whitehall to read the palms of Lord Horatio Kitchener. He prophesied that Kitchener would achieve his greatest career success in 1914. He also told Kitchener not to board a ship during his 66th year. At the outbreak of World War I in 1914, Kitchener was made secretary of war. At the age of 66, in 1916, Kitchener ignored Hamon's warning—as had Stead four years before—and boarded the battle cruiser H.M.S. *Hampshire*. The ship sailed from Scotland on its way to Russia, where Kitchener planned to meet with Czar Nicholas II. Less than a day out of port, the *Hampshire* struck a German mine and sank. Kitchener drowned.

King Leopold II of Belgium, King Humbert I of Italy, and King Edward VII of Great Britain also sought his services. Edward, in particular, became dependent on Hamon's advice; in 1902 he even asked him to pick the most auspicious date for his coronation. Hamon selected August 9 for the investiture and put Edward's mind at ease by informing him that his present illness was not fatal and that he would live to be 69. Through Edward, Hamon was introduced to Czar Nicholas II, who became one of Hamon's most avid fans even though he predicted that Nicholas and his family would meet with disaster in 1917. In 1904 Nicholas invited Hamon to Russia and entertained him at the Summer Palace. In St. Petersburg (now Leningrad), Hamon met the self-proclaimed religious prophet Grigori Rasputin. The meeting was a strange affair. The two accomplished hypnotists tried unsuccessfully to hypnotize each other. Finally, Hamon predicted that Rasputin would die in the icy waters of the Neva River after being poisoned, knifed, and shot, which is exactly what happened to Rasputin 11 years later.

Allegedly, Hamon used his hypnotic powers in the pursuit of one of his favorite activities—amorous seduction. He seems to have preferred married women, since his name frequently appeared in divorce court proceedings. In order to contend with his female clients' jealous husbands, he became an expert with a revolver and a master of jujitsu. Nevertheless, Hamon was once stabbed in the side by a husband whose wife had allowed the prophet access to more than her palms.

Hamon's love affairs are cited as one of the reasons for his extensive travels. His journeys through the Americas, Asia, and Europe supposedly kept him from having to settle down with one woman. Whatever the reasons, Hamon led an adventurous life. He served as a war correspondent in 1895 during the Sino-Japanese War and in 1905 in the Russo-Japanese War. According to one biographer, he also served in British Intelligence during World War I. It is thought that his connection with the British Secret Service led Hamon into his affair with the infamous spy and nude dancer Mata Hari. Hamon was fascinated by, but never in love with, Mata Hari. After reading her palms, he foretold that she would reach the crisis of her life at the age of 37 in 1917. In that year and at that age, she was executed by a French firing squad for espionage.

Besides his personalized predictions for his clients, Hamon made numerous prophecies on world events. He accurately foretold the outbreak of the Boer War and World War I, the Russian and Chinese revolutions, and the Great Depression. He predicted that the Jews would return to Palestine, where they would establish their own country, named Israel. He foresaw India's independence and its partition into Muslim Pakistan and Hindu India. For Spain, he predicted the rise to power of a dictator (Franco).

Some of Hamon's prophecies have yet to come true. He predicted that a dictatorship would assume control in France, and that Japan and China would unite politically and control Asia. He foretold that a large part of New York City would be destroyed by an earthquake, while Russian airplanes would level London. He also foresaw Armageddon—the war of wars—which would take place when Russia, Libya, Ethiopia, and Iran invaded Palestine. Strangely enough, Libya and Ethiopia have never been allied with Russia until recently, and not until 1979 did Iran move away from a pro-U.S. position.

In 1930 Hamon moved to Hollywood, Calif., after deciding to try his hand at screenwriting. In Hollywood he established a school of metaphysics and again practiced palmistry; his clientele included movie stars Lillian Gish and Mary Pickford and famed director Erich Von Stroheim. On October 8, 1936, Hamon died at his home at 7417 Hollywood Boulevard.

—R.J.F.

HOMER LEA (1876-1912)

Lea was a remarkable American, a spindly hunchback who led Chinese insurgents in battle, a brilliant and perspicacious military

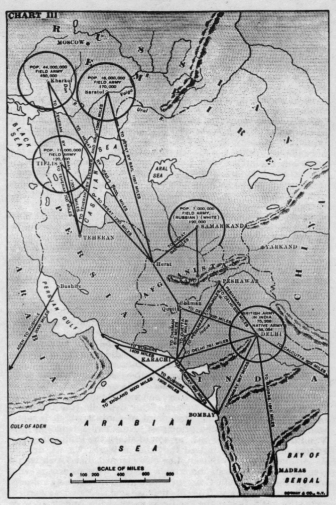

Homer Lea's 1912 map predicted a Russian
invasion of Afghanistan.

strategist who warned the U.S. of a Japanese sneak attack on Hawaii decades before Pearl Harbor. As early as 1912, his thoughts anticipated the Soviet invasion of Afghanistan in 1980.

Homer Lea was born in Cripple Creek, Colo., and raised both there and in Los Angeles. His congenital twisted spine grew progressively worse, and by age 12 he had grown to his full height of 5 ft. and was permanently hunchbacked. Despite his handicap, he dreamed of becoming a soldier. In fact, he had recurring dreams that he was a Chinese warrior fighting under the nickname "the Martial Monk." He drilled playmates, using broomsticks for arms and firecrackers for artillery.

In 1894 he enrolled at Occidental College, where he befriended a Chinese cook, learned his language, and studied military history. He showed a great aptitude for military strategy. Three years later he transferred to Stanford University and fell in with members of the Pong-Wong-Wui, an organization working to topple Tzu Hsi, China's empress dowager. In San Francisco he attended a lecture by Dr. Sun Yat-sen, who so impressed the youth that he volunteered that night to join Sun's movement to liberate China. After hearing of his genius for military strategy, Sun made Lea his chief of staff.

In 1899 Sun asked Lea to accompany him to China to work for the revolution. Understandably, Lea's father tried to dissuade his frail, crippled son from undertaking such a strenuous mission and even threatened to cut off his allowance if he should set sail. But Lea was determined. "All great careers have been carved by the sword," he boasted to a friend. "I intend to carve mine, now." Lea arrived in China just in time to take part in the Boxer Rebellion, the anti-Western uprising that the empress had privately hoped might rid her country of the "white devils." Although he played no major role in the conflict, he did raise and train a band of insurgents, with whom he made a raid on a Chinese arsenal and otherwise harassed the empress's troops. With a price now on his head and his ranks depleted, Lea took refuge in a Buddhist temple for a time before returning to California in 1901.

From makeshift headquarters in Santa Monica, he trained Chinese patriots for battle against the throne. He went on lecture tours and fundraisers in Chinese communities, promoting the revolution. At one such meeting in San Francisco, he exhorted an audience of 5,000 Chinese to cut off their queues, the traditional symbol of loyalty to the Manchus. The entire throng did so under his gaze in the first mass queue removal of the revolution.

Although he continued to play an active role in Sun's movement, he also began to take a critical look at his own country. He grew alarmed at the lack of U.S. defenses and in 1909 published *The Valor of Ignorance*, in which he warned, "This Republic [the U.S.] and Japan are approaching ... that point of contact which is war." Employing what he called principles of military science, he predicted that the Japanese one day would attack the Philippines in a pincers movement, as indeed they did in World War II, driving MacArthur's forces to Bataan. Lea also claimed that Japan would eventually attack Hawaii and cripple the U.S. fleet. After surveying much of the U.S. Pacific Coast, he pronounced it extremely vulnerable to Japanese invasion. The only defense against Japan, he warned, was a strong U.S. fleet in the Pacific, an expense few Americans were willing to make in the peaceful days before World War I.

Although the U.S. government largely ignored Lea's book, it was avidly read overseas, especially in Japan. Two people who enjoyed it were British Field Marshal Lord Roberts and Kaiser Wilhelm II of Germany. At their invitation, Lea met with both separately. To the kaiser, Lea directed another bit of prophecy. Germany could never win a war in Europe, he told him, unless it first captured the neutral states of Denmark and The Netherlands. Many believed that Germany's failure to do just that cost it World War I. Twenty years later,

Adolf Hitler also read Lea and incorporated some of his ideas into *Mein Kampf.*

In 1912 Lea published a second prophetic book, *The Day of the Saxon.* In it, he warned that the days of the British empire were numbered. "In this epoch of war upon which the [British] empire is about to enter, hopes of peace are futile," he wrote. Dominance of the seas was no longer enough to resist certain and overwhelming German aggression, he asserted two years before the outbreak of World War I. Only a great land power like the U.S., he said, could crush Germany.

In 1911 Sun Yat-sen was elected president of China. At Sun's invitation, Lea attended the inauguration ceremonies and received a hero's welcome. While in China he suffered a paralytic stroke, and on November 1, 1912, he died at his home in California. His last words were "Guard America. Make her secure."

He had been planning a third geopolitical book, tentatively titled *The Swarming of the Slav.* In it he predicted that after wars among Great Britain, the U.S., Germany, and Japan, the survivors—Great Britain and the U.S.—would confront a still greater threat from Russia. Prior to the Bolshevik Revolution, he foresaw an expansive Russia, straining at the borders of least resistance: "Oceanic in its greatness, [Russia] is oceanic in the expression of its forces." Germany and Japan might be vulnerable to Russian conquest, but even if these western and eastern flanks were impregnable, Lea believed, Russia still could push south, probably into India. Almost as if he were looking directly into the 1980s, Lea saw Russia advancing "on the left flank by Afghanistan, and on the right flank by Persia [Iran]."

—W.A.D.

EDGAR CAYCE (1877–1945)

The most famous clairvoyant and psychic healer of our century was a nondescript, unassuming, good-natured American farm boy named Edgar Cayce. During his lifetime, while in a trance, Cayce diagnosed illnesses and recommended treatments for over 14,000 patients who consulted him—usually after their own doctors had pronounced them incurable. Unlike most psychics, Cayce kept complete transcripts of his trance-induced utterings. These transcripts, together with the follow-up research done on his patients, proved that Cayce's methods had an amazingly high success rate. Cayce's prophecies have also been uncannily accurate.

Born on a farm near the town of Hopkinsville, Ky., on March 18, 1877, Edgar Cayce grew up a quiet, religious boy who appeared to be below average scholastically. In fact, his first psychic experience resulted from a problem he had with his schoolwork. At the age of nine, young Cayce was called an idiot by his teacher after he re-

Edgar Cayce.

peatedly failed to spell the word *cabin* correctly. That evening Edgar's father tried to teach his son the elements of spelling but failed completely. Finally, he left his son alone for half an hour. As Cayce reported later, during that time he heard a voice say, "Sleep now and we will help you." Cayce dozed off with his spelling book under his head. To the amazement of both father and son, Cayce knew every lesson in the book when he awoke.

Throughout his childhood, there were incidents that suggested Cayce possessed unusual powers. His career as a healer began after Cayce himself was seriously injured when he was struck by a baseball. After falling into a sleeplike trance, he began speaking, ordering his mother to apply a certain poultice to his injured spine.

He promptly recovered. With the help of a local amateur hypnotist, Cayce continued to go into trances during which he diagnosed illnesses and offered remedies for ailing friends.

Cayce dropped out of school after the ninth grade to become a clerk, and later he worked in a bookstore. In his hometown he was respected but treated as a kind of freak because of his occult abilities. Since he didn't charge for his trance consultations, Cayce continued clerking for a while, then sold life insurance, and later tried photography. He married and fathered two sons, but despite his psychic adventures he remained an unsophisticated country bumpkin who read his Bible daily.

Slowly, news spread of this young man with little education, who spouted complex medical terminology while in a trance. Scientists and doctors arrived in Hopkinsville to test his abilities. His name appeared in medical journals and newspapers, and a Hearst paper invited him to demonstrate his powers in Chicago. Letters arrived from people who sought cures not only for themselves but for friends and relatives. Cayce would recline on his couch, breathe deeply, and go into a trance while his wife read the letters aloud. Still in a trance, he would analyze the illness involved and prescribe treatment. He told a diabetic who consulted him to take a potion derived from Jerusalem artichokes. (It has recently been discovered that these vegetables contain a naturally occurring form of insulin.) Cayce ordered castor-oil packs for a variety of disorders, while one of his more exotic cures consisted of plantain—a fuzzy-leafed herb—boiled in milk to form a lotion, coupled with an internal dose of sulfur, Rochelle salt, and cream of tartar mixed together.

Because an increasing number of people were asking for help, Cayce decided to devote all his time to psychic healing, charging a modest fee of those who had money while offering his services free to those who were indigent. In 1927 wealthy believers in Cayce's ability to contact what he called the "Universal Consciousness" built him a hospital in Virginia Beach, Va. However, Cayce did not meet with total acceptance; the medical profession denounced him as a dangerous quack. The local authorities also took a dim view of his activities. He was arrested twice—once for practicing medicine without a license and once for fortune-telling in New York City—although all charges were subsequently dismissed.

Cayce was not only a psychic healer but a renowned prophet. In April of 1929, a broker consulted Cayce about the stock market, which had been booming for several years. Cayce went into his sleeplike trance and predicted that the market would suffer "a downward movement of long duration" and that there would be a "panic in the money centers," including Wall Street. Finally, Cayce urged his client to "dispose of all [he] held." Unfortunately, the broker failed to heed Cayce's warning, and six months later he was ruined when the market crashed on Black Friday. Cayce also accurately predicted the beginning and end of both world wars. He foretold the independence of India and Israel; he predicted the deaths of President Franklin D. Roosevelt and President John F. Kennedy; and he envisioned the discovery of the Dead Sea Scrolls and the invention of the laser. A hurricane in Japan, an earthquake in California, and a tidal wave in the Philippines in 1926 were all correctly predicted by Cayce.

Perhaps his most famous prediction was his prophecy that California would fall into the Pacific Ocean. In the 1960s, contemporary clairvoyants studied the transcripts of Cayce's trances to determine the date of this calamity, since Cayce himself had not given it. Somehow they decided that California would take its fatal plunge in April, 1969. This prediction was widely publicized, causing a panic on the West Coast which motivated a number of Californians to leave the state during that month. Fortunately, the prediction was incorrect.

Cayce made numerous prophecies for the closing years of the 20th century. According to Cayce, democracy will not only replace communism in China but will spread throughout the entire world. On a more somber note, he foresaw drastic and sudden physical changes in the earth's surface before the year 1998 because of shifts in the polar axis, as a result of which northern Europe will disappear below the ocean "in the twinkling of an eye"; Japan will be destroyed by earthquakes and volcanic eruptions; and southern Alabama, Georgia, and both North and South Carolina will be submerged under the sea. World War III will erupt in 1999, and within a year civilization as we know it will end.

A believer in reincarnation, Cayce had a dream in 1936 in which he saw himself reborn in 2100 A.D. in Nebraska, which by then will be on the west coast of the U.S. In this vision, he was trying to convince a group of scientists that he had lived some 200 years before. In order to collect evidence of his former life, he flew east in a cigar-shaped metal airship to an island where workmen were clearing rubble and rebuilding a city. When he asked where he was, a worker replied that he was in the former city of New York on Manhattan Island.

On January 1, 1945, while confined to a convalescent home in Roanoke, Va., 67-year-old Cayce predicted that his own funeral would occur four days later. He was correct.

—R.J.F.

IMMANUEL VELIKOVSKY
(1895–1979)

In 1950 Russian-born author and scholar Immanuel Velikovsky touched off the most bitterly contested scientific controversy of the century. That year saw the publication of his book *Worlds in Collision*, the thesis of which was, to say the least, cosmic. He announced that, during a 52-year period around 1500 B.C., the earth had been struck twice by the tail of an enormous comet that had erupted from the planet Jupiter.

The collisions brought cataclysm in their wake—tidal waves, earthquakes, and volcanic eruptions—and radically altered the face of our planet. Whole continents like Atlantis and Lemuria sank into the sea, and new landmasses were born. The sky rained fire, noxious

Could a comet such as this have struck
the Earth around 1500 B.C.?

gases, and red-hot gravel. Velikovsky believed that the comet threatened the earth for around 800 years, and in approaching Mars nearly caused that planet to collide with our own. The earth's crust shifted upon its molten core, and the polarity of the whole globe was reversed. This so altered the earth's orbit around the sun that the length of days, months, and years changed accordingly. Central to Velikovsky's theory was his belief that the heavenly maverick was recognized, feared, and worshiped throughout the ancient world. The comet was, he said, today in business under an assumed name—the planet Venus.

As might have been expected, Velikovsky's theories were far too incredible to gain acceptance readily within the scientific community. But Velikovsky was confident that future experimentation would prove the worth of his work, and since 1950 some of his theories have been proved right by technological breakthroughs generated by the space program. He predicted that the surface of the planet Venus would be found to be extremely hot, owing to its recent birth, a fact later confirmed by space probes. Moreover, he correctly described Venus's hydrocarbonaceous atmosphere and the planet's disturbed rotation. He said the moon would be found to have remnants of strong magnetic activity, and he predicted the presence there of carbides and aromatic hydrocarbons. Apollo astronauts later reported these facts. He spoke of what was to be dubbed the Van Allen radiation belt around the earth, and accurately predicted the discovery of radio emissions from the planet Jupiter.

A physician and psychologist by training, Velikovsky used *Worlds* as a bridge into the jealously guarded preserves of astronomers, astrophysicists, and anthropologists. Yet his biography is hardly that of a scientific heretic. He was born in the small Russian town of Vitebsk in 1895, the son of a Hebrew scholar and publisher. When the family moved to Moscow, the brilliant lad enrolled in the Medvednikow Gymnasium, graduating with high honors in 1913. He attended lectures at Edinburgh for a term and then dabbled in economics, law, and ancient history at Moscow's Free University.

Finally, he settled upon medical studies and graduated as a physician in 1921 from the University of Moscow. The new doctor went on to postdoctoral work in Berlin, where he became one of the founders of Scripta Universitatis, a series of scientific and cultural books by Jewish scholars. One of his colleagues was Albert Einstein, who edited volumes on physics and mathematics.

Velikovsky decided to specialize in the fledgling practice of psychoanalysis and returned to Vienna in 1933. It was there, spurred on by Freud's writings about Oedipus, Moses, and Ikhnaton, that he began to delve into ancient history and ethnology. The idea for *Worlds in Collision* was born of his observation that all of the ancient peoples—Greeks, Samoans, American Indians, and Chinese—had left behind accounts of an enormous natural holocaust, which had occurred roughly at the same time in each history.

In 1939 Velikovsky moved to New York City—more specifically to the Columbia University library—and immersed himself in ancient history and biblical research. He came to believe that he was chronicling a happening which took place 3,500 years ago, practically within recent times by archaeological reckoning. He dated his comet's first appearance as being at the time of Exodus in the Old Testament, of Prometheus in Greek mythology, and of the Middle Kingdom in Egypt.

He was particularly interested in the biblical account of the sun's standing still in the sky, and dated this event about 1450 B.C., when a host of other cultures also described a seemingly endless night. He believed they were all describing the comet's second approach to earth.

Such were the ideas that elicited howls of anguish from the world's scientists when Velikovsky burst upon the scene like the comet he described. Such an assault on the scientific heterodoxy was bound to draw fire and did, much of it aimed below the belt. Velikovsky was immediately blacklisted by scientific journals, but he was not a man to be put off by censure. He arranged to have his work published in popular magazines like *Reader's Digest, Harper's,* and *Collier's.* Next there was a desperate attempt by several scientists to block publication of Velikovsky's book, and when it was finally published, they succeeded in having it suppressed. As soon as Macmillan issued *Worlds,* the company was faced with a boycott of its scientific textbook division, and thus found itself in the awkward position of having to dump a national best-seller. At the time that Macmillan gave publication rights to Doubleday, the book had been on *The New York Times* best-seller list for several weeks.

His subsequent books were described as "fallout from a single central idea." *Ages in Chaos* appeared in 1952 and dealt with his interpretation of the social chronology of the Middle East of the period between the first collision and 687 B.C. He followed it up in 1955 with *Earth in Upheaval,* which was devoted to defending his comet theory by citing his archaeological and geological research. To his ultimate satisfaction, Dr. Velikovsky lived long enough to see proved many of the theories which had been so soundly denounced 20 years before.

—M.J.T.

KARL ERNST KRAFFT (1900–1945)

On November 2, 1939, Karl Ernst Krafft wired the Nazi State Security Office that between November 7 and 10 Hitler's life would be in danger. "There is a possibility of an attempt at assassination through the use of explosive material," predicted Krafft.

Krafft's telegram was pigeonholed in Berlin. Six days later, however, amidst a brownshirt beer-hall crowd, a bomb exploded. When the smoke cleared, the rostrum from which Hitler had been addressing his cronies was a pile of rubble. Seven people were dead, 60 injured. Had Hitler not unexpectedly departed ahead of schedule, most certainly he too would have been a casualty.

Who was this man who apparently had foreseen the explosion? Small, dark-haired, and with eyes that "burned with an inner fire," Krafft was a Swiss astrologer of German ancestry. Born May 10, 1900, he was brought up in an "oppressively bourgeois" household in

Basel, Switzerland, where his father managed a local brewery. Krafft did well in school and showed a natural flair for mathematics. Over the protests of his parents, who hoped he would enter a practical profession such as banking, he enrolled as a science student at the University of Basel in 1919. That same year his younger sister died, and Krafft received his first exposure to occultism when séances were held in an attempt to contact her spirit. After that his interest in the occult sciences, astrology in particular, grew rapidly. In 1921, while a student at the University of Geneva, he began trying to discover an underlying statistical basis for astrological predictions—a study which was to consume the rest of his life. Considering himself a genius of Isaac Newton's caliber, his obsession with astrology bordered on the psychotic.

In 1938 Krafft laid the groundwork for his reputation when he analyzed the horoscopes of two anonymous individuals for Virgil Tilea, the Romanian minister in London. The first chart, Krafft said, indicated a person with Jewish blood who would probably not live beyond November, 1938. The second chart showed a man of great prominence who would fall from his lofty position in September, 1940. Krafft's astrological interpretations proved amazingly accurate. The first chart belonged to Corneliu Zelea-Codreanu, the half-Jewish leader of the Romanian Fascists, who was killed on November 30, 1938. The second chart was that of King Carol of Romania, who abdicated on September 6, 1940.

Confident that his own horoscope aligned him with the Nazi rulers, the highly ambitious Krafft was anxious to gain further attention. The day after the bomb exploded, he bypassed the bureaucracy and wired Deputy Führer Rudolf Hess of his successful prediction. Both Hitler and Minister for Propaganda Joseph Goebbels saw the telegram this time, and the following day the Gestapo arrested Krafft. After satisfying his interrogators that he was not involved in the assassination attempt, Krafft was released. Soon after that the Nazis decided that his talents could be put to good use.

Four centuries earlier, the famous 16th-century seer Nostradamus had predicted that a man named "Hister" (Hitler) would lead Germany in a great war. Nostradamus had also foreseen a major crisis in both Great Britain and Poland in 1939. Learning that the Swiss was an expert on this early seer, Goebbels enlisted Krafft to deduce from Nostradamus's writings the inevitability of a Nazi victory.

The first of Krafft's full-time studies for the Nazis foretold the imminent invasion of Holland and Belgium by German forces. Reputedly it contained additional astonishing predictions, but the material was so severely censored at the time that little of the original manuscript is extant today. After further study of Nostradamus, Krafft declared that southeast France—the seer's birthplace—would not be affected by hostilities. This prediction was quoted in leaflets which were scattered over France by plane. The result: Thousands of French civilians made their way to southeast France, leaving the approaches to Paris and the Channel ports relatively open when the German armies advanced.

Although Krafft was imbued with patriotic zeal for the "unjustly abused and slandered Third Reich," his predictions were not always optimistic. At a private gathering in the spring of 1940, he revealed to Nazi leaders Robert Ley and Hans Frank the results of his latest graph of Germany's future. Krafft warned that Germany would have a major military reversal in the winter of 1942–1943. When Ley and Frank responded that the Fatherland would surely be victorious before then, they were badly mistaken. The war dragged on, and in January, 1943, the predicted debacle occurred when German forces suffered a crushing defeat at Stalingrad.

As events soon proved, Krafft's fate was inextricably bound up with that of the Third Reich. On May 10, 1941, Rudolf Hess flew to Scotland, hoping to negotiate a peace with Winston Churchill. Hess was acting on the advice of his astrologers. Hitler's horoscope showed unfavorable signs, they said, and the likelihood of Germany's winning the war was deteriorating. The Nazis reacted to Hess's astrologically-induced defection by cracking down on all "astrologers, fortune-tellers, and other swindlers" and hauling prominent occultists off to jails and concentration camps. Krafft was among them.

In prison Krafft was forced to misinterpret horoscopes of statesmen and other public figures. For example, he produced a false astrological analysis of President Franklin Roosevelt which was used for propaganda purposes. His observation that British Field Marshal Montgomery's lucky-in-war Scorpio sign was "certainly stronger" than his rival Rommel's was rudely dismissed. Only interpretations favorable to the Nazi cause were acceptable. Depressed and humiliated by the fact that a man of his reputation should be asked to provide astrological falsehoods for propaganda hacks, Krafft suffered a nervous breakdown. Early in March, 1943, he contracted typhus.

On January 8, 1945, the 44-year-old astrologer died while being transferred to the infamous Buchenwald concentration camp. Although ill and in mental collapse, Krafft nonetheless had a parting prediction. He prophesied that British bombs would rain down on the German Propaganda Ministry as a punishment for its despicable conduct.

—P.G. and F.B.

13

THE 6 GREATEST
PREDICTIONS
OF ALL TIME

Malachy O'Morgain, an Irish priest, in the year 1139 accurately forecast the identity of every single Roman Catholic pope who reigned from 1143 to the current John Paul II. He predicted there would be only two more popes after this one.

At a dinner party in Paris in 1788, a clairvoyant in attendance, Jacques Cazotte, accurately predicted the deaths of six other guests and the fate of a seventh within six years—and then accurately predicted his own death on the guillotine.

In 1898, Morgan Robertson, a New York writer of sea stories, published a novel, *The Wreck of the Titan*, about a British luxury liner that sinks after hitting an iceberg in the North Atlantic. Fourteen years later, the *Titanic*, a British luxury liner, hit an iceberg and sank in the North Atlantic.

SPURINNA'S PREDICTION FOR THE IDES OF MARCH

The oligarchic republic was collapsing. Pompey, champion of the ruling Roman nobility, had been killed in civil warfare. His father-in-law and conqueror, Julius Caesar, dreamed of a Pax Romana stretching from Spain to Parthia, with the senate representing all free men of the empire, not just Roman nobles. Declared dictator for life in 44 B.C., at the age of 55, he hoped to be acclaimed king in order to expedite a national reconstruction.

The first intimations of disaster came in January of 44 B.C. when Roman settlers in the city of Capua unearthed the tomb of Capys, the city's founder, and discovered a bronze plaque that read, "When once the tomb of Capys is brought to light, then a branch of the Julian house will be slain by the hand of one of his kindred." A relative was already involved in an assassination plot against Caesar. Marcus Brutus, supposed descendant of a Brutus who had routed a monarchy, was finally goaded into joining the 60 conspirators by graffiti on statues of the original Brutus that taunted, "Your posterity is unworthy of you." A double-edged gibe, since many, including Caesar himself, believed Brutus to be Caesar's natural child.

As the time of the Senate convocation drew nearer, terrible signs of upheaval began. Wild birds roosted in the Forum, and fiery men were seen fighting together. As chief priest, Caesar killed an animal that seemed to have no heart. One priest was able to determine the

Julius Caesar being warned of the
Ides of March by Spurina.

focus of these evil omens. Vestricius Spurinna, a practiced augur, found by examining the entrails of a beast sacrificed during religious ceremonies that Caesar faced a great danger that would culminate on the Ides of March, the day the Senate would convene. The assassins planned, in fact, to murder Caesar in full view of all the senators to give the deed an air of righteousness.

Although Caesar did not take Spurinna's warning seriously, death was on his mind as the 15th approached. When told of a possible conspiracy, he had once joked, "Brutus will wait for this old skin of mine"; now, on the evening of March 14, he suddenly remarked that the best death would be unexpected. That night the weather was gusty and changeable. In bed with his wife, Calpurnia, he was awakened when a sudden wind burst open the doors and windows. He roused Calpurnia, who was having a nightmare, and she begged him to postpone the meeting of the Senate, since she had dreamed that their house was crumbling and that Caesar lay dead in her arms. Calpurnia's fears shook Caesar, the more so since she had never been superstitious. He agreed to have further sacrifices made and to abide by the results.

The sacrifices were inauspicious, and Caesar decided to dismiss the Senate. Fearing that they would soon be discovered, the conspirators delegated Decimus Brutus Albinus, one of Caesar's heirs, to tell Caesar that the senators were ready to vote him king, and that he might never have another chance. Still uneasy, Caesar accompanied Albinus.

The steps of the meeting place (erected by Pompey) were crowded with men waiting to speak with Caesar, and when Artemidorus urgently pushed a warning note into his hand, the throng was so pressing he was unable to read it. As he mounted the steps he encountered Vestricius Spurinna, wearing the purple-edged mantle that was a sign of his office.

"Well, Spurinna," bantered Caesar, "the Ides of March have come."

"Yes, Caesar," answered the priest, "come, but not gone!"

In keeping with tradition, Spurinna performed his augury before Caesar entered the Senate. The first chicken he sacrificed had defective entrails, a portent of imminent disaster. Repeated sacrifices revealed similar abnormalities. The conspirators became increasingly restless about this unexpected delay and urged Caesar to make haste. Finally breaking free from Spurinna, the dictator advanced to meet his fate.

Once inside the Senate chambers Caesar was kept busy by Tillius Cimber until the assassins had gathered around, when Cimber bared Caesar's neck as the signal to begin. Brandishing his blade, Casca drew the first blood, but Caesar grasped the sword and shouted for help. The assassins, drawing their daggers, closed in on him then, but he kept them at bay until Brutus stepped forward and cut him in the groin. Horror-struck, Caesar gasped, "You, too, my child?" Realizing that there was no hope, he covered his face with his robe and fell at the foot of Pompey's statue, pierced by 23 wounds.

The assassins' blood mingled with Caesar's. They had struck so avidly in the crush that they had cut their own hands and arms.

At last, Spurinna's Ides of March had passed.

—S.D.

ST. MALACHY'S PAPAL PREDICTIONS

Malachy O'Morgain (1094?–1148) was an Irish priest and prophet who foretold the identities of 112 Roman Catholic popes, from the reign of Celestine II in 1143 to the present time and beyond.

But not *far* beyond. According to St. Malachy, whose predictions have proven amazingly accurate so far, only two popes will succeed the current supreme pontiff, John Paul II. The second of these will be "Petrus Romanus," or "Peter the Roman," of whom Malachy wrote: "In the final persecution of the Holy Roman Church there will reign Peter the Roman, who will feed his flock among many tribulations; after which the seven-hilled city will be destroyed and the dreadful Judge will judge the people."

The first formally canonized Irish saint, Malachy was born into a wealthy and learned family in Armagh. From early childhood he was drawn to the religious and mystical life, and while still a youth he apprenticed himself to St. Imar, a hermetic monk. In his 20s Malachy was made vicar of Armagh. During the ensuing years he embarked upon a program of church reform and is also credited with performing miracles of healing. Malachy succeeded to the archbishopric of Armagh in 1132, but desirous of a simpler existence, he gave up the post five years later.

Malachy's predictions reputedly were made in 1139 while he was on a pilgrimage to the Vatican, where he was appointed papal legate for Ireland. (On his last trek to the Holy See, in 1148, Malachy accurately predicted the place and time of his own death: Clairvaux, France, on All Souls' Day, November 2, of that same year.) Malachy "saw"—and committed to paper—a series of Latin phrases describing the popes to come. Except for the final apocalyptic note about Petrus Romanus, these are brief lines of no more than four words. They usually refer to a pope's family name, birthplace, coat-of-arms, or office held before election to the papacy. Some of the phrases contain ingenious wordplay or even puns; some are multiple prophecies.

Adrian IV, for example, Malachy designated as "De Rure Albo," which means either "of the Alban country" (England), or "from a white country." Adrian, "the English pope," was indeed born in the "Alban country," near the Abbey of St. Albans, no less. He then served as papal legate to Denmark, Sweden, and Norway, returning from those "white countries" to ascend the throne of St. Peter in 1154.

Pius III, who reigned for only 26 days in 1503, was aptly described as "De Parvo Homine," or "from a little man." Pius's family name was Piccolomini, Italian for "little man."

Some Catholic scholars insist that St. Malachy never saw the prophecies which bear his name, and the official Church attitude holds that they are a forgery dating from the 16th century. If hindsight *was* responsible for the early predictions, then the accuracy of the predictions should have *decreased* sharply after 1600. But consider what Malachy foresaw for some later pontiffs—all of whom reigned during the 20th century.

Benedict XV was given the chilling appellation "Religio Depopulata" ("religion laid waste"). Unfortunately, it was accurate.

Benedict served from 1914 to 1922, when World War I "laid waste" the religious populations of several continents.

John XXIII occupied the Vatican from 1958 to 1963. Malachy called him "Pastor et Nauta," or "pastor and sailor." Certainly a great pastor to his own people, John "modernized" his Church and wrote one of the most brilliant papal documents in history, *Pacem in Terris*. He was also a true pastor of the world, loved and admired by millions of non-Catholics. From 1953 until he became pope in 1958, John was the patriarch of Venice, a city full of sailors. When he convoked the Ecumenical Council in 1962, John chose two symbols for the council badge—a cross and a ship.

His successor, Paul VI, was represented by "Flos Florum" in Malachy's vision: "flower of flowers." Paul's coat of arms depicted three fleurs-de-lis.

John Paul I, who succeeded Paul in 1978 and held office for only 34 days, was referred to as "De Medietate Lunae," or "from the half moon." John Paul's papal mission was undoubtedly less than "half" completed when he died. His given name was Albino Luciani, or "white light"—such as that given off by the half-moon in Malachy's prophecy.

One of Malachy's strangest predictions concerned the pope who would follow "De Medietate Lunae." He is designated as "De Labore Solis," or "from the toil of the sun." Applied to John Paul II, this phrase reveals nothing less than a *double prophecy*. The current pope, the first non-Italian elected in 456 years, is a native of Krakow, Poland. Krakow is the city where, in the 15th and 16th centuries, Copernicus "toiled" for years to prove his heretical theory that the earth revolved around the sun. Many of Malachy's interpreters also suggested that the "sun" reference indicated a young pope. Fifty-eight years old at the time of his election, John Paul II is the youngest pope in over a century.

John Paul II's successor is called "Gloria Olivae," or "glory of the olive." Traditionally, the olive branch has been associated with peace, but in both the Old and New Testaments it also serves as an emblem for the Jews. Putting the two together, some commentators believe that the reign of this pope will be a peaceful one during which the prophesied conversion of the Jews will take place. However, Malachy's description may instead refer to St. Benedict's 6th-century prophecy that a member of his order will lead the Church in its fight against evil just before the Apocalypse. The Benedictine Order is known by another name: Olivetans.

After Gloria Olivae comes Petrus Romanus, the final pope of Rome, during whose reign "the seven-hilled city will be destroyed." The Church particularly—and understandably—repudiates St. Malachy's last, black prophecy. But it is striking that at least one pope had a similar mystical vision.

In 1909, while granting an audience, Pope Pius X leaned back and closed his eyes. Suddenly he "awoke" and cried out: "What I see is terrifying. Will it be myself? Will it be my successor? What is certain is that the pope will quit Rome, and in leaving the Vatican, he will have to wade over the dead bodies of his priests."

Pius's prophecy was fulfilled neither in his own time nor in that of the next pontiff. According to Malachy's vision of the Church's "tribulation," it applies to the successor of Gloria Olivae—the next pope but one.

—M.S.S.

CAZOTTE'S PREMONITION
OF DEATH

On a pleasant summer evening in 1788 in Paris, France, the Duchesse de Gramont—a wealthy patroness of the arts—held a dinner party in her salon. Present were writers, scientists, philosophers, lawyers, and courtiers. The dinner was magnificent and the guests were in a gay, jovial mood. However, this lighthearted ambience was temporary since the guests, by the end of the evening, had heard a prophecy which foretold violent death for almost all of them.

After dinner, the servants brought dessert and opened numerous bottles of Malvoisie wine. The sophisticated conversationalists turned their attention to politics and to the works of the predominant political thinker of that century, Voltaire. The guests agreed that Voltaire's Age of Reason was at hand and that the revolution, which would sweep away the old unenlightened forms of government, including France's decadent autocracy, was imminent. They saw this revolution as an intellectual movement in which men of learning would revamp French institutions and usher in the time when reason would rule government. The only problem seemed to be that they might not live long enough to witness this new age.

Sitting alone on a bench near a fountain—away from the other guests but within hearing range—was the poet Jacques Cazotte, a man of 70, who was best known for his book *The Devil in Love*. A devout Catholic, Cazotte was also a clairvoyant who often fell into trancelike sleeps. However, in an age of intellect and reason, when mysticism was dismissed as superstition, few paid attention to Cazotte's occasional prophetic statements. This night Cazotte had entered into another trance, and when he came out of it, he heard Chrétien Guillaume de Malesherbes—a lawyer and minister during the reign of Louis XVI, present the toast: "Here's to the day when reason will be triumphant in the affairs of men—a day which I shall never see."

This impelled Cazotte to return to the other guests. "Sir, you are wrong," he announced. "You will see that day." The guests laughingly commented that Cazotte must have had another of his visions and asked him for more details on their individual fates.

Cazotte looked grimly about the room, searching the faces of the various guests, then turned and addressed the Marquis de Condorcet, a mathematician and philosopher: "You will die on the stone floor of a prison cell, having taken poison to cheat the executioner—poison which the bliss of those times will oblige you to carry always on your person."

Next, he confronted the renowned playwright Sébastien Chamfort. "You will cut your veins with a razor 22 times, but you will not die until some months later."

At this point, Dr. Félix Vicq-d'Azyr slyly began to chant the "De profundis," whereupon Cazotte solemnly told the doctor that, lacking the strength to do it himself, he would ask a prisonmate to slash his veins for him. As for the famous astronomer Jean Sylvain Bailly, Cazotte said that he would die on the guillotine, where he would be joined by Chrétien de Malesherbes and two of the other guests in the room, Jean Roucher and M. de Nicolai.

Jacques Cazotte.

Jean de Laharpe, an atheist playwright who was Cazotte's personal enemy, asked Cazotte whether he would be allowed to join his friends on the scaffold so they could hiss at the mob together. Cazotte replied that Laharpe would not die in the revolution; instead, he would become a devout Christian. Someone jested that, if they were not to die before Laharpe became a Christian, the guests would be immortal. Cazotte replied that his predictions would come to pass within six years and added that he himself would also be killed.

With their spirits dampened by Cazotte's silly yet gloomy predictions, the guests retired from the party. Laharpe went home and recorded the predictions verbatim in his diary so that in six years he could discredit and disgrace the lunatic Cazotte. However, the next year—in 1789—the revolution swept France.

The Marquis de Condorcet at first took an active role in the revolution, but later he opposed the radical Reign of Terror and was arrested and imprisoned. In 1794 he took poison to escape the guillotine's blade. In 1793, threatened with arrest, Chamfort slashed his wrists 22 times but lived on for another two months before improper medical treatment of his wounds caused his death. Dr. Vicq-d'Azyr did not die as Cazotte had foreseen. Under great pressure from the Revolution and from seeing his many friends die in the manner Cazotte had predicted, the doctor came down with a violent fever and died in a delirium. Bailly, who at one time was a prominent revolutionist and mayor of Paris, together with Malesherbes, Roucher, and Nicolai, died during the proletarian Reign of Terror on the guillotine, just as Cazotte had foretold. While imprisoned in a dungeon, Laharpe had a spiritual experience and was converted to Christianity. Upon his release, he entered a Catholic monastery, where he remained until his death in 1803. His diary, with its record of Cazotte's predictions, was published in 1806.

Almost exactly four years after the Duchesse de Gramont's dinner party, Cazotte was arrested as a counterrevolutionary. His last prediction was fulfilled when he was guillotined on September 25, 1792.

—R.J.F.

MORGAN ROBERTSON'S VISION OF THE *TITANIC* DISASTER

He did not know he was making one of the greatest predictions of all time. He was a writer, and he was simply writing one more story.

His name was Morgan Robertson. He was born in 1861, and his father was a ship's captain on the Great Lakes. After a brief education limited to the lower grades, Robertson went to sea serving as a cabin boy. At 16 he signed on in the merchant marine as an ordinary seaman. After 19 years he had risen to the rank of first mate. In 1886 Robertson quit seafaring, traveled to New York, and studied at Cooper Union to be a jeweler. Eventually, he opened a jewelry store, specializing in the setting of diamonds. In 1894, when he was 33 years old, Robertson married Alice M. Doyle. Two years later, when his trade began to affect his eyesight, he sold his business. Shortly thereafter, in financial straits and with a frail wife to support, he desperately sought a new means of making a livelihood.

One day he read a sea story by Rudyard Kipling. This inspired him to make use of his own experiences at sea. Robertson determined to become a writer. He sat down and wrote his first short story overnight, and sold it to a magazine for $25. The next year he wrote 20 short stories that brought him a total income of $1,000. In that period his wife became a full invalid, and Robertson was forced to write steadily to keep them both alive. Writing did not come easy for him.

Handicapped by a lack of both education and a facility with words, Robertson found it painfully difficult to produce each story. But produce them he did.

One evening in 1897, in the New York study of his 24th Street apartment—a room with a porthole and nautical decorations—Morgan had the idea for a new sea story. It would be longer than a short story, yet not as long as a novel. It would be a novelette. It would be about the maiden voyage of a modern unsinkable luxurious British sea liner—he would christen his ship the *Titan*—and about John Rowland, a drunken derelict of a crewman on that ship, and Myra Selfridge, a woman Rowland had once loved but who had rejected him. Myra, now married, and her young daughter were passengers aboard the ship. Robertson visualized a disaster at sea, which Rowland's onetime love survived, while Rowland saved her daughter.

Morgan Robertson began to write his story, with the help of an invisible "astral writing partner." He entitled his novel *The Wreck of the Titan, or Futility.* What appeared to interest him most as he wrote, and what he could picture clearly in his mind, was the disaster at sea that befell the *Titan,* his make-believe luxury liner. When he came to the scene of the disaster, Robertson wrote it vividly:

> "Ice," yelled the lookout; "ice ahead. Iceberg. Right under the bows." The first officer ran amidships, and the captain, who had remained there, sprang to the engine-room telegraph. . . . But in five seconds the bow of the *Titan* began to lift, and ahead, and on either hand, could be seen, through the fog, a field of ice, which arose in an incline to a hundred feet high in her track. The music in the theater ceased, and among the babel of shouts and cries, and the deafening noise of steel, scraping and crashing over ice, Rowland heard the agonized voice of a woman. . . .
>
> Seventy-five thousand tons—dead-weight—rushing through the fog at the rate of fifty feet a second, had hurled itself at an iceberg . . . a low beach, possibly formed by the recent overturning of the berg, received the *Titan,* and with her keel cutting the ice like the steel runner of an iceboat, and her great weight resting on the starboard bilge, she rose out of the sea, higher and higher—until the propellers in the stern were half exposed—then, meeting an easy, spiral rise in the ice under her port bow, she heeled, overbalanced, and crashed down on her side, to starboard.
>
> The holding-down bolts of twelve boilers and three triple-expansion engines, unintended to hold such weights from a perpendicular flooring, snapped, and down through a maze of ladders, gratings, and fore-and-aft bulkheads came these giant masses of steel and iron, puncturing the sides of the ship, even where backed by solid, resisting ice; and filling the engine-and-boiler-rooms with scalding steam, which brought a quick, though tortured death, to each of the hundred men on duty in the engineer's department.
>
> Amid the roar of escaping steam, and the beelike buzzing of nearly three thousand human voices, raised in agonized screams and callings from within the inclosing walls, and the whistling of air through hundreds of open dead-lights as the water, entering the holes of the crushed and riven starboard side, expelled it, the *Titan* moved slowly backward and

launched herself into the sea, where she floated low on her side—a dying monster, groaning with her death-wound.

. . . Then the fog shut her out, though her position was still indicated by the roaring of steam from her iron lungs. This ceased in time, leaving behind it the horrid humming sound and whistling of air; and when this too was suddenly hushed, and the ensuing silence broken by dull, booming reports—as from bursting compartments—Rowland knew that the holocaust was complete; that the invincible *Titan*, with nearly all of her people, unable to climb vertical floors and ceilings, was beneath the surface of the sea.

Morgan Robertson finished his story in 1897. It was published as a short novel in 1898. The book was to be the highlight of Robertson's career and make him immortal, not as an author but as a prognosticator.

After that, Robertson's career was all anticlimax. He wrote slowly, steadily, never making more than $5,000 in a single year. For a while, the financial pressure and worry about his ailing wife temporarily unhinged his mind. He committed himself to the psychopathic ward of Bellevue Hospital. There a psychologist encouraged him to give up writing and take up invention. Released, Robertson invented a practical periscope for submarines. It might have made his fortune, except he could not get it patented because a science fiction story in a French magazine had once described the same invention.

The *Titanic* disaster was predicted
14 years in advance by novelist Morgan Robertson,
in *The Wreck Of The Titan.*

Disheartened, Robertson went back to writing. In all, he published 200 short stories and nine books. "But my punch was gone," he admitted. His stories sold less and less. He was all but impoverished when friends rallied around to assemble and publish a special edition of his works. This helped briefly. In March of 1915, in an Atlantic City hotel room, Robertson suffered a heart attack. He was found leaning against a bureau. In death, he was still on his feet.

His legacy was the fictional *Titan*.

Fourteen years after he had created his luxury liner, made it hit an iceberg and sink to the bottom of the Atlantic, a real-life luxury liner, the British-made *Titanic*, the largest and—allegedly—safest ship afloat, put out to sea on its maiden voyage. Sailing at full speed south of Newfoundland, in the late night hours of April 14, 1912, the great *Titanic* smashed into an iceberg. Its bow ripped open, cold water poured through the gash, the mighty *Titanic* was upended, and the wounded monster sank to the bottom of the Atlantic Ocean. At least 1,513 persons were drowned. It was history's most dramatic disaster at sea.

A few readers who recalled Morgan Robertson's story of the *Titan* in 1898 now sought it out and compared it to the news stories of the *Titanic* in 1912. Here is what they found:

	Titan	*Titanic*
Displacement tonnage	75,000 tons	66,000 tons
Length of ship	800 ft.	882.5 ft.
Watertight compartments	19	16
Number of propellers	3	3
Number of lifeboats	24	22
Persons aboard	3,000	2,224
Speed on hitting iceberg	25 knots	23 knots

The biggest sea liner. The safest. Maiden voyage. April in the Atlantic. The iceberg. The terrible collision. The sinking. The enormous loss of life.

Morgan Robertson had called it all 14 years earlier. He had written history before it happened. No writer had ever made a more incredible prediction.

—I.W.

THE PROPHECIES OF OUR LADY OF FÁTIMA

January 25, 1938: A weird glow illuminated the evening sky over western Europe. In some places the light was so intense that nightshift workers had no need of electric lights, and one newspaper compared the visual phenomenon to "the fires of hell." At the Reich Chancellery in Berlin, Adolf Hitler reviewed a file folder marked

"Case Otto"—top-secret plans for the invasion of Austria. Case Otto was to be brutally executed in March, one long step on an insane journey which would not end until 1945, by which time Europe would be devastated.

It was exactly as "Our Lady of Fátima" had predicted in 1917: "When you see the night lit up by a great, unknown light, know that it is a sign that God gives you that punishment of the world by another war, famine, and persecution of the Holy Church and of the Holy Father."

Our Lady had also prophesied events which were to take place after World War II. This third prophecy of Fátima was entrusted to the Vatican with instructions that it be opened in 1960. It was, but to this day the third prophecy is a mystery. According to Omar Garrison's *Encyclopedia of Prophecy:* "A source inside the Vatican reported that one day the Pope [John XXIII] confided to a few friends how he had read the third secret of Fátima and that upon reading it, 'he had trembled with fear and had almost fainted with horror.'"

The "Lady of the Rosary," as she first identified herself, appeared near the little Portuguese town of Fátima on May 13, 1917. She could be seen and heard only by three shepherd children: Lucia de Jesus dos Santos (aged 10) and her cousins Francisco and Jacinta Marto (aged 8 and 7, respectively). Other observers reported seeing a "bright cloud" overhead during the Lady's visits. The children described her as a young, beautiful being in the sky.

These visitations occurred at a time when Portugal was convulsed by anti-Catholicism. Some of the irreligious civil leaders, who had claimed they would wipe out Catholicism in the country "within two generations," became alarmed when news of the vision spread and crowds started following the children. On June 13, about 50 people joined the children to witness the Lady's second appearance at the Cova da Iria (Hollow of St. Irene).

On July 13, there were more than 5,000 people. On that date, the cosmic visitor told Lucia dos Santos: "Continue to come here on the thirteenth of each month. In October I will say who I am and what I desire, and I will perform a miracle all shall see so that they believe."

Lucia, Francisco, and Jacinta did not keep their appointment with the Lady on August 13. They had been kidnapped and jailed by the civil authorities. Despite hours of interrogation and threats that they would be boiled alive (among other punishments) the children refused to renounce their visions as a "Catholic hoax," and they were subsequently released. That month, our Lady appeared to them on the 19th and repeated her promise about October 13, which was to be her last visit.

Fátima was hit with a hard rainstorm on October 13, 1917, but 50,000 to 80,000 people jammed the roads to the village. The faithful were drawn by the prophecy of a miracle, not at some indeterminate time in the future, but on a specific date. A good many professional nonbelievers made the pilgrimage as well; reporters from every major newspaper in Portugal attended.

They were not disappointed. The reporters called it a "mysterious solar occurrence," but others had a more colorful term: "The Dancing Sun." By all accounts, the sun whirled on its axis like a pinwheel, throwing out white, blue, and green lights; after this colorful display, it turned blood-red and seemed to move closer to the earth, before "bouncing" back to its normal place in the sky. This happened three times.

Our Lady of the Rosary made a revelation to the three children as she had promised she would do. She identified herself as the Virgin Mary and said she desired that humanity change its ways, lest her three awful prophecies come true. And she related the predictions.

The first was a gruesome and graphic depiction of a very real Hell, a place of eternal damnation for the unrepentant.

The second threatened a Second World War unless humankind mended its ways. One portent would be the "great unknown light" in the night skies, signaling an outbreak of war "within the next pontificate." (The next pontiff, Pius XI, died in 1939, the year Hitler invaded Poland and "officially" started World War II.)

The third prophecy has been the object of much educated guesswork. In 1963 a German newspaper published an alleged "complete text," which the Vatican wisely neither confirmed nor denied. It is a grim document which states that "A great war will break out in the second half of the 20th century. . . ." Two things are common to virtually all interpretations of the third prophecy. There will be a holocaust in which several entire nations will be wiped out, and a persecution of the Catholic Church which will include the assassination of a reigning pope.

—M.S.S.

JEANE DIXON AND
THE DAY IN DALLAS

In 1952 an astrologer and crystal gazer named Jeane Dixon stood in front of a statue of the Virgin Mary at St. Matthew's Cathedral in Washington, D.C. It was part of a familiar ritual for her, but on this day she was to have a vision that would eventually mark her as the most famous of the modern prophets.

A dazzling vision of the White House—with the numbers 1-9-6-0 above it—appeared before her. She saw a young man with blue eyes and a shock of brown hair poised before the main door. An inner voice told her softly that the young man, a Democrat, would be elected president in 1960 and suffer a violent death while in office.

It was not the last vision Dixon had about the murder of John Kennedy before November 22, 1963. In the intervening years—in fact, up till the very day of the Dallas assassination—the "Washington Seeress" blurted out her fears to such a variety of solid notables that her prediction became virtually the only thoroughly documented one among many that later surfaced.

In 1956 she repeated the prophecy to investigative reporter Jack Anderson, who published it in *Parade* magazine. In October, 1963, she related to parapsychological researcher Dr. F. Regis Riesenman and newspaper columnist and psychic Ruth Montgomery another, more recent vision: Dixon had seen black hands, representing death to her, removing Vice-President Lyndon Johnson's nameplate from his office door. She felt that this was not due to any intention on Johnson's part.

Jeane Dixon also saw a man and a hazy image of his name; it had two syllables and five or six letters, she said. The first letter looked like an *o* or a *q*. The second was definitely an *s*. The last letter appeared to "have a little curve that went straight up." The name Oswald fits this description.

Many others among Dixon's prominent Washington acquaintances recall hearing these and other prophecies about Kennedy's killing as Dixon became increasingly anxious at the approach of November, 1963. She tried to warn JFK through mutual contacts, but apparently without success. It would scarcely have mattered, though; the brash Kennedys had little use for psychics and a devil-may-care attitude about personal security. JFK was quoted as saying, "If they want to get you, they're going to get you."

On November 22, 1963, Dixon was attending a small luncheon at Washington's Mayflower Hotel with Mrs. Harley Cope, widow of the rear admiral, and Mrs. Rebecca Kaufmann. Mrs. Kaufmann chided

The shirt worn by President Kennedy
on the day of his assassination.

393

Dixon for only picking at her eggs Florentine. The two witnesses say Dixon replied, "I just can't. I'm too upset. Something dreadful is going to happen to the President today."

While the matronly trio were dining in Washington, President Kennedy's car was wheeling into Dealey Plaza in Dallas. A bullet suddenly pierced the back of his neck; a second slammed into his brain. The President was pronounced dead at 1:00 P.M. at Parkland Hospital.

The dining room's orchestra conductor interrupted to tell the trio that "Someone just tried to take a shot at the President." Excited chatter speculated that the President may not have even been hit by the gunman. The morose Dixon said, "No, the President's dead ... you will learn that he is dead."

The Kennedy assassination prophecy is not the only accurate prediction that Dixon has made, according to her many chroniclers. She is said to have also predicted the murders of Mohandas Gandhi, Martin Luther King, Jr., and Robert Kennedy; the death dates of U.N. Secretary-General Dag Hammarskjöld and Secretary of State John Foster Dulles; Marilyn Monroe's suicide; and the U.S. race rioting of the early 1960s.

Were Dixon a pro baseball player, though, her batting average might not earn her a fat contract. Among her failed predictions: a world war started by Red China in 1958; Russia to be the first to put a man on the moon; and a stunning wave of suicides in the U.S. She also stated repeatedly that President Nixon had "excellent vibes" and would be remembered as one of the great modern presidents. Dixon explains: "When a psychic vision is not fulfilled as expected, it is not because what has been shown is not correct; it is because I have not interpreted the symbols correctly."

Born to German immigrant parents in 1918, Dixon was taken by them as a small child to California, where she says a gypsy fortune-teller told her of her psychic gifts. Perhaps because she is a devout Roman Catholic who considers her prophetic abilities to be a gift from God, some of Dixon's predictions for the long range echo orthodox religious prophecies of centuries' standing. She foresees: an attack on the U.S. by the barbaric forces of the third world during which America will pay with blood and fire for its moral degeneracy; enormous fatalities from germ warfare; a successful ideological attack upon the Catholic Church and the assassination of a pope; and, very finally, catastrophic world war in 1999.

—R.E.

14

THE WORST PREDICTIONS
OF ALL TIME

THE 41 WORST PREDICTIONS
OF ALL TIME

1. CHRISTOPHER COLUMBUS'S VOYAGE TO THE NEW WORLD

Christopher Columbus's plans to sail west to find a shorter route to India were considered impossible because: (1) A voyage to Asia would require three years. (2) The Western Ocean is infinite and perhaps unnavigable. (3) If he reached the Antipodes (the land on the other side of the globe from Europe), he could not get back. (4) There are no Antipodes because the greater part of the globe is covered with water and because St. Augustine says so. (5) Of the five zones, only three are habitable. (6) So many centuries after the Creation it was unlikely that anyone could find hitherto unknown lands of any value.

> —The consensus of a royal committee appointed by King Ferdinand and Queen Isabella of Spain, 1490. (Cited by Samuel E. Morison in *Admiral of the Ocean Sea*.)

2. GALILEO'S DISCOVERY OF JUPITER'S MOONS

"Jupiter's moons are invisible to the naked eye and therefore can have no influence on the earth, and therefore would be useless, and therefore do not exist."

> —Pronouncement made by a group of Aristotelian professors who were contemporaries of Galileo's, c. 1610.

3. USING GAS LIGHTING IN BRITISH CITIES

"[They] might as well try to light London with a slice from the moon."

> —William H. Wollaston, British chemist and physicist, early 1800s.

4-6. LOCOMOTIVES

"What can be more palpably absurd than the prospect held out of locomotives traveling twice as fast as stagecoaches?"

> —*The Quarterly Review*, 1825.

"It is far from my wish to promulgate to the world that the ridiculous expectations, or rather professions, of the enthusiastic speculist will be realized, and that we shall see [locomotives] traveling at the rate of 12, 16, 18, or 20 miles an hour: Nothing could do more harm towards their adoption, or general improvement, than the promulgation of such nonsense."

> —Nicholas Wood, British civil engineer, 1825.

". . . any general system of conveying passengers—at a velocity exceeding 10 miles per hour, or thereabouts—is extremely improbable."

> —Thomas Tredgold, British railroad designer, 1835.

By 1846 locomotives traveled at an average speed of 30 mph; by the 1890s, over 60 mph; and today they travel at an average speed of 80 mph.

7. THE INTRODUCTION OF ANESTHESIA

"The abolishment of pain in surgery is a chimera. It is absurd to go on seeking it today. *Knife* and *pain* are two words in surgery that must forever be associated in the consciousness of the patient. To this compulsory combination we shall have to adjust ourselves."
—Dr. Alfred Velpeau, French surgeon, 1839.

Anesthesia was introduced only seven years later, and Dr. Velpeau used it in the years following.

8. THE SUEZ CANAL

"All mankind has heard much of M. Lesseps and his Suez Canal. . . . I have a very strong opinion that such canal will not and cannot be made; that all the strength of the arguments adduced in the matter are hostile to it; and that steam navigation by land will and ought to be the means of transit through Egypt."
—Anthony Trollope, British novelist, 1860.

The canal was opened only nine years later and proved to be one of the most heavily used shipping lanes in the world until its closing during the 1967 Arab-Israeli War.

9. THE GRAND CANYON

". . . The region last explored is, of course, altogether valueless. It can be approached only from the south, and after entering it there is nothing to do but leave. Ours has been the first, and will doubtless be the last, party of whites to visit this profitless locality."
—Lt. Joseph C. Ives, U.S. Corps of Topographical Engineers, 1861.

10-11. THE PURCHASE OF ALASKA

"The possession of this Russian territory can give us neither honor, wealth, or power, but will always be a source of weakness and expense, without any adequate return."
—Orange Ferriss, U.S. congressman, 1868.

"In support of the proposition of the utter worthlessness of this territory there are several general tests of a most important and convincing character. Conclusive proof of it is that Russia would sell her territory. If it was not valuable to her, it will never prove of any value to us. Russia is not a Power to surrender a foothold upon earth unless it should be an actual and annoying burden to her."
—John A. Peters, U.S. congressman, 1868.

12. SURGERY

"There cannot always be fresh fields of conquest by the knife; there must be portions of the human frame that will ever remain sacred from its intrusions, at least in the surgeon's hands. . . . The abdomen, the chest, and the brain will be forever shut from the intrusion of the wise and humane surgeon."
—Sir John Erichsen, British surgeon, 1873.

In 1881 Dr. Albert Christian Theodor Billroth performed the first successful operation for stomach cancer. Though chest surgery made its greatest progress during the 1930s, successful simple surgeries for emphysema and tuberculosis were performed as early as 1879. Sir William Macewen successfully operated on a brain tumor the same year.

13. THE INCANDESCENT LAMP

Edison's ideas for developing an incandescent lamp were described as "good enough for our transatlantic friends ... but unworthy of the attention of practical or scientific men."
    —A committee of the British Parliament, 1878.
Thomas Edison demonstrated his incandescent light on December 20, 1879. Only three years later the Pearl Street central power station in New York City was completed and the city lit up.

14. ALTERNATING ELECTRICAL CURRENT

"There is no plea which will justify the use of high-tension and alternating currents, either in a scientific or a commercial sense. They are employed solely to reduce investment in copper wire and real estate."
    —Thomas A. Edison, U.S. inventor, 1889.
Alternating-current-powered electric streetcars appeared in the U.S. by the early 1890s, and by 1895 power generated from Niagara Falls serviced its first customer, the Pittsburgh Reduction Company (later known as the Aluminum Company of America).

15. THE AUTOMOBILE

"The ordinary 'horseless carriage' is at present a luxury for the wealthy; and although its price will probably fall in the future, it will never, of course, come into as common use as the bicycle."
    —The Literary Digest, October 14, 1889.

16. THE PANAMA CANAL

"The Panama Canal is actually a thing of the past, and Nature in her works will soon obliterate all traces of French energy and money expended on the Isthmus."
    —Scientific American, 1891.
The Panama Canal was opened on August 15, 1914, and became one of the two most important man-made waterways in the world (the Suez is the other).

17. THE SUBMARINE

"I must confess that my imagination, in spite even of spurring, refuses to see any sort of submarine doing anything but suffocating its crew and floundering at sea."
    —H. G. Wells, British novelist, in Anticipations, 1901.
The development of the submarine proceeded rapidly in the early 20th century, and by World War I submarines were a major factor in naval warfare. They played an even more important role in World War II. By the 1960s and 1970s submarines were considered among the most important of all strategic weapons.

18–21. AIRCRAFT

"May not our mechanisms ... be ultimately forced to admit that aerial flight is one of that great class of problems with which man can never cope, and give up all attempts to grapple with it? ... The construction of an aerial vehicle which could carry even a single man from place to place at pleasure requires the discovery of some new metal or some new force. Even with such a discovery we could not expect one to do more than carry its owner."

—Simon Newcomb, U.S. astronomer, 1903.

"We hope that Professor [Samuel] Langley will not put his substantial greatness as a scientist in further peril by continuing to waste his time, and the money involved, in further airship experiments. Life is short, and he is capable of services to humanity incomparably greater than can be expected to result from trying to fly. . . . For students and investigators of the Langley type there are more useful employments."

—*The New York Times,* December 10, 1903.

Exactly one week later, the Wright brothers made the first successful flight at Kitty Hawk, N.C.

"I confess that in 1901, I said to my brother Orville that man would not fly for 50 years. . . . Ever since, I have distrusted myself and avoided all predictions. . . ."

—Wilbur Wright, U.S. aviation pioneer, 1908.

"The popular mind often pictures gigantic flying machines speeding across the Atlantic and carrying innumerable passengers in a way analogous to our modern steamships. . . . It seems safe to say that such ideas must be wholly visionary, and even if a machine could get across with one or two passengers the expense would be prohibitive to any but the capitalist who could own his own yacht.

"Another popular fallacy is to expect enormous speed to be obtained. It must be remembered that the resistance of the air increases as the square of the speed and the work as the cube. . . . If with 30 horse power we can now attain a speed of 40 mph, then in order to reach a speed of 100 mph we must use a motor capable of 470 horse power . . . it is clear that with our present devices there is no hope of competing for racing speed with either our locomotives or our automobiles."

—William H. Pickering, U.S. astronomer, c. 1910, *after* the invention of the airplane.

The first transatlantic commercial scheduled passenger air service was June 17–19, 1939, New York to England. The fare one way was $375, round trip $675—no more than a first-class fare on an ocean liner at the time. On October 14, 1922, at Mount Clemens, Mich., a plane was flown 216.1 miles per hour.

22. HIGHWAYS

"The actual building of roads devoted to motor cars is not for the near future, in spite of many rumors to that effect."

—*Harper's Weekly,* August 2, 1902.

Conceived in 1906, the Bronx River Parkway, N.Y., when completed in 1923, was the first auto express highway system in the U.S.

23. RADIO

"[Lee] De Forest has said in many newspapers and over his signature that it would be possible to transmit the human voice across the Atlantic before many years. Based on these absurd and deliberately misleading statements, the misguided public . . . has been persuaded to purchase stock in his company. . . ."

—A U.S. district attorney prosecuting inventor Lee De Forest for selling stock fraudulently through the U.S. mails for his Radio Telephone Company, 1913.

The first transatlantic broadcast of a human voice occurred on December 31, 1923, from Pittsburgh, Pa., to Manchester, England.

24. BOLSHEVISM

"What are the Bolsheviki? They are representatives of the most democratic government in Europe.... Let us recognize the truest democracy in Europe, the truest democracy in the world today."
—William Randolph Hearst, U.S. newspaper publisher, 1918.

25-27. ROCKET RESEARCH

"That Professor Goddard and his 'chair' in Clark College and the countenancing of the Smithsonian Institution does not know the relation of action to reaction, and of the need to have something better than a vacuum against which to react—to say that would be absurd. Of course he only seems to lack the knowledge ladled out daily in high schools...."
—*The New York Times,* January 13, 1920.
The New York Times printed a formal retraction of this comment some 49 years later, on July 17, 1969, just prior to the Apollo landing on the moon.

"No rocket will reach the moon save by a miraculous discovery of an explosive far more energetic than any known. And even if the requisite fuel were produced, it would still have to be shown that the rocket machine would operate at 459° below zero—the temperature of interplanetary space."
—Nikola Tesla, U.S. inventor, November, 1928.

"The proposals as outlined in your letter ... have been carefully reviewed.... While the Air Corps is deeply interested in the research work being carried out by your organization ... it does not, at this time, feel justified in obligating further funds for basic jet propulsion research and experimentation."
—Brig. Gen. George H. Brett, U.S. Army Corps, in a letter to rocket researcher Robert Goddard, 1941.

28-29. AIR STRIKES ON NAVAL VESSELS

"The day of the battleship has not passed, and it is highly unlikely that an airplane, or fleet of them, could ever successfully sink a fleet of navy vessels under battle conditions."
—Franklin D. Roosevelt, U.S. assistant secretary of the navy, 1922.

"As far as sinking a ship with a bomb is concerned, you just can't do it."
—Rear Adm. Clark Woodward, U.S. Navy, 1939.

30. JAPAN AND THE U.S.

"Nobody now fears that a Japanese fleet could deal an unexpected blow on our Pacific possessions.... Radio makes surprise impossible."
—Josephus Daniels, former U.S. secretary of the navy, October 16, 1922.
See headlines December 7, 1941.

31. COMMERCIAL TELEVISION

"While theoretically and technically television may be feasible,

commercially and financially I consider it an impossibility, a development of which we need waste little time dreaming."
> —Lee De Forest, U.S. inventor and "Father of the Radio," 1926.

32. REPEAL OF PROHIBITION

"I will never see the day when the Eighteenth Amendment is out of the Constitution of the U.S."
> —William Borah, U.S. senator, 1929.

The Eighteenth Amendment was repealed in 1933. Borah was alive to see the day. He did not die until 1940.

33. HITLER

"In this column for years, I have constantly laboured these points: Hitler's horoscope is not a war-horoscope.... If and when war comes, not he but others will strike the first blow."
> —R. H. Naylor, British astrologer for the London *Sunday Express*, 1939.

34. THE ATOMIC BOMB

"That is the biggest fool thing we have ever done.... The bomb will never go off, and I speak as an expert in explosives."
> —Adm. William Leahy, U.S. Navy officer speaking to President Truman, 1945.

35. INTERCONTINENTAL MISSILES

"There has been a great deal said about a 3,000 mile high-angle rocket. In my opinion such a thing is impossible for many years. The people who have been writing these things that annoy me, have been talking about a 3,000 mile high-angle rocket shot from one continent to another, carrying an atomic bomb and so directed as to be a precise weapon which would land exactly on a certain target, such as a city.

"I say, technically, I don't think anyone in the world knows how to do such a thing, and I feel confident that it will not be done for a very long period of time to come.... I think we can leave that out of our thinking. I wish the American public would leave that out of their thinking."
> —Dr. Vannevar Bush, U.S. engineer, in a report to a Senate committee, 1945.

36. LANDING ON THE MOON

"Landing and moving around the moon offers so many serious problems for human beings that it may take science another 200 years to lick them."
> —*Science Digest*, August, 1948.

It took 21 years.

37. ATOMIC FUEL

"... it can be taken for granted that before 1980 ships, aircraft, locomotives, and even automobiles will be atomically fueled."
> —David Sarnoff, U.S. radio executive and former head of RCA, 1955.

Skirts for men—
typical fashion of the 1970s.

38–40. THE VIETNAM WAR

"The war in Vietnam is going well and will succeed."
—Robert McNamara, U.S. secretary of defense, January 31,
1963.

"... we are not about to send American boys 9,000 or 10,000 miles away from home to do what Asian boys ought to be doing for themselves."
—Lyndon B. Johnson, U.S. president, October 21, 1964.

"Whatever happens in Vietnam, I can conceive of nothing except military victory."
—Lyndon B. Johnson, in a speech at West Point, 1967.

41. FASHION IN THE 1970s

"So women will wear pants and men will wear skirts interchangeably. And since there won't be any squeamishness about nudity, see-through clothes will only be see-through for reasons of comfort. Weather permitting, both sexes will go about bare-chested, though women will wear simple protective pasties."
—Rudi Gernreich, U.S. fashion designer, 1970.

—K.H.J.

FROM BAD TO WORSE: ON THE ACCURACY OF SOME PSYCHIC PREDICTORS

Twice a year the *National Enquirer* publishes a roundup of predictions by leading psychics. In an effort to determine the accuracy of these "sensitives," we checked up on the past predictions of the 10 most frequently quoted psychics. The years covered are 1976 through 1979.

	Right Predictions	Wrong Predictions	Batting Average
Olof Jonsson	1	25	.038
Clarisa Bernhardt	1	32	.030
Florence Vaty	1	33	.029
Page Bryant	1	35	.028
Fredrick Davies	0	34	.000
Kebrina Kinkade	0	34	.000
Jack Gillen	0	36	.000
Bill O'Hara	0	37	.000
Shawn Robbins	0	46	.000
Micki Dahne	0	48	.000
	4	360	.011

In other words, the *National Enquirer* psychics were 98.9% wrong. Here are some highlights from each of the predictors.

• OLOF JONSSON •

Best Prediction: In July, 1976, picked Carter over Ford.
Worst Prediction: Muhammad Ali will be elected to the U.S. Congress in 1979. (Note: 1979 was not an election year.)

• CLARISA BERNHARDT •

Best Prediction: Kate Jackson will marry in 1978.
Worst Predictions: In late 1979, a deal with Mexico and an oil strike in Arizona will solve U.S. gasoline problems for good; Ted Kennedy will run for president with John Connally as his running mate.

• FLORENCE VATY •

Best Prediction: In July, 1976, picked Carter over Ford.
Worst Predictions: In December, 1978, Jackie Gleason will temporarily disappear in the Devil's Triangle; in 1978 a revolution will topple Russia's government and Glenda Jackson will win an Oscar for her portrayal of Renée Richards; Elizabeth Taylor will win the 1980 Best Actress Oscar for a role in an X-rated movie.

• PAGE BRYANT •

Best Prediction: Cher will finally divorce Gregg Allman in 1979. (She filed for divorce in January, 1978.)
Hardest Prediction to Verify: In 1977 the ghost of Freddie Prinze will visit his widow, Kathy.

• FREDRICK DAVIES •

Best Prediction: None.
Worst Predictions: In 1976 Princess Caroline of Monaco will marry an African property developer, and in the spring of 1979 she will marry a Wyoming rancher; in 1977 Billy Carter will win acclaim for his sensitive portrayal of a priest in a movie; Miss World 1979 will be an Eskimo.

• KEBRINA KINKADE •

Best Prediction: None.
Worst Predictions: Ethel Kennedy will marry Andy Williams in the summer of 1977; Anwar Sadat will be assassinated in 1978.

• JACK GILLEN •

Best Prediction: None.
Worst Predictions: President Carter will be injured in a hang-gliding accident between April 8 and 10, 1979; in 1978 a government study will be released proving that women who watch soap operas live longer than those who don't.

• BILL O'HARA •

Best Prediction: None.
Worst Predictions: In 1979 Debby Boone will join a commune, Roy Rogers and Dale Evans will divorce, and men will start wearing miniskirts. Also in 1979, Spiro Agnew will win a cinema acting award.

• SHAWN ROBBINS •

Best Prediction: None.
Worst Predictions: In 1978 Frank Sinatra will give up show business and become manager of a minor-league baseball team in Arizona. Also in 1978, General Motors will introduce a "thoughtmobile" which is operated by the driver's thoughts.

• MICKI DAHNE •

Best Prediction: None.
Worst Predictions: Redd Foxx will become an evangelist in 1977; Barbara Walters will become a lobbyist for a Mideast oil country in 1977, and in late 1977 Fidel Castro will fall in love with Walters and travel to the U.S. to be close to her. In 1978 Elizabeth Taylor will help

settle the Israeli-Arab dispute. John Travolta will marry Priscilla Presley in 1979; in late 1979 Pope John Paul II will visit Disney World, aliens in UFOs will contact tourists in West Palm Beach, Fla., and Billy Graham will experience a vision which will lead to the arrest of the murderer of Marilyn Monroe.

—D.W.

15

PREDICTIONS LISTS

SECRET DOCUMENTS TO
BE RELEASED IN THE FUTURE

Year *Item*

1984 **EARL WARREN'S PERSONAL PAPERS**
(LIBRARY OF CONGRESS)

In 1953 President Dwight D. Eisenhower named Earl Warren
as chief justice of the Supreme Court. The choice seemed a
wise one. Warren, at the age of 62, was a Republican with a
long and distinguished career including three terms as governor of California. However, Eisenhower later said that the
Warren appointment was "the biggest damnfool mistake" he
ever made. During his 16 years in the Supreme Court (1953–
1969) Warren presided over the greatest legal revolution in
American history. The Warren court handed down the school
desegregation ruling of 1954 *(Brown v. Board of Education of
Topeka).* It ruled against prayers and Bible reading in the
public school. It dictated that a suspect must be informed of
his or her right to remain silent *(Miranda v. State of Arizona).*
In addition to his service on the court, Warren presided over
the presidential commission that investigated the assassination of John F. Kennedy. Warren's will bequeathed his personal papers to the Library of Congress—to be made public
10 years after his death. The chief justice died in 1974.

1988 **ELEANOR ROOSEVELT/LORENA HICKOK**
LETTERS REVIEWED—POSSIBLY RELEASED
(FRANKLIN D. ROOSEVELT LIBRARY)

In 1978 the Franklin D. Roosevelt Library released more than
3,000 letters written by Lorena Hickok and Eleanor Roosevelt
to each other. Full of love and tenderness, the letters—
spanning 30 years—reveal the intimate relationship that
existed between Hickok, a prominent journalist, and the First
Lady. Hickok was an intense part of Mrs. Roosevelt's life for
only a few years. However, Eleanor Roosevelt remained the
core of Hickok's life from 1932 until the First Lady's death in
1962. The correspondence was donated to the library by
Hickok with the condition that nothing be released until 10
years after the journalist's death. Hickok died in 1968. The
materials subsequently became the basis for *The Life of
Lorena Hickok: E.R.'s Friend,* written by Doris Faber and
published in 1980. However, library officials held back approximately 12 letters because they contain material that may
"embarrass, harass, or injure a living person." Those letters
will again be reviewed—and possibly released—in 1988.

2001 **KISSINGER'S "DEAD KEY SCROLLS"**
(LIBRARY OF CONGRESS)

From 1969 to 1976, Henry Kissinger played a dominant role in
American foreign policy—as national security adviser and as

secretary of state. During those years, his telephone had a special button—a "dead key"—which allowed his secretaries to monitor conversations. After taping or taking shorthand notes, a secretary would prepare a transcript of a designated call. The original tape or notes would then be destroyed. When Kissinger left the State Department, he took the thousands of pages of "dead key scrolls" with him. In 1976 he donated them to the Library of Congress with the stipulation that they remain secret for 25 years. The action caused an uproar among groups such as the Reporters Committee for Freedom of the Press and the American Political Science Association. These groups took the case to court, claiming that the papers were official government records and were subject to the Freedom of Information Act. In March, 1980, the Supreme Court ruled in favor of Kissinger.

2003 DAVID HALBERSTAM'S VIETNAM PAPERS (BOSTON UNIVERSITY)

For 15 months during 1962–1963, journalist David Halberstam was *The New York Times* war correspondent in Vietnam. According to Halberstam, he went out "to the boondocks, to isolated posts, to strategic hamlets." He told of political problems within the Diem government as well as the buildup of Vietcong troops in the Mekong Delta. Also, he exposed American-claimed victories as being, in truth, defeats. As he later said, "It is all so futile; for years now the only question left on Vietnam is how much damage we will do to ourselves as a society." U.S. officials denounced his reports as inaccurate and sensationalized. However, in 1964 Halberstam received the Pulitzer Prize for international reporting. His numerous writings on the war include the highly acclaimed *The Best and the Brightest*. Halberstam's Vietnam papers, covering his war correspondent days, are at Boston University. They will be opened in 2003.

2014 WARREN G. HARDING/CARRIE PHILLIPS LOVE LETTERS (LIBRARY OF CONGRESS)

In 1964 a large cardboard shoe box—full of love letters—was accidentally discovered in the home of Mrs. Carrie Phillips of Marion, O. Mrs. Phillips, who had been dead for four years, was the wife of James Phillips—a department store owner in Marion (the President's hometown). Written by Harding between 1909 and 1920, the letters show his passion and devotion to the beautiful Carrie. Often, he used their special code names—his was "Constant" and hers was "Sis." One letter, dated Christmas, 1914, contains a poem:

> I love you more than all the world.
>   Possession wholly imploring
> Mid passion I am oftimes whirled
>   Oftimes admire—adoring.
> Oh, God! If fate would only give
> Us privilege to love and live!

Much has been written about Harding's extramarital affairs, particularly his liaison with Nan Britton, who wrote a book,

The President's Daughter, which claimed that Harding was the father of Britton's daughter, Elizabeth Ann. However, Carrie Phillips supposedly was the most important woman in Harding's life. Historian Francis Russell read the Harding/Phillips letters, but a lawsuit, brought against him by the Harding heirs, prevented him from publishing them in his book *The Shadow of Blooming Grove: Warren G. Harding in His Times.* However, Russell did comment: "The letters, if they can be considered shocking—and some of them can—are more so because they were written by a President of the United States than through the tumescence of their content. When I first read them, I felt a sense of pity for the lonely Harding; for Carrie Phillips was clearly the love of his life, and he was more loving than loved." Library of Congress officials say that "slightly more than 100 letters from Harding to Phillips" will be released in 2014 (50 years from the date that they were found).

2027 MARTIN LUTHER KING, JR., TAPES MADE BY THE FBI (NATIONAL ARCHIVES)

The FBI, under Director J. Edgar Hoover, maintained 16 bugs and 8 wiretaps on Martin Luther King, Jr. This cam-

paign against the civil rights leader existed in 1965 (perhaps earlier) and lasted until King's death on April 4, 1968. The wiretaps and bugs were placed in King's office, home, and supposedly in hotel rooms where King was engaged in alleged sexual activities. Thousands of hours of tapes exist. Reasons for the electronic surveillance have never been adequately explained. However, Hoover's personal distaste for the Baptist minister was never a secret. In public Hoover called King "the most notorious liar in the country." In private the director called King a "degenerate."

2030 TEAPOT DOME PAPERS (UNIVERSITY OF WYOMING)

In 1922 Secretary of the Interior Albert B. Fall secretly leased U.S. oil reserves at Teapot Dome, Wyo., to oil magnate Harry F. Sinclair of the Mammoth Oil Company. Shortly afterwards, Fall leased U.S. oil reserves at Elk Hills, Calif., to Edward L. Doheny of the Pan American Petroleum Company. For his efforts, Fall received a gift of $200,000 and a "loan" of $100,000. When the scandal erupted in 1923, both Republicans and Democrats ran for cover as the U.S. Senate began a full-scale investigation. In the resulting furor, Fall was tried,

Hired killers for the Johnson County Cattle War.

convicted of accepting a bribe, and sent to prison. Doheny and Sinclair were tried on a charge of bribery but were acquitted. Is there anything more to be learned about Teapot Dome? The year 2030 may reveal some new information when the William L. Connelly collection is opened at the University of Wyoming. Connelly was vice-president of the Mammoth Oil Company during the Teapot Dome years.

2039 WILLIAM FAULKNER MEMENTOS (NEW YORK PUBLIC LIBRARY)

The 30-year romance between William Faulkner and Meta Carpenter began in the early 1930s when the novelist went to Hollywood to work on a screenplay for *The Road to Glory*. Carpenter was a script girl for the film's director, Howard Hawks. In her book, *A Loving Gentleman*, Carpenter paints a detailed portrait of Faulkner, whom she calls "the great joy of my life—my lover, my friend, my spar in a raging sea. . . ." She also mentions several Faulkner items which she donated to the New York Public Library for release in 2039. The small collection contains a copy of Faulkner's *A Green Bough* (with handwritten erotic inscription by the author), an erotic letter from Faulkner to Carpenter, and some erotic drawings. According to Carpenter, "One series [of drawings] shows us, recognizable, in the act of lovemaking, with a final sketch of Bill stretched out beside me, visibly exhausted. . . ."

2050 WATERGATE SPECIAL PROSECUTORS' FILES (NATIONAL ARCHIVES AND RECORDS SERVICE)

On October 20, 1973, Archibald Cox, Watergate special prosecutor, was fired by Solicitor General Robert Bork at President Richard Nixon's direction. The dismissal resulted from a legal battle over the controversial Nixon tapes. A brilliant lawyer and legal scholar, Cox said, "Whether ours shall continue to be a government of laws and not of men is now for Congress and ultimately the American people to decide." Days later, Leon Jaworski was appointed as the new prosecutor. He held the job until after Nixon's resignation in 1974. All files belonging to the special prosecutors have been sealed until 2050.

2052 1980 CENSUS INFORMATION (NATIONAL ARCHIVES AND RECORDS SERVICE)

In 1980 approximately 226 million Americans were counted in the nation's 20th census. While U.S. law allows summary statistics to be published, individual questionnaires remain confidential for 72 years. As in previous censuses, the questionnaires are put on microfilm which is kept in a special Census Bureau facility in Pittsburg, Kans. Original census forms are shredded, dissolved in acid, and recycled as paper pulp.

2100 JOHNSON COUNTY WAR CORRESPONDENCE (UNIVERSITY OF WYOMING)

The Johnson County War of April, 1892, was one of the most gory, notorious events of the American West. For years cattle barons had tried unsuccessfully to stop the cattle rustling which was prevalent throughout this Wyoming county. Taking the law into their own hands, the wealthy cattlemen put together a 50-man army (including 25 hired gunmen from Texas) to rid the land of the rustlers. Carrying a hit list with 35 names, the armed men began their work on April 9 by murdering two so-called rustlers. Small independent cattlemen rose up to retaliate. Federal troops were called in and quickly stopped the fighting. The "invaders" were brought to trial but were subsequently freed. While much has been written on the war, the subject can still cause tempers to flare. The war was not simply an invasion. It had been preceded by six years of intermittent killings and was followed by yet another two years of violence. Many Johnson County citizens believe the war was a hostile and very personal conflict between the haves and the have-nots. There is still an undisclosed "body of correspondence" concerning the war at the University of Wyoming. However, library officials will not divulge the nature of the correspondence or the names of those involved. When the materials are finally released in 2100, they will be more than 200 years old.

—C.O.

THE WORLD'S TOP JOURNALISTS PREDICT THE BIGGEST HEADLINES FOR 1985

In 1980 we polled a small, select list of newspaper and newsweekly editors, writers, columnists, and television newspeople and asked them to give us their educated or intuitive guesses on five future headlines that would appear in 1985.

We wrote the well-known journalists as follows: "These 1985 top stories might be in any field ranging from the international situation (SOVIET TROOPS POUR INTO YUGOSLAVIA), to the scientific realm (FIRST EXTRATERRESTRIAL LIFE FOUND IN OUTER SPACE), to the field of medicine (CURE FOR CANCER FOUND), to social or religious issues (POPE ADMITS WOMEN TO THE PRIESTHOOD)."

We posed to each renowned journalist one provocative question: *What do you foresee or forecast might be the five biggest headlines or news stories in 1985?*

Here are the responses we received.

• FROM JIM BELLOWS,
editor: *Los Angeles Herald Examiner*
(Los Angeles, Calif.) •

1. RUSSIA AND CHINA OPEN NUCLEAR WARFARE
2. TOUCHY-FEELY TELEVISION BEGINS
3. WOMAN BECOMES POPE
4. THREE-DAY WORKWEEK DECLARED
5. ERA FINALLY PASSED IN U.S.A.

• FROM DARRYL D'MONTE,
editor: *The Indian Express*
(Bombay, India) •

1. CHINA AND THE SOVIET UNION UNITE AGAINST U.S.
2. ARREST OF POPULATION GROWTH ALARMS DEMOGRAPHERS
3. MEN'S COSMETICS INDUSTRY OUTSTRIPS WOMEN'S
4. SCHOOLS CLOSING FOR LACK OF CHILDREN
5. GREAT BRITAIN NOW AN UNDERDEVELOPED COUNTRY

• FROM R. J. DOYLE,
editor: *The Globe and Mail*
(Toronto, Canada) •

1. MAJOR EARTHQUAKE IN CALIFORNIA
2. CRISIS IN OIL SUPPLY
3. PAKISTAN BORDER WAR

• FROM SIDNEY GOLDBERG,
executive editor: *Independent News Alliance*
(New York, N.Y.) •

1. BOMB KILLS 17 IN CROAT SENATE; U.S.S.R.: WE'LL DEFEND SERBIA
2. MONDALE NAMES KENNEDY AMBASSADOR TO IRELAND
3. WORK STARTS ON CAUSEWAY LINKING ALASKA, SIBERIA
4. PONTIFF NAMES 11 MORE TO COLLEGE OF CARDINALS
5. ARMY SEIZES KREMLIN: ANNOUNCES REFORMS

• FROM A. E. INSOBIA,
editor: *Newsday*
(Long Island, N.Y.) •

1. U.S. SEEKING WAYS TO CUT OIL IMPORTS
2. INFLATION INCREASES; FED TIGHT MONEY POLICIES FAIL
3. 782 DIE IN WORST AIR DISASTER
4. CASTRO CALLS CARIBBEAN SUMMIT
5. QUEBEC BECOMES 51ST UNITED STATES STATE

• FROM K. J. KAVANAGH,
editor: *The Courier Mail*
(Brisbane, Australia) •

1. NEW ZEALAND SINKS INTO SEA
2. LAST WHITE LEAVES AFRICA

• FROM FREDERIC S. MARQUARDT,
senior editor: *Arizona Republic*
(Phoenix, Ariz.) •

1. WORLD WAR III ENDS IN STALEMATE
2. U.S. INAUGURATES FIRST WOMAN VICE-PRESIDENT
3. FAMINE SWEEPS WORLD
4. IMELDA MARCOS BECOMES PHILIPPINE PRESIDENT
5. DOW-JONES INDUSTRIAL AVERAGE HITS 1600

• FROM IAN A. NIMMO,
editor: *Evening News*
(North Bridge, Edinburgh, Scotland) •

1. NORTH SEA OIL: THE WELL RUNS DRY
2. KING CHARLES NAMES HIS QUEEN
3. £2 MILLION SOCCER POOLS SCOOP
4. RHODESIA: IT'S CIVIL WAR
5. SOUTH AFRICA: THE WHITE EXODUS
6. AMERICA QUALIFIES FOR THE WORLD CUP

1. MUSLIMS UNITED: INVADE U.S.S.R.
2. SOLAR ENERGY HEATS 75% OF NATION'S HOMES
3. UNITED NATIONS DISBANDS
4. NIXON NAMED AMBASSADOR TO CHINA
5. INFLATION 23% IN '84: NEW RECORD

· **FROM JESSICA SAVITCH,**
network correspondent: *National
Broadcasting Company* (New York, N.Y.) ·

1. HUMAN LIFE SYNTHESIZED
2. $20,000 YEARLY INCOME NOW POVERTY LEVEL
3. MASS-PRODUCED AUTOS RUN ON GRAIN FUEL
4. FIRST WOMAN (OR BLACK) ELECTED VICE-PRESIDENT
5. GEORGE BUSH ELECTED TO SECOND TERM AS PRESIDENT

· **FROM HARVEY WOOD TYSON,**
editor: *The Star*
(Johannesburg, South Africa) ·

1. WORLD'S FIRST ARTIFICIAL HEART TICKS ON
2. HOME-MADE NUCLEAR BOMB IN NEW YORK: MASS EVACUATION
3. BRITAIN MOVES TO PERMANENT 3-DAY WORK-WEEK
4. ESCAPED GERM WARFARE ON RAMPAGE—U.S.S.R. SEEKS WORLD AID
5. SPACE TRANSMITTER RECEIVES ANSWERING SIGNAL. IS IT FROM ANOTHER SOLAR SYSTEM?
6. NORTH AMERICAN DROUGHT THREATENS MASSIVE WORLD FAMINE

Mr. Tyson adds: "A colleague suggests—'1984 didn't happen. So there!' "

· **FROM ANDREW VIGLUCCI,**
editor: *San Juan Star*
(San Juan, Puerto Rico) ·

1. PRESIDENT BROWN LAMENTS WIDESCALE DESTRUCTION IN SAN FRANCISCO EARTHQUAKE
2. PUERTO RICO ADMITTED INTO UNION AS THE FIFTY-FIRST STATE

NOBEL PRIZE LAUREATES PICK FUTURE WINNERS OF NOBEL PRIZES

In 1980 we took an international poll of living Nobel Prize laureates in the six award categories—literature, physics, chemistry, physiology and medicine, peace, economic science.

We asked each Nobel award gold medalist the same question: *Who do you feel will—or should—win the Nobel Prize in your field in the decade ahead?*

Six previous winners declined to participate on the grounds that as laureates they were expected to officially nominate future winners and that the Nobel committees had "ordered" them to keep their choices "strictly confidential." As medical laureate Dr. Baruch S. Blumberg explained, "I do not think that it would be appropriate for me to prepare such a prediction. As you pointed out, former laureates are permitted to nominate candidates for the Nobel Prize. The Nobel committee has asked us to keep these proceedings private. If I were to make a prediction . . . it would be contrary to their policy."

As a matter of fact, the Nobel Foundation has no official stricture against predictions. Many of the Nobel Prize judges themselves, before every annual vote, leak their own predictions to the press.

A number of other laureates declined to participate on other grounds. One of them, Professor Konrad Lorenz, wrote from Austria: "I do not feel competent to make any predictions about future Nobel Prize winners without previous investigations about the work of the innumerable scientists working in this field. For this I do not have the time, as, at my age, I feel compelled to accomplish those tasks which I have already begun." Another laureate, P. W. Anderson, gave a different reason for not wishing to predict future winners: "It will raise too many hopes or disappoint too many expectations."

Nevertheless, from around the world, eight great Nobel Prize winners felt it was quite proper to name 27 others in their fields who would be—or should be—Nobel Prize laureates in the 10 years ahead. Herewith, then, the Nobel predictors and their exclusive predictions:

• PREDICTIONS FROM MILTON FRIEDMAN, NOBEL PRIZE IN ECONOMICS, 1976 •

Name:	GEORGE J. STIGLER
Affiliation:	University of Chicago
Discovery or Advance:	Industrial organization
	Economic analysis of politics
Name:	GARY H. BECKER
Affiliation:	University of Chicago
Discovery or Advance:	Human capital theory

Name:	MARTIN FELDSTEIN
Affiliation:	Harvard University
Discovery or Advance:	Tax efforts
Name:	ROBERT LUCAS
Affiliation:	University of Chicago
Discovery or Advance:	Rational expectations
Name:	FRANCO MODIGLIANI
Affiliation:	Massachusetts Institute of Technology
Discovery or Advance:	Monetary and cyclical theory

• PREDICTION FROM JOHN H. NORTHROP, (shared) NOBEL PRIZE IN CHEMISTRY, 1946 •

Name:	ALBERT BRUCE SABIN
Affiliation:	Weizmann Institute of Science
Discovery or Advance:	Oral polio vaccine

• PREDICTIONS FROM JAMES RAINWATER, NOBEL PRIZE IN PHYSICS, 1975 •

Name:	CHIEN SHIUNG WU
Affiliation:	Columbia University
Discovery or Advance:	Contributions to knowledge of weak interactions
Name:	LEO LEDERMAN
Affiliation:	Columbia University, on leave from Fermi National Laboratories
Discovery or Advance:	Many contributions to elementary-particle knowledge

• PREDICTIONS FROM PHILIP NOEL-BAKER, NOBEL PRIZE FOR PEACE, 1959 •

Name:	HIS EXCELLENCY MINISTER GARCÍA ROBLES
Affiliation:	Permanent representative to the U.N. Conference of the Committee on Disarmament, Geneva, Switzerland
Discovery or Advance:	For distinguished work in the Special Session of the U.N. General Assembly devoted to disarmament, 1978
Name:	HIS EXCELLENCY OLOF PALMÉ
Affiliation:	Former prime minister of Sweden

Name:	ARTHUR BOOTH
Affiliation:	International Peace Bureau in Geneva, Switzerland
Name:	LOUIS DOLIVET
Affiliation:	Filmmaker in Paris, France
Name:	MONSIGNOR BRUCE KENT
Affiliation:	Pax Christi
Discovery or Advance:	Campaign for nuclear disarmament

• PREDICTIONS FROM HOWARD MARTIN TEMIN, NOBEL PRIZE IN MEDICINE, 1975 •

Name:	WORLD HEALTH ORGANIZATION in Geneva, Switzerland
Discovery or Advance:	Eradication of smallpox
Name:	BARBARA MCCLINTOK and ALEXANDER BRINK
Affiliation:	Cold Spring Harbor Laboratory in Cold Spring Harbor, N.Y. (McClintok) University of Wisconsin (Brink)
Discovery or Advance:	Original discovery of movable controlling elements in maize, now believed to be transposable element
Name:	SEWALL WRIGHT
Affiliation:	University of Wisconsin
Discovery or Advance:	Pioneer in population genetics and physiological genetics
Name:	HUGH HUXLEY
Affiliation:	Medical Research Council Laboratory of Molecular Biology in Cambridge, England
Discovery or Advance:	Mechanism of muscle contraction
Name:	S. TONEGAWA
Affiliation:	Basel Institute of Immunology in Basel, Switzerland
Discovery or Advance:	Discovery of somatic genetic changes in antibody formation
Name:	SUNE BERGSTROM, BENGT INGEMAR SAMUELSON, JOHN ROBERT VANE
Affiliation:	Karolinska Institute in Stockholm, Sweden (Bergstrom) Department of Medical Chemistry, Royal Veteran College in Stockholm, Sweden (Samuelson) The Wellcome Foundation in Kent, England (Vane)
Discovery or Advance:	Work with prostaglandins

• PREDICTION FROM HUGO THEORELL, NOBEL PRIZE IN PHYSIOLOGY AND MEDICINE, 1955 •

Name:	BRITTON CHANCE
Affiliation:	Johnson Research Foundation, University of Pennsylvania
Discovery or Advance:	For his brilliant methods for studying the very rapid enzyme process on the molecular, subcellular, and cellular level and for the fundamental discoveries made thereby

• PREDICTIONS FROM WILLARD LIBBY, NOBEL PRIZE IN CHEMISTRY, 1960 •

Name:	DONALD CRAM
Affiliation:	University of California at Los Angeles
Discovery or Advance:	Organic chemistry
Name:	HANS SUESS
Affiliation:	University of California at San Diego
Discovery or Advance:	Geochemistry
Name:	HENRY EYRING
Affiliation:	University of Utah
Discovery or Advance:	Kinetics

• PREDICTION FROM ANWAR SADAT, NOBEL PRIZE FOR PEACE, 1978 •

Name: JIMMY CARTER

In personal correspondence with *The Book of Predictions*, President Sadat stated:

"I firmly believe that President Jimmy Carter is most qualified to receive this award. No one can match his record of promoting peace and understanding among nations. No living statesman has worked as vigorously and diligently as he did for the cause of peace. His key role in bringing about a just and comprehensive peace in the Middle East was indispensable. He remains firmly committed to pursue this noble goal until a solution to the Palestinian problem is reached and implemented. Throughout my dealings with him, I found him a man of vision, conviction, and strong sense of morality. His faith in God and human nature is unshakable.

"His compassion towards fellow men is formidable and he is genuinely determined to alleviate human suffering and oppression in all four corners of the globe. In short, the awarding of the Nobel Peace Prize to President Jimmy Carter would do justice to the cause of universal peace and friendship."

14 PREDICTIONS
MADE IN DREAMS

In the 4th century before Christ, the Taoist mystic Chuang-tzu dreamed he was a butterfly. Upon awakening, he asked himself, "Am I Chuang-tzu who dreamed he was a butterfly or a butterfly now dreaming I am Chuang-tzu?"

1. THE DEATH OF HENRY II (1559)

In April, 1559, the Peace of Cateau-Cambrésis was signed, ending a 33-year war between France and Spain. To cement the alliance, King Henry II of France betrothed his 14-year-old daughter Elizabeth to Philip II, the widowed king of Spain. He then called for a period of celebration, which was to commence the last week of June. The main event was a week-long sword tournament between Henry and a succession of opponents. Henry demonstrated his skill ably the first two days, defeating his rivals one after the other. The evening of the second day, Blaise de Monluc, the marshal of France, dreamed he saw the king's face covered with blood. He heard contradictory voices proclaiming, "He is dead," and "He is not dead."

Henry was challenged on the third day by Gabriel, Comte de Montgomery, captain of the Scots Guards. As the two men were jousting, the count's splintered lance penetrated the king's visor and entered his brain through one of his eyes. At first, spectators were unable to discern whether the king was dead or alive. He survived for 10 days, in horrible agony, ultimately dying on July 10, 1559.

2. THE DEATH OF GENERAL TOUTSCHKOFF (1812)

In the summer of 1812, when Napoleon's armies were advancing into Russia, Countess Toutschkoff, the wife of a Russian general, dreamed she was in a hotel room in an unfamiliar city. Her father entered the room, holding her small son by the hand. "Your happiness is ended," he said. "Your husband has fallen. He fell at Borodino." The countess had the dream twice more before telling her husband. Together they combed maps looking for a place called Borodino, but to no avail.

In the fall of that year, the French armies moved toward Moscow, and General Toutschkoff's forces made a vain effort to arrest them 70 mi. outside the city. The countess had taken a room in an inn near the battlefield. One morning her father and son entered the room. Suddenly the countess was overwhelmed with grief. As she looked about her, she recognized the room as the scene of her recurring dream three months before. "He has fallen. He has fallen at Borodino," her father said. The bloody battle had been fought on the banks of the Borodino River, near which stood a little-known village of the same name.

3. THE DEATH OF PERCY BYSSHE SHELLEY AND EDWARD WILLIAMS (1822)

Shelley is recognized as one of the great British romantic poets. In 1822 he was living in Italy with his wife, Mary and their friends Edward and Jane Williams. On the night of June 23, Shelley rushed into Mary's room screaming. He had dreamed that he had seen "the lacerated figures of Edward and Jane covered with blood, who staggered into his room supporting each other, and shouted, 'Get up, Shelley, the sea is flooding the house and all is coming down.' "

Two weeks later, Shelley and Williams planned to sail Shelley's yacht from Leghorn to their home in Lerici. A storm was gathering offshore as they prepared to leave, and a captain in the lighthouse saw waves breaking on the ship's decks as it faded into the foggy horizon. Although a sailor from a nearby ship shouted to them to lower their sails or their ship would be lost, Shelley was reportedly seen stopping one of his crewmen from effecting the maneuver. The ship was lost at sea on July 8, 1822. Ten days later, the bodies of Shelley and Williams washed ashore near Viareggio. The flesh on Shelley's face and arms was so torn away that his bones were exposed. The lacerations were similar to what he had seen on Edward and Jane Williams in his dream two weeks before.

4. THE FATE OF SIR JOHN FRANKLIN (1847)

Franklin, the noted British admiral and explorer, vanished in the Arctic Circle in the summer of 1847 while on an expedition that was searching for the Northwest Passage. Public opinion held that he was alive. His wife Jane solicited funds for search parties and wrote letters to foreign dignitaries pleading for financial assistance. Shortly after Franklin's party was reported missing, his friend Walter Snoo had a tragic dream in which Franklin perished. As soon as Snoo

The discovery of the body of Sir John Franklin
was foreseen in a dream 12 years earlier.

422

woke up, he took a pencil and paper and drew what he saw—a scene depicting snow formations, abandoned boats, and the frozen bodies in the snow. Snoo's vision would not be confirmed until 12 years later, when, in 1859, an expedition headed by Capt. Leopold McClintock discovered the icebound wreckage of Franklin's ship. Scores of bodies were found frozen in the snow, just as Snoo had seen them in his dream. Franklin's was among them.

5. THE DEATH OF MARK TWAIN'S BROTHER (1858)

In May, 1858, Samuel Clemens, who later adopted the pen name Mark Twain, had a dream so vivid he awakened convinced it was real. He saw his 21-year-old brother Henry lying dead in a metal casket placed upon two chairs. Henry was wearing one of Samuel's suits, and on his breast was a large bouquet of white roses with one red rose in the center. Two weeks later, Henry met with a terrible accident. He was aboard the steamship *Pennsylvania* when it exploded near Memphis, and his lungs were severely scalded by the steam he inhaled. Samuel was at his side as soon as possible. Although a week later Henry passed the crisis point, he died shortly afterward from an accidental overdose of morphine administered by an inexperienced young physician. Samuel went to view Henry's body the day after his death. As he entered a room filled with pine caskets, he saw that only one corpse was lying in a metal coffin. It was Henry, and was wearing one of Samuel's suits. As Samuel stood startled, remembering his dream, an elderly lady came up to the casket and placed a bouquet of white roses on Henry's breast. When Samuel moved closer, he saw a single red rose in the center.

6. THE CONFEDERATE MARCH ON WASHINGTON (1862)

It was 1862 and the second summer of the Civil War. The Union armies had just suffered a crushing defeat at the Second Battle of Bull Run. Gen. George B. McClellan, chief of the Union armies, was now put to the crucial test of defending Washington, D.C. President Abraham Lincoln not only wanted a decisive Union victory, he wanted Confederate Gen. Robert E. Lee's troops destroyed.

McClellan sat at his desk late one night plotting his strategy. He began to feel drowsy, and then, while in a trancelike state found the room bathed in light. Before him stood a vision of George Washington. "General McClellan, do you sleep at your post? Rouse you, or ere it can be prevented, the foe will be in Washington. Note what you see. Your time is short." When McClellan awakened, he found pencil marks on his maps denoting the Confederate army's plans. This knowledge enabled Union forces to arrest the Confederate advance at Antietam on September 17, 1862. Unfortunately McClellan failed to pursue Lee's armies and destroy them. For this blunder Lincoln removed McClellan from his command.

7. THE MURDER OF LLOYD MAGRUDER (1863)

Magruder was a seasoned Idaho packer who made regular trips to Virginia City to exchange goods for gold. In August, 1863, he departed from Lewiston, Ida., for the 300-mi. journey. Three onlookers—Lowry, Howard, and Romain by name—watched the caravan leave laden with goods, and they decided it would be to their advantage to follow it. They gave Magruder a 10-day head start and then joined him on the trail, acting as if it were a chance meeting. Magruder welcomed the unexpected company, and when the four men reached Virginia City, Magruder sold his merchandise for $30,000 in gold and engaged several men for the trip back to Lewiston.

Lowry, Howard, and Romain decided to make their move on the return trip. Late one night while Magruder and his companions were asleep, Lowry killed them with an ax and tossed their bodies into a nearby gorge. The murders would never have been discovered had it not been for a hotel proprietor named Hill Beechy. One night after Magruder's caravan had left Lewiston, Beechy had a dream in which he saw him being murdered with an ax. Beechy also saw the face of the murderer clearly. When Lowry showed up in Lewiston to purchase stagecoach tickets, Beechy recognized him and suspected his dream had come true. The bodies were discovered, and Lowry, Howard, and Romain were convicted of first-degree murder on January 26, 1864. All three were hanged on March 4.

8. THE DREAM OF E. A. WALLIS BUDGE (1878)

Budge was a Semitic scholar who gained world renown for his translation of the *Egyptian Book of the Dead*. As a young student, he experienced a remarkable dream which was the turning point in his academic career. In 1878, when he was 21, Budge was scheduled to take a fellowship examination which, if he passed it, would enable him to continue his studies at Cambridge. The night before the exam, the exhausted Budge fell asleep at his desk. He dreamed that he saw himself alone in a shed with a murky skylight. A tutor walked in and took from his pocket an envelope containing examination questions. Budge had the same dream three times in a row; when he awakened two hours later he remembered the questions and studied them for the remainder of the night. When he arrived at school the following day, he was surprised to hear that the examination hall was full. He was taken to a room that was an exact duplicate of the one in his dream and he was given the same questions that he had dreamed about the night before. He won the fellowship.

9. THE DREAM OF AN EGYPTIAN KHEDIVE (1891)

Heinrich Karl Brugsch was a renowned Egyptian scholar. In 1891 he left Egypt—where he had directed the School of Egyptology—for his native Germany. He was scheduled to depart on another journey from the north German port of Bremen when he received a telegram from the khedive requesting his immediate return to Cairo. Brugsch obeyed the command and boarded a Lloyd steamer for Trieste. En route, the captain announced the tragic news that the last steamer to leave Bremen had exploded, inflicting a great number of casualties. Brugsch thought to himself that a great stroke of luck had saved his life. He also assumed the khedive would have an important communiqué to deliver, but when he arrived in Cairo, the khedive greeted him in a casual manner. When Brugsch inquired about the reason for the telegram, the khedive explained that he had dreamed a great misfortune would befall Brugsch if he did not return to Cairo.

10. THE DREAM OF HERMANN HILPRECHT (1893)

Late one night in 1893, Hilprecht, a noted Assyrian scholar, fell asleep at his desk in Philadelphia. He awakened to a vision of a priest from the temple of Baal in Nippur (in present-day Turkey). As he looked about, he realized he was no longer in his study but was seated on a giant stone step. A hot wind circled his body. The priest beckoned for him to follow, saying, "I will help you." They walked through deserted streets to a magnificent building. "You are in the temple of Baal at Nippur, between the Tigris and the Euphrates," the priest said. Hilprecht asked his guide to show him the secret treasure room, where he discovered some agate fragments bearing inscriptions. As he began to read the words, the vision faded and he was back in his Philadelphia study, the priest still by his side. On a paper on his desk was written "Nebuchadnezzar," translated by the priest as "Nebo, protect my boundary." Hilprecht awoke. The vision of the inscriptions and their translations provided Hilprecht with the missing link he needed to complete *Old Babylonian Inscriptions, Chiefly from Nippur*, which he published later that year.

11. THE ERUPTION OF MT. PELÉE (1902)

John W. Dunne was a well-known British aeronautical engineer who experienced clairvoyant dreams throughout his life. In May, 1902, when he was stationed in South Africa, he awakened one night from an "unusually vivid and rather unpleasant dream." He saw an island that was about to be destroyed by a tremendous volcanic eruption. Before awakening, he remembered hearing himself shout, "Four thousand people will be killed unless . . ." A few days later a news dispatch arrived at his post. The *Daily Telegraph* headline read: VOLCANO DISASTER IN MARTINIQUE PROBABLE LOSS OF OVER 40,000 LIVES. In retrospect, Dunne postulated that he had *not* experienced a premonition of the eruption itself, but instead had foreseen the *Daily Telegraph* headline. He added that he had been "ought by a nought" in projecting the number 4,000 instead of the reported 40,000. Later reports placed the death toll at 30,000 lives.

12. THE TRAPPED LOVERS OF BEDEILHAC (c. 1930)

A French anthropologist named Joseph Mandemant dreamed one night about the prehistoric cave of Bedeilhac in France. He saw drawings on the ceiling and a group of primitive Magdalenian hunters gathered around a campfire. In the shadows, he saw two lovers on a corner ledge whispering and stroking each other affectionately. He then heard a thundering sound and saw the roof of the cave collapse. He awakened convinced he had gone back in time to witness a prehistoric earthquake, and he was determined to travel to Bedeilhac and uncover the skeletons of the two trapped lovers. Before leaving, he detailed his vision on paper and placed the document in a bank vault. Upon arriving at Bedeilhac, he discovered that the cave was exactly as he had pictured it in his dream. With the help of some local workmen, he broke through the rock wall and found the corner ledge where he had seen the two lovers. But to his amazement, the ledge was empty. Mandemant concluded that in the confusion caused by the falling rock, he had not noticed that the lovers had escaped to safety.

13. *MANNA* WINS THE DERBY (1922)

Oscar-winning screenwriter T.E.B. Clarke *(The Lavender Hill Mob*, 1951) had a curious dream about Britain's Derby. In 1922, when he was 15 years old, he dreamed he saw a newspaper with the headline DERBY RESULT. When he woke up, he remembered that the winning horse was named *Manna*. Two years later, he noted that a horse called *Manna* was entered in a 2-year-old race. "The horse had probably not even been born when I had my dream," Clarke thought to himself. Certain that the horse would win the Derby the following year, he decided to back it with two weeks' pay. *Manna* won the Derby at odds of 9 to 1.

14. THE CRASH OF AMERICAN AIRLINES FLIGHT 191 (1979)

On May 15, 1979, a Cincinnati man named David Booth awakened from a terrifying dream. As he described it, "I was standing beside this one-story building. . . . I look up in the air and there's an American Airlines jet. . . . Then it starts to bank off to the right. And the left wing goes up in the air and it's going very slow. . . . Then it just turned on its back and went straight down into the ground and exploded." On May 24, after having experienced the dream for the tenth time, he woke up weeping. The next day Booth arrived home from work distraught and terribly depressed. When he turned on the TV after dinner, a news story was broadcast about American Airlines Flight 191, bound for Los Angeles from Chicago's O'Hare Airport; it had crashed shortly after takeoff, killing all 271 passengers. The DC-10 crash was the worst domestic air disaster in U.S. flight history. Booth had called the FAA on May 19, six days before the crash, to warn it of an impending disaster. But he had no date or flight time, so there was nothing the FAA could do. Later, when asked what action he would take if told of an impending plane crash, a public relations man from one of the major U.S. airlines replied, "Absolutely nothing. I'd ignore it. We discount the occult here. It goes against everything scientific and logical to even discuss such a damn thing."

—L.O.

6 BIBLICAL PROPHECIES

1. APPEARANCE OF THE MESSIAH

Prediction: There are many biblical references to the "coming of the Messiah." Theologians have found more than 300 such predictions. For example, Matthew 2:4–6 says: "And when [Herod] had gathered all the chief priests and scribes of the people together, he demanded of them where Christ [Messiah] should be born. And they said unto him, In Bethlehem of Judea: for thus it is written by the prophet. . . ."

Commentary: The Jews and the Christians part company on the issue of whether or not the prediction has been fulfilled. The Jewish view is that the Messiah is yet to appear; the Christians believe He has already come in the form of Jesus Christ.

2. TRAGEDY FOR EGYPT

Prediction: Isaiah 19:5-10: "And the waters shall fail from the sea, and the river shall be wasted and dried up. And they shall turn the rivers far away; and the brooks of defense shall be emptied and dried up: the reeds and flags shall wither. The paper reeds sown by the brooks . . . and everything sown by the brooks shall wither . . . and be no more. The fishes also shall mourn, and all they that cast angle into the brooks shall lament, and they that spread nets upon the water shall languish. Moreover, they that work in fine flax, and they that weave networks, shall be confounded. And they shall be broken in the purposes thereof, and all that make sluices and ponds for fish."

Commentary: Isaiah reveals that at some future time Egypt will have more tragic circumstances take place than just the drying up of the Nile River. In Isaiah 19:4 and 19:20, he warns the people of Egypt that they will also be given into "the hand of a cruel lord; and a fierce king"—sometimes referred to as the Antichrist—will rule over them. However, all of this will change ". . . for they shall cry unto the Lord . . . and He shall send them a saviour . . . and He shall deliver them."

3. REBUILDING OF JERUSALEM

Prediction: Daniel 9:25: ". . . from the going forth of the commandment to restore and to build Jerusalem unto the Messiah the Prince shall be seven weeks, and three score and two: the street shall be built again, and the wall, even in troublous times."

Commentary: The prophecy of the Jews' rebuilding Jerusalem did come closer to reality when in the 1967 Arab-Israeli six-day war, the Jews took possession of the Old City in Jerusalem. The Israeli troops had been on a pilgrimage to the Western Wall (or "wailing wall"), which is greatly revered by the Jews as having been part of the First Temple (built by Solomon and destroyed in 586 B.C. by Nebuchadnezzar's army). Defense Minister Moshe Dayan declared: "The Israeli defense forces liberated Jerusalem. We have reunited the torn city, the capital of Israel. We have returned to this most sacred shrine, never to part from it again."

4. ARRIVAL OF THE ANTICHRIST

Prediction: Revelation 13:4, 5, and 7: "And they worshipped the beast, saying, who is like unto the beast? Who is able to make war with him? And there was given unto him a mouth speaking great things and blasphemies; and power was given unto him to continue forty and two months. . . . And it was given unto him to make war with the saints, and to overcome them; and power was given him over all kindreds, and tongues, and nations."

Commentary: Biblical scholars have speculated that the Antichrist will be a powerful political leader. He will gain respect of the masses by solving some serious world problems and also by using his powers to perform what appear to be "miracles." He will align himself with an important and powerful religious leader, and he will use the media to gain the attention of the world. Jeane Dixon, the American psychic, has predicted the exact date and place of the Antichrist's birth—February 5, 1962—somewhere in the Middle East. If

427

her predictions are correct, he will come into power, first among the youth, around 1992 at the age of 30 in Jerusalem. Supposedly his reign will last only 3½ years ("40 and 2 months"), although it will be filled with incredible deception and devastation.

5. CHRIST'S SECOND COMING

Prediction: Revelation 1:7 and 20:2: "Behold, He cometh with clouds; and every eye shall see Him, and they also which pierced Him: and all kindreds of the earth shall wail because of him. . . . And he laid hold on the dragon, that old serpent, which is the Devil, and Satan, and bound him a thousand years. . . ."

Commentary: Fundamentalists, interpreting the Bible literally, take an apocalyptic view of Revelation. They believe that the appearance of the Antichrist will be followed by a war which will devastate the earth. It is at this time that Christ will return, presaging 1,000 years of bliss.

Another explanation is that the second coming of Christ will not be a physical incarnation, but will be a state of altered consciousness. Christ consciousness—the universal symbol of compassion and love—will be experienced and manifested in all living things. Luke 17:20–21 reinforces this theory. Jesus told the Pharisees, "The kingdom of God cometh not with observation: Neither shall they say, Lo here! or Lo there! for, behold, the kingdom of God is within you."

6. THE APOCALYPSE

Sir Isaac Newton once said of the Apocalypse: "To explain this book perfectly is not the work of one man or of one age; but probably it never will be understood till it is all fulfilled."

The impermanence of the world has always been one of the chief concerns of humankind. The oldest record of apocalyptic ideas dates back to Babylonian times. In the Judeo-Christian theology which concerns itself with the "final events" in the history of the world, creation occurred only once and destruction of the world as we know it will come once. A new and better world will emerge, and the "chosen"—those who have faced the temptations of the world and have remained loyal to God—will be saved.

The final book of the New Testament, The Revelation of St. John the Divine, is the most famous of the apocalypses. It is said to have been written by John the Apostle around 90 A.D. on the Greek island of Patmos. It has been the inspiration for many doomsday prophecies.

The central theme of Revelation concerns a book which is held closed by seven seals. The breaking of each seal reveals another aspect of the apocalypse. The first four seals bring to life the famous four horsemen of the apocalypse riding a white, a red, a black, and an ashen-colored horse. The four horsemen personify the evils of war—Conquest, Slaughter, Famine, and Death. The broken fifth seal reveals martyrs who have been slaughtered "for the word of God." They are each given a white robe and told to rest a little longer and await the arrival of more martyrs.

A violent earthquake takes place upon breaking the sixth seal; the sun becomes black "and the moon became as blood . . . and every mountain and island were moved out of their places." Some biblical scholars have interpreted this to refer to a change in the earth's poles. Any change whatsoever in the earth's axis and its orbit around the sun can directly affect the climate. Some physicists have theorized that polar reversals in the past have caused dramatic changes; one brought the magnetic north pole off the California coast some 600 million years ago.

The breaking of the seventh seal is followed by silence in heaven. Seven angels then appear and are given trumpets. The sounding of each horn brings a new disaster on earth. Hail and fire mingled with blood are cast upon the earth, and a third of the trees and all green grass are burned up. A third of the sea becomes blood, and a third of the ships upon it are destroyed. The waters of the earth are polluted by the falling star Wormwood; and many die from the bitter water.

When the fourth trumpet is sounded, darkness covers the sky. John sees an angel flying above calling out: "Woe, woe, woe to the inhabitors of the earth, by reason of the other voices of the trumpet of the three angels, which are yet to sound!"

As the fifth angel sounds the trumpet, a star falls to earth and opens the bottomless pit, out of which comes smoke which produces swarms of locusts. They are told to hurt "only those men which have not the seal of God in their foreheads." The torment they inflict is like the sting of a scorpion and causes people who are stung to wish for the refuge found in death, but they are denied it. The locusts wear "crowns like gold." Their faces are like the faces of men, their hair the hair of women, and their teeth those of lions.

With the sounding of the sixth trumpet, four angels are released to lead an army of 200 million to kill a third of humankind. The horses they ride into battle have heads like lions "and out of their mouths issued fire and smoke and brimstone."

In Revelation 11:15 "... the seventh angel sounded; and there were great voices in heaven, saying, The kingdoms of this world are become the kingdoms of our Lord ... and He shall reign forever and ever." However, this chapter also states that "the nations are angry." And in heaven occurred lightning and thunder, "an earthquake, and great hail."

In Revelation 13, a terrible beast appears. This marks the arrival of the "Antichrist" and deception and devastation throughout the world. It is at this time that many fundamentalists feel the Messiah will come to save those who have survived the trials and tribulations of evil. They will find "the tree of life ... [and] the grace of our Lord Jesus be with you all. Amen."

—D.B.S.

10 PEOPLE WHO PREDICTED THEIR OWN DEATH

1. ST. MALACHY (1094?–1148), Irish

Ireland's greatest prophet predicted both the time and place of his death—All Souls' Day at Clairvaux, France. As St. Malachy was leaving on what he knew was to be his last trip to Rome, Catholicus, an epileptic monk who depended upon the prophet for strength, wept bitterly, for Catholicus dreaded the idea of facing his attacks alone. Malachy hugged him, saying, "Rest assured, my child. You shall not be troubled again until my return." Malachy stopped on his journey at Clairvaux to visit his old friend St. Bernard. There he came down with a slight fever, and although St. Bernard and the other monks who nursed him insisted his ailment wasn't serious, Malachy died just before midnight on November 2, All Souls' Day. As predicted, the monk Catholicus never suffered another epileptic attack—for Malachy did not return. (See Chapter 13, "The 7 Greatest Predictions of All Time," for a full account of St. Malachy's predictions.)

2. JOAN OF ARC (1412–1431), French

Throughout her crusade, the future saint spoke often of the limited time she had to accomplish her task of saving France from English domination. True to her pronouncements, two years after the beginning of her mission, she was captured by English soldiers. While she was in prison, Bishop Cauchon, one of the judges who presided at her trial, asked Joan when she thought she would be delivered from imprisonment. She told him to return in three months to find out. On May 30, 1431—three months later to the day—Joan of Arc was burned at the stake and "delivered" from imprisonment and all mortal authorities.

3. THOMAS WOLSEY (1475?–1530), English

When Cardinal Wolsey failed to convince Pope Clement VII to grant Henry VIII of England an annulment of his marriage to Queen Catherine, his fate as a leading statesman was sealed. Enemies at court turned Henry against Wolsey, and he was arrested on November 4, 1530. As the king's soldiers escorted him back to London, Wolsey became ill with dysentery and had to rest at a monastery in Leicester. Upon entering the monastery, he remarked to the abbot, "I am come to lay my bones among you." On the morning of the second day of his illness, Wolsey asked what time it was. When told it was eight o'clock, he said, "That cannot be, for at eight o'clock you will lose your master." The following day, precisely at 8:00 A.M., Wolsey died.

4. DAVID FABRICIUS (1564–1617), German

The astronomer and Protestant minister who discovered the variable star Mira Ceti predicted his death would occur on May 7, 1617. On that gloomy day, he was afraid to go outdoors or see anyone and didn't leave his room. At ten o'clock that night, he laid aside his fear in order to get some fresh air. Once outside, he was attacked and killed by a member of his church whom Fabricius had intended to expose as a thief.

5. SPENCER PERCEVAL (1762–1812), English

The prime minister of Britain from 1809 to 1812, Perceval foresaw his death in a dream he had on the night of May 10, 1812. In the dream he was accosted in the lobby of the House of Commons by a man wearing a dark green coat with brass buttons. The man appeared half-crazy and waved a pistol menacingly toward Perceval. There was a shot and everything went black. The next morning, Perceval told friends and family of his dream and, despite their warnings, left for work as usual. In the lobby of the House of Commons, he was

Joan of Arc predicted her own death
three months before it occurred.

shot and killed by a man wearing a green coat with brass buttons. Ironically, assassin John Bellingham apparently had intended to kill another member of the House of Lords, who had ruled against him in an embezzlement suit. Perceval's murder was a case of mistaken identity.

6. ABRAHAM LINCOLN (1809–1865), U.S.

One evening in 1865, the President was in a particularly melancholy and quiet mood. After much prodding, his wife convinced him to talk about what was bothering him. He spoke philosophically about dreams for a short while, and then mentioned a recent one that continued to disturb him. "Somehow the thing has got possession of me," he said, "and like Banquo's ghost, it will not down." He went on to describe the dream. "There seemed to be a deathlike stillness about me," he said. "Then I suddenly heard subdued sobs as if a number of people were weeping." Determined to find out what was going on, Lincoln wandered from room to room of the White House until he reached the East Room. There he saw a corpse wrapped in funeral vestments, surrounded by mourners. "Who is dead in the White House?" Lincoln demanded. "The President. He was killed by an assassin," came the reply. This was followed by a loud wailing which woke Lincoln from his dream. Only a few days after Lincoln related his dream, he was shot and killed by John Wilkes Booth while attending a play at Ford's Theater.

7. MARK TWAIN (1835–1910), U.S.

America's most beloved humorist was born in 1835 on the same day that Halley's Comet appeared in the sky. Seventy-three years later, in anticipation of the return of the comet, Twain said to his friend and fellow writer A. B. Paine, "I came in with Halley's Comet in 1835. It is coming again next year, and I expect to go out with it. It will be the greatest disappointment of my life if I don't go with Halley's Comet. The Almighty has said, no doubt, 'Now here go those two unaccountable frauds; they came in together, they must go out together.' " Twain was not to be disappointed. Halley's Comet lit up the sky on April 20, 1910, and Twain left with it on the following day.

8. ARNOLD SCHÖNBERG (1874–1951), Austrian

The famous composer was obsessed with the number 13. Born on September 13, he became convinced in later life that he would die during his 76th year, because the numbers 7 and 6 totaled 13. Even worse, July 13 of that year fell on a Friday, a traditional harbinger of bad luck. That day Schönberg remained in bed, firmly believing that his end would come soon. The day passed uneventfully, however, and late that night his wife visited his bedroom to reassure him that he was foolish to have worried. When she entered the room, Schönberg uttered the word *harmony* and died—at exactly 13 minutes before midnight.

9. GROW HUNT (1860–1938), U.S.

A Pennsylvania dairyman, Grow Hunt was known for his antics and his boisterous spirits. Although many stories circulated about him during his lifetime, the most famous tale concerned his foretelling his own death. When Hunt's wife died in 1923, he ordered two monuments made—one for her and one for himself. On his monument he requested that the year of his anticipated death—1938—be inscribed. Although the workman protested, Hunt got his way. Just as he had predicted, Hunt died 15 years later in 1938. He was buried next to his wife in a cemetery in Austinburg, Pa., where the markers still stand.

10. EDGAR CAYCE (1877–1945), U.S.

The well-known prophet and faith healer knew 20 years before his death how he would die. In a dream he had in April, 1926, Cayce saw himself being scalded to death in a tub of hot water. His interpretation of this dream was that one day his body would be immersed in water and that he would die shortly thereafter. The cause of his death was pulmonary edema, which causes fluids to build up in the lungs and results in strangulation. Cayce also predicted the day of his funeral. On New Year's Day, 1945, he said, "I am to be healed on Friday, January 5." It was understood by friends and family that he did not mean a physical healing. He was buried on January 5, 1945. (See Chapter 12, "The 19 Greatest Predictors of All Time," for a full account of Cayce's life and prophecies.)

—K.H.J.

THE 20 STRANGEST METHODS OF PREDICTING THE FUTURE

1. ALEUROMANCY

Divination by predictions written on slips of paper and baked in cakes that are chosen at random by interested persons, like Chinese fortune cookies. This has also survived in the custom of baking a coin or ring in a large cake, which is then divided among guests, one of whom is lucky and finds the gift.

2. AXINOMANCY

Primarily used as a mode of finding a guilty person, this consisted of heating an ax head, setting it upright, placing a marble on it, and turning it slowly until the marble rolled in someone's direction. Treasure can presumably be uncovered by the same procedure. Another way is to suspend a hand ax or hatchet from a string attached to its handle, start it twirling, and see to whom it points when it stops. A third and perhaps the best method is to drive the ax blade into the top of a post and let it waver there, while a group dances around the post. When the ax finally falls, its handle is supposed to point to the culprit if he is still around. If he has gone, it will point to the direction that he took.

3. CATOPTROMANCY OR CATOXTROMANCY

Divination with the aid of a magic mirror. This originated in Persia and spread throughout the ancient world. Two techniques were used: In one, the mirror was suspended in a pool of water; in the other, it was turned to catch the light of the moon. Either way, it showed mysterious reflections revealing future events. This practice increased through the years, reaching its peak during the Middle Ages with such remarkable results that it is highly probable that concave mirrors were used to reflect distorted images or other scenes. However, simple magic mirrors are still used, their surface being painted a glossy black, and some persons who gaze into their depths claim to see visions there.

4. CEPHALOMANCY

A weird and long-obsolete rite of boiling a donkey's head for divinatory purposes.

5. CHALCOMANCY

Divination by striking bowls of copper or brass. The tones this produced were given definite interpretations at the ancient Oracle of Dodona.

6. CROMNIOMANCY

Onions figure in this long-range divinatory process. Names or other significant items are written on different onions, which are planted with due ceremony. Careful check is kept of each, and the first onion that sprouts will represent the person or thing chiefly concerned. A good way to predict next year's election or the winner of a pennant race.

7. DAPHNOMANCY

An ancient Greek divination in which questions of great moment were answered in varying degrees of "yes" or "no" by throwing laurel leaves on a fire. The louder the leaves crackled, the better the omen; the more profound the silence, the worse. Since the laurel had to be plucked from a grove sacred to Apollo and tossed on an equally sacred fire, it is doubtful that the process would work now, even if it did back then.

8. EROMANCY

An Oriental form of divination in which a person covers his head with a cloth and mutters questions above a vase of water. Any stirring of the surface is regarded as a good omen.

9. GELOMANCY

Predictions gained by translating hysterical laughter into tangible terms. Probably a carry-over from the ancient oracles, where persons inhaled natural gas from volcanic fissures and babbled incoherent utterances which gifted listeners interpreted as prophecies that determined the fate of nations. A useful device for political conventions.

10. GYROMANCY

Originally performed by persons moving around a circle marked with letters or symbols, until they became dizzy and stumbled, thus spelling out words or enabling a diviner to interpret the symbols. From this, according to some authorities, developed wild, whirling dances by fanatics who uttered prophecies after collapsing in a state of complete exhaustion. Rolling down the side of a hill can produce a similar state of ecstasy for those who care to try it.

11. MOLYBDOMANCY

Dropping hot lead on a flat surface to divine the future by interpreting the shapes that result. Hot lead may also be dropped in water and conclusions drawn from the hissing sounds.

12. OMPHALOMANCY

Contemplation of one's own navel as a mystical procedure that promises divinatory results. Often recommended in connection with yoga exercises.

13. ONYCHOMANCY

Divination by studying the reflection of bright sunlight upon a person's fingernails and noting any symbols—real or imaginary—that may appear there. These are interpreted in accordance with established rules, as with crystal gazing or teacup reading.

14. PHYLLORHODOMANCY

Clapping rose leaves against the side of the hand and noting the sounds that they make. This trifling pastime was used for divination by the ancient Greeks.

15. SCAPULOMANCY OR SPEALOMANCY

Divination from the markings on the shoulder bone of an animal, particularly a sheep.

16. SCARPOMANCY

A modern method of reading character from a study of a person's old shoes.

17. SPLANCHOMANCY

A form of anthropomancy practiced by the ancient Etruscans, involving predictions gained from a study of the entrails of sacrificial victims.

18. SYCHOMANCY

This consisted of writing names or messages on leaves of a fig tree and letting them dry out. If they dried slowly, it would bode well for whoever or whatever was mentioned; if rapidly, a bad omen. This ancient form of augury can be tested with leaves from sycamores or other trees. There is a modern version involving ivy leaves, which are placed in water for five days and then examined. If still fresh and green, good health should attend the person named thereon, but a spotted, darkened leaf denotes illness or misfortune in proportion to the number of such sinister marks.

19. TIROMANCY OR TYROMANCY

A curious form of divination based upon observation of the coagulation of cheese and its results.

20. XYLOMANCY

Interpreting the forms or appearance of fallen tree branches or other wood seen on the ground; also the positions of logs burning in a fire. If a log falls suddenly, a surprise is due.

SOURCE: From *The Complete Illustrated Book of Divination and Prophecy* by Walter Gibson. Copyright © 1973 by Walter B. Gibson. Reprinted by permission of Doubleday & Company, Inc.

PREDICTION ODDS AND ENDS

1. AN EAR TO THE GROUND

On February 8, 1971, Mrs. Ginger Hainsworth was sitting at home in Anaheim, Calif., when she heard seven loud beeps in her left ear. She ignored the strange experience and went to bed. The next morning a massive earthquake rocked southern California. Since 1971, Mrs. Hainsworth has had additional experiences in which she has heard beeps prior to earthquakes in various parts of the world. She also had premonitory dreams a week before California's Sylmar quake, a few days before a major quake in Spain, and a few days prior to the Nicaragua catastrophe. Her premonitory dreams extend back to 1941 when, six months before the Pearl Harbor attack, she had a vivid nightmare about the Japanese. With regard to her gifts, Mrs. Hainsworth says, "I hope some day I may be able to tell the world exactly where the earthquakes will be. But as of now, only our Lord Jesus and God know the answer."

2. THE DOOM OF THE SEAFORTHS

Coinneach (Kenneth) Odhar, known as the Brahan Seer, was a 17th-century Scottish mystic with the gift of second sight. At the height of his fame he was consulted by the Countess of Seaforth, who had become alarmed over her husband's long-delayed return from Paris. Odhar looked into his divining stone and said with a smile that Lord Seaforth was "well and merry." When the countess pressed him for details, he divulged that his lordship was in the company of a beautiful woman. Enraged, Lady Seaforth accused Odhar of slander and ordered his execution. Before his death, he foretold the fate of the Seaforth family. He predicted that the future of the Seaforths held "extinction and sorrow." The last head of the household would

Mrs. Ginger Hainsworth is warned of
major earthquakes by beeps in her left ear.

witness the death of all his sons before he himself died, deaf and
dumb, and the estate would pass into the hands of "a white-hooded
lassie from the East," who would kill her sister. All that the seer
predicted eventually came to pass. The last male heir to the Seaforth
estate was Francis Humbertson Mackenzie, who became deaf after a
childhood bout of scarlet fever. By the time of his death in 1815, he
had seen his four sons die and had become completely mute. The
estate passed into the hands of his eldest daughter, Lady Hood, who
had returned from India (the East) white-hooded—the traditional
sign of mourning—due to the recent death of her husband. A few
years later, the carriage she was driving overturned, mortally injuring her younger sister. Although it had taken nearly two centuries,
the prophecy was finally fulfilled.

3. A PROPHETIC SELF-PORTRAIT

In 1938 Victor Brauner, an expatriate Romanian surrealist, was in
the company of two friends in Paris. An argument erupted between
his companions, and when one threw a glass at the other, Brauner

was caught in the crossfire. The broken edge of the glass struck Brauner in the face and gouged out his eye. Although two operations were performed to replace it, they were unsuccessful. For Brauner, the incident was almost a relief. Seven years earlier he had painted a self-portrait in which his eye dangled from its socket, and this portrayal was followed by a series of paintings in which he depicted partial or total blindness. Friends said that the actual accident seemed to free him from his obsession, and in the ensuing years his career soared.

4. THE POLISH VISIONARY

Recognized as one of Poland's three great romantic poets, Juliusz Slowacki considered himself a prophet and a spiritual leader of his nation. Slowacki often had prophetic dreams and visions. On August 16, 1831, while living in England, he was awakened by a frightening dream in which he was caught in the midst of riots. He learned later that political riots had broken out in Warsaw on August 15 and 16. In 1848 Slowacki wrote a visionary poem which predicted that a new Slavic pope would be elected who would have a beneficial influence on the world. Slowacki's vision was realized 130 years later when, in 1978, John Paul II was elected pope. He was the first non-Italian pope since 1522 and the first pope to come from Poland.

5. THE MONEY-MAKING "BROWNIES"

Arthur Stilwell, a wealthy financier and railroad builder, attributed his success to the "brownies," or "spirits" who had been speaking to him since he was 15. These voices urged Stilwell to build railroads and told him where to place the lines and where to develop towns. While constructing an important line that was to link Kansas City with the Gulf of Mexico in the late 1890s, Stilwell listened to his "brownies" when they told him to avoid ending the line in Galveston. Stilwell instead terminated his railroad at a desolate spot in Texas which was named Port Arthur in his honor. When a hurricane later devastated Galveston, Stilwell was more than grateful for the sound advice of his "brownies." The voices guided him in other ways, too. Four years before he married, they told him the name of his future wife, and they also dictated some 30 books to him. In one of those books, he revealed that in 1910, four years before World War I, his "brownies" had told him of a "Great War" that would "deplete" the world.

6. THE PATRICIA HEARST PARALLEL

In 1972 a small publishing company in California issued a sex novel called *Black Abductor*. Its plot was uncannily similar to the events in the Patricia Hearst kidnapping case two years later. In the novel, a young college student named Patricia, the daughter of a wealthy and prominent family, is kidnapped while she is with her boyfriend. Her kidnappers are a multiracial revolutionary group led by an embittered black man. At first she resists her abductors but eventually joins their group. The novel at times appears to be a near blueprint for the Hearst kidnapping, although there are important divergences. For example, the novel has no daring bank robbery. Still, the similarities appeared striking enough to have provoked the FBI's curiosity. The author, who writes under the pseudonym Harrison James, reportedly was amazed that his novel had foretold so accurately the Hearst kidnapping.

7. THE ILLITERATE "DOC"

Arthur Roberts, known as "Doc" to his clients, gained a reputation as a psychic detective in Milwaukee. In one of Wisconsin's famous murder cases, Roberts predicted that the suspect, Erdman Olson, would never be found alive. Olson was never found. In 1935 Roberts astounded Milwaukee residents when he predicted that two banks, a city hall, and an unknown number of police stations would all be blown up. In addition, there would be a big "blow-up" south of the Menomonee River on November 4. Following that, the explosions would cease. Alerted by Roberts, the police took extra precautions. Eight days after his warning, the bombings began to occur. A village hall, two banks, and two police stations exploded, just as "Doc" Roberts had foretold. On November 4, the Menomonee district of Milwaukee was jarred by the sixth and final explosion. The two young men responsible for the bombings were working on their last bomb when it accidentally detonated and killed them. Although his psychic successes continued, Roberts remained illiterate until his death in 1940. He believed that education might ruin his special abilities.

8. HITLER'S SENSE OF DESTINY

Adolf Hitler was a soldier in the German army during World War I. One night in 1915, while he was eating dinner in a trench, he heard a voice telling him to move to another area. He duly moved 20 yd. away, responding to the voice as if it were a military order. Immediately afterward, a stray shell hit the part of the trench that he had just left and killed everyone sitting there. This incident enhanced his sense of destiny. A few weeks later, the future führer predicted to his comrades, "You will hear much about me. Just wait until my time comes."

—F.B. and L.L.L.

16

PROPHETS OF DOOM

MARCHING TOWARD DOOMSDAY

YEAR AND PROPHET

992-BERNARD OF THURINGIA

In 960 Bernard, a visionary in the former German state of Thuringia, announced that the world would end on the day the Annunciation of the Virgin coincided with Good Friday. This was to occur in 992. His prophecy was the cause of great alarm throughout Europe.

DECEMBER 31, 999—THE APOCRYPHA

Historically we are led to believe that the year 1000 was greeted with great panic because the Apocrypha had prophesied that the Last Judgment would occur 1,000 years after the birth of Christ. Legend has it that thousands journeyed to Jerusalem to await the coming of Jesus. Reportedly, homes and jobs were neglected and every phenomenon of nature was greeted with terror. Today we are told that the first published account of these incidents did not appear until 700 years later, and historians Jacques Barzun and Henry F. Graff have called the panic story a phony. They say that the year 1000 sounds impressive but in the Middle Ages people used Roman numerals. The year would simply have been "M" with no magic property attached to it. Furthermore, numerical dates had little meaning for medieval people. Their lives were guided by the feast and fast days of the Church, not calendars. It is believed that the myth concerning the year 1000 was largely created during the 18th century by such writers as Voltaire and Gibbon. Wishing to discredit the Middle Ages, many writers exaggerated the superstitious and credulous nature of medieval Christians.

SEPTEMBER, 1186—JOHN OF TOLEDO

In 1179 astronomer and astrologer John of Toledo calculated that a major calamity would occur in September of 1186. All the planets would unite under the sign of the Scales (Libra) and the result would be terrible storms and earthquakes. His prediction made a great impression throughout Europe and Asia. People in Germany began to dig shelters, while those in Mesopotamia and Persia readied their cellars for occupation. The Byzantine emperor had all the windows of his palace boarded over, and in England the Archbishop of Canterbury declared a national fast of atonement. Astronomically, John was correct in his prediction, but the catastrophes failed to materialize. John of Toledo later announced that his prophecy was meant to be symbolic of the Hunnish invasion and so had actually been correct.

FEBRUARY 1, 1524—ASTROLOGERS

In June of 1523 a group of London astrologers concurred that the end of the world would begin with the destruction of London by a deluge on February 1, 1524. Because so many astrologers agreed with this prediction, people accepted it as fact. By the middle of January, at least 20,000 had left their London homes for the higher ground of Kent and Essex. The prior of St. Bartholomew's even went so far as to build a fortress at Harrow-on-the-Hill and stock it with a two-month supply of food. February 1 arrived and nothing happened. The next day astrologers reexamined their figures and discovered a tiny error in their calculations. It was in 1624—not 1524—that the world was to end.

FEBRUARY 20, 1524 AND 1528
—JOHANNES STOEFFLER

"The world will end by a giant flood on February 20, 1524." So said German astrologer and mathematician Johannes Stoeffler (1452–1531) in 1499. A faculty member at Tübingen University and adviser to royalty, Stoeffler was regarded as a believable source. As 1524 drew near, more and more people began to prepare for the disaster by building boats. Among those seeking refuge on the Rhine was the Count von Iggleheim, who had ordered a three-story ark constructed for his family. When it began to rain on February 20, the crowd on the docks became panicky and attempted to board the huge ark. Drawing his sword, the count tried to defend his domain. He managed to kill one of the intruders before being trampled to death by the stampeding mob. Before the day was over, hundreds had been killed fighting to reach the supposed safety of the craft. Although the world hadn't ended, the violence of the storm had made it a close call, thereby greatly enhancing Stoeffler's reputation as a seer. However, when Stoeffler again predicted the end of the world, this time for 1528, very few people paid any attention to him.

1533—MELCHIOR HOFMANN

Famous Anabaptist leader Melchior Hofmann (1495–1543) taught his followers that in 1533 Christ would return to earth. He said that at this time the world would be consumed by fire but the kingdom of righteousness would prevail in Strasbourg, which would become the New Jerusalem. From there the true gospel and true baptism would spread over the earth. His followers believed him, and many sold or gave away all of their possessions. They renounced the worldly life and dedicated themselves to self-sacrificing devotion. When 1534 arrived and there was no Second Coming, the Anabaptists, undaunted, increased their efforts to convert the world.

OCTOBER 18, 1533—MICHAEL STIFEL

German monk and mathematician Michael Stifel (1487–1567) calculated that according to the Book of Revelation, doomsday would occur October 18, 1533. When his prophecy did not prove correct, Stifel was given a sound thrashing by the townspeople of Lochau.

1665—SOLOMON ECCLES

In 1665 London experienced the last large outbreak of the Black Plague. With hundreds dying every day, it was not difficult for people to believe that the end of the world was at hand. Solomon Eccles, a Quaker prophet, entered St. Mary's Church in Aldermanbury during one Sunday service. Dressed only in a goatskin loincloth and balancing a chafing dish filled with burning coals on his head, Eccles ran down the center aisle crying out that all should repent because the end of the world was near. He led the worshipers from the church to an enormous pit that was filled with the bodies of plague victims. Again he called for repentance. During the following weeks he roamed London, spreading his tale of impending doom. People believed him, and many of his followers also had visions of the approaching end. Finally Eccles was arrested and the hysteria abated. Eventually he followed George Fox, founder of the Quakers, to the West Indies. Soon Eccles was inciting the black slaves to riot with his stories of doom. For this he was shipped back to England, where he died three years later.

MAY 19, 1719—JACQUES BERNOULLI

The fear of comets has been with humans throughout history. In his *Treatise upon the Comet,* Jacques Bernoulli (1654–1705), an eminent Swiss mathematician, predicted that the comet of 1680 would return with a terrible crash on May 19, 1719. He said that the head of the comet would not be dangerous but that the tail would be an infallible sign of the wrath of heaven.

OCTOBER 13, 1736—WILLIAM WHISTON

William Whiston (1667–1752), the famous English divine and mathematician, announced in 1736 that "the beginning of the end" was to be the destruction of London on October 13. Hundreds of panic-stricken Londoners headed for high places to escape the predicted deluge. Hampstead Heath and Islington Fields were jam-packed, but instead of the expected day of disaster, it turned out to be a day of rejoicing for believers and a field day for pickpockets.

APRIL 5, 1761—WILLIAM BELL

On February 8, 1761, London was rocked by an earthquake, and on March 8 another severe tremor rumbled through the capital. A soldier in the Life Guards—William Bell by name—noted that exactly four weeks had elapsed between the two quakes. Subsequently Bell made dozens of speeches throughout the town predicting the complete destruction of the world 28 days later, on April 5. Panic spread quickly. As the dreaded day approached, Londoners left in droves for outlying villages, where exorbitant prices were charged by villagers eager to take advantage of the mass hysteria. Many people anticipated a flood, so all of the boats on the Thames were filled to capacity. Nothing happened. On the following day, Bell was seized and thrown into Bedlam, London's notorious madhouse.

1806—AN EGG

In the autumn of 1806, a tavern in Leeds, England, was the sight of an unusual occurrence. Mary Bateman's hen began laying eggs inscribed with the words "Christ Is Coming." Curious crowds gathered and Mary told them that God had revealed to her that the hen would lay 14 such eggs and then the world would come to a fiery end. Even as she spoke, the hen laid another egg, causing great pandemonium among those present. Mary announced that there was hope of salvation but it would cost everyone a penny to hear it. Everyone paid. She then explained that God would allow those bearing a piece of paper sealed with the inscription "J. C." entry into heaven immediately after the last egg appeared. The price for such a paper was a shilling. Almost everyone paid. As each new egg was laid, news spread to other communities and thousands came to the tavern in Leeds to get "sealed." By now the town officials were curious about the recent events. On the day the last egg was to be laid, they went to the tavern. Bursting in, they surprised Mary just as she was inserting an inscribed egg into the egg duct of an angry hen, and arrested her. After her release, Mary continued to prophesy, but eventually she was convicted as an abortionist and hanged.

OCTOBER 19, 1814—JOANNA SOUTHCOTT

The daughter of an English farmer, Joanna Southcott (1750–1814)

began to write rhymed prophecies when she was 42. She developed a following and in 1802 opened a chapel in London. When she was 64 years old, she announced that a voice had spoken to her and said that on October 19, 1814, she would bear a divine child known as the Shiloh who would be the Second Messiah. This event was to mark the end of the world. Joanna was examined by 21 doctors and, impossible as it seemed, 17 agreed that she was indeed pregnant. Upon hearing the verdict, people congregated in Manchester Street, where Joanna lived, to await the messiah's birth. They kept a long vigil, and many collapsed from exhaustion. Three people died. As it turned out, Joanna was not pregnant but desperately ill. She died 10 days after the date set for the messianic birth. Greatly disappointed, the crowds slowly dispersed to their homes.

MARCH 17, 1842—DR. JOHN DEE

Hundreds of people believed that the famous Elizabethan astrologer Dr. John Dee (1527–1608) had predicted that St. Patrick's Day in 1842 would mark the end of Europe. This belief was based on a poem written by Dee in 1598 which allegedly was in the Harleian Museum. Although only the "uneducated classes" believed Dee's prophecy, hundreds of people took to their boats in order to be on the safe side. Only later was it revealed that no such prophecy or manuscript could be found in the museum. (See Chapter 12, "The 18 Greatest Predictors of All Time.")

APRIL 3 AND JULY 7, 1843, AND MARCH 21 AND OCTOBER 22, 1844—WILLIAM MILLER

(See "The Millerites," which follows this chronology.)

1866—REV. ETHAN SMITH

In his *Dissertation on the Prophecies Related to Antichrist and the Last Times* (1811), Reverend Smith of Poultney, Vt., concluded that the world was due to end in 1866. He felt that with heresy rife throughout the U.S. and dire events occurring in Europe, the world was experiencing its "last days" preceding the return of Christ to earth.

1881, 1936, AND 1953—THE GREAT PYRAMID

According to early experts who interpreted the measurements of the Great Pyramid of Cheops, the Second Coming and the Day of Judgment should have occurred in 1881. Later experts set 1936 as the fateful year. When these experts were also proved wrong, 1953 was chosen as the date for the end of man. (See Chapter 12, "The 18 Greatest Predictors of All Time.")

NOVEMBER 13, 1900— THE BROTHERS AND SISTERS OF RED DEATH

In czarist Russia, a district called Kargopol (about 400 mi. from

St. Petersburg, now Leningrad) contained a 200-year-old sect which called itself the Brothers and Sisters of Red Death. They shared some provocative ideas. Marriage was forbidden but sexual intercourse was allowed, providing the sinners immediately submitted themselves to suffocation with a large red cushion. Believing that the world was due to end November 13 (November 1 Old Style), 862 members thought it would please God if they sacrificed themselves by being burned to death. When news of this plan reached St. Petersburg, troops were rushed to Kargopol. They were too late. More than 100 members had already perished. When the appointed day passed without catastrophe, the sect disbanded.

OCTOBER, 1908—LEE T. SPANGLER

Remembering a prediction he had made after coming out of a trance at the age of 12, Lee T. Spangler announced that the world would end in fire during October of 1908. Spangler, a grocery store owner from York, Pa., convinced a number of people with his prophecy. However, the only thing that fell on York in October was a light rain, on the last day of the month.

1910—THE PRESS

In 1910 some scientists made the announcement that the world would pass through the tail of Halley's Comet. The press began to print dire predictions about poisonous gases asphyxiating all life on earth. In Sydney, Australia, people were warned to remain indoors on the day that the earth would be enveloped in the tail of the comet.

DECEMBER 17, 1919—ALBERT PORTA

Born in Italy, Albert Porta emigrated to the U.S. in 1875. An expert seismographer and meteorologist, Porta settled in San Francisco and published regular weather forecasts in a small Italian newspaper. Due to his accurate predictions of several earthquakes, he began to receive worldwide attention. Therefore, people sat up and took notice when he announced that on December 17, 1919, there would occur a conjunction of six planets. This would result in a magnetic current that would pierce the sun, cause great explosions of flaming gas, and eventually engulf the earth. There was widespread alarm. Weather stations were besieged with calls and a statement was issued which said that while there would be such a planetary conjunction, it would not be dangerous. As December 17 approached, suicides and hysteria were reported throughout the world. The fatal day arrived and all the planets aligned, but the world still remained. Porta returned to predicting the weather.

FEBRUARY 13, 1925, AND OCTOBER 10, 1932—ROBERT REIDT

A young Los Angeles, Ca. girl named Margaret Rowan announced that the Archangel Gabriel had told her that the end of the world would take place at midnight on Friday, February 13, 1925.

This intelligence was seized upon by Robert Reidt, a Freeport, Long Island, house painter. He immediately placed large advertisements in New York newspapers summoning the faithful to join him on a hilltop at the hour of doom. His followers—all dressed in white muslin robes—gathered on the hilltop and waited, and exactly at midnight they threw up their hands and chanted, "Gabriel! Gabriel! Gabriel!" Nothing happened. Reidt announced that the hour of doom was to be on Pacific rather than Eastern Standard time, so there were three hours yet to wait. When nothing happened at 3:00 A.M., Reidt turned on the press, blaming the news photographers' flashbulbs for the failure. Seven years later, after Reidt had immersed himself in the Book of Revelation, he came up with a revised doomsday date. Quoting from the Second Epistle of Peter, Reidt thundered, "Before the year is out 'the heavens shall pass away with a great noise, the elements shall melt with fervent heat, the earth also and the works that are therein shall be burned up.'" Joined by his revived followers, Reidt awaited October 10, 1932, which was to be the day of disintegration. But the target day came and went without noise, heat, or burning. Reidt got the message and permanently retired from doomsdaying.

1931—THE PROPHETICAL SOCIETY OF DALLAS

The year set for the end of the world by the Prophetical Society in Dallas, Tex., was 1931. Believers, however, were disappointed.

AUGUST, 1944—MUNOZ FERRADAS

Much of South America was thrown into a panic by Munoz Ferradas, a Chilean astronomer, who said that in August, 1944, a comet would collide with the earth and all life would come to an end. Many people were terror-stricken and sold their homes. Several committed suicide. Drinking increased dramatically and sexual orgies and murders were the result. Many people went off to hide in the mountains, refusing to return until at least a month had passed after the predicted date of destruction.

SEPTEMBER 21, 1945—REV. CHARLES LONG

It was the middle of the night in 1938 when Reverend Long was mysteriously awakened in his Pasadena, Calif., home. At the foot of his bed he saw a blackboard on which a ghostly hand wrote 1945. A voice later whispered that the world would end at 5:33 P.M. on September 21 of that year. Reverend Long felt duty-bound to spread the news about the coming destruction. He wrote a 70,000-word tract outlining how, on the fatal day, the earth would be vaporized and all human beings would be turned into ectoplasm. He mailed copies to the world's major leaders. Long also rented the Pasadena Civic Auditorium, where his son held meetings during which he urged members of the audience to repent and be baptized. Together they impressed a number of people and developed a following. Seven days before doomsday the Longs and their followers gave up food, drink, and sleep . . . presumably forever. They sang and prayed fervently during the last hours, but nothing happened. The group eventually disbanded.

JANUARY 9, 1954—AGNES GRACE CARLSON

The Children of Light was a Canadian religious sect based at a farm near Keremeos, about 30 mi. from Vancouver. Their leader, Mrs. Agnes Grace Carlson, announced on December 26, 1953, that the end of the world would come the following January 9. She collected 35 faithful converts, including 8 children, in a farmhouse and awaited the final day. They passed their 17-day vigil by singing hymns and sitting in awed silence while Mrs. Carlson sought inspiration. Meanwhile, the local school had obtained summonses under the School Attendance Act, and when the local sheriff called to serve them, the farmhouse congregation quickly dispersed.

MAY 24, 1954—ITALIAN PROVERB

An Italian adage that "Rome and the world are safe, so long as the Colosseum stands" brought mass hysteria to Italy in 1954. On May 18, engineers were alarmed when huge cracks appeared in the 1,800-year-old amphitheater. Someone suggested it was a "sign" and set the day of destruction for Monday, May 24. Thousands besieged the Vatican, hoping that the pope would absolve them from their sins. Despite a sharp rebuke from a Vatican prelate, who added, "The world will see Tuesday and more Tuesdays to come," thousands appeared in St. Peter's Square on May 24. The prelate was proved right, and builders were sent to repair the Colosseum.

JUNE 28, 1954—HECTOR COX

For many years Hector Cox had been one of London's best-known and most colorful talkers at the famous Speaker's Corner in Hyde Park. His main topics were the truths he had discovered in the Egyptian *Book of the Dead*. On Sunday, June 27, he startled his audience by announcing that the world would end within 24 hours. For Cox, his prophecy proved right; the following day he was found dead. Police ruled out foul play, although a knife had been plunged into his heart.

DECEMBER 20, 1954—DR. CHARLES LAUGHEAD

Forty-four-year-old Dr. Charles Laughead, a Michigan State College physician, was a much-respected, down-to-earth professional man. It was a surprise to all who knew him when he suddenly became a doomsday prophet. This transformation was largely due to the influence of medium Dorothy Martin. Dr. Laughead claimed that with Mrs. Martin's help, he had had communications with a cosmic civilization. These voices told him that there would be worldwide upheaval. America's Atlantic Coast would submerge and France, England, and Russia would become big seas. The date set for these events was December 20, 1954. As the time approached, Dr. Laughead and his followers had all-night sessions with Mrs. Martin. They learned from cosmic voices that a spaceship would land and pick them up, and they would be saved. Everyone anxiously awaited the ship, but in vain. The next morning, Dr. Laughead announced to the press that "God had stopped it all." The doctor's relatives tried to have him committed to a mental institution, but a court ruled that even though he had "unusual ideas" he was not mentally ill.

JULY 14, 1960—ELIO BIANCO

The Community of the White Mountain was a 40-member-strong sect led by Elio Bianco, a 46-year-old Italian pediatrician. He claimed that in 1958 his sister Wilma, since deceased, had warned him that at exactly 1:45 P.M. on July 14, 1960, an accidental thermonuclear explosion of the secret American "E" bomb would destroy the world. Bianco kindly informed the press and then, with the help of his 40 followers, proceeded to build a 15-room ark 7,000 ft. up Mont Blanc. The appointed hour came and passed safely. At 1:58 P.M., Dr. Bianco issued a statement: "Anyone can make a mistake. Be happy that I have. Our faith has not collapsed because of that." Bianco was later charged by police with spreading false reports.

FEBRUARY 2, 1962—HINDU ASTROLOGERS

For the first time in four centuries, eight planets were due to line up in a spectacular planetary conjunction as they entered the House of Capricorn. This was to happen on February 2, 1962, between 12:05 and 12:15 P.M. Indian astrologers regarded this as a terrible portent signifying the end of the world. Although Prime Minister Jawaharlal Nehru described the whole affair as "a matter of laughter," throughout the whole subcontinent millions gathered in nonstop prayer meetings in hopes of calming the anger of the gods. In one marathon invoking Chandi Path, the goddess of power, 1½ tons of pure butter and thousands of marigolds were burned. The Hindu liturgy was intoned 4,800,000 times by a relay of 250 priests. U Nu, the prime minister of Burma, released 3 bullocks, 3 pigs, 9 goats, 60 hens, 60 ducks, 120 doves, 120 fish, and 218 crabs in the hope of averting the evil forces. Millions waited, and when the hour of doom passed they all gave thanks that their prayers had been answered.

APRIL 18, 1965—A COLOMBIAN PREACHER

A Colombian preacher in Bogotá warned his congregation that the world was about to explode on April 18, 1965. One faithful believer, Nelson Olmeido, spent his life's savings in one almighty spree. When April 18 passed without incident, he sued the preacher.

DECEMBER 25, 1967—ANDERS JENSEN

On *The David Frost Show*, in front of millions of TV viewers, Anders Jensen, the Danish leader of the Disciples of Orthon, predicted Christmas Day would mark the Apocalypse. The sect chose a field near Copenhagen to build an underground bunker with a 20-ton lead roof to see them through the danger period. Fifty disciples spent Christmas Day underground. The expected nuclear explosion failed to happen. One by one the disciples reappeared from their shelter and were applauded by delighted sightseers. Jensen said, "We expected to see ash covering the ground, a red glow in the sky, and everything destroyed. It's all a bit disappointing, but we are confident there is a simple explanation." The disciples later sold the bunker at a profit.

FEBRUARY 20 AND MARCH 17, 1969—MARIA STAFFLER

Self-appointed "Popess" Maria Staffler told her subjects that the world would suffer a disaster on February 20, 1969. She invited the faithful to follow her to the safety of a mountaintop. When only a few showed up, Maria shrewdly moved the date to March 17. On that day a few more of the faithful appeared and waited with Maria inside a specially built hut. When nothing catastrophic happened, the people became restless. They were told, "Wait for one hour." The hour passed, and still all was peaceful. This time everyone left and the hut was demolished.

1970—TRUE LIGHT CHURCH OF CHRIST

Based on Bible interpretation and study, the leaders of the True Light Church of Christ in Charlotte, N.C., prophesied that the world would end in 1970. They adhered to the traditional belief that the world would end 6,000 years from the time of creation. They placed creation at 4000 B.C. and reasoned that 30 years were lost from the first century of the Christian calendar. In anticipation of the end, 17 True Lights resigned their jobs. The members were shocked and surprised when their prediction failed to come true. However, they said that the failure of this prophecy did not cause them to doubt other church doctrine.

SEPTEMBER, 1975—VIOLA WALKER

In September of 1975, Mrs. Viola Walker of Grannis, Ark.—then 67 years old—announced to her relatives that she had received a message from God. The Second Coming and the end of the world were close at hand. Exactly 21 kinfolk joined Mrs. Walker in a vigil which took place in a three-bedroom house. They stopped paying bills and took their children out of school. The vigil lasted 10 months and was not brought to an end until July 16, 1976, when two deputy marshals went to the house. Everyone was evicted because the bank had foreclosed on the vigil-house's mortgage. A spokesman for the group said that they would now continue the vigil in their hearts and that their faith was not shaken.

1978 AND 1979—JOHN STRONG

In his book *The Doomsday Globe* (1973), John Strong, a businessman from Melbourne, Australia, predicted a nuclear attack by the Soviet Union. He based his prophecy on parts of the Bible and his own calculations on the size of the great pyramids in Egypt. In preparation, Strong and 70 followers constructed a "doomsday city" where they planned to wait out the attack. Strong reasoned that the fateful day would fall sometime in October, 1978. If the attack did not occur on October 2, it would be either on October 15 or October 31. In any event, the world would certainly be destroyed by September 23, 1979.

1980—LELAND JENSEN AND CHARLES GAINES

Originally scheduled for April 29 at 5:55 P.M., the end of the world was postponed until the early morning hours of May 7 by cultists Leland Jensen and Charles Gaines. Leaders of a splinter sect of the Baha'i faith (which officially disclaims them), the two men said that revised calculations—based on the *Book of Revelation* and the Great Pyramid in Giza—clearly indicated that World War III would break out on May 7. Sect members in the Rocky Mountains—from Missoula, Mont. to Durango, Colo.—stocked their fallout shelters in preparation for the inevitable. Asked how he reacted to being scoffed at for his dire prediction of nuclear holocaust, Gaines replied, "They laughed at Noah."

1998—PROPHETS

Christ died in the 1,998th week of his life, according to some prophets, who have chosen this year as the fateful one.

1999—CRISWELL

Criswell, a psychic prophet, claims that a black rainbow (a magnetic disturbance) will suck the oxygen off the earth in 1999. Then the planet will race into the sun, incinerating everyone and everything.

2000—JEANNE LE ROYER

A lay sister in a convent in Brittany, Jeanne Le Royer (1732–1798) foresaw wars, earthquakes, and social upheavals before the coming of the Antichrist. She predicted the end would come about the year 2000, following the end of the papacy.

MAY 5, 2000—STELLE GROUP

In 1973 a group of people began building the small town of Stelle in the middle of a cornfield 100 mi. southwest of Chicago, Ill. About 800 people have lived there for varying periods of time. They all were drawn to Stelle after reading *The Ultimate Frontier* (1963) by Richard Kieninger, the group's spiritual leader. He claims that a secret ancient organization chose him to establish a community in Illinois and lead its members to the Kingdom of God in the Pacific. The group believes that on May 5 in the year 2000 tidal waves, earthquakes, floods, and volcanoes will destroy the world. It plans to survive by building lighter-than-air vehicles which would float above the turmoil and land them safely in a new city in the Pacific called Philadelphia. The Stelle group concentrates its efforts on technology, feeling that therein lies survival. The members are strongly family-oriented, and the traditional male and female roles are strictly observed. Negative influences, such as violence, are carefully screened out of the community. In 1975 they expelled Mr. Kieninger on charges of womanizing. He is now setting up another community near Dallas, Tex., but visits Stelle once a month.

APRIL 25, 2038—NOSTRADAMUS

The famous French prophet and astrologer Nostradamus (1503–1566) predicted that the world would end when Easter fell on April 25. So far this has happened in 1666, 1734, 1886, and 1943. It will occur again in 2038. (See Chapter 12, "The 18 Greatest Predictors of All Time.")

3936—ST. VINCENT FERRER

In 1399 St. Vincent Ferrer (1350–1419), a Spanish Dominican monk, said that the world would end in another 2,537 years. He based his prediction on the number of verses in the Book of Psalms.

—A.T. and J.B.

THE MILLERITES—

October 22, 1844—the last possible day on which the world could end and Christ appear again, according to William Miller—was over-

William Miller—Prophet of Doom.

cast and windy. Believers—the Second Adventists, sometimes called Millerites—gathered by the thousands on hilltops in New England, many in the crotches of trees, so that they would be closer to heaven when it came time to leap into the hereafter to enjoy eternal life while the sinners fried in hell. Some, it was said, carried umbrellas, laundry baskets, and washtubs to facilitate rising. A group of Philadelphia ladies waited in a group apart, not wanting to ascend with the common herd.

Stories of that Awful Last Day range from the horrifying to the amusing, while many have proved to be untrue. It was said that the believers wore white ascension robes; that two children, neglected in the fervor of coming redemption, died of exposure; that a Chicago woman tied herself to a trunkful of new clothes so that she would be fashionable in heaven. And it was told that a farmer brought his cows, also in white robes, so that the children would have milk on the trip. And that a man in Worcester, Mass., put on turkey wings, climbed a tree, flapped, and fell. He broke his arm. A Philadelphian who flew from a third-story window was not so lucky.

All night they waited. Morning came. The world was still there. Miller, who had kept vigil at his home, wept.

They called it The Disappointment.

It was amazing that an old, palsied, stammering prophet could have aroused such hysteria among so many people—1 in every 85 Americans, according to one estimate. True, the zeitgeist of the time favored such movements, and several other prophets had also predicted the Second Coming. However, none attracted and held people in such large numbers as did Miller. Perhaps it was because he believed in the prophecy with all his heart.

It was a long road to that prophecy. Born in 1782, William Miller grew up in Low Hampton, N.Y., the oldest of 16 children. Though inclined to be bookish, he received only a minimal frontier education. In 1803 he married and settled in Poultney, Vt., where—influenced by the works of Thomas Paine, David Hume, and Voltaire, all available at the town library—he became a Deist.

After serving in the army as a captain during the War of 1812, he came home "completely disgusted with man's public character." Perhaps he was suffering from postwar ennui, for he said that it appeared to him "that there was nothing good on earth ... the heavens were as brass over my head, and the earth as iron under my feet ... I was truly wretched and did not understand the cause." It was the kind of emptiness from which religious conversion naturally arises. In 1816, Miller became a fervent Baptist. The ridicule of his Deist friends drove him to the Bible for counterarguments. Intrigued by its prophetic passages, he reached the conclusion that Christ would return to earth about 1843. For 15 years he studied the Bible to back up his prophecy, following his "Rules of Interpretation," in which biblical words were to be taken as standing for something else. For instance, to Miller the word *mountains* stood for governments, and *day* stood for year. Arithmetic led him to the year 1843 in four separate exercises using Bible verses. For example, Daniel 8:13–14 states, in answer to a question about how long the "vision" concerning the transgression of desolation was to be: "For 2,300 evenings and mornings; then the holy place will be properly restored." Assuming that the desolation began in 457 B.C., when Ezra was ordered to rebuild Jerusalem, and that an "evening and morning" was really a year, Miller came up with:

2,300 "evenings and mornings,"   2,300 years
Minus year Ezra was ordered to rebuild

$$-457 \text{ B.C.}$$
$$\overline{1843 \text{ A.D.}}$$

After hearing a voice say, "Go and tell it to the world," Miller started preaching. His dictum, "If you wish people *to feel, feel yourself*," may have been partially responsible for his enormous appeal. Or it may have been his "strong, mellow voice" with its "northern-antique pronunciation." Or his blue eyes that beamed "shrewdness and love." He spoke of "last trumpet sounds" and the bursting of the bowels of the earth. He envisioned the parting of clouds to reveal the throne on which God sat. He warned of "the horrid yells of the damned spirits."

In 1833 a magnificent meteor shower recalled to many doubters the prophecy in Revelation that after "the stars of heaven fell unto the earth," the heavens would roll up like a giant scroll. Doubters started believing.

The Reverend Joshua V. Himes, a talented organizer and public relations man, joined Miller in 1839. Newspapers—*Signs of the Times, The Midnight Cry,* and others—were started.

In 1842, 30 camp meetings—with attendance numbering in the thousands—were held in various locations in the East and Midwest. Poet John Greenleaf Whittier described the ". . . white circle of tents; the dim wood arches; the upturned earnest faces; the loud voices of the speakers, burdened with the awful symbolic language of the Bible. The smoke from the fires, rising like incense from forest altars . . . ." Two canvas sheets, he said, were used to illustrate lectures. On one ". . . was the figure of a man, the head of gold, the breast and arms of silver, the belly of brass, the legs of iron, and the feet of clay—the dream of Nebuchadnezzar. On the other were depicted the wonders of the Apocalyptic vision—the beasts, the dragons, the scarlet woman . . . mystic symbols, translated into staring Yankee realities, and exhibited like beasts of a traveling menagerie."

On January 1, 1843, Miller published a synopsis of his prediction, saying the end would come sometime between March 21, 1843, and March 21, 1844, according to the ancient Jewish calendar. Various dates in that interval were seized upon as Judgment Day. They came and went quietly, although once an ominous comet streaked across the sky. And finally March 21, 1844, arrived—without the Second Coming. Scoffers teased believers: "What! Not gone up yet? We thought you'd gone up! Aren't you going up soon? Wife didn't go up and leave you behind to burn, did she?"

Now Miller changed the date to October 22, 1844. Hysteria grew. There were stories of insanities, killings, suicides; of people crawling with others on their backs to represent Christ entering Jerusalem on the back of an ass; of merchants giving their stock away; of farmers leaving crops to rot in the fields.

The scoffers called Miller "the end-of-the-world man." Hoaxers blew trumpets outside Millerite meetings.

On the Great Day, a Millerite saw Ralph Waldo Emerson and Theodore Parker out walking. They were quite calm. When the Millerite asked whether they realized that the end of the world was coming, Parker replied, "It doesn't much concern me. I live in Boston."

Emerson added, "The end of the world doesn't bother me. I can get along without it."

Miller died in 1849, less than five years after The Disappointment. His movement grew into several modern-day churches, among them the Seventh-Day Adventist Church with a membership worldwide of 3,016,338.

—A.E.

ACCORDING TO SCIENCE—
11 WAYS THE WORLD CAN END
(MEANING OUR PLANET EARTH
OR ALL LIFE ON IT)

1. SUCKED INTO A BLACK HOLE

A black hole is believed to be a large dead star which has collapsed and become so incredibly dense that even light can't escape its intense gravity, which proves to be a fatal attraction for any matter floating nearby. Astronomers using radio techniques think they might have detected large black holes, and the hole closest to earth may be grazing in the constellation Cygnus, a safe 6 quadrillion mi. away. According to the laws of space, everything in the universe is moving, and an unexpected rearrangement of cosmic real estate might find us on a collision course with one of these galactic vacuum cleaners. Black holes come in all sizes, and some scientists suggest that a micro–black hole was responsible for the mysterious leveling of an entire Siberian forest in 1908.

Timetable for Disaster: The odds against the earth's colliding with one of its celestial companions are astronomical, but black holes, if they really do exist, could cause scientists to recalculate the chances. A voracious black hole might sneak up on earth at any time, or it could be a billion years before one drifted into our solar system for a snack.

2. CLIMATE CHANGE—THE BIG FREEZE

The earth is currently in a million-year cycle of ice ages. The glaciers have advanced four times, for periods lasting several thousands of years each time. Then they recede, and earth enjoys a mild spell, known as an interglacial, which seldom lasts longer than 10,000 to 20,000 years. The last ice age ended 15,000 years ago. What triggers an ice age is still unknown, but one fact is clear: The world has cooled off 1°F since World War II. Humankind managed to survive the last four waves of ice, but the next one will find over 8 billion of us trying to squeeze onto 30% less land. With the acreage available for farming reduced, famine will be inevitable.

Timetable for Disaster: 2,000 to 10,000 years.

3. CLIMATE CHANGE—THE GREENHOUSE EFFECT

Don't buy a lifetime supply of long johns and earmuffs yet, because we may be parboiled before we freeze. The burning of fossil fuels such as coal and oil has caused a 10% increase in carbon dioxide in the earth's atmosphere since the late 1950s. Carbon dioxide acts as a one-way mirror, allowing sunlight in but preventing heat from escaping. If the rate at which we're burning fuel continues to increase 4% annually, scientists predict that the atmosphere will be 6°F warmer by the year 2030. Russian scientists say that an increase of 7°F will cause the polar regions to thaw. If the Antarctic ice sheet and the Greenland ice cap both melt, ocean levels could rise 200 ft. and flood, among other areas, the U.S. Gulf States, northern Germany, the British Isles, eastern China, and the Netherlands. Much of the world's population would have to retreat to higher ground, and widespread food shortages would follow. Climatologists speculate that the effect of the atmospheric heat combined with the giant ice cubes floating in the oceans would produce drastic changes in global climates, perhaps rearranging the world's deserts and fertile regions. The Corn Belt of the U.S. could become a large arid prairie, while the Sahara would be populated by alligators and other swamp-loving creatures.

Timetable for Disaster: 70 years. If the increase in fuel burning can be cut to only 2% annually, we can postpone this catastrophe for another 15 to 20 years.

4. COLLISION

Although Dr. Immanuel Velikovsky believed in the possibility of planets grazing against each other, the scientific community agrees that it would take a monstrous intruder from outside our solar system to force the planets out of their orbits and start them slamming together like billiard balls. Hold that sigh of relief, however, because the solar system is filled with bits of celestial garbage which could threaten earth's well-being.

Comets are fuzzy-looking ice balls which begin to melt and grow long tails of poisonous vapor when they approach the sun in the course of their oval-shaped orbits. They are fickle and will dramatically alter their course if disturbed by the gravitational pull of a large planet. It's estimated that there could be 100 billion comets circling around the sun, and several of their paths cross the earth's orbit. Even with 400,000,000-to-1 odds against a direct hit, collisions with comets' heads have probably occurred about 50 times during the earth's 4 billion years of existence. (A comet has also been blamed for the leveling of that Siberian forest.) Comets' tails are millions of miles long, and the chances of earth passing through one are great. In fact, the earth did cross the tail of Halley's Comet during its last visit in 1910, but it wasn't dense enough to cause any damage.

When comets die, the dusty debris that remains is transformed into meteors and meteorites. Meteors are small fragments which glimmer briefly as shooting stars until they disintegrate in earth's atmosphere. Meteorites are larger pieces which make it through the atmosphere and strike the earth's surface. About 500 meteorites crash annually, and the largest, located in Namibia, in southwest Africa, weighs 66 tons. If a very large meteor crashed into New York City, it could demolish Manhattan and kill millions.

Asteroids are even greater threats because they are larger than meteorites and are composed of stone or metal, which are much more deadly than a comet's icy head. Asteroids are really small planets, and most of them are content to frequent the asteroid belt located between Mars and Jupiter. Like comets, asteroids can be persuaded to roam by strong gravitational influences. One such stray, named Hermes, whizzed within 500,000 mi. of earth (a close call in astronomical terms) in November, 1937. Over half a mile in diameter, Hermes could have inflicted enormous damage if it had whammed into a heavily populated area.

Timetable for Disaster: Don't worry about it. The lowest estimate claims a comet can be expected to hit earth during the next 100,000 years, while one or two small meteorites tumble down daily. Complacency isn't advised, though, for tomorrow's batch might bring a whopper. An asteroid strike is scheduled for every 1,000 years, but it's possible the next offender will find us capable of blowing it up, creating a spectacular shower of falling stars as a by-product.

5. ZAPPED BY COSMIC RAYS

The earth's magnetic field usually keeps this threat at bay, but the magnetic field waxes and wanes during its normal 150,000-year cycle of polarity reversal. It's waning at present, and by the year 4000 it could decline to zero, leaving earthlings unprotected for 500 years. Some scientists have theorized that the same phenomenon was responsible for the sudden extinction of dinosaurs 70 million years ago. If a nearby star (30 light-years away or closer) should explode and become a supernova, or if our sun were to belch a giant solar flare, the earth would be blasted by the cosmic rays such events radiate. This penetrating radiation is capable of causing genetic mutations. The chance of the magnetic reversal coinciding with a supernova close enough to inflict catastrophic damage is remote, since such a supernova occurs only once every 100 million years. And a solar flare intense enough to send life-threatening radiation our way will have to be stronger than any witnessed by astronomers in the last 20 years.

Timetable for Disaster: 2,000 years.

6. GRAVITY LOSES ITS GRIP

About 14½ billion years ago, our universe started off with a big bang when a cosmic fireball exploded and spewed matter out in every direction. The universe has been expanding ever since, and some physicists speculate that as it grows larger the gravitational forces holding the celestial bodies together are weakening. Ultimately this would mean that the earth's atmosphere will dissipate, and the sun's grip on the earth will also weaken. As our orbit spirals outward into space, taking us farther away from our solar heat source, the earth's temperatures will plummet until the planet resembles a spherical deep-freeze.

Timetable for Disaster: It will be at least a billion years before the effect becomes noticeable enough to make lead shoes fashionable.

7. THE DEATH OF THE SUN

This is viewed by scientists as the ultimate disaster; however, there are no odds to debate, because this holocaust is inevitable. Our sun has been burning its hydrogen fuel for 5 billion years, and its supply can hold out only for another 8 billion years at the most. Recent research indicates that this estimate may be on the high side. Physicists are trying to prove the existence of gravity waves, the elusive and universal ripples which were predicted in Einstein's general theory of relativity. If gravity waves do exist, they could be shuttling energy from the sun's hot interior to its surface, causing the sun to cool down a million times as fast as anyone cares to believe. In either case, the sun will heat up during the last billion years of its life, boiling away earth's oceans and baking earth's crust until it is red hot. Optimists point out that since we do have some advance notice of our impending cinderhood, humankind should be able to throw together an escape plan, and move on to other solar systems heated by more youthful suns. (This escape clause is suggested for several of the astronomical-disaster scenarios. Its success is dependent upon being able to spot imminent disaster, having the sophisticated technology necessary to transport a number of people extraordinarily long distances, and locating a hospitable planet somewhere in the vast expanses of the universe.)

Timetable for Disaster: From 5 to 7 billion years, or maybe sooner if the gravity-wave theorists are correct.

8. THE STRAYING MOON AND THE SLOWING EARTH

This situation is fraught with opportunities for ringing down our final curtain. Like every other object in the universe, the moon is on the move, pulling 2 in. farther away from the earth annually. The ocean tides are slowly braking the earth's rotation, helping to shove the moon farther out into space. (This tidal action has already lengthened the earth day from 21 to 24 hours in the past 400 million years. Ultimately a day will last 37½ hours.) As the earth continues to slow and the days get longer, dramatic climate changes, perhaps violent enough to wipe out humanity, will develop. The earth's gravitational forces will allow the moon to stray only 20% farther away from its current position. Then these forces will start very slowly pulling the moon back toward our planet. As it moves closer, chaos will reign on earth; when the moon is 6,000 mi. out and revolving around earth every 90 minutes, it will spark volcanoes, trigger earthquakes, and draw massive tidal waves which will be powerful enough to pound across entire continents. Then the days will grow shorter, clocking in at less than 10 hours as the earth's rotation speeds up. When the moon is 5,000 mi. away, it will break up, forming a ring similar to those around Saturn. Eventually, large chunks of moon rock will bombard the earth.

Timetable for Disaster: The whole process will take hundreds of billions of years, and unless the sun unexpectedly gets a new lease on life, both the earth and the moon will be annihilated before the cycle is completed.

9. THE YO-YO UNIVERSE

Will the universe continue to expand forever? Many astronomers think not, contending that gravity will eventually apply the brakes to this cosmic sprawl. Then the far-flung galaxies will slowly start moving backward, picking up speed as they go. As the universe contracts, it will push lethal radiation ahead of itself. Finally, the individual pieces of the cosmos will rush together to form another ylem (pronounced "eyelem," meaning primeval matter) like the one which exploded about 14½ billion years ago to form our universe. Some astronomers say the universe will never recover from its spectacular collapse. Others assert this ylem will go the way of the last by exploding to create another universe, and instant replays of the entire process will keep matter on the move for infinity. One thing is certain: Not one astronomer will be around to collect on the bets.

Timetable for Disaster: Don't expect the Big Stop for about half a trillion years, and it will be another half a trillion years before Son of Ylem is born.

10. HEAT DEATH

The latest measurements indicate that the universe's gravitational forces are only 1/10 strong enough to bring its expansion to a standstill. Unless more mass can be located to aid in making up the gravity deficit, the recycling universe theory will have to be scrapped in favor of one involving omnipresent atrophy.

A finite amount of hydrogen is the basic fuel of the universe, and when it is exhausted, the birth of new stars will be out of the question. Although the celestial bodies will continue drifting forever farther out into the black void of space, one by one the stars will all die. When the last one is extinguished, the universe will be defunct, and heat death will be the culprit.

Timetable for Disaster: A trillion, perhaps several trillion years.

11. NUCLEAR WAR AND ITS AFTERMATH

This is a familiar, fear-provoking disaster scenario. Whether triggered by the desperation of hunger, nationalism, or the need for resource-rich territory, the next major war will undoubtedly be launched by the use of nuclear weapons. According to a study conducted by the U.S. Office of Technology Assessment, a full-scale thermonuclear attack could kill up to 88% of the U.S. population, and a maximum of 50% of the Soviet citizenry. Additional deaths from radiation exposure and fallout would follow, along with widespread genetic mutations of both animal and plant life.

The fathers of the first atomic bomb wondered whether its explosion—or a subsequent explosion—might set off a runaway chain reaction in the hydrogen atoms in the water which covers 85% of the earth, causing the entire planet to disintegrate. An article published in the respected *Bulletin of the Atomic Scientists* in 1975 states that this question has not been satisfactorily answered, and suggests a computer calculation of the odds for and against such a cataclysm's occurring be run before it's too late.

Even though the world's nuclear inventory holds the explosive equivalent of about 10 tons of TNT for every human on this planet, most experts agree that enough people would survive a nuclear war to repopulate the earth. A combination of nuclear arms, however, with deadly and unpredictable bacteriological and chemical weapons could prove universally fatal.

Timetable for Disaster: The greatest threats to survival we will face in our lifetimes are entirely man-made. It's possible we will be able to avert or escape from the rest of the disasters which might befall the human race with the assistance of our burgeoning scientific and technical knowledge. But how do we defuse nuclear power and check the people who control the bombs? We are balanced precariously today, and one slip tomorrow could see mushroom clouds blossoming on the horizon.

—L.S.

17

A CHRONOLOGY
OF THE FUTURE

A CHRONOLOGY OF
THE FUTURE

There have been countless published chronologies of events that happened in the past. This chronology is different. It is a chronology of events that will, or may, happen in the next 50 years or so. The events that will happen—or are most likely to take place—are events that have been scheduled, like a sports event, an election, a heavenly cycle, an anniversary. These more or less sure things will be indicated by two asterisks—thus**. All the other events entered in this history of tomorrow are predictions made by experts in various fields of knowledge. Based on their learning in their specialized fields these experts are forecasting what your future may bring.

But, you may wonder, is it all—or any of it—believable? Are the forecasts made for the years from 1982 to 2002 possible? Can these predictions come true?

To convince yourself that they are possible, we suggest you take a look over your shoulder. Look back to a similar time period covered by the years 1962 to 1982. Had someone told you in 1962 that the 20 years ahead would bring you portable computers, videotape machines, digital watches, microwave ovens, birth-control pills, supersonic passenger planes, and test-tube babies, you might have had doubts. Had someone told you in 1962 that the next two decades would bring you heart and kidney transplants, moon walks, spacecraft on Mars and Venus, discovery of DNA, satellite broadcasts, a Polish pope, an Israeli Jerusalem, a resigned U.S. president, you might have scoffed.

But it all happened, it actually happened. In the light of the recent past, there is no reason to disbelieve the advent of new miracles, advances, changes in the next 20 years.

Open your mind.

Make way for tomorrow.

1982

• A massive earthquake hits northern Iran, taking a large toll of lives. The inability of the government to deal with the crisis leads to its downfall. The Ayatollah Khomeini (or his heirs) is overthrown by a coalition of minorities.
• Automobile gas rationing takes effect throughout the Western world.
**Spain hosts the 12th World Cup Soccer Championship.

1983

• The U.S.S.R. puts into operation a particle-beam accelerator that can protect the nation against any guided-missile attack.
• The Soviet Union achieves clearcut strategic nuclear superiority

over the U.S., the NATO alliance, Communist China, and Japan combined.
• Saudi Arabia and Libya lose their oil wealth. In each nation, a democratic form of government takes over.
• With the crash of the U.S. stock market, a long economic depression begins.
**The U.S. spacecraft Pioneer 10, launched 11 years earlier, is just passing the planet Neptune.
• Launching of the first space telescope, which revolutionizes astronomy.

1984

**The XXIII Summer Olympics, staged in Los Angeles, goes on. Maybe.
**The U.S. elects a president.
• The risk of nuclear war peaks, with central Europe and the Middle East presenting special dangers.

1985

• Israel formally annexes the West Bank and Gaza Strip.
• People work a 4-day, 32-hour week.
• Most family homes have installed flushless toilets that compost wastes. (One brand of toilet uses a sound track that makes a flushing noise whenever the toilet lever is pressed, even though no water is used in the system.)

Flushless composting toilet.

- Your home television set has 300 different channels.
- Using expensive digital synthesizers, if you are able to play one musical instrument, you are able to play any instrument.
- A national health insurance goes into effect in the U.S. This federal insurance covers 90% of your medical costs.
- The U.S. government nationalizes all gasoline stations.
- Gasohol totally replaces gasoline for use in motor vehicles.
- First nonscientist passengers carried into orbit by space shuttle.
- A private company, selling to any customer, launches a satellite into space. The company's first customer is China.
**Halley's Comet soars through the skies once more. It is most clearly seen in November and December.

1986

- The People's Republic of China places an astronaut into orbit—and becomes the third nation with a man in space.
- A computer program beats the world chess champion.
**Colombia hosts the 13th World Cup Soccer Championship.
- The majority of working people are on Flextime—setting their own hours for going to work and leaving work.
**Sirhan Sirhan, who was convicted of murdering Robert F. Kennedy, is up for parole.

1987

- Most courtrooms are open to television coverage. Criminal and civil courtroom proceedings are so popular they have replaced soap operas and game shows.
- Your television screen can project three-dimensional pictures through use of laser holography.
- A bottle of hard liquor costs $125, a double martini at a bar costs $20, and a pack of cigarettes costs $5.
- The U.S. legalizes marijuana. Some of the leading brands for sale in your liquor store or tobacco shop are *Connoisseur Colombian, Santa Marta Gold, Primo Mexican,* and *Californian Sinsemilla.* (Colombia legalized marijuana two years earlier.)
- The British sport of cricket becomes a national sport in the U.S.
- A computer chess champion proves superior to almost all grandmaster human chess players.
**The bicentennial of the signing of the U.S. Constitution is celebrated.
- Since winters in the U.S. East have become harder, almost all large corporations are transferring their headquarters to California and Florida.
- One of three California cities—San Diego or Los Angeles or San Francisco—suffers several destructive earthquakes along a major fault line.
**A locust plague sweeps the eastern U.S.
- The U.S. public school system collapses and is replaced by one-room local schools in every neighborhood.
- A woman priest is ordained in the Roman Catholic Church.
- New scientific experiments prove that Einstein's theory of relativity is partially wrong.
- In South Africa, black resistance increases as black leaders resort

to urban terror. The white government makes dramatic concessions to blacks in social and economic fields, but the whites continue to hold military and political power.

1988

• The track record for the mile is now 3 min. 32 sec.
• Women compete in the Olympic marathon for the first time.
• A 1,000-seat jetliner has its inaugural flight.
• Most laborers working on assembly lines are replaced by robots.
• West Germany and East Germany fight an undeclared war. No other nation is involved.
• Both the U.S. and the U.S.S.R. invade Iran, the Soviets occupying the Iranian provinces of East and West Azerbaijan and the U.S. landing on the northern shore of the Strait of Hormuz. The incident ends peacefully.
• A terrorist group gets its hands on an atomic bomb.
**A U.S. presidential election is held.
• The first human being is cloned.

1989

• The median age in the U.S. is 32.5.
• Roger Maris's home-run record of 61 is broken. Someone hits 63.
• Weather forecasting achieves accuracy for 30-day periods.
• A computer makes an original scientific discovery and its program is nominated for a Nobel Prize.
• Because of excessive unemployment due to increasing automation, work riots occur in most industrialized nations.
• Nuclear war breaks out between India and Pakistan, destroying major population centers.

1990

• Spanish joins English as an official language in the U.S.
• Areas of Texas and California split off to form new states.
• Vegetarians outnumber meat eaters in the U.S.
• Most large corporations provide paid educational sabbaticals.
• Control of outer space shifts from civil to military authority in the U.S. NASA gives way to the U.S. Department of Defense.
• A male astronaut in outer space shoots and kills a crewmate in an argument over a woman.
• All school buildings vanish as students receive their education from portable communications-linked appliances which are cast on pieces of semiconductor silicon.
• Every automobile is equipped with microcomputer, sensor, and control actuator for self-operation by voice command. Also, every auto is equipped with collision-avoidance electronic gadgetry.
• Wrist telephones are popular.
• Daily body checkups by computer provide ample warning of any impending illness.
• In the past 10 years, heart disease has decreased 37% due to improved diet and exercise.
• Diabetics have pumps implanted in their bodies to feed them insulin automatically as they require it.

- Artificial eyesight is invented for blind people.
- Chemicals are produced that arrest senility in the aged.
- The Soviet Union's communist government is overthrown by a social democratic faction working inside the party.

1992

- The common cold is treated successfully with interferon.
- The first human is brought back to life after being frozen and thawed.
- 27% of Americans are illiterate. (It was 1% in 1980.)
- Over 90% of the households in the U.S. play electronic television games for recreation.
- The average secretary earns $25,000 a year, but inflation continues to soar.
- Four or five women judges are on the U.S. Supreme Court.
**U.S. presidential election is held.

1993

- After a U.S. stock market crash and major depression, the U.S. ceases to be a great power. The Soviet Union dominates most of the world.

1995

- A new do-it-yourself device for music lovers comes on the market. You can buy an electric baton and conduct a recorded orchestra, actually controlling the tempo and volume of the music.
**Ceremonies celebrate the 50th anniversary of the signing of the U.N. charter.

1996

- In order to protest the rising rate of cancer among their ranks, workers at several nuclear reactors and processing plants set off a series of nuclear "accidents."
**U.S. presidential election is held.

1997

- Most U.S. companies install locker rooms and give time off for exercise.
**The longtime British lease on Hong Kong expires, and Hong Kong reverts to Chinese control unless the lease is extended.

1998

- First tourist service to outer space. All seats booked a year in advance.
- A special gadget built into men's suits and women's dresses enables people to change the color, pattern, and shape of their garments.
**Israel celebrates its 50th anniversary of independence.

1999

• The capital of the U.S. moves from Washington, D.C., to Minneapolis, Minn.

**Pluto regains its position as the outermost known planet in our solar system, a position Neptune had held for 20 years.

**On December 31, the U.S. turns the Panama Canal over to the Republic of Panama.

2000

**Over 600 million people are living in "absolute poverty." More than half the world's population is living in cities.

• Most couples live together before getting married.

**According to the Library of Congress, in this year all nonfiction books published between 1900 and 1940 will be disintegrating because of acid in their paper, poor-quality ink, and pollution, and will be rendered useless.

• Computer printout terminals in every neighborhood publish and bind any book while you wait.

**Presuming no preventative action has been taken, the noise level on U.S. highways this year will be 50% greater than it was in the year 1980.

• Cocaine is legalized in the U.S. It is sold in liquor shops, packaged in snuffboxes bearing such names as *Peruvian Flake* and *Bolivian Rock*.

• Almost all illnesses are treated electromagnetically. Cells of the body are "fooled" into producing antibodies, coagulants, new tissue,

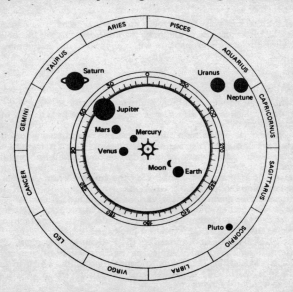

This chart shows the position of the planets relative to the sun on May 5, 2000.

and chemicals when they are exposed to certain kinds of electric and magnetic fields. This drugless treatment revolutionizes medicine.
• All Persian Gulf countries run out of oil. Most new autos around the world use alcohol or liquids converted from farm and forestry waste. On such fuels, each car gets 100 miles to the gallon.
• A shortage of oil starts a large-scale migration of people from cold parts of the world to warmer parts.
• The world's oceans are being used extensively as a source of minerals and energy. Ocean floor and subfloor mining is accomplished by automated systems and remotely controlled robots.
• More than 90% of the people over 16 in the world will recognize that a Power Control Group (including Allen Dulles, Lyndon B. Johnson, J. Edgar Hoover, Richard Nixon, some members of the U.S. Joint Chiefs of Staff, and others) conspired to murder President John F. Kennedy; probably arranged the assassinations of Robert Kennedy and Martin Luther King; tried to assassinate George C. Wallace; and probably assassinated Adlai Stevenson, Walter Reuther, and others.
**A U.S. presidential election is held.
• 50,000 people are living and working in space.
• The first children are born off the earth.
• An interplanetary ship brings back to earth an alien virus that kills a tenth of the world's population.

2002

• If caught in the early stages, every kind of cancer is now curable.

2005

• All the walls of your living room are video screens. You can activate Dial-an-Environment and have the interior of the Taj Mahal projected on the screen so that you will feel you are inside the mausoleum.

2010

• A robot can now cross a busy highway without being hit.
• Football coaches still direct their teams from the bench—but their teams consist of robots.
• Because of rising inflation, the U.S. issues a new currency to soften the impact of high prices. Many realistic people turn to barter.
• There is an open market for used and reconditioned human body parts.
• An artificial brain—as complex as the human brain—proves to have conscious thoughts and emotions.
• Authoritarian governments in various nations are using mind- and behavior-control chemicals on their subjects to suppress dissent.
• The Soviet Union attempts to change its history by using tachyons, particles that can carry information backward in time.
• The black pope of Rome transfers the Vatican to Jerusalem.
• International terrorists, employing nuclear weapons, destroy a major world capital. This leads to police repression, which in turn leads to a worldwide disarmament conference. As a result, all nuclear-weapon systems are scrapped.
• One million people are living permanently in space colonies.

2011

• Japanese investors open factories in the South Bronx in New York City.
• The U.S. passes laws banning the indiscriminate use of sugar, white flour, salt, artificial colorings, flavorings, and all additives in food.
• Polio has been totally eliminated in all Western countries.
• In South Africa, revolutionary developments provoke the intervention of the Big Powers, which will ultimately lead to black majority rule.
• Following the collapse of the American economy, there is a civil war in the U.S.
• The majority of people leaving earth for permanent jobs in outer space are female.
• The first hominid with upright posture, almost 8 million years old, is found near the Swailik Hills in India.

2012

• The Catholic Church ends its opposition to contraception. The Church also permits priests to marry.

2015

• The American Medical Association (AMA) is disbanded.

2017

**The first total eclipse of the sun since 1979 is observed by the peoples of the U.S. and Canada.
• A U.S. spacecraft reaches Mars, moves over the planet, and picks up samples of soil, which are examined in an orbiting Spacelab to avoid contamination of planet Earth. A sensational discovery—the fossil of a tiny creature—is made. Proof that Mars once possessed life.

2020

• Newly married couples are spending their honeymoon on the moon or in outer-space spas.
• More than 65% of all married women and 75% of married men have committed adultery during their married lives.
• A robot is developed with an IQ of over 100.
• Earthquakes are prevented by injecting water into wells along fault lines.
• Nighttime is eliminated from the earth. Through the use of solar satellites, which store the sun's rays, nights are fully illuminated. People enjoy 24 hours of daylight.

2025

• During the winter of this year, a new, unidentified, and particularly lethal influenza virus appears in India, leapfrogs to Southeast Asia, attacks Europe and the U.S. Untold thousands die everywhere. The virus burns out in six months. Only the people of Argentina, Chile, and sub-Saharan Africa are spared.

2027

**Sealed in the U.S. National Archives for over half a century, the secret tapes made of Martin Luther King, Jr., by his enemy J. Edgar Hoover and the FBI are finally released to the public. These tapes—made by FBI bugging devices and wiretaps placed in King's home, office, and hotel rooms—sought to compromise him by exposing alleged sexual activities.

2028

• Solar-powered satellites supply 90% of the world's energy.

2030

• The average secretary earns over $600,000 a year—but $10 will barely buy a cup of coffee.
• Computers and robots have become more intelligent than human beings, and they make major economic, social, and technical decisions using reasoning that is beyond human comprehension.
• Antarctic icebergs are being melted to relieve water shortages.
• Advances in our understanding of crystal structures enable us to grow buildings.
• The average consumer is able to trade in his or her body for a new custom-built improved model.
• People under 21 years of age are no longer deformed, sick, stupid, neurotic, undernourished, or ugly.
• The average human being lives to an age of 120 or more.
• Despite decades of experimental work, scientists have failed—thus far—to see *inside* the atom and to demonstrate the existence of gravity waves.
• A democratic United States of the World is established. All wars are outlawed.
• Nuclear weapons stockpiled by the world's armies are sent into space to capture asteroids and bring them into orbit around the earth, where they are used as raw materials for space industrialization.
• Over 250 million people are living on High-Orbital Mini-Earths (H.O.M.E.s). Of these, 100 million were born on the new worlds.
• Spacekind issues a Declaration of Independence from Earthkind.

2087

• A young physicist develops a unified field theory (first proposed by Einstein 150 years before) which provides the theoretical basis for faster-than-light travel.

3000

• More people are living in space than on earth.

18

THE BOOK OF
PREDICTIONS CONTESTS
·
HOW TO WIN A
REAL ROBOT PREPARED TO
HELP AND SERVE YOU

2 SUPER
PREDICTIONS CONTESTS

We believe you do *not* have to be an expert or trained psychic to have the ability to make accurate predictions. We believe that everyone, to varying degrees, has the ability to predict the future. But some people are better at this than others. To find out who among you are the best predictors, we are sponsoring two contests. All of you are eligible to enter and to win our unusual top prizes.

The first of these two contests is THE FORECASTING CONTEST. You are given a series of questions to answer. You are also given some factual information to help you with those answers. While answering correctly does depend on your intuitive ability to see ahead, this contest also gives you a chance to make an educated guess. The information provided offers you an opportunity to add a bit of logic to each of your predictions.

The second of these two contests is THE PSYCHIC CONTEST. To provide the right answers here, or close to the right answers, you must be truly psychic. You must be psychically sensitive, able to conjure up a premonition, a vision, a bolt from the blue, in order to fill in the answer to each question.

You can make predictions in one or both contests, as you wish. You can answer all or some of the questions. The persons in each contest who have the most correct—or nearly correct—answers will be the winners.

Let us look at the prizes and rules for both contests.

• 6 SENSATIONAL PRIZES •

To the three winners of THE FORECASTING CONTEST:

First Prize
A HOUSEKEEPING OR OFFICE-CLEANING ROBOT. (If a ROBOT is not available at the time, then an equivalent fascinating prize worth at least $2,000.)
PLUS ROUND-TRIP PLANE FARE TO LOS ANGELES, PREPAID HOTEL, AND MEALS FOR 2 DAYS FOR WINNER AND ONE GUEST.

Second Prize
AN UNUSUAL GIFT WORTH $500 OR MORE.

Third Prize
AN UNUSUAL GIFT WORTH $250 OR MORE.

To the three winners of THE PSYCHIC CONTEST:

First Prize
PERSONAL APPOINTMENTS WITH 8 WORLD-RENOWNED PSYCHICS AND MYSTICS IN LOS ANGELES (INCLUDING AN ASTROLOGER,

PALMIST, GRAPHOLOGIST, PSYCHIC READER, TAROT AND I CHING READERS, PSYCHOANALYST, AND PHRENOLOGIST) PLUS ROUND-TRIP PLANE FARE TO LOS ANGELES, PREPAID HOTEL, AND MEALS FOR 2 DAYS FOR WINNER AND ONE GUEST.

Second Prize
AN UNUSUAL GIFT WORTH $500 OR MORE.

Third Prize
AN UNUSUAL GIFT WORTH $250 OR MORE.

Special Bonus: The top winner of the contests will be honored guests at a Crystal Ball Awards dinner, at which they will receive their first prizes and enjoy a futuristic meal. All winners will be presented actual crystal balls with stands bearing their names.

• RULES FOR ENTERING CONTESTS •

1. To enter either or both contests print your name, address, city, zip code, telephone number, *and* your predictions on a postcard or a sheet of paper.
2. Mail your entry to PREDICTIONS CONTEST, P.O. Box 49699, Los Angeles, Calif. 90049. Entries must be postmarked on or before June 30, 1982, and received by July 10, 1982. No more than one entry per person per contest.
3. Winners will be selected based on the total number of correct predictions for each contest. Answers involving numbers, if within 5% of correct answer, will receive half credit. An answer involving words or names, with no more than two letters misspelled in an otherwise correct answer, will receive half credit. In case of ties, the earliest postmarked entry will be declared the winner.
4. Winners will be announced on January 15, 1984—and each winner will be notified by mail.
5. All employees of, and contributors to, *The Book of Predictions*—and their families—are ineligible to enter these contests. Also, all employees of *The People's Almanac,* William Morrow and Company, and Bantam Books are ineligible to enter these contests.
6. All federal, state, and local taxes on prizes, if any, are the responsibility of the individual winners.
7. A list of the final correct predictions, as well as a list of the contest winners, can be obtained by sending a stamped self-addressed envelope to PREDICTIONS CONTESTS WINNERS' LIST, P.O. Box 49699, Los Angeles, Calif. 90049.
8. All winning entrants grant to *The Book of Predictions*, without limitation, the right to use their names and likenesses for any advertising and promotional purposes.
9. Void where prohibited.

THE BOOK OF PREDICTIONS
FORECAST CONTEST

1. ACCORDING TO THE U.S. BUREAU OF LABOR
STATISTICS, WHAT WILL BE THE U.S. INFLATION
RATE FOR 1983—AS OF OCTOBER 31, 1983?

Background:

Year	Inflation Rate
1980	12.4%
1979	13.0%
1978	9.0%
1977	7.0%
1976	5.0%
1975	7.0%
1974	12.0%
1970	5.5%
1965	2.0%

2. WHICH TELEVISION SERIES WILL HAVE THE
#1 NIELSEN RANKING FOR THE 1982–1983 SEASON?

Background:

Season	Series
1980-1980	Dallas
1979–1980	60 Minutes
1978–1979	Three's Company
1977–1978	Laverne and Shirley
1976–1977	Happy Days
1975–1976	All in the Family
1974–1975	All in the Family
1973–1974	All in the Family
1972–1973	All in the Family
1971–1972	All in the Family
1970–1971	Marcus Welby, M.D.

3. ACCORDING TO THE U.S. BUREAU OF LABOR
STATISTICS, WHAT WILL BE THE AVERAGE PRICE OF
A GALLON OF GASOLINE IN THE U.S. IN JULY, 1983?

Background:

Month and Year	Price per Gallon
July, 1980	$1.25
July, 1979	91¢
July, 1978	63¢*
July, 1977	63¢
July, 1976	60¢
July, 1975	60¢

*A new method of computing lowered the price about 2¢ per gallon.

4. BASED ON STATISTICS FROM SCOTLAND YARD
AND THE NEW YORK CITY POLICE DEPARTMENT,
WHAT WILL BE THE TOTAL NUMBER OF HOMICIDES

COMMITTED IN LONDON AND NEW YORK
CITY DURING 1982?

Background:

Year	Total Homicides
1980	1,993 (London 179, New York City 1,814)
1979	1,912 (London 179, New York City 1,733)
1978	1,621 (London 118, New York City 1,503)
1977	1,694 (London 142, New York City 1,552)
1976	1,767 (London 145, New York City 1,622)
1975	1,790 (London 145, New York City 1,645)

5. OF THE 435 SEATS TO BE CONTESTED IN THE 1982 U.S. ELECTIONS TO THE HOUSE OF REPRESENTATIVES, HOW MANY WILL BE WON BY WOMEN?

Background:

Year	Women Elected
1980	19
1978	16
1976	18
1974	19
1972	14
1970	12
1968	10

6. OF THE 435 SEATS TO BE CONTESTED IN THE 1982 U.S. ELECTIONS TO THE HOUSE OF REPRESENTATIVES, HOW MANY WILL BE WON BY LAWYERS?

Background:

Year	Lawyers Elected
1980	194
1978	205
1976	222
1974	221
1972	221

7. IN THE 1982 U.S. ELECTIONS TO THE HOUSE OF REPRESENTATIVES, WHAT PERCENTAGE OF SEATS WILL BE WON BY CANDIDATES WHO SPENT MORE MONEY ON THEIR CAMPAIGN THAN THEIR OPPONENTS?

Background:

Year	Percent
1978	84%
1976	84%

8. WHO WILL WIN THE WOMEN'S SINGLES CHAMPIONSHIP AT THE 1983 WIMBLEDON TENNIS TOURNAMENT?

Background:

Year	Women's Singles Winner
1980	Evonne Goolagong Cawley
1979	Martina Navratilova

1978	Martina Navratilova
1977	Virginia Wade
1976	Chris Evert
1975	Billie Jean King

9. WHAT WILL BE THE CLOSING U.S. DOW-JONES INDUSTRIAL STOCK AVERAGE ON JULY 1, 1983?

Background:

Date	Closing Average
July 1, 1980	872
July 2, 1979	834
July 3, 1978	813
July 1, 1975	879
July 1, 1970	688
July 1, 1965	872
July 1, 1960	641

10. IN 1982, WHAT PERCENTAGE OF ELECTRICITY IN THE U.S., ACCORDING TO THE U.S. DEPARTMENT OF ENERGY, WILL BE GENERATED BY NUCLEAR POWER (TO THE NEAREST 1/10 OF A PERCENT)?

Background:

Year	Percent Nuclear-Generated Electricity
1980	11%
1979	11.5%
1978	12.5%
1977	11.8%
1976	9.4%
1975	9.0%
1974	6.1%
1970	1.4%
1965	.4%

11. WHICH ARTIST OR GROUP WILL HAVE *BILLBOARD*'S #1 L.P. AND TAPE FOR THE WEEK OF NOVEMBER 15, 1982?

Background:

Date	Artist(s)
November 15, 1980	Bruce Springsteen
November 17, 1979	Eagles
November 11, 1978	Donna Summer
November 12, 1977	Fleetwood Mac
November 13, 1976	Stevie Wonder
November 15, 1975	Elton John

12. WHO WILL WIN THE ACADEMY AWARD FOR BEST ACTOR FOR 1982 (AWARDED IN 1983)?

Background:

Year	Best Actor
1980	Robert De Niro
1979	Dustin Hoffman
1978	Jon Voight
1977	Richard Dreyfuss

1976	Peter Finch
1975	Jack Nicholson
1974	Art Carney
1973	Jack Lemmon
1972	Marlon Brando
1971	Gene Hackman
1970	George C. Scott

13. WHICH COUNTRY WILL THE WINNER OF THE 1983 MISS UNIVERSE BEAUTY CONTEST COME FROM?

Background:

Year	Country
1980	United States
1979	Venezuela
1978	South Africa
1977	Trinidad and Tobago
1976	Israel
1975	Finland
1974	Spain
1973	Philippines
1972	Australia
1971	Lebanon
1970	Puerto Rico

14. HOW MUCH MONEY WILL BE COLLECTED BY THE U.S. INTERNAL REVENUE SERVICE IN THE FISCAL YEAR ENDING SEPTEMBER 30, 1982?

Background:

Year	U.S. Tax Collections
1980	$519 billion
1979	$451.0 billion
1978	$400.0 billion
1977	$358.0 billion
1976	$302.5 billion
1975	$294.0 billion
1970	$196.0 billion
1965	$114.0 billion
1960	$ 92.0 billion

THE PSYCHIC CONTEST

1. What title will be #7 on *The New York Times* hardback fiction best-seller list on July 5, 1983?
2. Which horse will finish second to last in the 1983 Kentucky Derby?
3. What will be the banner headline in the *Los Angeles Times* (morning final edition) on July 1, 1983?
4. Which television program will get the lowest Nielsen rating for the week beginning May 8, 1983?
5. Who will finish 47th in the 1983 Boston Marathon?

GLOSSARY OF WORDS USED
IN THIS BOOK

Actuator A mechanical device used instead of hands to move or control an object.

Antigen A substance not usually found in the body. Its presence provokes the production of antibodies, which fight the antigen by combining with it. This immunological system causes allergies—the overreaction of some individuals' antibodies to harmless antigens—and also is responsible for the rejection of organ transplants.

Biomass The amount of living (bio) matter (mass) in a given habitat.

Cloning Asexual reproduction in which "fertilization" is accomplished by implanting a cell nucleus from an individual into an egg cell which has had its nucleus removed.

Cryonics The practice of freezing a body at death with the intent to resuscitate it when medical science is advanced enough to do this.

Dyad Two people (e.g., a husband and wife) who are involved in a significant relationship.

Dystopia The opposite of *utopia*. A depressing imaginary place where people live a wretched and fearful life. *Anti-utopia* is an alternative expression for *dystopia*.

Ecosystem An ecological community and the nonliving factors of its environment, considered as a unit.

Endogenous Growing from or on the inside, developing in the wall of a cell, or orginating within the body.

Endorphins Morphinelike proteins found in the brain and other tissues.

Euthanasia The act of "mercy killing," when people or domestic animals who are terminally ill are either killed or allowed to die naturally instead of being put on life-support systems.

Fusion reactor Device of the future which will extract the energy produced when two light atomic nuclei combine at high speeds to make a heavy, stable nucleus. When this process is perfected, it will be three times as efficient than present-day nuclear fission reactors and will provide ample and inexpensive power because "deuterium"—the type of hydrogen atom used in the process—is found in abundant quantities in the world's oceans.

Gamete bank Similar in nature to a sperm bank, this service would store both frozen sperm and egg cells for future use.

Geosynchronous Identical in meaning to *geostationary*. When an artificial satellite travels at the same speed as the rotation of the earth, it is moving in a geosynchronous manner. In its orbit, the satellite appears to stay in the same place.

Glacial rebound Return of the glaciers—large bodies of ice which move slowly on land.

Hegemony A strong and significant authority over something or someone, particularly of one country over another.

Heisenberg uncertainty principle States that the exact measurement of velocity of a subatomic particle during observation produces uncertainty concerning the exact point the particle is at, and vice versa. This is also called "the Heisenberg indeterminacy principle."

Holograms Three-dimensional pictures made on film or plates with a beam of light instead of a camera.

IMF International Monetary Fund, an organization of 138 countries, headquartered in Washington, D.C. It promotes stabilization of international currencies.

Immunosuppressive Acting to suppress the natural immune responses of the body.

Interface Common boundary where independent systems meet and communicate with each other. The man-computer interface point is the computer terminal, where a person can ask the computer questions and receive its replies.

Interferons Proteins which cells produce when invaded by viruses.

In utero When the fertilization process occurs in the uterus.

Inverse-square law When a measurable quantity changes inversely according to the square of its distance from a source. The force of gravity is subject to this law. For example, an astronaut weighing 160 lb. on the surface of the earth (4,000 mi. above its center) will weigh only 40 lb. when he's 4,000 miles above the surface of the earth (8,000 mi. above its center).

Ion rocket Method of aeronautical propulsion created by ejecting charged atomic particles at a speed high enough to produce sufficient thrust.

Isotopes Atoms which are different varieties of the same element, differing only in the number of neutrons present in their nuclei. Hundreds of isotopes have been identified, including radioactive ones. Isotopes have been manufactured in the laboratory.

Libertarianism The concept which upholds the principle of free will, or freedom in action and thought.

Mass driver rockets Originally designed for magnetically levitated trains, this launching system is being adapted for use with reusable space shuttles. A loaded carrier vehicle, or bucket, is placed in a tunnel and accelerated by superconducting electromagnetic coils. The payload is launched from the buckets at the end of the tunnel. These rockets will be useful for transporting raw materials from the moon to manufacturing centers located in space.

Megastructures Unusually large structures. This word is now being used to refer to a total environment under one roof where work, living accommodations, and leisure activities will all be contained.

Neurotransmitter Chemical substance which aids in sending nerve impulses across the gaps between nerve cells.

Neutron rays Rays which are composed of uncharged particles that have a similar mass to protons. The neutron is found in the nuclei of all atoms except hydrogen.

OECD Organization for Economic Cooperation and Development. Formed in 1961 with 24 countries, OECD seeks to further world economic development. For example, it has agreed to set limits through 1985 on the importation of oil.

O'Neill-type space colonies Named for Gerard K. O'Neill, professor of physics at Princeton University, these self-supporting artificial planets would be located halfway between earth and the moon at a point called Lagrange 5, or L5. The habitats are designed to be built completely from materials found on the moon and would be powered by solar energy. O'Neill feels space colonization is the answer to world population problems and will be ideal for manufacturing using space materials.

Peptide Compound formed when two or more amino acids bond together in a specific arrangement. Protein molecules are composed of amino acids linked by peptide bonds.

Phages A shortened term for the word *bacteriophages*. These are bacteriolytic viruses or bacteria-destroying agents which are usually present in body by-products and sewage.

Pluralism A metaphysical theory that there is more than one kind of ultimate reality.

Polyandry The practice in which a woman has more than one male mate or more than one husband.

Polymer A natural or synthetic chemical compound produced by the union of monomers, which are simple molecules. This union creates products with more strength, flexibility, resistance to cold, etc.

Prostaglandins Fatty acids which act like hormones.

Psionics Science of electronic machines which deal with psychic phenomena; usually used in connection with the diagnosis of disease and prescription of therapy.

Psychometry The intuitive perception of facts concerning an object or its owner through contact with or proximity to the object.

Psychopharmacology The study of the effect of drugs on behavior and on the mind.

Recombinant DNA technology A form of genetic surgery by which genes can be separated out from a DNA molecule and spliced together with those from an unrelated organism.

Red shift Light from a moving source tends toward high-frequency violet when the source is approaching, and low-frequency red when it is receding. When spectrum photographs of galaxies show a displacement of a spectrum towards red—indicating that the universe is expanding—this is called a red shift.

Right brain and left brain functions Two hemispheres with separate but overlapping functions form the human brain. The left side of the brain controls the right side of the body and specializes in speech and logic. The right side of the brain controls the "wiring" of the body's left side and specializes in images and acts which are hard to put into words—things which are often attributed to intuition or native ability.

Statism A highly centralized form of government which exerts control over all economic planning.

Subcutaneously Under the skin.

Synergy Combined action or operation.

Telemetry The process of using radio waves or wire to transmit data—such as pressure and radiation intensity—recorded by electrical instruments to a distant station where it is recorded.

UNCTAD U.N. Conference on Trade and Development. Formed in 1964 in Geneva to discuss the trade needs of developing countries and to promote international trade.

Index

491

G

H

Picture Credits

ABOUT THE AUTHORS

DAVID WALLECHINSKY, creator of *The People's Almanac* and *The People's Almanac #2*, coauthored both books with his father, Irving Wallace. They just finished work on *The People's Almanac #3*. David is also coauthor of *Chico's Organic Gardening and Natural Living, Laughing Gas, What Really Happened to the Class of '65?, The Book of Lists,* and *The Book of Lists #2*. He is married to Flora Chavez, and they live in Santa Monica, California.

AMY WALLACE, Irving Wallace's daughter, is a graduate of the Berkeley (Calif.) Psychic Institute and has developed such psychic skills as clairvoyant reading and psychic healing. Besides coauthoring *The Book of Lists, The Book of Lists #2,* and *The Psychic Healing Book,* she has written, with her father, *The Two,* a biography of the original Siamese twins, and with her family, *The Intimate Sex Lives of Famous People*.

IRVING WALLACE is one of the most widely read novelists in the world, with estimated worldwide sales of his twenty-five books, in all editions, at 145 million copies. His first great international success was with *The Chapman Report*, followed by *The Prize, The Man, The Seven Minutes, The Word, The Fan Club, The People's Almanac* (with his son, David), *The R Document,* and *The Pigeon Project*—all major best sellers. His most recent novel is *The Second Lady*. He lives with his wife, the writer Sylvia Wallace, in West Los Angeles, California.

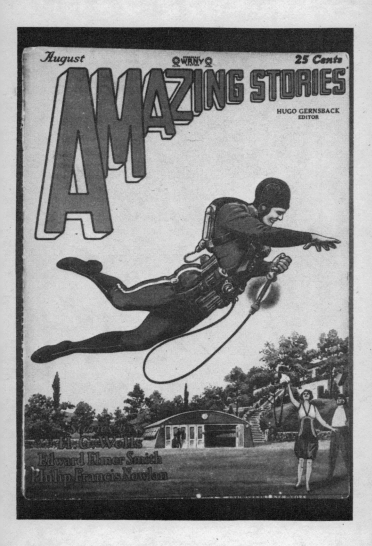

RELAX!
SIT DOWN
and Catch Up On Your Reading!

We Deliver!

And So Do These Bestsellers.

Facts at Your Fingertips!

June 1982 US Bombed
⅓ psp die!